Steel Sh...

The Sons of Annie McKenna

by David Quinn

The McKenna Cross
Emyvale, County Monaghan

STEEL SHAMROCKS
The Sons of Annie McKenna

iUniverse books may be ordered through booksellers or by contacting:

iUniverse LLC
1663 Liberty Drive
Bloomington, IN 47403
www.iuniverse.com
1-800-Authors (1-800-288-4677)

ISBN: 978-1-4917-3434-6 (sc)
ISBN: 978-1-4917-3435-3 (e)

Library of Congress Control Number: 2014910834

Printed in the United States of America.

iUniverse rev. date: 07/11/2014

"... history, the rival of time, repository of great deeds, witness to the past, example and adviser to the present, and forewarning to the future."
Miguel De Cervantes

To The Reader

This story, like those which preceded it, has been the result of my love for the confluence of genealogy and history. In *It May Be Forever—An Irish Rebel on the American Frontier* and *Leviathan's Master—The Wreck of the World's Largest Sailing Ship,* I relied upon the true life tales of my own ancestors. However, it has long been my ambition to turn my attention to the fascinating McKenna family of Pittsburgh, Pennsylvania, the family of my loving wife, Betsy.

Though, at first glance, there are parallels between the unlikely rise of Mike Quinn and the McKenna brothers—Barney and Charles. The differences are fundamental and real. Mike Quinn's life was largely a case of sacrificing love and family in the pursuit of fortune. The McKenna rise to prominence finds its impetus in the ambition for public service.

The accomplishments of my characters are emblematic of the energy and determination of the immigrant to achieve a better life in America. But they are also testimony to the opportunities afforded by their adopted country for those who would strive.

Where available, actual quotations from characters or contemporary publications are presented in italics.

Acknowledgements

I would like to recognize the help received from Daniel M. Curtin for the valuable trove of letters from Charles F. McKenna during his Civil War service. I would be remiss indeed if I did not mention the constant and valuable assistance and encouragement offered by my dear wife, Elizabeth (Betsy) McKenna Quinn.

About the Author

David M. Quinn was born in Oak Ridge, Tennessee in 1945 and grew up in the Washington, D.C. area. He studied political science at Wheeling Jesuit University (B.A.) and Fordham University (M.A.). In 1999, after thirty years in the telecommunications industry, David made the decision to leave the corporate world. Following his passion for genealogy led him to uncover remarkable stories within his family history. First was that of his great, great uncle Michael Quinn, as told in the historical novel, *It May Be Forever—An Irish Rebel on the American Frontier.* Later, drawing upon his maternal ancestry, David gave us the remarkable story of Captain George W. Dow, who is the narrator of the true story, *Leviathan's Master—The Wreck of The World's Largest Sailing Ship.*

Steel Shamrocks recounts the story of his wife's ancestors, the McKennas of Pittsburgh, Pennsylvania. David and his wife Betsy reside in Frederick, Maryland. They have three grown children and five grandchildren.

Principal Characters

Hugh McKenna (Anacramp)
m. Catherine McMahon

↓

•James McKenna m. Annie Mullan ----------→ •James McKenna m. Ellen Collins
•Nancy McKenna McAlavy   •Hugh McKenna
•Catherine McKenna O'Brien   •Patrick H. McKenna
•Charles McKenna m. Ann McAffee → Ellen   •Catherine McKenna
• Mary McKenna O'Hare   McKenna   •Bernard (Barney) McKenna m.
•Bridget McKenna Cullen   Mary A. McShane
•Hugh McKenna   •Charles F. McKenna m. Virginia
•Ellen McKenna Delaney   White
•Edward McKenna   •Edward M. McKenna m. Margaret
•Patrick McKenna   Manning
•Bernard McKenna

                                    •Charles B. McKenna
                                    •Catherine (Kitty) McKenna McNulty
                           ----------•James F. (Frank) McKenna m.
                                        Elizabeth (Bess) Heyl
                                    •Charles F. McKenna
                                    •William B. McKenna m. Clementine Heyl

                    •William H. McKenna

Principal Characters (Continued)

Will McKeever (Anacramp)
m. Catherine Mullan

↓

•Catherine McKeever
•Rev. Edward McKeever

James McShane (Dungannon)
m. Alice Mellon

↓

•James McShane (Pittsburgh)
m. Ann Daugherty

↓

•Mary McShane McKenna

Prologue

Late Spring, 1942

Bill McKenna stabbed out his cigarette in disgust. The glass ashtray on his plain wooden desk, between the squat lamp and the black, bakelite telephone, was already brimming with stinking butts from that morning. It was nearly time for his meeting with his boss, Tom Gregory. It was an encounter he was not looking forward to. The tall, lean, sandy-haired McKenna went to the gray metal cabinet in the corner his office. He removed his dingy dress shirt, shoving it into the paper laundry bag on the floor of the cabinet. Then he donned his afternoon, white shirt in the long-standing ritual of Pittsburgh executives in the day-time dark and soot-laden atmosphere of industrial Pittsburgh. There was no bad blood between himself and Tom, the president of Hanlon-Gregory Galvanizing Company. No, it was the subject of the meeting that had Bill so out of sorts.

As he adjusted his tie and pulled on his suit jacket, he scanned the factory floor through the observation window that made up most of one wall of his office. A hive of activity forty feet below struggled to cope with the constant stream of structural steel, ship plates, bolts, nuts, and rivets headed for a bath of molten zinc. Virtually all of the company's output was now related to the war effort. Bill's gaze was particularly directed to the performance of a cadre of new hires. Many of these were blacks from the Hill District, replacements for employees drafted or who had volunteered for military service. The introduction of this altered racial mix to skill positions was a social experiment that required close supervision.

William H. (Bill) McKenna

He descended the metal staircase that linked his office to the shop floor and acknowledged the nodded greetings of busy foremen and long-time employees. Just shy of thirty years of age, he walked briskly as he crossed the asphalt yards full of steel items awaiting processing. You wouldn't know it was spring, save for the mild temperatures, he thought. The industrial strip in Lawrenceville, between Butler Street and the Allegheny River, was nearly devoid of the greening trees and emerging flowers to be found around his Highland Park home. He entered the corporate office, a grim one-story brick building facing 55th Street.

"Hi, Margaret. Tom back from lunch yet?"

Gregory's secretary, a pleasant matron with dyed red hair, quickly closed her Life magazine and gave a nervous smile. "Yes, Mr. McKenna. He returned early from town . . . asked me to have you go right in."

Gregory's office was somewhat modest in size and decor, but comfortably furnished nevertheless. Tom was a couple of decades senior to Bill, with a head full of thick, graying hair and the beginnings of a paunch. He peered above his reading glasses as Bill entered. Dropping the piece of correspondence in his hands, he rose from behind his uncluttered desk. Gesturing to one of two wing chairs, he offered, "Hi, Bill. Take a seat. Shall we have Margaret bring in some coffee?"

Bill sat casually, crossed his long legs, and adjusted the crease of his trouser to the middle of his knee.

"Thanks, Tom, but we'll have to make this somewhat brief. The folks at Dravo have asked for a delivery update on those LST components and, frankly, we're running a bit late on that order. I'll have to drive down this afternoon and smooth some feathers."

Tom sat casually on the edge of his desk. "OK, I'll make this like the old woman's dance—short and sweet. I spoke to the staff at the War Production Board again yesterday. Their position hasn't changed. While they salute your patriotism and desire to enlist, they insist that your current duties must take priority. Any Joe Doakes can carry a rifle, Bill. But there's damn few men that can push war materiel out the door—on-time, on-spec, and on-budget."

"I figured to make officer—maybe the Corps of Engineers," he glumly replied.

"I'm sure you would." Tom paused, removed his glasses, and rubbed the bridge of his nose. "But with all these demands of the war, I don't know how I'd manage without you. I'd be competing with the military and my competitors to find a capable replacement. And, there's hardly ever been a time when there wasn't a member of your family helping to run this company."

McKenna impatiently pulled a cigarette from a pack of Camels and lit it. Both an uncle and his father had acted as treasurer for Hanlon-Gregory at various times in the past. He knew the history and didn't need it rehearsed again.

"I can't say I'm surprised at the WPB decision. Still, I was hoping for a different answer. You must know what it is like,

Tom . . . . I've got five brothers in uniform, and here I am—young, fit, and willing to serve—but staying behind in safety and comfort!"

Tom listened patiently as he polished his glasses with his tie. "Surely, they realize what you're doing for the war effort. I can't imagine any criticism . . . ."

"No, no! Nothing like that. They've never said a word. But that damned newspaper article has caused some talk among our neighbors and friends!"

Tom smiled, barely suppressing a chuckle. "Oh, I see. 'The Fighting McKennas', wasn't that the headline? I remember they joked that your father was organizing his own regiment. Well, Bill, it may rankle for a while. Still, I need you here, and so does your country. And then, there's Ronnie and the kids. You'll just have to ignore such foolish talk. I hope, in time, you'll accept the value of your service here . . . . Now—I'd better let you get off to Neville Island."

"Right. Well, thanks for, at least, putting the question to the WPB for me, Tom. I'll let you know tomorrow if you need to call anyone at Dravo."

"The Fighting McKennas"
(left to right, Robert, Charles, Bernard, J. Frank Jr., and David)

Fall, 1945

The Grant Building was, in the pre-war years, the premier corporate address in Pittsburgh. An imposing design combining beaux arts and art deco elements graced the forty-story structure. It was located close to the Courthouse and City-County Building and infested with attorneys. Among these were Bill's father, J. Frank McKenna, and a cousin, Edward J. McKenna. They took offices there immediately after it was completed in 1930. The fact that the building's developer was the older brother of Frank's long-time law partner, Eugene Strassburger, probably had something to do with the choice.

Riding the elevator to the office suite on the 25th floor, Bill wondered what had prompted this rare invitation to join his father for lunch. The old man, now in his late sixties, was a warm person, but quiet—hardly the "let's do lunch" type. As expected, the meal was ordered in from a nearby delicatessen. It was to be consumed in a conference room adjoining his father's office. Bill sat and fidgeted while Frank wrapped up a telephone conversation with a client. He looked at his watch; it was already twelve-thirty. He needed to be back at the plant well before two.

The room was graced by a long, mahogany table capable of accommodating a football team. Around the table were matching chairs, upholstered in green leather. The effect on prospective clients might well have been: If you don't have a great case for *pro bono* treatment, be prepared to pay handsomely for services rendered. Frank's secretary had laid out two place settings of china, silverware, and cloth napkins around one end of the table—a client style of hospitality to grace their meal of chicken salad sandwiches. Coffee at the side-board was a welcome discovery and Bill poured himself a cup.

Frank entered and patted his son on the shoulder; then he moved to his place at the head of the table. "Sorry to keep you waiting, Bill. How are things up at the plant?"

"Good afternoon, Father . . . . We're still busy, but it's not the defense boom anymore. I'd say orders are down twenty percent since the war ended. We've even had to let some men go, . . . just when soldiers are back home, looking for work. Can I pour your coffee?"

"Thanks, I'd like that. I'm dry from all the talk this morning." He shook out his napkin and then lifted the edge of his sandwich, peering at it as if some foreign substance might be lurking within. Apparently satisfied, he took a bite.

The two men ate in silence for several minutes. Then Bill, rising to refill his coffee cup, broke the spell. "It's been quite some time since I've seen you at your office, Father. I'm sure that you have an agenda for us today. You rarely object to eating your lunch alone."

Frank chuckled, pushed his chair back and crossed his legs. "Well, I must confess that I didn't drag you into town just for the company. Of course, I'm always happy to see you. But I do have an agenda, as you say. Nothing sinister, mind you. I just wanted us to have a chance to talk without wives and children rushing about. I hope you don't mind."

J. Frank McKenna, Sr.

Bill pulled an ashtray close and lit up. "I'm all ears, Father. What's on your mind? I'm not in trouble, am I?" Bill grinned to underscore the intended jest. Despite his effort, there was a tension in the air that drained the humor from his remark. This was unchartered territory, to be summoned like a schoolboy at the age of thirty-three.

"I wouldn't put it that way, son." Frank turned and gazed out the window at the blackened cityscape. It was a brief pause to choose his words carefully. "I suppose I came away from last week's homecoming party a bit worried about you. You didn't seem very engaged or comfortable at what was supposed to be a happy occasion."

Bill squirmed a bit, absent-mindedly opening and closing the cap of his Zippo lighter. "Father, I'm sure you know that I'm as happy as any of us that my brothers are home again, safe and uninjured . . . . I guess I wasn't the life of the party, however."

Frank uncrossed his legs and leaned forward, looking deep into his son's eyes. "What is it, then? It's really quite unlike you to withdraw like that. And I found you showing up at the bar that night more frequently than I liked."

Bill sprang to his feet like a circus cat responding to the crack of the whip. "I don't imagine you'd understand, Father . . . . I'm tired of playing the wall flower to returning war heroes." He paced back and forth. "Of course, I admire their service. It just seems to be laid on a bit heavy—like I spent the last four years doing nothing for the war effort. They don't pin ribbons on your chest for going to work each day."

"I see." The old man smiled, relieved to know the pebble in Bill's shoe. He paused an uncomfortable minute before resuming. "Sit down, son. I want to tell you a story you may find most interesting . . . . You never knew my father, Bernard—Barney, they called him." Frank leaned back in his chair, his eyes raised as if experiencing a vision of the long-deceased parent. "You might be surprised to learn that he faced a situation very similar to your own."

Bill slumped back into his chair, embarrassed at his outburst. Still, he was relieved that the tension he felt before was now quickly dissipating. He lit another cigarette and waited with a hint of curiosity.

"When Barney was a young man, about twenty I suppose, the Civil War was on. Many of the boys in the Fourth Ward were either enlisting in the state militia or joining the regular army. You know our family had been solid Democrats; still, they were strong for the Union. Not least in his loyalty was young Barney. He was anxious to go, just like his younger brother, Charles. But there was a problem . . . ."

Bill sat up, now. His emotions having subsided, he found himself being drawn into his father's tale.

"You see, Barney was the one son in the family helping my grandmother, Annie, run the boarding house that was the family's livelihood. It wasn't a huge place, but it was a lot of work. Annie was in her sixties by then. Charles and Edward were just teenagers. My uncle Hugh had run off to the California gold rush, years before. The eldest brother, James, had a big position at the post office and a wife to support. So it fell to Barney to stay and help run the business. He was not happy about it.

"Of course, Charles saw a lot of action during the war. His unit was present at all the great battles in the east, from Antietam right through to Lee's surrender at Appomattox."

Frank stood and slowly paced before the bank of windows at one side of the room. His thumbs wedged into the slit pockets of his vest. "In later years, Charles became prominent in the G.A.R."

"Hmm, the G.A.R.?"

"Yes, the Grand Army of the Republic . . . . There was always some commemoration event or tribute being offered to him and his former comrades-in-arms. My father would not speak of it, but I believe it was a sore point between them. I'm not suggesting a serious rift, but each them was conscious that one had to stay while the other was free to go."

Bill interrupted, "And Barney didn't even have a war industry position to point to! I guess I knew Charles had gone to war, but I never gave a thought to what your father had done—aside from becoming the mayor of Pittsburgh. I don't know much about him or the rest of the family . . . . We never really talked much about these things as I was growing up."

Frank was gazing out the window at the miniature-like figures moving along the street below. Now he turned and faced his son, a sad expression crept across his face. "I guess I should have made a point of it . . . I may have been too busy, or at least I thought I was. It's easy to neglect such things when you're raising a family and pursuing a career."

He walked over to Bill and again placed his hand upon the young man's shoulder. "It's too bad. These people were giants! They accomplished so much . . . against great obstacles. How different our lives are from theirs!"

Chapter One

<u>Winter, 1828</u>

It's less than three miles from Anacramp to Derrygooly, but a rainy day can make it feel like ten. A heavy drizzle had been falling since before dawn, as it seemed to be doing all winter long. It made the journey even more bone-chilling. Even the wrens and the magpies hid themselves in the depths of thick hedges. Hugh McKenna shivered as he drove a rickety, two-wheeled cart. Beside him on the seat was his daughter-in-law, Annie. She sheltered in his lee, a scarf pulled tightly over her head. His youngest daughters Nancy, Ellen, and Bridget huddled in the bed of the cart. Behind and beside the cart his sons (James, Hugh, Edward, Patrick, Charles and Bernard), his elder daughters (Mary and Catherine), and their husbands straggled along in the wind and wet. At least the walk allowed their bodies to generate a bit of warmth, Hugh envied.

They progressed slowly along the muddy boreen, threading their way between hedge rows and stone-walled pastures. The ground was littered with the droppings of cattle that used this path as they were shifted from one pasture to another. The pace suited just fine the gaunt donkey between the wagon shafts.

Also in the bed of the cart was a simple, bare-wood coffin containing the body of Catherine McMahon McKenna, Hugh's wife of thirty-three years. In the constant cold and damp of the season, Catherine had contracted, and finally succumbed to, pneumonia. The rustic chapel in Derrygooly would today afford her a Catholic requiem and burial, a right denied to previous generations of Irish Catholics under the harsh Penal Laws. It was, therefore, a memorial all the more precious in the eyes of her devoted husband.

Annie pressed herself against her father-in-law as a blast of weather came upon them. She felt no inhibition in doing so. She had always held Hugh and Catherine in the same circle of affection as her own father and mother. Her family, the Mullans, were also a farming family of Anacramp. They had been friends of the McKennas for decades. Annie was a slight woman of average height, with brown hair. Her face was somewhat plain; she had a strong chin and a wide line of a mouth. Her kindly, caring demeanor endeared her to all who knew her. Now she pushed the dirty weather and the day's sad occasion out of mind. She passed the journey watching her husband James as he walked beside the cart. Hugh's eldest son was a handsome fellow with sandy hair and his father's blue-gray eyes. Well-spoken and blessed with a ready smile, he made friends readily. He was as popular in the village of Caledon as he was in the townland. He and Annie had married two years prior but, as yet, were childless.

At mid-morning, they approached Hop's Fort, a hilltop clearing surrounded by a hedge of hawthorn that originally hid the "Mass rock" where outlawed liturgies were kept from prying British eyes. Now it was the site of a proper chapel, partly thatched and partly slated. It was the only Catholic chapel in the area, accommodating a large congregation from the length and breadth of the Caledon estate. Already arrived separately were members of the McMahon family, the Mullans, the McKeevers, and other neighbors and friends. The dark sky and, now, pelting rain drove everyone into the chapel in hurried fashion. There, solemn and teary-eyed faces watched in silence as the six McKenna sons carried their mother's coffin into the shelter of the nave.

It was early afternoon when the rituals were completed. Please God, the rain had stopped before the prayers at grave-side. Normally, folks would linger afterwards to comfort the grieving— women exchanging a bit of gossip, men off enjoying their white, clay pipes. But today, the threatening sky and hostile wind sent mourners back to their homes without delay. Hugh gathered his large family about him for the journey home. The sight of them all, especially his six strapping sons, evoked some considerable pride and comfort in the fifty-eight-year-old. He would miss his Catherine desperately. Their marriage had been a long and happy one. Still, he had these young ones upon whom he would rely in his old age.

* *

Hugh was a rough-hewn farmer with thick graying hair and pale blue-gray eyes. He was of medium height, but his frame was full and strong—signaling a life of strenuous labor. He was a thoughtful man who esteemed education, though he had little himself. He and Catherine had made a priority of having their children attend the little National school in nearby Ramaket. At three shillings per quarter per pupil, it was a sacrifice, but one they were happy to undertake. The family sustained themselves on potatoes, cabbages, and the sheep and swine they raised. They also grew oats as a cash crop, reserved for the grain market in the one-street village of Caledon. Though their lives were hard enough, it was not to be compared to the years of the Great Hunger that would come nearly twenty years later. Centuries of British landlordism had enured these Irish peasants to the rigors of the present. Life was as it had been and, therefore, as expected. Still for some, there lingered a hand-me-down memory of an earlier, freer time.

From medieval days, the green, fertile lands of this region were held by the venerable Irish clan of Uí Néill (O'Neill). In later years, the great Hugh O'Neill, the second Earl of Tir-Owen (Tyrone) fought the might of English armies through the Nine Years War (1591-1601). In that conflict, O'Neill allied himself with many other Ulster clans, including Clan McKenna. The McKennas had established themselves just across the Blackwater River in nearby County Monaghan as early as the 8th century. In the end, however, these forebears of Hugh McKenna were dispossessed of their holdings by the English invaders. The remnants of the O'Neill dominion were forfeit in 1646 when Phelim O'Neill's insurrection against English rule was put down in bloody finality.

Now, the Anglo-Irish Earl of Caledon was lord of a vast estate running along the southern border of County Tyrone and east into County Armagh. A demesne of 650 acres was surrounded by large landholdings in various townlands where tenancies were let to farmers and cottiers. The estate had been assembled through a series of purchases and leases, beginning in 1776, by James Alexander, a Derry merchant and former colonial official in India. Despite his status as newcomer to this area, and his lack of blue bloodlines, James was made a Baron in 1790, and a Viscount in 1797. Finally in 1800, he won the title of Earl in return for his political support of the Act of Union that abolished the Irish Parliament in Dublin. James died in 1802 and was succeeded by his son, James DuPre Alexander, the current Earl and landlord of the McKennas' modest leasehold in Anacramp. Notably generous, the Earl and his wife gave regular subsidies to the schools, the dispensary, and to the poor of the estate. As landlords went in 19th century Ireland, one could do much worse than the Alexanders of Caledon.

Daylight was nearly gone by the time the McKenna family returned from the funeral. Hugh returned the borrowed cart and donkey and retired to his home and hearth. Throughout the evening, his daughters and sons made repeated but subtle efforts to comfort their father. After the evening meal of gammon and cabbage, Ellen announced a special finale. "Here, Da! Nancy's made your favorite dessert—apple-barley flummery." Her father smiled and nodded his thanks.

Edward stoked a cheery fire in the hearth, while young Bridget brought pipe and tobacco to her father. But the old man was quiet all evening, lost in thoughts that owned no words. He sat up late, well after the others had retired. A vacant chair, long favored by his Catherine, repeatedly pulled his gaze. The turf fire was gray ash before he finally surrendered to nodding head and heavy eyelids.

The clachan where the McKennas resided consisted of a scattering of modest cottages—white-washed, mud-walled structures with thatched roofs. But glass windows and plank floors relieved any sense of abject poverty among the inhabitants. Hugh shared his dwelling with his unmarried children. James and Annie had a cottage of their own nearby. The married girls, Catherine and Mary, lived with their husbands in Caledon.

After their supper that evening, Annie complained, "James, I'm for bed . . . can't shed the chill of the day. You must be knackered yourself. Will you be comin' to bed now?"

James rose from the table and yawned. "Not just yet, dear. Will McKeever offered a visit and a wee measure of poteen. It's been a long and tirin' day, but I could use a good, strong drink. I shan't be too late."

He gave her a long hug and a kiss on the forehead. Then donning his still-wet coat and cap, he made his way through dark and muddy paths to the McKeever cottage. As he went, James rehearsed a prior conversation he and Will had shared. Weeks before, he had expressed to Will the worry and frustration he and Annie were feeling about their future and that of the extended family.

"As the first-married son, 'tis decided that I should be searchin' for a new leasehold. But my brothers will marry someday, and their new families will not be fed on the produce of Da's ten acres. But there's no vacant leasehold to be found in Anacramp."

Will had commiserated. "Perhaps another townland within the estate. Or another estate might have tenancies available."

"Aye, I must look into that. Da had to move away from his family in Errigal Truagh when he and Mother wed. A leasehold might suit my brothers, but what I'm wantin' is a business or trade. I respect the farmin' life, but I'm not lookin' to follow in Da's footsteps. The routines of a farmer are lonely, arduous, and borin'. Why shouldn't I be master of my own business? No more the tenant with the downcast eyes, the doffed cap, the yes, mi'lord, no, mi'lord. Ach! I want more than that!"

"Is it Caledon or Omagh where you might be findin' some business to do?"

"Omagh, perhaps. There's nothin' to be had for a papist farm boy in Caledon. The flour and the corn mills are owned and staffed by Protestants only. And I'll not be joinin' Annie's brothers as stone masons. That job makes the farm seem like heaven, it does."

Tonight, James would report his findings and continue this conversation interrupted by his mother's recent illness and death. Will greeted him at the door. "Ah, James, welcome." Shaking water drops from his cap, James entered the McKeever's common room, a modest space combining aspects of parlor, dining area and kitchen. It was dimly lit by candles and the glow from the hearth. Will's widowed mother was shooing her youngest children off to bed. James called out as they tumbled into their pallets in the sleeping loft. "A blessin' on this house and a peaceful night!"

Will was a farmer, some years younger than James. A lean fellow with a narrow face and red hair, he was friendly and had a good sense of humor. Drawing two chairs close to the turf fire, he poured their drinks and offered a toast in subdued voice. "Sláinte! God rest your sweet mother's soul. 'Twas a grand service they gave her this day, . . . well attended, given dirty weather."

James gave a deep sigh and nodded. "Sláinte!" He sipped his moonshine. The warmth it gave to his still-chilled body was most welcome. He stretched his legs closer to the fire, anxious for warmth beneath his damp clothing. After a few minutes of exchanged complaint over the persistent rains, James raised the postponed topic that was his greater worry. "You'll recall, Will, the leasehold question we discussed. Well, I've made my inquiries . . . . 'Tisn't good news. There's no lease to be had in the entire estate. I suppose one must wait upon a farmer dyin'! I'll be lookin' elsewhere, but findin' a landlord the like of Caledon may be a fool's errand."

Will pushed back an ember just fallen from the grate. "Too true, too true . . . . Have you a mind at all to go to America?"

James rocked back a bit in surprise. "I really haven't given it much thought. There's many who have gone . . . even from Aghaloo parish. You'll know Annie's older sister Mary. She's the one married to Edward McShane in Dungannon. Well now, Mary says McShanes have family in America for ten years now. To hear them tell, it be a fine country, a place where a Catholic lad might do well. But I'm not sure. I'm not one to slip family ties so easy, I'm thinkin'."

Will cast an eye to the loft, taking care as to who might be listening. "I have been weighin' it a bit," he admitted in a lowered voice. "Where does she say they are? America, 'tis a big place after all."

"Aye, she says they be livin' in a townland called Pittsburgh."

Will reached for the crock again and topped each glass. James winked his thanks.

"Are you serious about this, Will? After all, you have your father's leasehold. Would you really quit from home and kin? Who will mind your mother and the girls?"

"My uncle in Aughnacloy is willin'. But, arrah, I be talkin' only, friend. I might, and then I might not. Better than diggin' praities? Still, 'tis somethin' to think about of an evenin'."

Will did not act on the notion of emigrating to America. But the subject continued to be a bone for picking. And though James was somewhat intrigued by the career possibilities, he put the thought away when, several months later, he was surprised to find a leasehold after all. It wasn't a death that made his luck, but the emigration of another Anacramp family. While this eased his immediate dilemma, it left unresolved the challenge for his brothers. And it still left James in an occupation he could only endure, never embrace.

* *

In 1829, landlords throughout Ireland were moving land from tillage to grazing. Many were pressed by debts incurred

17

in living the aristocratic life, supporting country manor houses as well as town homes in Dublin or London. Others were convinced that the population of small tenants was outstripping the availability of arable land. All aspired to the greater profit to be had in selling to the export market their butter, beef, pork, and lamb. But this would mean displacing tenant families from existing leaseholds.

Small farmers, including Hugh McKenna, began to recognize that leases would be dwindling as they came up for renewal. Because his sons were hard pressed to find work or leaseholds for themselves, they were not well placed for taking wives. Even worse, Hugh might find himself displaced when his lease expired. So, the subject of emigration came up repeatedly for discussion within the family. The experience of the McShanes of Pittsburgh was cited frequently as young Hugh, Patrick and Bernard voiced their readiness to go. The McShanes might assist in their settlement, they argued. But Charles was adamantly opposed and James and Edward were unsure. James was especially concerned about the hardships of travel as Annie had become pregnant that summer. The young girls cared mostly that their family not be severed by the western ocean. They would greatly miss their older sisters who were fully settled.

The harvest that year was a good one. Hugh and his sons took in a fine crop of oats and sold them at good price at the Caledon market. Hugh reckoned these cash proceeds, and what might be had for his livestock, might pay for passage to America. He convened his children to see if a decision might be reached on this subject of emigration.

It was an atypically warm September. The long summer evenings of north latitudes were waning, but the glow of this evening's sunset was enough to light their meeting. Hugh spoke to his assembled young people as they sat together in the yard outside his cottage. He paused at first, staring at his rough, calloused hands. When the chatter of the others subsided, he began.

"My children, your father is no longer young. 'Tis not a time of life when one welcomes great changes. These fields of Anacramp have received the sweat of my brow for near forty years; my dear Catherine is buried nearby." He paused again, struggling to hold his emotions in check. He looked up into the dusky sky, took a deep breath, and allowed the wave to pass. "Leavin' this place will tear at deep-set roots I have put down here. And yet, there is no denyin' we have become too many for my poor acres. And my leasehold is not secure. I know very little of America. I have no assurance that life in the townland of Pittsburgh will be any better than what we have here. I only know that I cannot bear to lose what's left of my family. And that will surely happen if we do nothin'."

Nancy, a female image of her father in color and features, could not bear keeping silent. "Oh, Da! We'd never be leavin' you at all. If some must go, all should go!"

But Charles jumped in, his somber expression previewing his comment. He was a stocky fellow with dark hair and bushy eyebrows. A skeptic of emigration, his attitudes were unchanged, even in the face of economic pressure and the urging of his siblings. "I'm for stayin'. We don't know what's so grand about this place called Pittsburgh. And there are the dangers of the voyage."

James squeezed Annie's hand. "I'll not be takin' my wife, heavy with child, upon the sea for three or four weeks. I, too, want our family to stay together. But I cannot risk the life of our unborn child or its mother. Who can say what we will face on such a journey?"

Patrick, brown haired and brown-eyed, spoke next. He was the keenest proponent of emigration. "We accept what you say, Brother. None of us wish any harm. Still, you must agree that we cannot continue here in Anacramp. Lord Caledon may have his charity, but he will consolidate his lands for pasture!"

James spoke again without rancor. "I accept the truth of what you say. Still if goin' to America is your choice, we must remain here."

Undeterred, Patrick pressed further. "James, you've been wantin' an opportunity in business. The McShanes tell of many such in America, even for Catholics. This might be your best chance. Suppose we delay our departure until after Annie's baby arrives. Could you then consider joinin' in such a journey?"

James was now conflicted. Patrick may be right, he thought. In America, I might well become my own master. He looked at Annie. She knew well the ambitions of her husband and sensed that his winning ways were being wasted on the farm. It was part of what had attracted her so as they had begun courting. She shared his desire for a life beyond the fields and flocks. Now, she gave him a tentative nod, though her chin quivered with emotion. The thought of leaving home and her own family was daunting for her.

James shrugged. "'Tis no sure thing! If we do agree, Annie and the child must be healthy and strong."

Charles glared at his brother and sulked. "If you leave, James, perhaps I'll be havin' your leasehold."

Now a burst of vigorous debate ensued with the proponents of family unity pressing Charles. But it was soon interrupted by Edward. "Well, 'tis all grand that we might remain a family together. But the sums for passage and provisions will consume every penny of the oats money. There will also be the land journey to Pittsburgh, and then a period of gettin' settled—findin' lodgin', work, and all such. A considerable sum must be set aside for that."

Edward's voice of caution stilled the debate; everyone sensed he had put his finger upon an issue that must be resolved. As the evening darkened, Hugh stood again. "We must give it a bit more thought, children. Let's be in now."

Over the next few months, the differences of opinion narrowed somewhat. Though Charles was most unhappy, he had to reluctantly concede that being the sole holdout was untenable. Given his father's wishes, and the risk that the leasehold might be forfeit if he stayed, his opposition dissipated. Still, his attitude remained dour. The financial challenge of emigration, however, was yet to be resolved.

It was Nancy, who despite her youth, posed a partial solution. Her eyes shone with optimism as she addressed her father and siblings at table. "We have our leasehold yet! Not all need leave immediately. Suppose our men go beforehand and find employment. We girls can remain here, or with our sisters, until a home be made in America. Another crop of oats would easily provide money for our passage and more."

Hugh shook his head and offered his daughter a patronizing wave of the hand. "Nancy, you are well-said, but for two cautions. 'Tisn't right that you girls make such a journey without my protection or that of your brothers. There are dangers, and those who would do you dirty. And further, who will bring in another oats crop? Surely, not yourselves!"

Nancy dropped her gaze. To these points, she had no ready reply.

One evening several days later, James and Annie lay in bed awaiting the onset of sleep. Annie's little one was active this night, kicking and moving about, reminding her that it would not be long in making its appearance. She placed James' hand against her belly so that he might feel the strength of the child in waiting.

He laughed as he felt movement within. "Must be a lad in there; he's so strong!"

"Might be a daughter, Mr. McKenna. Don't be placin' any wagers. We Mullan girls are strong enough."

When the movements subsided, Annie turned the conversation to the events of the day just ending. Her younger sister, Catherine Mullan, was now virtually betrothed to Will McKeever. Any excuse would do to come by for a visit, in hopes of seeing him.

"James, Catherine was here today. She says Will is after goin' off to America after all. I'm thinkin' all this talk of Pittsburgh among us has peaked his interest."

"Is he really? He hasn't mentioned it to me lately. I know he's sore worried the Earl will have grazin' in Anacramp. Every family that chooses emigration adds to the land available for pasture and further whets the Earl's appetite."

"I said nothin' of this to Catherine, mind you. But, could it be, if Will is truly decided, that he and Catherine might bring your sisters to America when their time be right."

"'Tis an interestin' thought. They will marry next year. I must query Will when next I see him."

Early in 1830, Annie delivered a healthy boy, also named James—after his father. By then, an agreement had been struck between the McKennas and Will McKeever. Will agreed to come to Pittsburgh in the following year, bringing Nancy, Ellen, and Bridget with him. The McKenna men would put down a final crop of oats and potatoes before departing. The task of harvesting they would leave to Will and spalpeens. He would receive the major share of proceeds for his trouble and the balance would fund the sisters' passage.

The family being now in consensus, James wrote to the McShanes of Pittsburgh to advise them of an intended arrival later in the year. As spring came and went, the time of departure drew near. It was a wrenching and emotional day when the goodbyes were said to family and friends.

The McKenna daughters all gathered round their father and brothers in tearful embraces. Other farmers of Anacramp, many of whom had been Hugh's great friends for two or three decades, presented him with a fine, new burl pipe. And there were several suggestions that, perhaps, some others of the family being left behind might one day choose to make the great migration as well.

But the most difficult farewell for Hugh was that made in Derrygooly. There, he knelt and prayed and cried at the little white cross atop the grave of his beloved wife. Ach, Catherine, my love. Can you forgive my leavin' you, dearie, never to visit here again? You'll be knowin' that our farm in Anacramp cannot sustain us. Sure, somethin' must be done. I'm afraid to be goin' to America; but I'm afraid not to be goin'. I'll be carryin' you in my heart wherever the Lord may take us.

Chapter Two

The 25th of May, 1830 dawned bright and pleasant, a continuing spring-time blessing to the travelers from Anacramp. Their journey to the port of Derry had taken most of three days to cover the roughly sixty miles. Their route took them through the towns of Omagh and Strabane, as well as through lush, green country devoted increasingly to grazing. While the towns and villages along their route offered lodging options, they resolved to save their funds by sleeping in the open. The weather being unusually fine, it was no problem to occupy a fallow field to take their nightly rest. The party of nine consisted of Hugh, his sons, Annie, and her baby. Being the only woman in the group would present awkward moments for Annie, but she and James had ultimately decided that their little family would not be left behind.

The dirt road followed the valley of three interconnected rivers—the Strule, the Mourne, and finally the Foyle—their entrance to the sea and thence to America. Following these bodies of water, it was difficult for Hugh McKenna not think how their lives were being swept along with the currents to strange, new lands. Already, he was farther from home than ever before. Leaving the rolling hills, the fertile fields, and the stands of woodland pained his agrarian soul.

It was afternoon when they approached Wooden Bridge that spanned River Foyle and led them into the ancient, walled city that the English had misnamed Londonderry. Derry is the anglicized form of the Irish word "Doire" (meaning oak-wood). The city dates back to the 6th century when Saint Columba founded a monastery on the east bank of the Foyle. It was the Tudor invasions of the early 17th century that brought under British sway this strategic gateway to the land of the O'Neills. Derry was granted a Royal Charter in 1613. It was then that massive stone walls were raised to encircle the city, protecting the English and Scot settlers "planted" in the region. These same stone walls, never breached in various sieges, were still very much intact as our weary travelers paid the bridge toll and entered into the city proper.

The sights and sounds of this urban center bewildered and intimidated Hugh and his family. Previously, Omagh had provided the barest hint of city life to these farmers of Anacramp. The sheer variety of shops, the loaded carts of street vendors, the soldiers, sailors and stevedores, all presented new images and insights. A stooped and wizened keeper of the toll house had directed them to Ship Quay Street where the shipping companies were clustered. "Follow Bridge Street to Ferry Quay. Continue on to The Diamond, then a right turnin' and you're there."

Visibly puzzled, Hugh turned to his sons. "What must this Diamond be?"

James hoisted his baggage. "Whatever it may be, the day is dyin' soon. Shops will be closin' presently. We must find lodgin' now and leave bookin' passage till mornin'." He was especially concerned for Annie and her baby. They were visibly fatigued by the heat of the day and the long walk from Strabane. Though Annie made no complaint, her baby was now getting quite fussy.

Hugh readily agreed and sought out a public house. His choices were numerous, but of uncertain character. Being a busy port, Derry's waterfront district was a place for caution. Eventually they settled upon a hostelry in Ferry Quay and took their supper. While James and his family retired early, the others sat for a pint in the bar. Inevitably, talk turned to the impending voyage.

First, Charles ventured a bit of advice to the group. "I say we choose a ship bound for New York or Philadelphia. These ports must be closest to Pittsburgh."

But Patrick waved away such a thought. "Nay, the costs of passage will be too dear. We must seek the least price, whatever that may be. We'll need every spare shillin' for the land journey and beyond."

Their father pulled at his new pipe and thought for a moment. "Patrick makes good sense. I've heard the ships from Canada make the best offer. They deliver their cargo of timber to Belfast or England. They would return home empty save for any settlers they may carry. We should find a timber ship, I'm thinkin'." With that, Hugh drained his pint and stood to retire. "Don't be up late, lads. We must be out and about early in the morn."

The next day, leaving Annie and the baby at the inn, Hugh and his sons made the rounds of the shipping companies. Signs in the windows touted passage to America and Britain. As predicted, Canadian timber ships bound for Quebec were offering the cheapest passage, about fifteen shillings per adult. This compared to four to five pounds sterling to book a passenger ship bound for Boston, New York, or Philadelphia.

Selecting a company at random, the men entered a small office. A ticket agent was seated behind a counter. He was a young man in frock coat. His somewhat blemished face showed wispy beginnings of a beard. Responding to their query, he announced with feigned surprise, "Arrah, you be in luck, misters. There be a departure tomorrow—the bark *Sophia*, bound for Quebec. You must book today though, for the tide will be early!"

Hugh looked at his sons and each nodded. Pulling a leather bag from his pocket, he counted out the nearly seven pounds required. He had never seen his money spent so quickly. He gave a sigh of trepidation. Ach! I wish I was back in Anacramp.

"Don't forget, you must make all provisions for your party," the clerk chastened. "The company provides only drinkin' water. As there will be little chance for cookin', you'd be well served to purchase food what can be eaten cold."

Hugh nodded and picked up their tickets. Provisions, ah yes, provisions! As they turned to leave, their clerk laughed. "Will you not wish to know where your ship be docked?"

Embarrassed, they received directions to the quays at Kings Shores, where the *Sophia* was berthed. Young Hugh and Charles were dispatched to find the vessel and confirm the time of assembly. The rest of the group marched off in search of the many purchases required for the long sea voyage.

When Hugh and Charles approached the river, just downstream of the city center, they quickly became perplexed. There were twenty-one wharves spilling north along the Foyle. After making several queries, they found the *Sophia*. She was a three-masted vessel—two masts rigged for square sails and that closest to the stern rigged fore-and-aft. Its wooden hull was painted black and the gunnels white. There was rope strung everywhere. Sailors scrambled upon ratlines, mending and coating the rigging with pitch as needed. Charles gaped at the sight. "Jaysus, the masts seem to go to the heavens."

Various stevedores and crew were engaged in loading supplies from the wagon of a ship's chandler. This activity took place under the watchful eyes of a short, stocky gentleman in shirt-sleeves and wearing a planter's hat. He looked to be about forty-odd years, and when he spoke it was a dialect of English that sounded strange upon McKenna ears.

Charles queried a crewman who pointed to the gentleman giving orders. "Best ask the master, Captain Blake." Tentatively, caps in hand, Hugh and Charles ventured up the gangway during a break in the traffic moving to and fro. "Might we have a word, sir?"

Blake, unhappy with this distraction, impatiently motioned them aboard and out of the path to the hold. "Ayah, what's yer business?"

Charles made himself spokesman. "We've tickets for tomorrow's voyage, sir. Can you tell us the time we should assemble for boardin'?"

Blake pushed the brim of his hat back and surveyed the two farm boys. "We need to be underway by mid-morning. You ought arrive about seven. Have all your provisions in hand. I reckon there'll be nearly three-hundred passengers, so it will take a while to get everyone settled 'tween decks."

Charles and Hugh looked at the vessel and then at each other. Three hundred! Where will they put us all? Though they had never seen ships before, and certainly the *Sophia* seemed quite large, one could only wonder what the hold would be like with three-hundred people confined for a month.

"Thank you, sir. We'll be here on the wharf before seven."

Blake grunted and turned back to the loading process.

When the McKenna boys returned to the inn, everyone was engaged in packing their few clothes, some bedding, and all their newly purchased provisions into canvas bags.

"Ah, here they are!" Patrick announced as Charles and Hugh entered. "Grab your kit and get busy. Da, wants all made ready by supper."

Baby James dozed in the corner, undisturbed by the chaos. Annie ruminated as she packed. *Good job that I'm nursin' that wee one. There'll be no cow's milk on that ship . . . . What will I do for clean nappies?*

Next morning, they were all up before dawn. After breaking their fast and settling their account, the men each hoisted their burdens and marched off in the cool of an overcast morning. Charles and young Hugh led the way. James, Annie and the baby brought up the rear. At the wharf, there was already a sizeable crowd gathered. Families, couples, and solitary travelers all milled about, talking in low, expectant voices. The McKennas took their place in a straggly queue, soon followed by the next arrivals. Hugh fingered the tickets, trying to look composed. But he was all a'churning inside. *I wonder*, he thought, *what sort of leasehold I may find if we actually get to where we are goin'.*

About an hour of waiting ensued. The time was passed in casual conversation between parties, comparing homes left behind, desired destinations, and the motives prompting their leave-taking. An elderly woman in a blue shawl came over to chat. "Álainn babaí!" Seeing Annie's perplexed expression, she switched from Irish to English. "I said you're baby is cute."

"Sorry, mamó, I have little Irish. But, thank you . . . . I'm thinkin' he's a wee one for such a terrible-long journey."

"Arrah, you'd be a quare one were you not to worry. But the child seems he's doin' bravely. I'm cheered to see all the young ones among us, so I am. It suggests hope for new beginnin's."

"Please, God!" She dandled her baby to keep him happy. "I'm Annie McKenna. May I know your name? It'll be a long voyage and I'd welcome a friendly word now and again."

"Aye, I'm Mary McDevitt . . . from Dunfanaghy in County Donegal. My family are just there," she pointed. "Sure, I'd welcome your company and that of your babe as well."

"And have you a husband with you, mamó?"

"Ach, no, dearie. Mr. McDevitt, God rest him, was a fisherman, don't you know. I lost him in a storm twenty-two years ago. No, 'tis my only son, Sean, and his family. They're off to Philadelphia. And as there's none of mine still in Dunfanaghy, I'm after comin' along."

Now, the young clerk from the shipping company pushed his way past them, passenger list in hand. He was sporting a bowler hat, seemingly a size too small, for it caused his hair to stick out at queer angles. With some difficulty, he made his way to the gangway where he could be seen and heard. Under the watchful eye of Captain Blake, he called for a semblance of order.

"Boardin' will commence shortly . . . . Straighten that queue and be havin' your tickets ready for inspection."

With that, a great shuffling began. After a quick goodbye, Mrs. McDevitt hurried back to her brood. Wandering children were collected. Conversation died a slow death, and bags were hoisted again. Soon passengers were making their way up the gangway. The clerk checked off names on the passenger list as they stepped aboard. On the foredeck, several improvised privies had been cobbled together. There, human waste would be channeled through scuppers and out to the open sea. Several of the crew shepherded the arrivals to a broad staircase that led to the hold. "Watch yer steps, folks," the seamen called out in their broad, Boston accents. "Find a place and settle in. Single men aft, single ladies to the bow."

The McKenna family descended into a den of confusion amid cries of complaint, even anger, from their fellows. Charles was the first to voice his outrage. "Jaysus, Da! Will you be lookin' at where we must stay? I knew we should have stayed in Anacramp!"

His father grimaced. Where have I brought this family of mine?

The dark of the hold was barely relieved by a handful of whale oil lanterns hung from overhead beams. The rough plank flooring was still littered with the debris of timbers lately delivered to Deptford, near London. Rows of makeshift, wooden berths ran the length of the hold in double bunk fashion. An arm-load of straw in each offered meager comfort. At the center of the hold were many great casks of potable water arranged upon long, wooden racks. Spiders and various other insects reluctantly gave way to new occupants. Worst of all was the heat and lack of fresh air. A few small portholes on either side of the ship provided scant light and ventilation, especially for those near the center of the hold.

Bernard, the youngest, pushed forward. "Let's not be tarryin', the best spaces will all be taken." He rushed off in search of some unoccupied area proximate to a porthole, his brothers following his lead. James and his father escorted Annie and child through a pushing and shoving crowd. Finding no vacant berths near a porthole, the family had to accept something less.

About 10:30, the call "Cast off all lines!" was heard and soon the ship's movement could be felt. A towline was used to pull the *Sophia* from the quay and into the river current now running fast with the outgoing tide. The sound of sails being unfurled and the scamper of many feet on the deck above followed shortly. A miniature of landscape and sky passed each porthole, a last glimpse of land for many days to come. By afternoon, the *Sophia* passed through the mouth of the Foyle between Greencastle and Magilligan Point. Now, naught but open water was before them till Newfoundland and the Gulf of St. Lawrence.

Immigrant Ship at Sea
(The MultiText Project in History, University College Cork, Ireland)

The early days of the voyage were difficult for everyone. Though the weather was still relatively favorable, adjusting to conditions 'tween decks was a challenge to the senses. Noise persisted day and night—babies and young children crying, older children foostering and being scolded, men and women snoring, the sounds of ocean waves beating against the hull, decks creaking, and sailors shouting back and forth.

The smells emanating from such close quarters became increasingly noxious. Despite the straw and scant bedding, backs and limbs became cramped and achy. When the weather permitted, time above on the main deck was rationed among the passengers such that there be no interference with ship operations. These intervals were precious escapes from the unpleasant conditions below.

Though berthed in separate areas, the McKenna family gathered together for meals. Sharing out with parsimonious care, Hugh controlled the supply of hard cheese, salt-cured meat, black bread, and dried fruit.

Edward, the shy brother distinguished from his siblings by his carrot-red hair, took a protective attitude towards his sister-in-law, conscious that she was eating for two. "Here Annie, take some of mine." In time, other family members made similar offers. Finally Annie had to cry, "Enough, dear brothers! I'm thankin' you, but you overwhelm my appetite. You also must see to your own health."

Though the *Sophia* was a slow, somewhat plodding vessel, she did well angling into the westerly winds. The weight of her nearly three-hundred passengers, their baggage, and provisions was insufficient to steady the craft in choppy seas. She, therefore, carried from England a load of paving stones in the bottom of her hull as essential ballast.

The weather became stormy after five days. Rolling seas and driving rains made conditions markedly worse for passengers. Portholes remained closed to prevent the invasion of seawater. This requirement made the atmosphere even more foul, especially as many fell victim to seasickness. Visits to the main deck were eliminated during this period as well. Just keeping one's footing in moving about, as the ship did pitch and yaw, presented considerable danger. Mercifully, these days of foul weather lasted less than a week and brighter days and calmer seas returned.

Two weeks into the voyage, the first death among the passengers was reported; subsequently three others expired, two of them being infants. It was rumored there was a fever aboard, though some passengers appeared simply to be malnourished. Annie became frantic in her concern for her baby. Mary McDevitt tried to give some comfort, conscious that her own grandchildren were equally at risk. "Prayer, dearie. Prayer is the only way forward. Have you your rosary?"

Crowded hold of a typical emigrant ship.
(The MultiText Project in History, University College Cork, Ireland)

Late that night, James found Annie awake and crying. He reached over and pulled her close to himself. He stroked her hair and kissed her forehead.

"Oh, James, . . . I'm so scared . . . scared our little one will be catchin' the fever. 'Tis a thousand Ave's I've said, but I can't put it aside."

"Ach, Annie, I know. I worry as well, but for the both of you . . . . Now, are you not the woman who was after tellin' me some months ago how strong were the Mullan girls?"

With that, Annie began to laugh at herself through tears. "Aye, I am that woman . . . . I'll try to be strong, dear. I promise."

But Annie's worry was shared by the rest of the family. Her father-in-law chided himself constantly in the face of the daily hardships and dangers. One day, he commented to James, "Can you forgive your old Da for bringin' your wife and child into this hellish den?"

"Da, you are not to be blamed." There was a note of tension in James' voice. "'Twas a decision taken by all. Bad as it is, it cannot last much longer. Another fortnight? Let us pray for safety, above all." His father gave a half-hearted smile, but his anxieties persisted throughout the voyage.

On Sundays, Captain Blake would make an appearance to conduct a celebration of the Sabbath. This consisted of readings from his Bible, typically selections from the Psalms. He also used these occasions to reassure the passengers. "We've had a bit o' weather this last week and that has cost us some days due to strong headwinds. But now, we're progressing well. The winds have shifted in our favor," he claimed to no one's great comfort.

The last of these inspirational moments came on Sunday, June 27. They had been at sea for a month already. Blake arrived in the hold dressed in his usual Sunday, black frock coat. His graying, brown hair was wet-combed severely back from a wide, furrowed brow. Standing upon the staircase, several feet above the steerage, he addressed his captive, but not unwilling, congregation. After the usual sacred readings, he offered his progress report.

"My friends, you have done right well, enduring the hardships of life at sea. Now, I have a bit of encouraging news. Two days ago, we spotted the first gulls and land birds of British North America. We are now well into the gulf of St. Lawrence and will be on the river for another day or two. Quebec is not so far off."

This disclosure elicited cries of "Huzzah," smiles, and laughter among what had been a weary and anxious crowd. Annie took her baby from her husband and kissed the child repeatedly, murmuring, "We're almost there, son, almost there." But though they had traveled over two thousand miles, they would travel a great deal more before reaching their new home. From that day, visits to the main deck were spent searching the horizon for glimpses of the port of Quebec.

Chapter Three

On the afternoon of June 29th the *Sophia* arrived at Grosse Ile, just downriver from Quebec City. There, an inspection by the health authorities was required of all incoming vessels. In anticipation of prompt clearance, *Sophia's* passengers cheerfully dumped overboard the fetid straw that had lined their berths for so long. It was to their shock and regret that two more nights were spent aboard ship without the scant comfort that straw had afforded. On July 1st, they were cleared and arrived in the port of Quebec. But the river was crowded with ships at anchor, awaiting a wharf. Due to the delays they had encountered at sea, Captain Blake was as anxious as his passengers that they disembark promptly. He was already late for collecting his next cargo of timber. Rather than await a vacant pier, arrangements were made to ferry his passengers from the *Sophia* to the Quai Saint Andre in hired long boats. The McKennas were nearly crazy with excitement to be rid of their foul confinement. They waited upon the main deck, in the heat of a sunny, summer day, knowing the hold was even hotter. Finally, about mid-afternoon, they touched solid ground and rejoiced.

Quebec City in the 19th Century
(The MultiText Project in History, University College Cork, Ireland)

Old Hugh regained his spirits. "Let's find our lodgin', lads . . . .
I'll be welcomin' a proper meal!"

"A bed, my kingdom for a real bed," joked Bernard. James and
Annie exchanged glances. "I'm thinkin' a bath might be the first
thing each of us require," she announced to laughter from all.

Pushing into the city, they found suitable accommodation
in Rue Saint Paul. Their much diminished supplies of food they
would reserve for the journey ahead. This night, a modest feast was
arranged, though with some difficulty. Their host spoke only the
French of the Quebecois.

After an interval of looking and pointing at the various
offerings served to other patrons, they made their wishes known
and savored their first hot meal in almost six weeks. Though the
French-influenced cuisine was unfamiliar, it was pronounced
delicious by all. Then, full of exhaustion, their night's sleep carried
well into the following morning, though baby James ensured that
his parents awakened early for his feeding.

The weather being fine the next day, everyone chose to stretch their long-cramped legs in an exploration of the city. James, Annie, and the baby did not venture far. Annie had volunteered to see to the washing of the family's filthy attire. The others, however, attacked the heights of Cap Diamant, the high promontory upon which much of the city rested. From these heights, a dark, blue river, full of vessels and sea birds, presented itself in gleaming sunlight. The realization of being on land and in fresh air was a delight to all.

Old Hugh spied the cross-topped Basilica de Notre Dame de Quebec in the distance and called his sons to attention. "Children, let's be lookin' further there. Sure, that must be the grandest church in all the world! We have been preserved through much hardship, by the grace of God. 'Twould be fittin' that we give heaven our thanks."

The following morning the entire family returned for the Mass. Though stupefied by the glory of the ornate interior and totally lost by the homily delivered in French, Hugh and his children took great comfort in the reception of the blessed sacrament. Thanksgiving for a successful crossing was soon followed by supplications for a safe and speedy passage in the great land journey that lay ahead.

But how to get to their destination? What road to take? An inquiry with a police officer was of little use. He insisted that a packet steamer was the only way to the west and pled ignorance of optimal land routes into and through United States territory. At supper at the inn that night, another party of immigrant travelers were overheard speaking English. Leaving his meal, Hugh engaged them in conversation and learned that they were Irish, from Dublin. The leader of the party, one Michael McDermott, related that they were bound for Albany, New York and would be taking the steamer to Montreal. Thence, they would travel by land into the United States just above Plattsburgh.

"Ach, I was hopin' you might advise us," Hugh admitted. "We haven't a thought as to the best way to the townland of Pittsburgh."

McDermott was an educated man and far more knowledgeable about his intended country. "'Tis unknown to me the route to Pittsburgh, my friend. But I know this—many travelers bound for the west choose the packet boats on the Erie Canal. The route is direct and easier than walkin' the rough, isolated roads. Many roadways charge a toll for each coach or wagon."

Hugh was ashamed to admit that his purse would permit neither packet boat fares nor horse-drawn wagon. Still, it was interesting to learn of this canal to the west. He reasoned that where there is a canal, there ought be a towpath where travelers afoot might pass.

"How might one find this Erie Canal?"

McDermott scratched his well-trimmed beard and pondered. "Well, you could join us, as we will pass over the canal as we enter Albany. But another way, a better way, would be to meet the canal further west. It steers a northwesterly course. 'Twould make no sense to be travelin' as far south as we, only to turn north again. In Montreal, you must seek further directions."

Hugh thanked him for the advice and wished his party "Godspeed!" Yes, we must follow this river to Montreal. There, we will ask again of the authorities.

The rest of the day was spent in replenishing supplies and repacking their baggage. To lighten their burden, they made no attempt to provision for the entire trip to Pittsburgh. Periodic purchases would be made in the towns and cities along the way. They would leave early the next morning. There was no money for lingering in one place, especially in such costly lodging.

The Rue Saint Louis was quiet that Sunday morning, just after dawn. The McKenna party set out early, hoping to take full advantage of what would be a long, but fair, day. Most of the men carried bags; however, James carried his young son in his arms. Perhaps if Annie might be burden-free, he reasoned, we will make better progress. Later, Patrick improvised a sling of sorts in which the baby might ride without encumbering the arms of his father.

The cobbled street soon gave way to a dirt track the English called the Post Road and the French called the Chemin du Roi. This thoroughfare, generally paralleling the banks of the St. Lawrence, was the direct route to Montreal, about 170 miles away. They set a brisk pace in the cool of morning. At first, the dew kept the dust down; but by mid-morning, clouds of it hugged their ankles.

The sun was not yet high when they encountered a reality that would challenge their schedule and their purse repeatedly. They approached Cap Rouge only to discover the first of the many ferries they must use to pass over the tributaries of the St. Lawrence River. Each required a toll and often a wait while the ferry boat returned from a crossing, or loaded passengers and cargo. Annie would soon come to exploit these delays by using the time to feed or change the baby, still just four months old.

As the day went on, the number of travelers on the road increased significantly. The varied appearance of their fellow travelers was a wonder to the McKenna family. The styles of dress, the languages, and ethnicities were diverse to a degree to which they were unaccustomed. In Ireland, it was simple; there were three basic classes: the Irish peasant—typically Catholic, the middle-class farmer or tradesman—often Protestant, and the Anglo-Irish landlord or professional.

Here in Lower Canada, there were the Quebecois, those of French descent. These might be of any economic class: farmer, merchant, tradesman, trapper, or professional. Then there were the British: military, civil servants, shippers and traders. Finally, there was a significant indigenous population, Indians of various tribes, increasingly pushed away from the river settlements.

One day, as the family awaited the ferry at Cap-de-la-Madeleine, they were agog at the appearance of a fellow passenger who looked to be in his forties. He was of medium height, dark, with shaven head—save for the long, black queue tied with leather thong. A breastplate of bone-work hung upon his chest and a beaded choker encircled his neck. He wore a breechcloth, buckskin leggings, and moccasins. Around his shoulders was draped a woolen cape of red and black. A knife in a leather sheath hung at his waist; but his demeanor was quiet, dignified, and totally disinterested.

The McKenna party tried not to stare, but found their gaze returning repeatedly. They had heard stories of fierce warriors capable of cruel violence, though these were exaggerated and long out of date. Annie whispered to her husband. "I'll not be afraid, James. 'Tis his country, after all. It is we who are visitors."

"Well said, Annie dear. But I'm thinkin' the Brits have taken his land just as they have taken our own."

When they landed, the aboriginal went his way. The ferryman, noticing their trepidation assured, "Il est Abnaki, a paisible."

For the most part, the countryside they passed through was open, green, and cultivated in small-holding farms. Being early summer, the crops were just beginning to show their character.

Each night, the McKennas sought out a fallow field and a clear stream or well where they might encamp. When the weather turned, as in a sudden thunder storm, they had to seek shelter wherever they could find it. Sometimes this would be a farmer's barn or a village inn. More often a copse of trees was the best they could do.

Given the relatively slow pace, it took them four days just to reach Trois Rivières, the first sizeable town along their way. But they made no attempt to linger as they were anxious that their journey be concluded before the warmth of summer disappeared. Another five days brought them to the village of St. Joseph on the eastern edge of the island of Montreal. The island was dotted with numerous such villages. The McKennas' route hugged the southeastern coastline of the island. In each village, they sought guidance regarding the best route to New York's Erie Canal. But they received no meaningful directions. Usually, it was difficult just to find English speakers.

Upon reaching Vieux Montreal, their first priority was to find lodging. Afterwards, James was sent off to make further inquiries. As he wandered through the city, he found himself in the Place

D'armes, a public square graced with several impressive buildings. He gawked at another great church, also called Basilica de Notre-Dame. Nearby was the Seminary of St. Sulpice, one of the city's oldest structures. Just then, one of the Sulpician priests emerged from the seminary and James accosted him.

"Forgive me, your grace, have you any English at all?"

The young priest chuckled, amused at the misplaced honorific. "Oui, I speak some English. How may I serve you?"

James explained their journey and the search for the most appropriate route across the border and to the west. The cleric shook his head. "I am sorry, but I am unable to answer this. I will take you to the prefecture of police. They will certainly help you."

James readily accepted this kind offer. At least they will have English there, he mused. It was a short distance, and he thanked the priest profusely as they arrived. Inside, a corpulent police captain was summoned. A shower of dandruff bespeckled his fine blue uniform at the collar and shoulders. His manner was initially rather brusque and spoken with disdain. "Another Irish settler, eh? We see a great number of your kind here . . . . Well, come along. I have a map in my office." He brought James into a room furnished with several desks. These were covered with documents being attended to by clerks. The captain led James to a wall map and pointed.

"You must follow the river further west, you see. First, you will make the crossing to Ile Perrot and then another beyond. You want the road to Cornwall and thence to Prescott. There you will cross the river into New York. You will find a road to the Canal in the town of Ogdensburg."

James scribbled the instructions upon a scrap of paper the captain provided him. "'Tis a long distance!"

"You're walking, are you? Then it must be five or six days to Prescott."

Back at the inn, James beamed in his success. "'Tis all sorted!" He reported to his father and brothers all he had learned.

Old Hugh slapped him on his back. "Well done! Now, let's top up our supplies. At dawn, we will find the ferry for this island of Perrot."

The weather held fair and the family made good time. As they passed into the province of Ontario, the character of the country changed noticeably. The Quebecois influence waned rapidly and was replaced by an English and Scots-Irish culture. Here, they had no difficulty communicating with the locals, though they sensed an air of disdain in the attitudes of some. These transplants from Ulster, often members of the Orange lodge, had little use for a party of papist immigrants.

As they marched along, Hugh, ever the farmer, ruminated to James, "Have you noticed, lad, how different this land is from our home in Ireland. And, we've seen but little rain. No soft days such as back in Tyrone. The farms seem rich enough, but 'tisn't like home at all."

"Aye, even the trees are an unfamiliar sort. As for rain, perhaps 'tis just the season. Anyway, 'tis Canada and likely different entirely from what we'll be findin' in Pittsburgh."

As they approached Prescott, their last Canadian milestone, the littlest McKenna was taken with a high fever. The child was flushed and disconsolate. Annie was distraught. She pleaded with her husband. "Sure, we must stay in this town! The child needs a doctor. 'Twould be foolish to remain on the road."

"Don't be frettin', Annie. We will not be leavin' till the boy be well. But I must let Da and the others decide if they will wait or go. We mustn't drain their purse over our own trouble."

But Hugh was having none of that and he barked at his son. "No, that will not do! We've come this far as a family. I'll not be leavin' any behind." The brothers were also adamant that they would await young James' recovery. Though they were clearly concerned about the child, there were other motives in their minds as well.

Patrick pulled off his shoe and rubbed life back into his toes. "Begad! I'll be happy to let my poor feet rest a day or two."

They took lodging in Prescott to shelter the child from the elements. But the fever persisted and James sought a physician for the child. The innkeeper recommended a Scots-Irish gentleman named McDonald who lived in the town. James called upon him and explained their predicament. Then he led him to the public house and the room where Annie kept watch over the little patient. The doctor was a middle-aged fellow, affecting a full, graying beard. He was friendly, but business-like. He examined little James carefully. When he had finished his "ahhs" and "hmmms" he addressed the parents.

"The boy's pulse is a bit high, but his lungs are clear . . . . That's very important. It appears to be just a passing fever, something that he must fight off. I see no signs of any particular ailment. Cool his brow with a wet cloth and see that he sleeps as best he can. When the fever breaks, give him a thin gruel of oat or barley. He's old enough now to need more sustenance than mother's milk."

James and Annie nodded their understanding. She took the doctor's hand. "I'm thankin' you, Doctor. I can't tell you how relieved you've made me. We arrived on a timber ship some weeks ago and there was terrible sickness aboard! I was worried my babe had come down with that same fever. God bless you, sir!"

James, seeing the doctor's embarrassed reaction, cleared his throat. "Yes, thank you Doctor. Now, about your fee . . ."

But McDonald demurred. "Save your money . . . . I have done little enough! It seems you have a great journey ahead of you. But if the child worsens, come for me again."

Two mornings later, the boy awoke, free of fever. As instructed, Annie began to add a bit of solid food to his diet. By the following day, James announced that they might safely resume their trek. During the interlude, his brothers had sorted out the ferry to Ogdensburg. Hugh was also productive, searching out a money changer to acquire American silver for his British pounds and shillings.

They took the afternoon ferry to Ogdensburg, where they made further inquiries for the Erie Canal. "Continue upriver to the village of Morris," they were instructed by the postmaster. "From there, head south and stay on the road to Utica. The canal passes through the city on its way west."

It being too late in the day to set out for Morris, they found a field southwest of town in which to camp for the night. The next day, they made the fifteen miles to Morris. There, for the first time since arriving in Quebec, they abandoned the St. Lawrence river and turned south.

After the first ten miles out of Morris, the country gradually changed its character. Instead of farm country and a succession of villages, their route took them into an increasingly wild, rugged, forested area. Up and down hillsides, they plodded the rough track. The efforts they expended reduced the distance they could cover before dusk. This meant camping in a most remote and wild country.

Ever the optimist, Charles cautioned the group. "We may well be facin' a bunch of hostile Indians, or maybe wild animals."

Annie, hearing such talk, was plagued by strange sounds and sights, real and imagined. She nestled closer to her husband and child, listening and evaluating each animal cry or snap of twig. "James, did you hear that?" But his reply was only a deep snore. It was a long, restless night. Though she found the forest scenic and pleasantly cool by day, she was relieved to emerge into a more familiar, open country the next day as they approached the village of Antwerp.

It took another five days of trudging from Antwerp to Utica, their gateway to the Erie Canal. They crossed over the Mohawk River and shortly thereafter passed over the canal itself. An air of excitement came over the family. Hugh lit his pipe and puffed away in celebration. "It may be only a way-station, but this canal has been a destination of sorts. It makes me feel blessed to have found it, and safely so."

It was the first of August, one month after they landed in Quebec. They were tired, but now their feet were toughened and blisters were becoming rare. Their shoes, however, were showing the evidence of the almost six hundred miles they had already covered. They would be on the road for almost another five hundred miles before reaching Pittsburgh. Several members of the family invested in new footwear as they reconnoitered Utica, a town of eight thousand souls. After shopping for shoes and supplies, they returned to the canal to observe its operation and understand how best to proceed.

The Erie Canal was only completed from Albany to Buffalo five years prior. Its length was three hundred sixty-four miles. It was hailed as a world-class engineering marvel of the day. A series of locks enabled a rise in elevation of five hundred sixty-eight feet from east to west. Each lock was ninety feet long and fifteen feet wide. The ditch itself was four feet deep and forty feet wide. In addition, there were eighteen aqueducts constructed to allow passage over ravines and rivers along the route.

Freight vessels, known as line boats, were typically pulled by a team of mules, driven by a man known as a "hoggee." Passenger traffic was served by packet boats about sixty feet in length. Each was fitted with a multi-purpose room that functioned as lounge, dining area, and sleeping quarters (men's and ladies areas divided by a curtain). Because this interior space was often hot and stuffy, passengers regularly passed fair days seated on a roof-top deck. A boat might make the full-length journey in six days, a pace of roughly four miles per hour. Passenger fares were typically four cents per mile. Though the McKenna party was beginning their journey some one hundred-ten miles west of Albany, the packet fares were still well beyond their means.

As they watched boats slowly passing, young Hugh noticed many people walking the tow path. He queried a middle-aged farmer, bearded and wearing a broad straw hat. "Pardon sir, is the tow path available to folks walking their way west?"

45

"Oh, sure it is, friend. The canal was built with public monies. It's only proper that citizens might use the right-of-way. Just stay clear of the mule teams."

The tow path could be as narrow as ten feet in places, so pedestrian traffic was required to yield to any teams of mules or horses encountered along the way. Still, the freedom of the tow path confirmed the hope that had been kindled back in Montreal. It would be a clear path west for the family. They would take full advantage of that freedom at dawn the next day.

It was a rainy morning when the family set out. They had been blessed by good weather heretofore, but today was rather miserable. Annie took great pains to see that baby James was sheltered from the downpour by the broad-brimmed hat and coat of his father. Despite the weather, they made very good time as the path was beaten smooth and hard from constant traffic. It was only fifteen miles to the town of Rome, so they passed it by and made another ten miles beyond. The movement of traffic was constant, however, and in both directions.

After three days of walking, the family arrived in Syracuse where, unlike in Utica, the canal passed directly through the city center. The rain of previous days had passed and August heat and humidity returned. Most of the people they met along the way were friendly, though sometimes a hoggee would curse them if he felt they moved too slowly to clear his path. Once so chastised, Edward shook his head in dismay. "These drivers are a sour lot! All they must do is walk their animals down a narrow road. 'Tis easy enough . . . . Bad manners for lads so young."

The McKenna men were mesmerized when they passed a lock in active operation. Watching closely to understand the principles involved, old Hugh found himself intrigued by the elegant simplicity of the system. When a westbound boat approached a lock, the upstream gate being closed, the downstream gate was opened. As the boat approached the lock, its tow rope was released and the vessel was allowed to drift into the lock basin. Then the downstream gates were closed. After this, sluices in the upstream gate were opened and water rushed into the basin, gradually raising the water level and the boat to a point even with the upstream waterline. Once this was accomplished, the upstream gate would be opened, the tow rope re-attached, and the mules or horses urged back to their wearisome task.

Old Hugh laughed with enjoyment when the procedure was completed. "'Tis a fine invention, this canal system!"

"'Twould be even more grand if we could make further use of it," was the rejoinder from Charles.

His father turned away, his patience tested. "The towpath will suit us, God willin'."

And it did. Though the days were long and tiring, and though there was an occasional refusal from a farmer for the use of his field and water, there was progress each day. In four more days, they made it to Rochester, the largest city they had yet encountered in the United States. It was here that the canal was elevated upon an aqueduct and carried over the Genesee River. It was an impressive sight, all built of red, Medina sandstone. But it did have a tendency to leak a bit, the towpath users noted as they made their way through the center of the city.

ERIE CANAL AQUEDUCT, ROCHESTER, N. Y.

Three more days of travel brought the family as far as Lockport, where the canal dipped south to join the Tonawanda Creek. There, nature offered relief to canal builders, carrying boat traffic west, nearly to the Niagara River, the gateway to Lake Erie. At the village of Tonawanda, the canal reappeared and turned south again for the city of Buffalo. A day and a half's walk from Lockport brought an end to the McKennas' life on the towpath. A sense of excitement and relief again pervaded the party. The Erie Canal had proved itself a direct and hospitable route to the west.

Exiting the towpath at the Erie Basin, the port of Buffalo was just to their right. Here side-wheelers and sailing ships plied the waters of Lake Erie, delivering grain for eastern markets and taking on passengers and manufactures for Cleveland and Detroit. The family walked up Genesee Street, crossed through Niagara Square and entered Main Street in central Buffalo. There, they used their time to revisit their provisions and footwear for the last phase of their journey to Pittsburgh. It was necessary to take lodging, as the open country was too far to reach by nightfall.

That evening, after supper, Hugh took the opportunity to chat up the innkeeper, a pleasant German with a heavy brush of a mustache. His name was Anton, and Hugh discovered that he also had been an immigrant.

"Ja, to America from Koblenz, maybe twelve years, we come. Many German people here in Buffalo. No problem about religion; and I don't have to join army, that's the best! With my wife, this hostel I make a good business. Many settlers by the canal come."

Hugh sat back with an air of confidence. "I'm thinkin' this America is a good place to settle. Back in Tyrone, our Catholic faith was like a wall. It stood high between what little you had and what you might hope for. Maybe we will be havin' a good farm in America . . . . 'Tis just what my sons and I hope to find in this townland called Pittsburgh . . . . Is it a long way?"

"A fortnight maybe, I think. Never been there, but visitors who make the trek from Pittsburgh, sometimes, I get here."

Later, when Hugh shared this estimate with his sons, they rejoiced. An ebullient Patrick crowed. "We can do that by the end of the month, God willin' . . . . If weather is fine, maybe sooner."

Annie mused silently. Will our child ever settle in one place after livin' on the road so long?

The next morning, they walked through still-quiet streets as far as the banks of Buffalo Creek and the Hamburg Road. Their route would hug the shores of Lake Erie for the next five days. Its blue waters were often in sight as they passed through open farmland. The days were hot, the road dusty. But their enthusiasm remained high. They crossed into Pennsylvania, arriving in the city of Erie at mid-morning.

With the best part of the day remaining, they passed straight through Erie and headed south, reaching Waterford by nightfall. A summer thunderstorm drove them to seek shelter in a farmer's barn just beyond Leboeuf Lake. Though it was hot and dusty inside, the stacks of fresh hay offered some of the most comfortable bedding of the whole journey.

The towns of western Pennsylvania, small villages really, passed in rapid succession—Meadville, Mercer, Centerville, Unionville, and finally Butler, just two day's journey from Pittsburgh. The Butler Turnpike was mostly a downhill journey. The closer they approached the valley of the Allegheny River, the greater the descent. The sun of late afternoon lit up the countryside of greens and golds. Rolling hills and fertile fields were rich and ripe with crops approaching harvest.

Later, steep hills and heavily wooded slopes flanked the road and stole away the panoramic views. Further on, Butchers Run with its ramshackle structures assaulted the eyes and nose. The area was dominated by abattoirs of butchers serving the Pittsburgh and Allegheny markets. Everywhere were pens and corrals for the pigs and cattle awaiting slaughter. Smoky streets and adjoining alleys were beset by feral dogs, fighting over discarded scraps and licking the blood pooled on the ground.

Charles shuddered at the grim scene before them. He voiced the family consensus succinctly. "Ach, I hope Pittsburgh may be a better townland than this!"

It was mid-afternoon on August 29th when they broke out of these wooded hills and captured their first view of the river. It was wide and placid in this late summer season. Finally, they were on the cusp of concluding their fifty-six day walk of over a thousand miles. They had been told that once they reached the river, Pittsburgh would be within their grasp. Now the turnpike swung right at North Avenue and followed the Allegheny's gray-brown flow to Federal Street. In the distance was the city of Pittsburgh, sited on the opposite side of the river. In the foreground were high, wooded hillsides fronted by a narrow strip of land dotted with modest villages and small factories. Beyond these, the western skies wore a veil of gray smoke that nearly blotted out the afternoon sun.

Old Hugh suddenly lost his "end of the road" satisfaction. "Jaysus, the city is on fire!" With this mixture of surprise and trepidation, the family walked the few remaining miles, entered the city of Allegheny and paid the final toll to cross the St. Clair Street bridge into Pittsburgh. It was the biggest, busiest, dirtiest city they had ever seen.

Chapter Four

In 1830, Pittsburgh was the third largest city west of the Allegheny mountains. The city population totaled 12,600 residents. It is set at the confluence of the Allegheny and Monongahela rivers, where they form the mighty Ohio. Pittsburgh was a two square mile triangle, largely hemmed in by water and steep cliffs. This was the center of commercial, industrial, and residential development. The city was divided into five wards (North, South, East, and West—plus The Northern Liberties, an adjacent area slightly upriver on the Allegheny). Long before it became the "steel city," Pittsburgh was a rather diverse industrial and commercial community feeding commodities, manufactured goods and travelers to the west and south via the Ohio River. There were glass factories, (iron) rolling mills, textile mills, and numerous foundries and machine shops. These provided employment to a varied mix of ethnic groups—mostly descendants of the original English and Scottish settlers, but also the more recently arrived immigrants from Ireland and Germany.

The streets were narrow, roughly paved, and littered with garbage and horse dung. Dogs, hogs, and rats roamed freely, taking their sustenance where they might. The waters of the rivers were highly polluted with sewage and industrial waste, making periodic outbreaks of cholera unsurprising. Just two years prior, the city began its first provision of piped water to homes and businesses from a small reservoir on Grant's Hill.

What street lights existed featured whale oil lamps, to be lit and extinguished by a cadre of lamplighters. There was no police force as such, only a high constable and several deputies. Even these required a sealed warrant from the mayor or an alderman to undertake an arrest. Violent crime was commonplace, especially in the saloons and public houses where arguments were often settled with a cudgel, knife, or pistol. There was no city fire department, only a handful of volunteer companies. These bitterly competed, often violently, at the fire scene for the recompense due from city council or property owners.

* *

It was into this urban cauldron that the McKenna family set foot that late August evening. Tired, footsore, hungry, and dirty, they searched out the address of the McShane family. James McShane and his wife Alice had arrived in Pittsburgh with their five children in 1818. They made their home at 22 Irwin Street in the North Ward, a short distance from the St. Clair Street bridge. James had established himself in the grocery trade, the family living above the store. His children were now grown and mostly gone. But the youngest of these, twenty-two year old James Jr., was living with his parents and his older sister, Sally.

Hugh McKenna entered the grocery, his demeanor slow and shy. His entourage stood waiting out in the street. Best not overwhelm folks with a crowd the first thing, he reckoned. The store was small, no more than a somewhat cluttered counter and three walls of stocked shelving climbing out of reach. A rolling step-ladder stood to one side, waiting to close the occasional gap. The floor was rough wooden planks, well-trodden to the point of smoothness. Two smallish windows flanked the entry like half-closed eyes. Though the summer evening was still bright at this hour, the store's interior required its gas-lamp illumination. The atmosphere within was quite warm, despite open door and windows. James McShane the younger, tall, brown-haired, and brown-eyed, was attending the light, evening trade while his family was at supper.

Hugh spied him as he made ready for closing by sweeping up. "God bless this house and all within! . . . Is there a James McShane here, uncle of one Edward McShane of Dungannon?"

"Ah, you must be the McKenna!" The lad's eyes flashed with excitement. "I must call Father down from upstairs. I'll be less than a minute." He turned, and taking the stairs two at a stride, disappeared.

Momentarily, a thunder of feet upon the wooden staircase heralded father and son, Alice and Sally. The elder James, a husky man of middle age, pumped Hugh's hand like it was attached to a well. The ladies smiled and curtsied. "But where are the others?"

Hugh turned and pointed to the street. With that, short, plump Alice and lean, quiet Sally made a beeline for the door, anxious especially to meet Annie and her baby. Soon the whole family was herded inside, a flurry of different conversations overriding each other.

Alice quickly assessed the situation and took charge. "Praise be to heaven! You're arrived at last. Poor dears! I expect you will be famished. James, will you bring up the fixings for another supper?" She gently guided Annie to the staircase. "I've a room prepared for you and your wee one, my dear. Come along, you can refresh yourself and the child."

When the ladies had retreated, McShane reasserted himself. "Son, show the gentlemen to the privy and wash basin."

That night the McKenna men would bed-down on the floor of the grocery, flour sacks stuffed with straw their meager comfort. It sufficed, but clearly these sleeping arrangements were for one night only.

"There's a decent boardin' house here on Irwin Street," the elder McShane advised Hugh as they enjoyed their tea after supper. "'Tis run by a nice Irish couple name of Buckley. Tomorrow, I'll introduce you if you've a mind to try it. We told them long ago that you might be needin' accommodation."

"A kind offer! . . . Even if it's for a short stay, I'd be most grateful."

Hugh now shifted in his chair, his face contorted with anxiety. "James, if you'll forgive my sayin', this here Pittsburgh didn't show so well this evenin'. I don't mean to talk down your townland, but it do seem a bit rougher than what we were thinkin'."

McShane laughed and clapped Hugh on the knee. "We don't present the best appearance, do we? Not compared to your fine, green fields and fresh streams back in Tyrone. My own reaction was much the same twelve years ago, when we arrived here from Dungannon. But city livin' is not to be placed beside the country life . . . . I guess we've got used to what we couldn't change. Still, the Lord has blessed us with a fair business and a roof o'er our heads. My children find work and have their own households, after all."

Old Hugh now pressed on to his major concern. "Perhaps some way outside the city, a piece of land may be had upon a lease? My sons and I would do well to stick to farmin'. 'Tis what we know best."

McShane scratched at his close-cropped, graying beard, his eyes raised to heaven. "Ach, I'm afraid you'll be findin' the land about here is quite dear. Most farmers own their fields and tenants are not so common as back home. Settlers wantin' farm land generally keep goin' west, to Ohio and beyond. Richer land, and cheaper too."

Hugh's chin fell upon his chest. "Well, perhaps in time . . . . With seven of us employed, we might someday afford a bit of ground."

The family took up residence at the boarding house that McShane recommended. It was a three-story, clapboard structure at 28 Irwin Street. The elderly Buckley couple kept a clean house and accepted no rough persons as boarders. On the first floor was a modestly furnished parlor and a large formal dining room. Behind the dining room was the kitchen. At the end of a central hall, a rear door led to an outdoor privy in the barren, dirt yard. The two floors above accommodated twenty-odd guests, depending upon the mix of married and single persons. The common areas were lit by gas, but the halls and guest rooms depended upon oil lamps. Because the McKennas, excepting James' family, were able to share rooms, they all were able to squeeze into the limited vacancies.

To Hugh's continued regret, the dream of re-establishing the family farm in America was not to be realized. Immediate financial realities dictated that he and his sons find work in the city. After all, his daughters would be coming in the new year and expecting a home to receive them. Joining with sons James and Charles, he entered one of the few fields of self-employment for which a farmer's skills with animals would well apply. They became draymen, hauling freight to and from the docks at Water Street, along the Monongahela River. They used the low, two-wheeled, horse-drawn wagons suited to the narrow city streets.

* *

Pittsburgh was then the principal shipping point for manufactured goods destined for the Ohio and Mississippi valleys. The exports consisted of glass, iron, textiles, farm implements, leather, and various foodstuffs. The waterfront was also the recipient of lumber, pig iron, and produce arriving on boats and barges from western Pennsylvania counties. Steamboats coming up the Ohio brought sugar, molasses, and baled cotton. This constant flow of goods to and from the city supported a great number of draymen, about three quarters of whom were also Irish-Americans. Hugh's other sons found jobs as laborers in nearby factories and foundries which, while less satisfactory to them, at least produced earnings to help cover the family expenses.

Irwin Street, and much of the North Ward, was by no means the stereotypical, ethnic enclave of Irish Catholic immigrants. In these years before Ireland's Great Hunger, the Irish of Pittsburgh were predominantly middle-class, often Scots-Irish Presbyterians, and typically hailed from Ulster. Yet, even these were a distinct minority living cheek by jowl with the majority natives of Anglo-Saxon descent. A smaller contingent of German immigrants were a distant third in numbers. This composition of North Ward society meant that the housing stock also included many fine homes of the merchant and professional class, featuring gardens, and stables fronting intervening alleys. It was a turn of fortune that the McKenna family found themselves a place to settle wherein, by their pooled earnings and relatively competitive educational status, they were able to transition into something approaching a middle-class existence. Though Annie did not work outside the home, she helped defray their lodging expenses by assisting the elderly Mrs. Buckley with various household tasks.

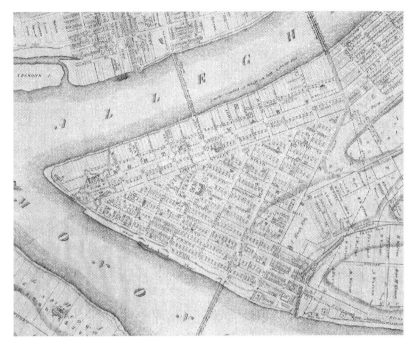

Pittsburgh and its environs, 1830
(Darlington Digital Library, University of Pittsburgh)

In 1831, Will McKeever and his new bride, Catherine Mullan, arrived safely with Nancy and Ellen in tow. To everyone's shock, they announced that Bridget had stayed behind with her older sisters. The poor girl had taken sickly upon the cusp of the departure. It was a bitter blow to Hugh who had always wanted his entire family around him. There was relief, however, that their journey wasn't nearly as arduous as that which he and his sons had endured. Indeed, the cash proceeds from that last oat harvest was sufficient to fund a voyage from Liverpool to Philadelphia on a proper passenger vessel rather than a Canadian timber ship.

A celebration of welcome was convened in the Buckley parlor, with cake, tea, and a drop of something stronger. The McShanes were invited as the two families had quickly become rather close. Even the Buckley's other boarders joined in, making the new arrivals feel at home. But for old Hugh, it was a bittersweet reunion and it was written in his eyes, belying his smile. Annie noticed what escaped the busy others and she approached him while they crowded about the honored guests.

"I know 'tis Bridget you're missin' this night, Da. She'll be comin' when she's able. Leave it to heaven to sort out. A bit o' good fortune is better than none at all."

Hugh sighed heavily. "Begorah, you are right, Annie. 'Tis a fine thing that Nancy and Ellen have arrived safely. Still, there's an empty place in my heart tonight."

Annie gave her father-in-law a hug. "I know I can't be Bridget for you. But I'll always be as much a daughter as I'm able . . . . And now, my Catherine is here and James has Will for a friend again. So there is much for which we must be grateful."

The old fellow nodded his assent. He took a deep breath. "I'm thinkin' this is supposed to be a party. Shall we be joinin' the celebration?"

But there were some logistics to be managed. The Buckley's boarding house was full. This came as no shock to the McKeevers. They had come with no expectations of moving in; but it was a bit awkward for Nancy and Ellen.

Young Hugh reassured his sisters. "No need to worry, Edward and I are after takin' lodgin' elsewhere. You girls will be havin' our room here." He winked at his sisters. "We are grown and ought be out from under our father's thumb."

But Ellen protested, hands on hips. "Now, Hugh. We'll not be puttin' our brothers out of their home."

"Arrah, we promised you a home upon arrival, and you shall have it!"

The girls looked about to appeal to their father, but found him nodding in agreement with his sons. A hint of a tear decorated the corner of his eye. In the face of such remonstration, the girls happily acquiesced.

This was not the only reunion to be noted, however. Annie's elder sister Mary and her husband Edward McShane arrived in Pittsburgh the following year, perhaps encouraged by safe arrival of these forerunners. Reunited and now settled, this network of related immigrants from Tyrone fixed their sights upon mastering the city life and adapting to American ways.

Meanwhile, the McKenna drayage business flourished as the city grew. It also benefited from cargoes carried by the Pennsylvania State System, a network of canals and railroads connecting Pittsburgh with Philadelphia. An aqueduct spanned the Allegheny River, delivering barge traffic to "The Basin," a freight terminal just above Liberty Street. For goods being trans-shipped, the canal continued across town, went through a tunnel, and exited at the Monongahela River on Try Street. Although there were two financial panics during the 1830s, the State System, and its attendant boom in east-west trade, meant new prosperity for draymen, including Hugh, James and Charles.

Nevertheless, city living and the drayman's task never sat well with old Hugh. The dream of a family farm in America died a slow, but steady, death. By 1834, this reality had depleted his spirit and his strength such that he left the business entirely. James, on the other hand, thrived in his profession. Together with Charles, they built a business of owned carts and hired drivers, no longer dependent upon their own physical labor. Charles supervised the operation, while James concentrated upon the commercial activity. His friendly, easy manner suited him well to the task of seeking and maintaining a broad base of shipper relationships. Annie was thrilled to see her husband finally able to reap the rewards of his hard work and social skills. James also turned his gregarious nature to the pursuit of local political affairs. He was so well received that local political leaders encouraged his participation in Whig Party affairs. Pittsburgh politics in those years was dominated by the Whigs, and James began to rise within the party apparatus.

But brothers Hugh, Patrick, and Edward were not so well situated. Cast in the role of unskilled labor, their earnings could not match their older brothers. Whether in the textile mill or foundry, their work was pure drudgery. There was little chance of advancement, as preferred, skill positions were reserved to the Protestant majority. Increasingly restless and unhappy, the Panic of 1834 drove them to the breaking point. Patrick and Edward had been laid off and young Hugh was feeling vulnerable to the same. That winter, they approached their father with difficult news. They caught the old man on the settee in the parlor, ready for his customary, after-supper pipe.

Patrick spoke first, his brothers behind him. "Da, there's somethin' we're wantin' to take up with you."

Old Hugh stopped loading his treasured, burl pipe. Reading their faces, he sensed the serious nature of the occasion. "Aye lads, sit. I'm listenin'." But he already felt a tightness rising in his chest.

Young Hugh and Edward now took a seat. Patrick, acting as spokesman, remained standing. "We feel, Da, that Pittsburgh has not been kind to us. The work we found has been lost and 'twasn't much to begin with. We're after thinkin' to push farther west, lookin' for somethin' better."

Their father countered with forced enthusiasm. "Sure, James and Charles will make room for you in the drayage . . ."

But Patrick shook his head at the thought. "Perhaps, they will, Da. But 'twill only push three other men out of work to do so. And besides, we'd not be happy workin' for our brothers as draymen. There must be better opportunities downriver!"

"But where? Have you prospects of anythin'? Will you be takin' leave of home and family with no prospect to hand?"

"We're hearin' good things about the city of Saint Louis, Da," Edward explained. "We've saved enough for the steamboat fare.

We're just askin' for your blessin'. But blessin' or no, our decision is made."

Old Hugh cleared his throat and cast his gaze about the room. Several other boarders sat quietly on the opposite side of the room, pretending not to be listening to the exchange. Finally, he responded in a low, quavering voice. "You are grown men. You come and go as you please. God knows, I'll not be here much longer . . ."

Young Hugh jumped to his feet, interrupting his father. "Da, 'tisn't that we're wantin' to leave you or the others. 'Tis that we feel life is passin' us by."

"Aye, I understand, lads. Were I in your place, I might well take the same decision. 'Tis just that . . ." Hugh's voice trailed off and he shielded his eyes from the curious gaze of his fellow boarders.

"Have we your blessin' then, Da?" Edward pressed.

"You have my blessin', so you do. Perhaps you'll be findin' a good farm in St. Louis." He then rose and left the parlor, retreating slowly to his room.

Before the week was out, the three young men were gone, much to the dismay of other family members. But old Hugh's loss was the greatest. His health continued its slow decline. Annie did her best to make him comfortable and cater to his needs. On Sundays, she and James would hire a carriage and accompany him to Mass at the new St. Paul's Church at Fifth and Grant. Their previous and much closer church, St. Patrick's, had long been dominated by Irish immigrants. But it was now ceded to a growing German Catholic population that wanted a church of their own and a German-speaking priest.

Hugh relished the attention he received. And his spirits were bolstered by the growing cadre of grandchildren presented him by the devoted couple. In addition to little James, now five years old, there was another Hugh and another Patrick in the brood. A daughter, who would be named Catherine, was on the way. In spite of these blessings, the old fellow still harbored a hope that somehow, someday, Bridget would make her way to America, back to her Da.

One morning in the spring of 1836, old Hugh's heart gave out. Nancy had called for him when he did not come down to breakfast. Receiving no answer, she entered his room and found him pitched to the floor in front of his chair. He was nearly dressed, one shoe on and the other on the floor beside him.

In short order, his children still in Pittsburgh gathered to grieve and support one another in their common loss. The Buckleys were more than gracious to the family, offering up their parlor for the wake that ensued that evening. Friends, neighbors, fellow draymen, and the other boarders all gathered for a rosary, followed by refreshments, conversation, and tributes.

James, Charles, and Bernard kept watch over their father through the night. Will McKeever and the three McShane men joined them. The elder James McShane provided a jug of whiskey to loosen tongues and freshen memories. They told stories of the old man and his life back in Tyrone.

James McKenna had been rather quiet, but now joined the conversation. "Wasn't it a blessin' to have him with us here these last six years? He'd never have lasted this long if put off his leasehold in Anacramp . . . . Too bad he found no farm in America!"

"He never took any comfort in city livin'," Charles replied. "He was always talkin' about his land, his crops, the animals . . . . He missed bangin' on with the neighbors about the weather and market prices."

Bernard refined the point. "He may have left his farm, but he would always be a farmer."

Edward McShane observed, "'Twas no small thing to be leavin' home and hearth at sixty years! Think of it—a month at sea and then the great land journey as well! He did it all to give an opportunity to his family and it turned out well."

As the dawn approached, Charles drained his glass and stood, unsteadily, to leave. The last few of the visitors were now long gone. "So, we're agreed, are we? I'll be writin' our brothers in St. Louis and the sisters in Tyrone. They all must be told as soon as possible. A funeral Mass must be arranged in Derrygooly. All of Anacramp will turn out, I'm certain."

James took his brother's hand. "Thank you, Charles. Bernard and I will see to the Mass here and burial, of course."

The requiem was held at St. Paul's. But the new parish, as yet, had no cemetery of its own. Thus, despite the new German regime at St. Patrick's, Hugh was buried in its old cemetery, among the graves of other, mostly Irish, immigrants.

* *

In the years that followed Old Hugh's passing, many other changes impacted family life. Nancy met and wed a fellow named McAlavy and they moved to Albany, New York. Charles married Ann McAfee, an Irish lass from County Monaghan. They established their home at Quarry Street in the Northern Liberties. Ellen McKenna met and married James Delany and they relocated to St. Louis, perhaps attracted by the prospect of reuniting with her older brothers.

James and Charles continued to enjoy prosperity in their drayage business. But in 1839, James approached his brother with a delicate issue. At the end of a busy day, a sudden downpour delayed their departure for home. Charles stood watching the rain course down the flooded alley where their animals were stabled. A nasty mix of rubbish, dung and straw was carried along the cobbled way as the furious storm beat down upon the city. The skies will be unusually clean tomorrow, he thought. James walked over and stood beside him to watch the deluge. When he spoke, he had to nearly shout to be heard above the din.

"Buckleys say they're after quittin' the boarding house. They'll sell and go live with the daughter."

Charles turned away from the open doorway. "Jaysus, 'tis about time! The missus is awfully frail. I don't know how they've lasted till now."

"I'm thinkin' I might offer to buy the place if the price is not too dear. 'Tis a decent business; Annie and I could run the place easy."

Charles raised his eyebrows in surprise. "And where will you be gettin' such a sum?"

"Well, I'm thinkin' to sell my share of the drayage, but I wanted to know how you would feel about it."

Charles glared at his brother, his cheeks nearly glowing with a scarlet tinge. "Not too damn well . . . . I'll not be havin' the funds to buy you out! That means someone else must become my partner . . . without my bye or leave."

James raised his palms in a gesture of surprised innocence. "Now brother, no decisions have been taken. I wanted to speak with you aforehand. There may be a way forward that would suit yourself. Of course, you must accept any new partner."

"And whilst you're keepin' house, who will be workin' the shipper community for me? Not only do I get a partner whether or no I'm happy to do. I must become the procurer as well as the manager of the whole bloomin' business!"

With that, Charles marched out into the pelting rain, his coat collar hauled up over his head. James quivered with shock at the explosive reaction he'd received. Though Charles could be counted upon to hold a jaundiced view of any great change, the two had always found a way of cooperating in matters personal or commercial.

As he waited for the storm to subside, James recalled the conversation he and Annie had shared after the Buckley's big announcement. As they discussed the possible purchase he admitted, "I know our savin's are not much. Somethin' must provide a livelihood for the family if heaven should call me. Buyin' a well-established boardin' house is just the thing, Annie. 'Tis a business that you and the children may depend upon if I'm not here for you."

But she chided her husband. "Oh, James, don't be talkin' such! You have your health, praise God. And what makes you think heaven should be in a greater hurry for yourself than your poor, overworked wife?"

They both laughed as he donned his coat to leave for work. "Well, 'tis a risk all the same." He paused at the door. I might as well tell her all. He took her by the hand and recovered his serious demeanor. "But 'tisn't just that, Annie. The Whigs are after me if I will run for office. They're wantin' me for Overseer of the Poor. There's never much support for the Democrats, so 'tis nearly guaranteed I'll win if I say yes."

"So, there 'tis!" Annie bristled with indignation. "You'll be overseein' the poor of Pittsburgh and 'tis my own good self that'll be runnin' the boardin' house!"

"Well, not entirely, dear. I'll be able to help some. And James may do small chores. But with my salary as Overseer, which will be considerable, you may hire a girl or two for skivvy. 'Twill work well, you'll see. Anyway, my first task is to get the money for Buckleys."

The cloudburst was easing as James finished closing for the night. He checked his animals, extinguished the lanterns, and locked the stable door, all the while rehearsing the argument for his ambitions. He would not forego this chance for an elective office that offered lengthy tenure and financial security.

There was no modern system of public welfare in those days. The Overseer of the Poor served both the city and Allegheny County. It was responsible for several poor houses. It had a taxing authority to support these and related efforts. The Overseer was charged to assist the able unemployed to find work, especially in public works such as building and maintaining the roads. He would also distribute financial relief to the disabled. He was charged with helping place dependent children as apprentices, gently directing the indigent to return to the district from which they came, and attempting to place insane persons within their extended families. James was anxious to accept the nomination. And he was also keen for the mission of the office. After all, many of those assisted would be immigrants, especially Irish immigrants.

But, it was a full-time job, and he couldn't possibly fulfill these official duties and do the drayage business as before. The only way to exit his partnership with Charles was to be bought out.

Later that week, James informed the Buckleys of his desire to buy their Irwin Street property. He would sell his share of the drayage business to fund the purchase. He assured them that existing boarders need not be disrupted. He just needed to find a new partner that Charles might accept. It would not be easy, he admitted to himself. Charles would forever find the lumps in the porridge of life. Still, he was right that what he needed was someone who could collect and keep customers. Perhaps my Whig friends would know of such a person, he pondered.

In the end, it wasn't some well-placed politician who found a partner for Charles. To his great surprise and relief, the new partner was his friend, Will McKeever. Long a drayman himself, Will agreed to replace James in the business. Pooling their resources, Will and Charles were able to purchase James' share. With these proceeds and some of his savings James consummated the boarding house purchase. The McKenna family fortunes would now rest on a firm foundation.

Chapter Five

The 1840s were turbulent years for the McKenna family and for Pittsburgh generally. James and Annie, now running their Irwin Street boarding house, added three more sons to their fold: Bernard (Barney) in 1842, and twin boys, Charles and Edward, in 1844. James was largely consumed with his duties as Overseer of the Poor, but his eldest sons, James and Hugh were now at an age where they might perform many of the household tasks that otherwise would befall their mother. When not engaged in this fashion, they, Patrick, and sister Catherine attended the public school at the corner of Cecil Alley and Penn Street.

The city was changing rapidly as well. The population had more than doubled since the McKennas' arrival. The wards of the city had been renamed. Much of the McKennas' old North Ward became the new Fourth Ward, while the Northern Liberties (also known as Bayardstown) now became the Fifth Ward. An influx of Irish immigrants, even before the Great Hunger, steadily grew— now including a greater proportion of Catholic Irish. The previous commercial focus of the city shifted increasingly to manufacturing, especially to the fabrication of iron products of all description. The ample presence in Western Pennsylvania of rich iron and coal deposits fueled this transformation. And with this increased industrialization came labor strife. Imposed wage reductions and the push for a ten hour workday precipitated marches and strikes. So much so that the Whig establishment saw political advantage in supporting the nascent workers' movement. They even adopted the campaign slogan, "Two dollars a day and roast beef!"

Perhaps 1845 was the year of greatest trial. The Mexican War was on and the political powers in Pittsburgh were bitterly split. The Democrat-leaning Pittsburgh Post took a strong position pro-annexation of Mexican territory. The Whig establishment and its client newspaper, the Gazette, strongly opposed the war, fearing an inevitable expansion of slavery into the newly acquired lands. In the midst of such debate, three Pittsburgh militia companies, the Duquesne Greys, the Jackson Blues, and the Irish Greens, enthusiastically participated with the Federal army for the duration of the conflict.

But a Thursday in April presented calamity far closer to home. The McKenna's first warning came from Charles as he brought a drayage cart at great speed into Irwin Street. Jumping down at the steps of the boarding house, he pounded upon the door. "Annie! Annie! There's fire in the city!"

Annie came to the door, a babe in her arms and young Barney clinging to her skirts. Not having understood the shouted message, she queried, "Charles, what is it? You're passin' fair for a ravin' banshee!"

"Jaysus, woman, the city is on fire! You must gather your brood. I've come to carry you to Allegheny. Will's gone for mine and his. Come, now!"

Annie was speechless momentarily, but soon regained her wits. "Charles, we've the children at the school! You must collect them! I'll give warnin' to all here and gather these wee ones. We'll wait here on the steps for you." With no time to argue, Charles leapt into the cart and dashed off to the elementary. As she turned from the door, Annie's mind raced with myriad thoughts. Ach, where might James be? Mother of God, pray for us!

A springtime drought and a windy day had combined as a washerwoman's unattended fire at 2nd and Ferry was whipped into a raging inferno. The wind carried the flames eastward, gobbling up the aging clapboard structures of early Pittsburgh days. Twenty city blocks, covering over fifty-six acres, were soon incinerated, despite the efforts of firefighters. They were equipped with a "modern" hand-pumping engine, but the drought had left the city's reservoir severely depleted. Without adequate water, they were forced to step aside and let nature run its course. The wooden Smithfield Bridge across the Monongahela was consumed. Twelve thousand residents were left homeless. However, there were only two fatalities and the wards along the Allegheny were almost completely spared. By evening the fire was spent and the McKenna families were able to return to their homes from Allegheny City. In future years, it would be noted that the "Great Fire of 1845" had made a clearance, enabling significant modernization and renewal of the city center.

View of the Ruins of the City of Pittsburgh from Boyd's Hill
(University of Pittsburgh Library)

The McKennas, however, were not wholly spared suffering during this decade. In the fall of 1845, newspaper accounts of a partial failure of the potato crop in Ireland reached them. Though the potato blight had not yet triggered widespread famine, James and his brothers became quite worried for those family members left behind in Tyrone. They began a letter-writing campaign, urging their siblings to join them in America. James' sister Catherine, her husband Edward O'Brien, and their four children quickly embraced the idea. They arrived in Pittsburgh early in 1846, despite the fact that Catherine was well into a final pregnancy.

By August, Ireland's Great Hunger had begun in earnest with another potato crop failure, this one nearly complete and nationwide. Faced with such reports, the McKennas in Pittsburgh dispatched funds to assist the emigration of the remainder of the family. Though Ireland's north was stricken by the potato blight, Ulster had never been so dependent upon that one crop as other regions of the country. Nevertheless, sister Mary, her husband Samuel O'Hare, and sister Bridget, with her husband Frank Cullen, readily accepted the financial assistance and promptly departed for America.

One evening that autumn, the first, real cold snap of the season chilled the dark, smoky streets of the city. James McKenna returned home late, emotionally exhausted. He had spent the entire day interviewing impoverished immigrant families recently arrived in Pittsburgh. Nearly all of these were refugees of the Irish famine. He found Annie in the kitchen, nearly finished with the aftermath of the evening meal. He sank into a chair at the rough kitchen table and sighed. Leaving the final touches to Judy, the scullery maid, Annie kissed him and set a place for his belated supper.

"Oh, James! You must be famished, so. I've kept a portion of lamb stew for you . . . and we've a fresh round of barmbrack as well."

He mustered a weak smile. "That'll be grand, love . . . No word of the sisters today? . . . . I keep thinkin' they'll be sittin' in my parlor some evenin' when I get home. I pray their journey goes well."

Annie retrieved his dinner from the oven. "Sure, it can't be long now . . . . They said they hoped to make a September sailin'. God save them! The papers are after tellin' the most desperate tales of sickness and hunger! The worst of it is said to be in Munster and Connaught." She set the steaming bowl of stew before him and took a chair opposite.

"Jaysus, Annie, you'd cry an ocean to see the poor waifs arrivin' each day. Those left with any physical strength, we try to match in public works or private menial labor. But most are not so healthy. They can only hope for some temporary relief in the county poor houses . . . . How they made it this far beggars the imagination . . . . 'Tis the children I find so distressin'. They look like little scarecrows, they do. Probably haven't had a decent meal for months . . . . I suppose I've missed my own children this night. I'm sorry to be so late."

"Ah, they're well in bed. James and Hugh were such a help tonight, God love them. They handled the twins for me, receivin' nary a fuss or a whimper. They're fine lads, those two! . . . But, I must go check on Catherine. She was feelin' a bit low this evening. Will you douse the lamps, dear, afore you come up?"

"Aye, I'll be up shortly." James returned to his stew. Mopping the last morsels with a crust of bread, he addressed the young, Irish maid. "So, Judy, how's your young man? Any luck in findin' a position yet?"

The wispy nineteen-year-old turned and smiled. "He's well, sir. Thank you for askin'. He's after seein' the alderman about a job with the city. We should hear somethin' in a week or so. Please, God, they take him on."

"Well, I wish him luck, for your own sake as well."

James quaffed the last of his tea and, stood to leave. "Thank you for the stew. 'Twas very fine. A grand night's rest now."

"Good night, sir," she replied with a hint of a curtsy. As he left the room, she began to put out the breakfast place settings. It was only a minute or two later that a sharp thud reached her ears from the hallway. Strange, she thought. All the boarders are long gone upstairs. Somethin' been dropped? She pushed the kitchen door aside and peered into the darkened hallway. In the shadows a shapeless form was barely visible on the floor ahead. A chill of apprehension coursed up her spine. Retreating to the kitchen, she fetched a taper, lit it, and returned to the first gas fixture in the hall. As the blue flame sprang to life, the darkness retreated. Twenty feet beyond lay the slumped body of her employer.

"Oh . . . oh no! Dear mother of God, no! . . . Missus McKenna! Missus!" She stepped past the unmoving figure and tore up the staircase, shouting all the more. Guest room doors opened. Candles flickered to life. The quiet house awoke to tragedy.

Annie, now dressed in her robe and slippers, came running, followed by her elder sons, James and Hugh. Finding her husband unconscious, she knelt and cradled his head. "James, oh dear James . . . . Hugh, go fetch the doctor! . . . James, you be callin' for Father Garland! . . . Ask him to come in all haste."

With the help of boarders, her husband was moved to the settee in the parlor. But he showed no vital signs. A rush of fears and questions flooded Annie's distracted mind. Dear God, he's too young for this to happen . . . . What shall become of us? . . . My children havin' no father! . . . Where's that priest now?

Reverend Garland arrived first. He administered the last rites and stayed on to console Annie and her children. When the doctor arrived, he recognized telltale signs of a cerebral hemorrhage. "He never knew what hit him, Annie. He will have lost consciousness in an instant . . . no pain or suffering at all." Turning to son James, now sixteen, he added, "It falls to you now, lad. You must be the man of the house, now that your Da is gone. God give you the strength to do."

Annie's brothers-in-law, Charles and Bernard, quickly came to her aid. So, too, did her sisters Catherine and Mary, the McKeevers, and the McShanes. They joined a circle of support and exorcised their grief through active measures. Annie was deeply saddened but responsibilities to her boarders and her children allowed her little respite. Her brother-in-law, Bernard, was particularly helpful in sorting out the practical and financial issues flowing from James' death.

Two weeks after James' funeral, his sisters Mary and Bridget arrived in Pittsburgh with their husbands. The extended family reconvened to welcome them. Instead of a happy reunion, news of the heavy loss befell them. Charles thought it ironic. "Just as all Da's children are safe in America, the eldest has up and died. Bad cess, I'm thinkin'."

Sorrow and mourning pervaded the McKenna boarding house, leaving the newcomers with a sense of awkward intrusion. That, and their strange, new surroundings in Pittsburgh, prompted a surprise decision. Both couples announced their intention to push on, joining sisters Catherine and Ellen, and brothers Hugh, Edward, and Patrick in Saint Louis.

* *

Winter arrived and the stream of Irish refugees swelled to a flood. Within the next three years, the Irish born would come to account for 21% of the population of Pittsburgh and 31% of the male workforce. Such a dramatic demographic turn provoked a strong, negative, nativist reaction. Though most of the arriving Irish would secure only menial, laboring positions, the competition for jobs and housing they represented was resented highly by the Anglo-Saxon majority, the Presbyterian Scots-Irish, and the Whig political establishment. Pittsburgh was not alone in its sectarian and anti-immigrant sentiments. There was a general wave of such sentiment in cities throughout the country. As early as 1844, there had been anti-Catholic riots in the sister city, Philadelphia. Now, cross-burnings, arson attempts, vandalism, and assaults, often from members of the Orange Lodges, were to be endured by Pittsburgh's Irish Catholic community.

It was in this environment of nativism and disorder that Annie McKenna was raising her youngsters. Caution dictated that neither she nor they should be found on the streets after dark. Even brothers-in-law Bernard and Charles would only sally forth in those hours when suitably armed.

A principal provocateur of this period was a soapbox orator from Bayardstown, Joseph Barker. Though well-dressed and clean-shaven, he seemed to have no regular occupation or visible means of support. His harangues against the papist Irish were nearly daily events. He attracted crowds of rowdies, happy to direct attacks upon Catholic clergy and laity alike. Barker was arrested at least six times on various charges. But in September 1849, he was arrested for pressing his attacks even to the steps of St. Paul's, now the cathedral for the diocese of Pittsburgh. The charges against him were obstructing streets, use of obscene language, and causing a riot. In his November trial, Barker told the jury to "go to hell" and warned Judge Benjamin Patton that he might well find himself hung from a lamp post.

The jury convicted Barker, and Judge Patton sentenced him to a $250 fine and one year in jail. But Barker's supporters, convinced that he was a martyr to a noble cause, circulated petitions to place his name on the mayoral ballot. On January 8, 1850, Barker was elected mayor of Pittsburgh, whilst in jail. He was pardoned by Pennsylvania Governor Johnston, but later arrested twice again, during his term of office, for assault and battery.

Law and order were severely tested in those years. There was an outbreak of arson and robberies. Many buildings and the Mechanic Street bridge across the Allegheny were burned down. Barker's successor as mayor, John B. Guthrie, appointed Pittsburgh's first meaningful contingent of municipal police and suppressed the problems of disorder in a wave of arrests.

* *

In 1851, Annie suffered another unexpected loss. Her second eldest son Hugh, then a nineteen-year-old iron moulder, came to her with an announcement. "Mother, I'm thinkin' to leave Pittsburgh. I want to go to California."

Annie's face went pale and she covered her mouth for fear she might scream. It took a moment to muster a reply. "'Tis the gold rush, is it? . . . Is Patrick after doin' this with you?"

Hugh's still beardless face flushed. "Oh, no, Mother. Patrick, he'll have no part of it. But my friends and I, we want to try our luck. If we do strike it rich, I'll come back and provide for you. I will, I promise."

"Oh Hugh . . . Hugh!" She collapsed into her chair and cried softly. Then she looked up. "Son, there are thousands and thousands who have gone before. What makes you think there's gold to be had for latecomers such as yourself?"

Hugh shifted his stance anxiously and tried persuasion. "We have discussed that, Mother. Even if the gold is all taken, we figure there will be great opportunities in business. The population there is growin' like a field of weeds. Anyway, I know I'm not meant for a life of workin' iron."

"But the journey itself will be hazardous . . . . If you go, 'twill be the last I'll ever see of you."

He placed his hand upon his mother's shoulder and kissed her forehead. "I'll not abandon you, Mother. I'll be back for visits. Besides, my uncles in St. Louis will advise me regarding safe passage to the West. Please, Mother, it's time I made my own way. I'm a child no more."

In the end, Annie realized she had neither the right nor the ability to stop Hugh from leaving. One way or another, he would go. Better, she concluded, that she accept it without rancor. He was, in fact, fully grown. And she still had James to help her with the business and fifteen-year-old Catherine to help mind the twins. Still, it nearly broke her heart when, a week later, Hugh left Pittsburgh, never to return.

* *

By the early 1850s Pittsburgh's population had again doubled to over 46,000. The advent of the railroads had occurred, first with the Ohio & Pennsylvania Railroad, offering connections to Cleveland and Cincinnati. Late in 1852, the Pennsylvania Railroad (PA.R.R.) extended its operations to Pittsburgh, cutting the travel time from Philadelphia from three days to fifteen hours. Subsequently, the PA.R.R. built a local spur down Liberty Street to serve its riverside freight depot at "The Point." But the draymen of the city erupted in protest at the potential reduction in their trade. And, though the railroad offered the concession that the spur wouldn't employ locomotives, the disruption of pedestrian and horse-drawn traffic was considerable.

One Sunday afternoon, Charles McKenna, his wife Ann, and their four children were visiting Annie and her family in Irwin Street. The dinner had ended and the children were playing in the street. Charles, still operating the drayage he founded with his father and brother James, was especially vocal in his opposition to the railroad spur. As he lit his pipe, he complained to Annie, "This rail line will cut the cartin' business by half! How's a man to make a livin' when the moneyed interests in Philadelphia can lay their tracks right through the center of the city, past homes and shops. 'Tis an unholy invasion!"

"Oh, Charles, you have it right, you do. The line is near to my own front door. I can hear the warnin' bell mornin', noon, and night."

"We'll not be takin' this lyin' down, Annie. There are bold fellows, draymen and others, which are after diggin' up the rails by cover of night! . . . Will and I just might lend them a hand." They did dig the rails out, but the railroad prevailed in the end.

Charles wasn't the only member of the family to face challenges in those years. In 1854, a bad outbreak of cholera carried off his brother Edward in St. Louis. Then in September, four hundred such fatalities were recorded in Pittsburgh. Such epidemics were not rare, but this occasion was the worst in memory.

Though Annie's youngest children were students at the Fourth Ward public school, James and Patrick had become young men, breadwinners working as iron moulders. Their earnings were a godsend for the family, especially during the financial panic of 1857. Business activity in Pittsburgh was greatly reduced, triggering layoffs, forced wage reductions, and labor unrest. Though making ends meet, Annie and her children were far from affluent. With the loss of several of her boarders, she was increasingly dependent upon the earnings of these elder sons.

* *

One afternoon that year, Annie received an unannounced caller. He was dressed in a black suit, and introduced himself as the Reverend William D. Howard, pastor of the Second Presbyterian Church. He was in his early forties, heavy-set, clean-shaven, and somewhat balding. His manner was formal, yet courteous and friendly.

"Mrs. McKenna, forgive this intrusion. If you will spare me only a few moments of your time, I have a matter of some importance I'd like to discuss with you."

Annie was visibly taken aback. Standing stolidly in her doorway, she argued. "My family and I are Catholics. Sure, we're not after joinin' some other church!"

Howard smiled his reassurance. "I'm sure that is the case, madam. My visit is, in no way, aimed at dissuading you from your chosen religion. Indeed, I'm here to discuss a business matter. May I come in where we might talk more comfortably?"

Still nervous, Annie led him into the parlor. She called Catherine. "Daughter, be puttin' on a pot o' tea!"

As the room was free of boarders at this time of day, the requested conversation would be conducted in private. Once seated, the clergyman began his explanation. "Mrs. McKenna, I am visiting you and several of your closest neighbors here on Irwin Street. You see, our congregation at Second Presbyterian has grown well beyond our modest structure on Diamond Alley. The elders and I have undertaken a search for a new site where we might erect a larger, more commodious house of worship."

When Catherine arrived with the tea service, she placed it before them and retreated without comment. The interruption afforded Annie a few moments to absorb what she had just heard.

76

After serving the tea, she queried her guest. "Are you suggestin' that you're after puttin' your new church here in Irwin Street?"

Howard paused as he brought the teacup to his lips. "To be totally forthright, that is the general idea. Of course, no final decisions could be made until you and your neighbors have all been consulted. But we are especially disposed towards the corner location here at Irwin and Penn. Given the age and condition of the several properties involved, we hope to acquire sufficient land at a price which we can afford and yet the residents would find rather generous."

Annie listened to this reply, her mind filled with questions and not a small measure of fear. She sipped her tea, waiting for some clarity of thought. Then she pressed Howard. "You'll know, sir, I'm a widow with young children. This boardin' house may seem most humble to you, but it's my only means of support. Even if your offer is fair, I cannot imagine where we might go or how we might get on."

Reverend Howard placed his teacup on the tray and leaned forward. His eyes were kindly, his words calm and disarming. "Mrs. McKenna, the Lord will not have His church built on the back of hardship for you and your neighbors. I very much appreciate your concern. Of course, you may find it impossible to accept the disruption of such a move to home and business. Nevertheless, if you and they agree, the elders and I are offering considerable assistance in seeing all of you are resettled properly. I take it you would wish to continue operating a rooming house, even in a new location?"

"Yes! 'Tis what I've been doin' for near twenty years, now . . . . I wouldn't know what else to do for myself and the children."

Howard rose to his feet and extended his hand. "Let's see how your neighbors respond. Once I have a sense of it, we must talk again. In the meantime, you will want to discuss this with advisors you trust. If I may call again, I will be prepared to discuss an offer amount for your consideration. Till then, madam, I wish you a very good day." With that he bowed slightly and departed.

As the family sat at supper that evening, Annie shared with James and Patrick the dilemma that now troubled her so. "The man was pleasant entirely, but I haven't an idea as to what we should do."

James was visibly excited by the proposal. "That, Mother, must depend upon the price that's offered. But this old house has seen better days. Even if we should stay, there will be repairs and costs to bear."

Patrick pushed his now-empty plate away and agreed with his brother. "Maybe, we should ask Uncle Charles."

Annie raised her eyes to heaven. "Oh no! I know what your uncle will say. He'll be tellin' me to send the left-footer packin'! Charles will only see the worst of it. No, I must rely on you boys to help me make a sound decision."

James sipped his tea and pondered. Then he concluded, "I'm thinkin' Pat and I should be lookin' about the ward. Perhaps we will find a property that suits . . ."

"Aye, and learn what prices are bein' asked," Patrick interrupted.

Fifteen-year-old Barney sat quietly through this discussion, as did his sister Catherine. Only when their brothers had left the table did they venture their opinions. Catherine was now twenty-one and a woman of deep religious faith. "It may be God's will that this old house be sacrificed for the buildin' of a church . . . even if it's not a church of our own."

But Barney's interests were less lofty. "If we do move house, Mother, can I be havin' a room of my own? Charles and Edward are after drivin' me mad."

"Your sister is right, young man. If it be God's will, you may get such a room. But, of course, it may not be His will."

Several days later Annie, with Barney in tow, made her usual visit to McShane's grocery. The store was now operated by forty-nine-year-old James Jr. Though the selection of goods offered was not as wide as that in the larger shops on Market Street, she knew she could trust what he carried. Too often bad eggs, rancid butter, or sugar cut with fine white sand were passed off by less conscientious merchants. As she completed her purchases, she related to McShane the visit from Reverend Howard and her current dilemma.

"Yes, I have heard as much from others on the street. Of course, Mrs. M, the price he offers must be considered," he opined as he bundled her items for Barney to carry. "But it is not just the offer that is important. Your neighbors on either side of you will receive offers as well. If they wish to accept, and you reject yours . . ."

"Ah, I'll be havin' me two new enemies," she finished his statement. "Oh, James, I'd never thought of that. I must take care not to spoil it for everyone. God love you! 'Tis a wise fellow you are."

When Reverend Howard and the elders disclosed their bids several weeks later, Annie and her neighbors were well pleased to accept. "You needn't move house immediately, Mrs. McKenna," the cleric assured. "First, we must find you a suitable property elsewhere. As I promised before, we stand ready to assist you."

Howard was as good as his word. His elders, well-connected in the business community, succeeded in identifying a property only two and a half blocks east, at 281 Penn Street. It was a newer structure, with plenty of rooms, though the increased traffic noise on Penn was a drawback. But the price was right. By mid-1858, the move was completed. And Annie's youngest children were able to remain at their Fourth Ward school. Though many of her boarders made the move, not all did. To fill the vacancies, young adult children of family friends took up residence. These included John and James McShane, sons of Edward and Mary McShane. Catherine and William McKeever, now adult offspring of Will and Catherine, moved in as well. In just a few months, a new normality settled upon Annie and her business. But it wouldn't last long.

Chapter Six

The iron industry featured prominently in the lives of Annie's sons. From their mid-teens, Hugh and Pat had worked as iron moulders in factories along "the strip"—as Bayardstown was informally christened. Having exhausted the elementary education offered by the Pittsburgh public school system, they spent their days in heat, smoke and dust. Their jobs were to assist the master moulders—typically those of English and Scots-Irish descent. Of course, Hugh had abandoned the trade for western adventure. Later, Patrick found a clerk's position with the railroad. But their younger brother, Barney, left the night school run by Christian Brothers at the Cathedral and followed them into iron moulding. At age fifteen, he had become an apprentice moulder at the firm of John C. Parry & Co. By 1860, he was well along in learning the craft of casting the components of iron stoves. He later moved to A. Bradley & Co. as a journeyman.

Barney had his mother's thin line of a mouth. His large nose and broad chin would prevent one from describing him as handsome. Yet, his gray eyes had a twinkle that, when combined with his ready smile, charmed people. He inherited his father's winning ways and his interest in politics. Making stoves wasn't all he was learning; as an iron worker, he found himself in the midst of Pittsburgh's emerging labor movement. From the first iron workers' strike a decade previous, through the founding of the Sons of Vulcan by iron puddlers in 1857, industry workers increasingly pushed back at forced wage cuts and hazardous working conditions. By 1859, a nascent International Iron Moulders Union (IIMU) represented twelve locals, with seven hundred members nationwide. And though Pittsburgh's moulders had no proper union yet, it was clear to Barney that the day was not far off. And he intended to have a role in making that happen.

His sixteen-year-old twin brothers, Eddie and Charles, entered other fields. The former found work as a clerk with the railroad, the latter as an apprentice to William Schuchman, a young German artist and Pittsburgh's first lithographer. Charles had always shown an aptitude for, and an enjoyment of, drawing and artwork. Even as a school child, he would amuse his classmates with quick, cartoon-like sketches capturing, often skewering, the traits and foibles of students and teachers alike. In Schuchman's shop, Charles was exposed to more formal artwork and techniques, along with the lithography trade. He worked diligently in his spare time, emulating the skills of his employer and the other artists whose works came his way. At night, he continued his education at a private academy operated by Jeremiah O'Donovan at 42 Congress Street. Even apart from his artistic pursuits, Charles showed a keen interest in all aspects of a liberal arts education.

Their elder sister, Catherine, had always assisted her mother with the boarding house operations. For years, she also spent considerable effort in shouldering childcare responsibilities for which Annie had limited time. At Catherine's knee, her younger brothers were supervised in their academic and religious instruction. A pious person herself, she instilled strong instincts of virtue and piety among her younger siblings. But now they were grown and off in their working careers, leaving her time to take work as a seamstress.

The year 1860 brought sad news from St. Louis. Just a few months apart Annie's brother-in-law Patrick and her sister-in-law Catherine McKenna O'Brien passed away. Recalling the shared journey of thirty years prior, Annie remarked to her daughter, "Ach, another of poor old Hugh's children gone! . . . I do wish you had known your uncle Pat. He was ever so kind on the long walk to Pittsburgh. Wasn't he always ready to carry baby James or dandle him on his knee should the child fooster. I don't think I ever told him how grateful I was for his many kindnesses."

Catherine gave her mother a long hug. "Don't worry Mother, he'll be knowin' it now."

✳✳✳✳✳✳✳✳✳✳✳✳✳✳✳✳✳✳✳✳✳✳✳✳✳

Busy as they were with their personal lives and the ups and downs of their jobs, the McKennas could not isolate themselves from larger events playing out nationally. Sectional conflicts between the slaveholding South and the more industrial/commercial North had been bubbling along for decades. Now however, they were about to boil over. South Carolina was championing a secession movement, even if that meant armed insurrection. The election of Abraham Lincoln that fall brought a further expectation of confrontation and violence.

In the waning days of President Buchanan's administration, further events centered in Pittsburgh brought the city to a fever pitch. It was late December and the Secretary of War was John B. Floyd, a former governor of Virginia and an ardent supporter of the Southern cause. After Lincoln's election, he took the decision to have federal armaments shipped to forts in Southern states on the brink of secession. The U.S. Army's Allegheny Arsenal, located in Lawrenceville, was a major producer of ordnance and a repository for a wide range of weaponry. Its commanding officer, Major John Symington, now received orders from Floyd to ship 124 large cannon to Federal forts at Galveston Harbor and at Ship Island, off the coast of Mississippi.

Major John Symington

Word of such plans was leaked by Arsenal staff and the news enraged the Pittsburgh citizenry. A mass demonstration was mounted at the steps of the neoclassic Allegheny Courthouse on Grant's Hill. Before long, the crowds overflowed Fifth and Diamond Streets. Annie McKenna's sons were swept up in this chorus of public indignation. Though the family shared a familiar Irish-American allegiance to the immigrant and labor-friendly Democratic Party, they nevertheless were strong in their support for the Union and thus for President-elect Lincoln.

Barney, having been exposed to the strong, anti-secession sentiment at his factory, came home the day after Christmas with a plan of action in hand. He gathered his younger brothers, Charles and Eddie, in his bedroom to privately share the scheme. No need to alarm Mother or Catherine.

"Now listen, lads, you may help us in the days ahead. A steamship, *The Silver Wave,* is at the wharf ready to receive armaments for shipment south. Many of our friends, Unionists all, are after setting a blockade above Water Street. If the Arsenal tries to move its artillery pieces to the docks, we aim to stop them by sheer force of numbers."

Charles guffawed at the thought. "Is that all you're needing us for, to be members of a crowd?"

Eddie was similarly unimpressed. "We thought you had something of importance for us to perform."

Barney waved away their objections. "Do you want to jabber at me or hear the rest of the plan? To be successful, we'll be needing to turn out a huge number of able-bodied men. To accomplish that, we must have plenty of warning that the transfer is in the offing. We can't expect the lads to mass at the docks for days on end waiting for the time. What we want from you, and others like you, is to be our eyes and ears. A watch must be manned! When the cannons begin to roll onto the streets of Lawrenceville, we must know at once!"

The frowning faces before him now lit up with excitement. "A schedule of watches has been established. You may sign on for the hours you are free to offer. The sooner you pick your times, the better choices you'll be having."

Eddie exchanged a glance with Charles. A nod and a grin sealed the deal. They would volunteer as spies.

Meanwhile, various public officials and private committees deluged President Buchanan with telegrams demanding rescission of Floyd's orders. On December 30th, Major Symington launched efforts to execute Floyd's instructions and the warning network sprung into action. Runners, including the McKenna boys, spread the word. Soon the angry crowds assembled to block any approach to the city's wharves. The line of artillery pieces, guarded by a detachment of Federal soldiers, paused between Virgin Alley and Diamond Alley awaiting word from Washington regarding a possible rescission of Floyd's orders. Eventually such notice was informally received from Attorney General Edwin M. Stanton. Symington relented and the cannons were returned to the Arsenal.

Coincidentally, Annie's family received a more direct report of events transpiring within the walls of Allegheny Arsenal. Their fifteen-year-old cousin, Ellen McKenna, was a daughter of Uncle Charles. Tall and lithe, with long, strawberry-blond hair, she had the green eyes of a Celtic princess. Though she was neither exceedingly pretty nor homely, her personality was friendly and fun-loving. She was one of 950 Pittsburghers working at the Arsenal. It had lately become the practice that young girls and women should be employed in the laboratory where rifle cartridges and artillery shells were assembled. Their slender and nimble fingers performed well the delicate and dangerous tasks. They also refrained from the wayward habits of their male predecessors who had been replaced for lighting matches and smoking in the presence of gunpowder.

At a family gathering in the New Year, Ellen confided to her cousins. "Thank God you men opposed Major Symington in his attempt to move those big guns. But mind you, 'twasn't only them cannon that were to be shipped to the slavery states."

Barney looked at her sharply. He nudged brother Pat who was busy reliving with Ellen's older brother, Michael, how they had barred the way to the wharves on the day.

"Ellen, tell us what you mean. What else has Symington been up to?"

Michael beamed with enthusiasm and pride. "Go ahead, Ellen. Tell 'em what you told Da and me. My sister, she keeps her eyes and ears open."

"Well, I didn't actually see it myself. 'Twas before all the foosterin' over them artillery pieces. One of the lads what loaded the crates told me what they had done. Major Symington has already shipped nearly 10,000 muskets and bayonets down river."

Barney snapped in anger at this revelation. "Wish that boy had said something in time to stop such treason! . . . What's done is done, however."

"'Twas only after the hue and cry that any of us thought what was afoot," Ellen offered meekly.

On the third of January, President Buchanan officially countermanded Floyd's directive at the urging of prominent

Pittsburgh citizens. This, together with a scandal in which Floyd was accused, prompted the War Secretary to resign. Symington dismissed any assertions of disloyalty to the Union. Indeed, he was reportedly heartbroken when his son ran away from home to join the Confederate Army. But the incident of the cannons was not the last time Symington's actions would be of concern to the McKennas.

* *

On February 14th, President-elect Lincoln made a visit to Pittsburgh on his circuitous route to Washington and the March 4th inauguration. Despite a delay of several hours and a steady rain, the citizens of Pittsburgh, including the McKenna family, turned out to welcome the man who had carried Allegheny County in the election by more than two to one. The President-elect was to stay a single night at the white, stone, five-story Monongahela House. The hotel had burned down in the Great Fire of 1845, but was rebuilt two years later in grand style, with white marble floors, black walnut staircases, and three hundred guest rooms. It was Pittsburgh's leading hotel, claiming Mark Twain, Charles Dickens, and Edward, Prince of Wales as prior guests.

Annie and her children huddled under shared umbrellas, having trudged the ten, puddled blocks to the corner of Smithfield and Water Streets. They found the crowd so vast that the Presidential party, when they finally did arrive, had difficulty entering the hotel. Soon, everyone's attention was fixed upon a small, second-story balcony above the Smithfield Street entrance. Repeated calls were made for Lincoln to address the gathering, but without response. Annie wondered impatiently, "Perhaps the poor man may be exhausted from his journey and has gone to bed. Come now, let's be home. You may catch your death on such a cold, wet night!"

Despite their disappointment and reluctance to leave, Catherine and her brothers made an effort to obey. But they found they could hardly move at all in the thicket of determined revelers. And the shouts of "Lincoln, Lincoln" would not be stilled. Finally a gaunt, newly-bearded figure emerged onto the balcony. An umbrella was held for him by an aide who was nearly too short for the task. Raising his hands to quiet the cheering crowd, the smiling Lincoln asked forbearance from a full address until morning. Then he added, "I have made my appearance now only to afford you an opportunity of seeing, as clearly as may be, my beautiful countenance. Good night."

Laughter followed and the President-elect retreated. Gradually the crowd began to disperse and Barney attempted to clear a path. "At least he has a sense of humor. He'll be needing such once he's sworn into office," Eddie chirped.

The next day, the boys returned to the Monongahela House to listen to Lincoln's promised address. Charles would assert in later years that he had the honor on that day to shake the hand of the future Great Emancipator.

Lincoln's Pittsburgh Address, February 15, 1861
(Black & White Image of Color Stained Glass Window
in the Smithfield United Church of Christ)

Edward was understating the requisite personal qualities the new president would require as he assumed office. The following month, the embattled Fort Sumter fell to rebel forces at

Charleston, South Carolina. Lincoln called for 75,000 volunteers for three months of service to suppress the rebellion. Recruitment in Pittsburgh began immediately. Only a few organized militia existed, most being remnants of the old Mexican War volunteer units. Nearly all functioned more as social clubs than proper military organizations. Command of such units was an elective office, voted upon by the members. Their choices were not constrained by the lack of military experience or training of the candidates. By the end of April, Pennsylvania Governor Andrew Curtin advised Mayor Wilson of his intent to establish military camps at Pittsburgh to receive new volunteer companies. The response in Allegheny County to the initial call for volunteers far surpassed Governor Curtin's quota for the region. Those in surplus left written notice of their willingness to respond if required in the future. Eventually some of these surplus volunteers were sent to the loyal "mountain state" region of Virginia or to other Union states struggling to fill their quota.

While other McKenna brothers were generally consumed with job or family concerns, Barney and Charles showed early interest in enlisting. Repeatedly they broached the subject with their mother. But Annie was adamant that her sons were needed at home.

"Who will support this family if you all are gone to war? Who will help my poor, aged self in managin' this roomin' house? Didn't Hugh leave me long ago, and nary a word since. Will you lads also leave me, never to return?"

Throughout that summer of 1861, Barney and Charles commiserated over their mother's firm opposition. One Sunday evening in August, the two brothers returned home from visiting several of their friends at Camp Wilkins at Penn and 29th Street. Though the sun was low in the sky, the lingering heat and humidity of the day drove them to the bank of the Allegheny River in search of a cooling breeze.

"The lads seemed greatly disappointed today, didn't they?" Barney observed as they skimmed stones out into the waters.

"Well it isn't surprising, cooped up as they are in that hot, dusty camp for weeks and weeks . . . . Even volunteers returning from the field said they saw little excitement in their months of service. Only the Zouaves were in real action and they took a licking!"

"This rebellion might go on bit, I'm thinking," Barney mused. "If it does, Mother must relent eventually. We can't be spending the entire war at home whilst others do the fighting. James, Pat and Eddie are showing no interest. Why can't they care for Mother and the household whilst we volunteer?"

"They should do! . . . But I'll be having a problem with Mr. Schuchman as well. I'd not wish to leave him without help after the many kindnesses he's shown. Perhaps if I gave him some months of notice, he'd be able to take on and train a new boy."

"My bosses will be needing none of that! I'll enjoy marching about the country in the fresh air rather than nearly melting in the heat of the foundry. We must try Mother again . . . perhaps after you sort out your position with Schuchman."

And so they left it until well into the following year. The burden of responsibility fell heaviest upon Barney. He had, in recent years, gradually become his mother's strong right arm in the family business and managed its finances. Though his patriotic fever was the equal of Charles', Annie's opposition to enlistment pricked his conscience deeply. He wanted to be off to war, but acknowledged to himself an inability to do so. But Charles was only stymied in his military ambitions temporarily. Indeed, he coaxed his mother into allowing his participation in a local "home-guard" organization, the Park Zouaves.

In the spring of 1862, Uncle Charles McKenna, drayman and brother-in-law of Annie, passed away leaving his widow Ann and seven surviving children. Though often a difficult personality, Charles was nevertheless loved and respected throughout the family. Annie remembered well his devoted support upon the death of her husband. With many of his siblings residing in St. Louis, only brother Bernard remained in Pittsburgh of the sons old Hugh had brought to America from County Tyrone. Now, Bernard and Annie rushed to support Charles' family in their time of grief.

* *

Lincoln's third call, for 300,000 volunteers, came in early July 1862. There was a general sense of crisis felt throughout the city. Despite General Grant's victories earlier in the year in Tennessee, Union campaigns in the East had been dismal failures. And there were rumors of an impending draft. This was just the lever young Charles needed to overcome his mother's deep opposition.

"Better that I volunteer now, Mother. I'll likely be drafted in any case, and then without honor. There's to be a grand, public meeting in Allegheny City on Thursday where I can freely choose my unit on the day. Please, Mother, it's a duty that someone from this family must answer!"

Annie wrung her hands in anguish and mopped at tears with the hem of her apron. "God save us, Charles, if you should go and be maimed or killed."

Now his sister Catherine intervened. She threw her arm around her mother's waist and argued, "You're not the only mother facin' such risk. If Charles should go to war, you'll still be havin' the rest of your sons and myself to lean on. Who knows? There may be some special service that Charles is meant to render."

Eventually, Annie conceded one son to the cause of Union, but she would go no further. Barney gritted his teeth but refrained from protest. He felt humiliated to see his younger brother given leave and himself bound by duty at home. He retreated from the discussion and marched out into the gathering dusk of evening.

Thursday, July 24th, dawned hot and humid; the skies were their normal smoky gray. Charles McKenna ventured forth, dressed in implausibly formal attire, given the weather. He crossed the St. Clair Street Bridge to Allegheny City, the same bridge that his grandfather used to first enter Pittsburgh thirty-two years prior. Making his way up Federal Street to South Common, he turned left towards the open public square just below the penitentiary. Already at noon, the crowds were impressively large, growing eventually to between 15,000 and 20,000 citizens. There were five speakers' platforms for the use of Governor Curtin and various local dignitaries. A chorus of singers was on hand to render a suitably patriotic medley of songs.

Interestingly, the meeting began with an invocation by Rev. William D. Howard, the man who had purchased the McKennas' Irwin Street rooming house just five years previously. Passionate oratory and numerous loyal resolutions ensued, bringing the crowd to a high pitch of patriotic fervor.

As the hours passed, the day got hotter. Doffing his coat and collar, Charles bought a lunch at one of the numerous vendor stands that dotted the periphery of West Common. He had as his ultimate destination the recruitment booths dedicated to filling the twenty-one new infantry regiments required of the State of Pennsylvania. When the meeting Chairman, General Thomas Howe, announced the opening of these booths and the officers assigned to each, Charles made his way to Booth #1, where the "Kier Rifles" and the "Hiland Guards" were the preliminary units being organized by interested citizens. Here recruiters stood ready to register the flower of Pittsburgh manhood in the great, now desperate, cause. They warned that "None but sober, steady men need apply."

They didn't have to devote much time inducing seventeen-year-old McKenna to inscribe his name on the rolls of the Kier Rifles. Numerous young ladies were on hand, looking on with admiration and approval as their beaus stepped forward to "fall in." After much handshaking and back-slapping, Charles left for home full of enthusiasm and self-satisfaction.

Barney greeted Charles glumly as he sat on the steps of the rooming house that evening, in retreat from the heat indoors. "When do you have to report?"

"Next week we must submit to a physical examination. Only then will we be told where and when to muster. There's talk of a new camp at Linden Grove over in the Sixth Ward, so perhaps I won't be too far from home to begin with."

"Mother will be glad of that." With this terse response, Barney returned to a book he had been reading.

Sensing his brother's lack of enthusiasm, Charles passed into the house to share his news and reassure his mother. The next day he gave a final notice to his employer, confident that the physical examination would present no challenge at all. He and his brothers were reasonably fit, having enjoyed years of boyhood, athletic pursuits in the old neighborhood in Irwin Street. When the time came, the physical examination proved to be casual and perfunctory, to say the least. Most of the recruits, being between fourteen and twenty years, readily demonstrated the requisite strength and flexibility with handsprings and other gymnastic feats. But a minority shirked the process for more pleasurable, last-minute pursuits—often to their ultimate regret. Some of these would eventually be lost to illness.

In August Charles was ordered to report to the newly-established military encampment at Linden Grove. Dubbed Camp Howe after acting Adjutant General Thomas M. Howe, the camp was set upon 150 acres in South Oakland and served by a street railway.

It took some days before the nascent infantry regiments were organized and officers assigned. In the meantime, ill-fitting blue uniforms, bleached underwear, and overly-large army shoes were issued. Ancient muskets were distributed, though without ammunition. The camp food was universally reviled. City boys routinely returned to their homes for the evening meal. Apart from drilling, there were games, music, and glee clubs to pass the time. Families and friends were frequent visitors to the camp each day.

Eventually, Private Charles McKenna found himself assigned to Company "E" of what would be designated the 155th Pennsylvania Volunteers. The entire 155th Regiment, consisting of ten companies, was under the command of Colonel Edward J. Allen. Late in August, Union forces suffered another defeat at the second Battle of Bull Run. Indeed, the city of Washington was deemed vulnerable to enemy attack. On September 2nd, Col. Allen was ordered to assemble his roughly one thousand men the following day at the rail station on Liberty Street to depart for Washington.

That night, Charles returned home for final goodbyes with family, friends, and long-time boarders. Besides his mother, uncle Bernard, and his siblings, they were joined by Irwin Street grocer James McShane and his family, and old friends Will and Catherine McKeever and their children.

Barney, despite his personal disappointment, took some satisfaction in the evening. For some months now, he had a marked interest in young Mary McShane, the grocer's eldest daughter. She and Barney were both twenty-years-old and had been schoolmates in years past. But as Mary became the attractive woman she was, acquaintance matured into friendship. And while he maintained a proper reserve through the evening, Barney's frequent glances her way did not escape the notice of family members.

After a fine meal, it was time to return to camp. Annie and Catherine cried. Brothers James, Patrick, Edward, and Barney embraced the young recruit. Uncle Bernard offered a prayer for the safe return of his nephew.

"I shan't forget all that you've taught me, Mother," Charles promised as he hugged her. "I'll serve with honor and virtue, God willing. And by His grace, I'll come back to you."

Chapter Seven

September 3rd dawned unusually hot and humid. Reveille sounded at 5:00 a.m. The Pennsylvania Railroad would need all day to assemble sufficient cars to carry the various regiments to Washington. Departure was set for 7:00 p.m., allowing fourteen hours to pack, assemble, and march the three miles from camp to the station. However, few recruits were able to name or recognize their officers, and vice-versa. There were no flags or designated assembly points at which to "fall in." Orders were given, countermanded, or ignored. Confusion reigned.

Many soldiers were weighed down with heavy knapsacks full of gifts, excess clothing, and equipment. Bibles, picture albums, shoe brushes, knives, forks, and spoons, cups and saucers, suspenders, gloves, neckties, mirrors, heavy blankets, fruits, preserves, and even some umbrellas, were among the non-essentials being toted. So untrained and undisciplined were these green recruits that a march of only two city blocks, to Fifth Avenue, caused some to fall out. In the heat of the day, they gathered at town-pumps and watering troughs to mop fevered brows and assuage fatigue.

It took three hours and numerous such rest periods for the bulk of the column to reach the Ross Street schoolyard in the Second Ward, where a flag presentation by grateful citizens was scheduled for 6:00 p.m. Judging the rate of progress so far, commanders dispatched a request to the Pennsylvania Railroad offices calling for a postponement of the departure to allow for stragglers to catch up with their units. Once arrived at the rail station, the soldiers were met by a crowd of families, friends, and well-wishers. Among these were enthusiastic young ladies dispensing hugs and kisses, not limited to sweethearts or family members. It was 9:30 p.m. before actual departure from Pittsburgh took place.

Early the next morning, the troop train arrived in Harrisburg, Pennsylvania where the soldiers were detrained, marched to Camp Curtin, and fed breakfast. Later, the Governor commissioned Col. Allen as regimental commander and gave the official designation of 155th Pennsylvania Volunteers. Then, at the State Arsenal, heavy Belgian rifles and cartridge boxes were issued. Some adventurous recruits took the opportunity to tour the city and State capitol before an afternoon departure for Baltimore. Very early on the morning of September 5th, the regiment bivouacked on the sidewalk of Eutaw Street in Baltimore for a stand-up meal of salt pork, hardtack biscuits and unsweetened black coffee.

* *

Private Charles McKenna was not, in the least, dismayed by the first days of deployment. He was confident that his regiment would prove to be "the banner regiment" of the entire Army of the Potomac. But he was surprised by the lack of public attention paid to their progress through Pennsylvania and Maryland. When there was no formal welcoming party upon their 6:00 a.m. arrival in Washington, McKenna reasoned that the President and Secretary of War Stanton must have been distracted by the burdens of putting down the Rebellion.

The officers of the 155th, having been met by no one upon arrival in Washington, quickly engaged in foraging for food for their tired and hungry soldiers. They quickly learned that a canteen, known as "the Soldiers Retreat", was located in Swampoodle (swamp puddle), a rough and ready shantytown just northeast of the U.S. Capitol. The Tiber Creek ran through this district and would often overflow, leaving the ground wet and puddled. This was where many Irish immigrants settled in the years following the Great Hunger. During the war, freed slaves also congregated in Swampoodle. The military canteen provided the most basic food and drink for newly-arrived soldiers throughout the day.

Standing in long lines waiting to be served, the soldiers groused that the vile menu was simply a replay of the unsatisfying fare experienced earlier in Baltimore.

Private James P. O'Neill remarked to Private McKenna as they passed through the line. "Charlie, these victuals are fit for neither man nor beast. Surely we can do better than this!"

O'Neill was also a member of Company "E". The two had become friendly during their time at Camp Howe. O'Neill was a lively, witty, adventurous fellow. One would hardly guess that he had left his studies for the priesthood at St. Michael's Seminary in order to enlist. Both were still seventeen and from Pittsburgh, so they had much in common. They would become "mess-mates," living together through much of the war.

Charles anxiously scanned the cityscape. "It is wretched stuff. There must be shops or restaurants nearby. But, of course, we may be missed."

"Then let's not tarry. We'll be fed and back before the entire regiment has their fill of this slop."

So the two set off, abandoning the Soldiers Retreat for nearby Washington markets where fruits of the season, coffee with cream and sugar, steaks, pies and buns were to be had. These constituted a memorable, if somewhat expensive, repast. After thus gorging their appetites, they proceeded to stroll along the muddy, unpaved Pennsylvania Avenue.

Jimmie's countenance brightened as a new idea occurred to him. "Let's be down to the White House! You met the man and shook his hand. Perhaps I may do the same."

"Right, but let's not be gone too long. It will upset our officers if we are late returning."

They hadn't progressed very far at all when they were accosted by several Provost Guards, U.S. Army regulars who filled their days rounding up stragglers and deserters.

A gruff sergeant strode across the street to meet them. "Where are your passes, you two?"

"We've none of those," Charles admitted. "We've only arrived in the city this morning. Our regiment is after taking refreshment at a place called Soldiers Retreat."

"Well then, lads, you had best high-tail it back to your regiment or we must place you under arrest for desertion. Now, double-time quick! We will follow you to be sure you arrive safely."

Jimmie and Charles hurriedly retraced their steps. But upon arrival at Soldiers Retreat they learned that the entire 155th had already departed for Camp Chase on Arlington Heights, just outside of Washington. It was only the Provost Guards' reluctant sympathy that availed the two an escort over the several hot, dusty miles to camp. They were relieved upon arrival to find their knapsacks, muskets, and cartridge boxes had made the trip successfully without them. Short of sleep and fatigued by the rigors of the day, they retired early. But their rest was interrupted when the regiment was subjected to a midnight "long roll" of drums. The order to rise quickly and "fall in" was a test of the soldiers' readiness to answer an unexpected call to arms.

* *

The 155th spent their first week at Camp Chase familiarizing themselves with their officers, their duties, procedural drills, and marches into the countryside to smoke out lingering Confederate forces. Having found none of the latter, they returned to Washington only to find the commissary totally bare of provisions. It was then that Col. Allen endeared himself to his troops forever. Rather than march his men, tired and hungry, back to Camp Chase, he procured a wagonload of oysters from Harvey's Restaurant. After an interval of confusion on the part of these Pennsylvanians, the colonel had to hire black "contrabands" from the city streets to tutor his soldiers in the proper technique for opening a bivalve.

Company "E" Captain Frank Van Gorder, had just been promoted to Regimental Quartermaster. He knew that the heavy, awkward Belgian rifles issued at Harrisburg were unfit for use.

With Allen's support, he arranged for their replacement with new muzzle-loading Springfield rifles. They were also issued "buck and ball" cartridges (each containing three buckshot and one bullet). The change was greatly welcomed by the soldiers, but the ammunition would later prove to be rather ineffective except at very close range.

On Sunday, September 14th, the green recruits of the 155th and the rest of the Division, under the command of General Andrew A. Humphreys, joined a march into the Maryland countryside. The eight regiments (about eight thousand men) were instructed to reinforce Gen. George B. McClellan's Army of the Potomac in their pursuit of Robert E. Lee's Confederate forces. They plodded their way fifteen hot, dusty miles that day and made their encampment that night just outside of Rockville, Maryland.

Private McKenna shared his evening with three messmates Jimmie O'Neill and the Tomer brothers, Corporal Tom and Private George. They still had no tents or gum blankets. But they washed the road dust from faces and hands and shared the salt pork, hardtack, and coffee which comprised most every meal when on the march.

Tom Tomer was the first to notice, raising his head from the remnants of supper. "What's that noise? Can you hear it, just faintly?"

Charles cocked an ear and listened closely. "Thunder? . . . Perhaps a thunder shower? Wouldn't I be grateful for one of those? Might clear the air and cool the evening."

"Dream on, McKenna," cracked 1st Sergeant Robert Thompson as he walked past their mess. Thompson, one of eight of their comrades hailing from the north of Ireland, was a friendly, if sardonic, fellow. "That be cannon fire from up at South Mountain. That's where McClellan has found the rebels . . . or been found by the rebels."

The next day was even hotter and more humid than before. As they continued their march, many soldiers were straggling. Some dropped from fatigue. Others began to dispossess themselves of knapsacks, heavy coats, and blankets, leaving them by the side of the road. The civilian teamsters, following with the military supply wagons, stopped and retrieved the discarded items for subsequent sale to citizens along their route.

On the evening of the 16th, a group of about a hundred footsore stragglers, many from Company "E," sought shelter for the night. They found it in a "young ladies' seminary," an abandoned schoolhouse possessed of fresh water and an orchard of peach and apple trees. This refuge had been occupied just two days prior by Confederate soldiers under General James Longstreet.

Jimmie O'Neill called to his comrades who were carrying in armloads of ripe fruit. "Will you look at this!" He pointed to what had once been clean, white-plastered walls. "Them dirty rebels have wrote their autographs and a load of insults against the Union and President Lincoln!"

Sure enough, in the corner of the room they found the charred sticks used as writing instruments days before. It did not take long before the boys of Company "E" were taking their revenge with answering graffiti of their own. O'Neill was soon joined by Theophilus Callen, Robert Douglas, and others in joyous rebuttals demeaning Jefferson Davis and the Confederacy. But it was Charles McKenna who distinguished himself that evening as a "lightning artist," dashing off caricatures so humorous and life-like, the assembly gave him three cheers and voted him the regimental artist.

* *

While Charles and his comrades were adapting to the rigors of the march, back in Pittsburgh there was a tragedy brewing. It involved a familiar character—John Symington, now a colonel but still the commandant of the Allegheny Arsenal. The Arsenal had become a premier production facility for ordnance and related supplies for the armies of the Union. Its campus, located in Lawrenceville, extended from Philadelphia Road down to the banks of the Allegheny River. It was bisected by Butler Street. The lower section consisted of the Main Armory, various workshops, storehouses, officers' quarters, barracks, and a central parade ground and a park. The portion above Butler Street included powder magazines, laboratories for the manufacture of shells and cartridges, stables, additional storehouses, some parkland and a fire-pond.

Six months prior, a private contractor had furnished a new road-bed of stone blocks. The way led to the principal ordnance laboratory, a wood-frame, single-story building. Safety concerns had necessitated the replacement of the heavily-rutted, dirt road that had caused gunpowder barrels to shift dangerously in the delivery wagons. The newly quarried stone was a hard limestone, tinged with iron and capable of striking off sparks when impacted by a hammer or a horseshoe. Upon discovering this problem, the contractor drew the issue to the attention of Symington. But the officer was reluctant to incur the expense of replacing the new surface with a different stone. Later Alexander McBride, supervisor of the laboratory, recommended that the roadway be covered with sawdust or sand. He knew that DuPont, the supplier of the gunpowder, was recycling barrels and that the lids of such often fit poorly. This allowed traces of powder to escape during transit. But Symington stubbornly rejected his concerns. When the roadway was finished, McBride on his own authority had the roadbed covered with cinders. But soon Symington discovered this initiative and reprimanded McBride. He ordered the cinders removed. Such was the state of affairs on the afternoon of September 17th.

About 2:00 p.m., a teamster was delivering powder barrels to the fourteen-room, main laboratory. Witnesses stated later that horse hooves struck sparks upon the roadway, igniting the dust upon its surface. The teamster, J.R. Frick, testified that he saw fire that made a "fizzling noise" between his wagon and the front porch of the laboratory. With that, a series of three separate explosions took place. The first of these caused McBride to flee the laboratory through a window, as his office was collapsing. He rushed to a nearby powder magazine to close its open door, which probably prevented it from exploding. As he was attempting to return to the laboratory, a second blast blew him thirty feet. The third blast disintegrated the building in which 156 of his employees were surrounded by nearly a full day's production of ordnance.

Allegheny Arsenal by Alina Josan
(Black & White Effect Added)

Charred wood, torn clothing, mutilated body parts, skirt hoops, fragments of dinner baskets, exploded and unexploded shells, and melted lead were scattered in an unimaginable scene of mayhem and chaos. Seventy-eight workers were killed, mostly women and young girls. McBride lost his own daughter, Kate. Many victims were never found or could not be identified.

News of the tragedy carried almost as fast as the deep, thunderous report heard even in the noisy city center. By late afternoon, details had reached the McKenna boarding house. When she heard the tragic news, Annie felt a knot tighten within her. It took only a minute, however, to determine what must be done. Rushing to the staircase, she summoned Catherine from her needlework and explained what had transpired. "I want you to run to Auntie Ann's home in Faber Street . . . . God have mercy on that poor woman who only just lost her husband and now, perhaps, a daughter. Wait there for news of Ellen."

Through her tears, the girl replied, "But Mother, what of Catherine?"

Catherine McKeever, Will's daughter (and Annie's niece), had lived for a time at the McKenna boarding house and was dear to all of Annie's family. She and Ellen McKenna had been friends and commuted together daily to and from their jobs at the Arsenal.

Annie now grabbed the girl by the shoulders and gave her a good shake. "Daughter! Just do as I say . . . . I'm off now to McKeevers. Bring me word there."

Early that evening Ann McKenna, Uncle Charles's widow, learned that her daughter Ellen was among the missing. Collapsed in grief, she was attended by her four sons and two other daughters. But it was a terrible night of prayerful vigils for many Pittsburgh families. Annie shuttled between the two stricken homes where her relatives awaited word of the missing girls. The next day, it was announced that Ellen's body could not be identified amidst the carnage and she would be declared dead. Somewhat later, the same disposition was made regarding Catherine. Sorrow was heaped upon sorrow. The scale of the Arsenal losses even prevented individual funerals for many victims. Fifty-four unidentified bodies were given a mass burial at the Allegheny Cemetery.

A coroner's jury was highly critical of Symington and several of his direct subordinates. But the colonel requested and received a military inquiry one month later. Claiming uncertainty as to the precise cause of the explosion, no knowledge of defective powder barrels, and pointing to likely breach of discipline by laboratory workers, Symington received complete exoneration from the military panel. But he was a broken man. After several months, he went on disability leave. He died in retirement two years later.

* *

The tragedy in Pittsburgh was dwarfed nationally by the coincident meeting of Confederate and Union forces in a major battle at Antietam Creek near Sharpsburg, Maryland. Beginning on the morning of September 17th the bloodiest day in U.S. military history ensued, leaving over 23,000 total Union and Confederate casualties. For Private McKenna and the entire Division, it was a missed appointment. Inexplicably the Union chief-of-staff, Henry Halleck, had ordered Gen. Humphreys to pause his march and encamp outside Frederick, Maryland. Perhaps Halleck harbored concerns about the vulnerability of the nation's capital and wanted reserves available in case of an attack.

By the time he and his staff realized the gravity of McClellan's situation and rescinded their order, the course of battle had been ordained. Now Humphreys led his men on a gallant and rigorous forced march through the night. As they had passed through the town of Boonsborough, they were at first cheered by the spectacle of hundreds of Confederate captives being marched away under armed guard. But the elation quickly dissipated when they encountered the great number of ambulance wagons full of desperately wounded Union troops, including many from the Ninth Pennsylvania Reserves from Pittsburgh. The sight of familiar faces contorted in agony and the sound of cries and groans in pain were the first exposure for Charles and his regiment to the desolation that was about to become commonplace.

The majority of the eight thousand troops forces under Humphreys' command arrived early on the morning of the 18th, too late to help McClellan's battered forces turn the tide of battle. About noon, the thousand or so remainder of foot-sore and weary stragglers finally caught up with their comrades. The division was then assigned to stand picket duty, protecting against any rear-guard action from Lee's departing forces. As they picked their way through the fields of battle towards the southwest perimeter, the ground was torn and marked by the most horrific evidence of the previous day's conflict. Bodies in blue and butternut lay rigidly in random congregation, bloated by the sun or ravaged by carrion birds.

As Charles carefully navigated his way through the cornfields littered with human and animal corpses, the sights and smells overcame him with revulsion and grief. "Ach, Jimmie, this is so much worse than anything I had imagined! Instead of a quick and clean dispatch by a single, well-aimed bullet, these poor ones have been torn to pieces or left to slow hours of agony . . . . This what we have signed on for?"

O'Neill removed the kerchief from his nose and mouth to respond. "God help us, Charlie, I believe it is, though I was as ignorant as yourself . . . . If I had completed my studies for the priesthood, I might be moving among these ravaged souls, administering the last rites. Instead, I'm carrying a musket and must add to the desolation."

"I don't ever want Mother or Catherine to realize all this . . . all that we must now face and, God willing, endure. I'll not be telling them, that's for sure."

After several weeks of picket duty on the north bank of the Potomac, Humphreys' division took up an encampment near Sharpsburg called Camp McAuley. It was poorly laid-out, with bad drainage, bad sanitation, bad food, and no medicine. Dysentery, diarrhea, even typhus, afflicted many of the soldiers, especially those who had dodged their enlistment physical. A significant number of deaths resulted. Others were discharged as unfit for duty and sent home. Meanwhile Col. Allen's request for better food, clean drinking water and medicines, endorsed by McClellan, was ignored by Washington.

Chapter Eight

In one of his first letters home, Charles wrote on October 8th:

". . . We are drilled severely, I might say, from seven till ten in the morning and from two till six in the afternoon. During these hours we have squad, company and battalion drills. The latter expose our officers and prove that they know nothing of the duties of their office . . . All the minor positions in the company are conferred. I asked none. Of course I would have accepted one, but I am not disappointed in not getting any. None of our mess, Jim O'Neill or the two Tomers got any 'posish', although as well qualified as those appointed."

Actually, Charles was not long in being selected for a responsible position. One day there was an order to detail a capable man to serve as "orderly" at Division Headquarters. Regimental Adjutant Ed Montooth sent for Private McKenna to fill this request. Upon reporting, Charles queried the freshly-minted adjutant as to the duties of an orderly. Montooth, a tall fellow with a walrus-like brush of a mustache demurred. "I'm not sure exactly. I suppose it might involve keeping things clean and tidy about the Division headquarters."

Charles bristled at the thought. "If it means cleaning muddy boots, washing dishes, or renewing ill-used cuspidors—I'll be off for home at once! I enlisted to fight, not for such menial tasks."

Montooth patted him on the back. "Ah now, don't do nothing rash. Give the post a try . . . . You'll be serving General Humphreys and his staff officers directly. Who knows? If you perform well, there may be a promotion in it."

Resignedly, McKenna left to report to the Division Adjutant General, the chief administrative officer within General Humphreys' command. Entering the tent office, the lowly private quickly approached the officer seated at his desk and extended his hand. "Good morning, General! How do you do?"

"HOW-DYE-DO, GENERAL?"

Sketch from "Under the Maltese Cross"

The senior officer, famous as a stickler for military discipline, jerked his head back in surprise and disgust. He ignored the proffered handshake. Rising from his chair, he leaned across his makeshift desk, his glaring eyes boring into those of the private.

"Who in Hades are you?"

Charles took a nervous step back. "Why, sir, I am the new orderly, detailed here as requested."

"Well, Private, has it possibly occurred to you that you might wish to salute a superior officer upon presenting yourself?"

"No one has ever explained such military affairs, sir. We were only told to be civil."

The adjutant resumed his seat, shaking his head. "How long have you been in service, Private?"

"Five weeks, sir."

This reply appeared to awaken a degree of sympathy within the officer's heart. For the next twenty minutes, he instructed his new orderly in postures, salutes, other strictures of military discipline, and signs of respect for ranking personnel.

Satisfied with this increment of training given, the officer turned to the stack of papers on his desk. "Now then, Private, I have your first order to fulfill. I want you to report to the camp of the 134th Pennsylvania Regiment. Give the following message to Colonel Matthew Quay: The Division Adjutant General sends his compliments and requests that the Colonel report immediately to Division headquarters."

McKenna smiled. "Yes, sir." This seems a duty I can easily perform. Remembering to salute, off he went. He found Colonel Quay, blouse open, cigar in mouth, and engaged in a friendly game of euchre with fellow officers. Charles saluted and delivered his message.

"All right, Private. You are dismissed." The Colonel studied his cards and showed no rush to comply.

Colonel Matthew S. Quay
134th Pennsylvania Volunteers

Private McKenna returned to his post, but failed to report back to his superior, as was his duty. After about a half hour, he heard the cry "Orderly!" from the Adjutant General's tent. Quickly he entered, snapped to attention, and delivered a smart salute.

"Did you inform Colonel Quay that he was wanted immediately?"

"That I did, sir." Charles beamed with self-satisfaction.

"Well, why did you not report such upon your return?" The adjutant's voice now reached a higher octave.

"I had no order to do so, sir."

The officer struggled to restrain an explosion of temper and profanity. A minute of silence ensued and the crisis passed. Pacing the length of the tent, he now issued Private McKenna a new message to deliver. Concluding a stream of colorful oaths, he added, "You go back and tell Colonel Quay that if he doesn't report here immediately there will be hell to pay!"

The orderly briskly returned to the Colonel's tent and delivered the message as verbatim as memory would allow, oaths and all. Since the rank of the Adjutant General was equivalent to that of Captain, and Colonel Quay was, in all respects, a superior officer, the delivered message produced both irritated surprise and an immediate response. Upon arrival at Division Headquarters, Col. Quay and the Adjutant General had a most stormy interview.

Private McKenna, confident that he had executed his instructions to the letter, returned to his post, blissfully unaware that it was the substance of the message that was expected, not to include all the decorative language that went with it. Sometime later, the cry of "Orderly" recurred.

He briskly responded to the adjutant's call. "Yes, sir?"

The adjutant's face was a mass of storm clouds. "Private, you are relieved of duty at these headquarters! . . . You are to return to your company . . . . And tell them that if there are any more goddamn fools there, keep them out of my sight!"

In shame and dejection, Charles returned to his unit and reluctantly related to Captain Joseph Sackett his brief career as Division orderly.

Several weeks later Sackett, anxious that Private McKenna have an opportunity to redeem himself, ordered him to the presumably-easier task of guarding the Division horse and mule stockade. Despite a total lack of instructions as to his duties or the procedures to be followed, our lowly guard went off to take up his new post.

After several days, General McClellan ordered his army to break camp and prepare to march. The now familiar Col. Matthew Quay arose that morning only to discover that his personal horse, a fine, well-bred charger, had been stolen during the night. Being commander of a volunteer regiment and not a member of the regular army, it was the custom for such officers to supply their own horses. Frantic not to be left afoot during a general mobilization, Quay instructed his regimental orderly, J.R. Swan, to conduct an immediate search of the camp.

"Don't neglect the Division stockade! Perhaps someone has discovered a horse without its rider. It may have been returned there."

Swan appeared at the stockade during the guard duty of Private McKenna. Being unacquainted with passwords and counter-signs, Charles welcomed the orderly and gave him free access to the inventory of mounts. Not finding his Colonel's missing horse, Swan selected a suitable, government-issue steed and requested its release to the Colonel. Such release was promptly agreed and Col. Quay was soon rejoining the forward march.

Later that day and some miles from camp, the Division Quartermaster took notice of Quay's new mount, which carried the brand "U.S." on its left hindquarter. Perplexed by the general problem of government-issued property going missing, the quartermaster took appropriate action. That evening, Col. Quay was confronted by a military guard who requested his sword and notified him that he was liable to court-martial for possession of government property without authorization. Private Swan was also placed under arrest. The next morning a stern General Humphreys convened a hearing at which Quay and Swan were brought forward.

Major General Andrew A. Humphreys & staff
(www.old-picture.com)

"The Colonel's horse was duly issued for his temporary use, sir, subject to return upon request," Swan testified to the dubious general.

The general replied testily. "May I inquire, Private, as to the identity of the issuing authority?"

After a considerable interval spent in a search, Private Charles McKenna was produced before the assembled court-martial. General Humphreys resumed the hearing and had Swan repeat his prior testimony. He then placed McKenna in his somber gaze. "Is this true, soldier?"

"It is General, sir." Reaching into his blouse pocket, Charles pulled out a written receipt, signed and dated by Private Swan. It confirmed the authorized release of the horse in question.

Hearing of the general's reputation for a rigorous adherence to military regulations, and given the severe countenance he had exhibited so far, McKenna was sure that he faced severe discipline indeed. However, upon hearing his testimony, and learning how recent was his entry into military service, Humphreys relaxed and complimented Charles for his foresight in demanding a signed receipt before issuing the animal to Swan. "You have shown promise for future service as a quartermaster, Private."

The general now turned his attention to Col. Quay. "Colonel, the charges against you are dismissed. But it is only by the initiative of this raw recruit that you have been saved from the adverse judgment of this court-martial!"

* *

Writing home to his sister Catherine, Charles makes no reference to his recent adventures, but reflects upon separation from home and family:

"Dear Sister, it would be altogether unnecessary for me to assure that your letters are welcome . . . They contribute greatly to my contentment. By the kind and tender sentiments expressed in them I see that your interest and love for me has only been strengthened by our separation . . . You speak the truth when you observe in your last letter that no son was ever more attached to home than I was, and I trust in God that it may not be 'ere long I am in your midst again . . . To you, dear sister, do I owe the knowledge of how to offer up my prayers to the Almighty . . . I will always endeavor to follow up the teachings of home . . . Prayer and the sacraments are the best weapons to defend myself with against the spiritual enemies by which I am surrounded . . . Giving my love to all and asking your prayers, I remain as ever your loving brother.

The spiritual enemies Charles found about him were real. Profanity, drunkenness, gambling, and pilferage were rampant. The latter was especially troublesome. The men attempted to supplement their meager army rations with purchases from the regimental sutler, but these often went missing. The sutler to the 155th was a civilian from Pittsburgh by the name of Samuel Pollock. Jolly and well-stocked with edibles, he offered his wares under a line of credit against the next monthly payroll. Still, there were complaints about the high prices, e.g. 15¢ for a half-pound of butter!

The days were full of training, drilling, inspections, parades, reviews, roll-calls, picket duty, and reconnaissance. Sergeant Robert Thompson was also the drill-master of Company "E." He drove his recruits hard, even on Sabbath mornings. His "hardie infantry tactics" transformed his soldiers from a green, undisciplined crowd into a proficient, organized, and resilient fighting force. Soon, they would need to be.

Chapter Nine

Back in Pittsburgh the McKenna family continued as before, but labored under the impression that the war would certainly be won promptly, and that Charles would be home soon. Charles encouraged this hope when he wrote:

> *"I hope the war may be over before New Year's so that I can give up the military business. For I need not inform you that it is a very disagreeable and uncomfortable pursuit to follow. But you know I expected hardships, harder than I have yet endured. I did not enter the army from a choice or love of it; but a desire to assist the govt. in putting down the rebellion, and it is that thought that consoles me in all my annoyances."*

But as the months passed, their confidence waned. The correspondence between family and soldier was sporadic, with brother James being the most reliable correspondent. Was Barney infrequent with his letters due to a lingering resentment of his confinement to the home front? Perhaps, but he had much to keep him busy. He continued to frequent the old neighborhood at Irwin Street, not least to keep up his continuing friendship with Mary McShane. Though Mary was receptive to his attentions, she made it clear that a serious courtship was premature.

She took his hand, attempting to soften the blow. "You must try to understand, Bernard. I have responsibilities at the store. Father's health is poor and Mother relies upon me for help with the children."

Barney's shoulders slumped at this statement. But he chose to accept it as a postponement, not a repulse. He forced a smile. "I'll not worry, Mary. Our friendship is strong enough to wait on better times."

But there was another purpose that brought Barney back to his old haunts. Irwin Street was the home of the Allegheny Volunteer Fire Company. It was probably not just the opportunity to serve his community that drove him to become a volunteer fireman. His older brother, Hugh, had been a member of the company prior to his departure for the California goldfields. But this precedent was not the motivator. Barney realized early on that, if he wanted to follow his father's footsteps into politics, the fire company was the best platform from which to begin. Indeed, the various fire companies of the day counted numerous future political leaders among their ranks. Getting to know the ambitious and engaged men of the city was a natural and beneficial result of signing on.

Though the longstanding tensions between fire companies had moderated somewhat, the tradition of bitter, even violent, competition was ever on their minds. The Allegheny Company, founded in 1802, was the second oldest in the city. Now, hand-pumped engines were replaced by steam-powered units. These and the proficiency and discipline of its members established a high reputation for the Allegheny Company. Laziness, drunkenness, or unreliable behavior were not tolerated. Being highly motivated and a teetotaler, it was easy for Barney to comply.

* *

The news from the military campaign in the east continued to be un-nerving. President Lincoln was convinced that McClellan was far too timid and cautious. In November, 1862 the president replaced him with Ambrose Burnside. Pressed by Lincoln to capture the Confederate capital of Richmond, Burnside reluctantly moved to comply. He advanced to the outskirts of Fredericksburg. There, he was confronted by Lee's army occupying high ground above the city. Well dug-in with artillery and entrenched rifle companies, Confederate forces looked down upon the city and the Rappahannock River. But Burnside was oblivious to the lack of any strategic value in capturing Fredericksburg and to the tactical advantage possessed by Lee.

Weeks went by as Burnside awaited the arrival of pontoon bridges from Washington. All this while, Lee improved his battlements. Finally, on December 13th, Burnside ordered his forces to cross the Rappahannock under withering rifle and artillery fire. General Humphreys' Division, which was ordered to cross last, sustained 1700 killed or wounded within their first ten minutes under fire. The 155th Regiment escaped the worst of the losses, suffering nine killed and fifty-eight wounded. But many other units of Burnside's army fared far worse. In particular, there was the Irish Brigade comprised of regiments from New York and Massachusetts. It was led by General Thomas Meagher, an Irish immigrant himself and a former rebel against the British occupiers of his homeland. Having taken 60% casualties at Antietam, Meagher had recruited replacements. They now entered the battle at Fredericksburg some 1600 soldiers strong. Showing remarkable bravery, they made numerous attempts to take the Confederate positions on the slopes of Marye's Heights. Only 280 men were left in the Brigade to fight the next day.

Burnside was intent on pouring more of his men into this suicidal attack, but his generals protested bitterly and President Lincoln intervened. The ensuing withdrawal took place under cover of dark and fog. Retreating to what would become Camp Humphreys near Falmouth, Va., the division went into a prolonged winter encampment. With the bitter defeat at Fredericksburg, following upon previous debacles for the Army of the Potomac, the morale of the troops was very poor. They were sick, undernourished, and long worn-out by the constancy of hardtack. The soldiers also had zero confidence in the intelligence and leadership of their top commander. When General Burnside ordered a January march in an attempt to flank Lee's positions across the Rappahannock, the effort was slow, noisy, and thus no secret to Lee's pickets. Then cold, steady rains turned the roads to a deep, muddy quagmire. Unable to proceed with his plan, Burnside was forced to order a return to camp.

In late January, President Lincoln replaced Burnside with "Fighting Joe Hooker," a handsome, genial, and aggressive commander who was popular among the troops. Hooker further endeared himself with the troops when he had them provisioned with fresh baker's bread, meat and vegetables. He also ensured payment of wages that had been delayed for months on end. The effect of these measures had a dramatic and positive impact upon morale. In the ensuing weeks, the health and strength of the men improved greatly. Hooker now entrusted the Fifth Corps (which included the 155th Pennsylvania Volunteers) to General George Meade. The well-loved and respected commander of the 155th Regiment, Col. Edward Allen, suffering greatly from inflammatory rheumatism, left on an extended sick leave. He was replaced by Lt. Col. John Cain.

Camp Humphreys was everything Camp McAuley never was. Well-designed with excellent sanitation and drainage, it housed men in three-man log huts, each with a fireplace and chimney. Indeed, one of the common pranks during the long winter was to smoke-out one's neighbor by placing a board over the chimney of his cabin in the middle of the night. Regular drilling and training in bayonet, skirmish tactics, and target practice were important parts of the daily regimen. But, there was a glee club. There were "hoe-downs," where-in the men danced with each other or alone. There were games such as quoits, football, and paddle-ball. Private McKenna reports in a letter to home:

> *"There are several sets of boxing gloves in camp; after much coaxing I was induced to try them on, with a verdant youth yesterday. I recollected sensations in my head produced by Eddy's left winders and others at the sport around Irwin Street. For fear of a repetition of these pains, I was reluctant . . . but was induced to try, first stipulating that there was to be no hitting hard. After maneuvering awhile, I found*

my opponent very timid. He knew less than I did, which was next to nothing. Accordingly, I . . . sent 'reconnaissances' out, right and left, and by vigorous work succeeded in causing my adversary to throw up the gloves—attracting a crowd and getting compliments for my science. Since then I have preferred to rest on my own easy-won laurels . . ."

Camp Humphreys, Virginia
Sketch by Charles F. McKenna

While in this hiatus, Private McKenna decided to put his artistic talents to work. His initial subject was a panoramic overview of Camp Humphreys. He sent the original drawing to his former employer, William Schuchman, requesting a supply of lithographic prints. These he then sold to eager comrades as souvenirs, at $1.00 a copy.

Later that winter, Charles took advantage of an unusually warm and sunny afternoon. Seated on the stump of a tree taken for cabin construction, he began to sketch from memory the impromptu "hoe-down" of the previous day. Music and dancing, even dancing with each other, had provided the soldiers a welcome respite from the boredom of winter camp.

Hoe-Down at Camp Humphreys
Sketch by Charles F. McKenna

Suddenly he became aware of someone quietly standing behind him. Somewhat annoyed, he stood to confront the uninvited visitor. "What the deuce . . . ?"

The stranger stepped back. "Sorry, soldier. I didn't mean to interfere with your work. I was just admiring your artistry."

Before him Charles found a large, heavy-set man with dark hair and a brush of mustache. Before he could give vent to his impatience, his glance met sergeant's stripes on the sleeve of the offender.

"Oh! . . . . Sergeant . . . ?"

"Fulton, . . . George Fulton. I'm assigned to the commissary. I was hoping to buy one of your prints of Camp Humphreys. Have you any remaining copies?"

Charles quickly relaxed, his frown now replaced by a smile of relief. "Yes, I have more in my cabin. Let me fetch one for you."

When he returned, Fulton queried him. "You have a wonderful talent. Are you a professional artist?"

"Oh no. These sketches . . . why, I have been doing these since I was a child to amuse myself. I doubt I could make a living as an artist as I have no formal training."

"Well, perhaps after the war you will further your education."

"I did attend night classes while apprenticed to Schuchman, the lithographer. I might do so again as I did enjoy them greatly."

Fulton nodded approvingly. "I encourage you to do so, Private. Of course, I am prejudiced on the subject. Before enlisting I was a school principal in Fayette County. I even brought a number of books to camp as several of my pupils enlisted with me."

Charles raised an eyebrow. "Would you consider a bit of a trade of goods? . . . I will make a gift of my print in return for the loan of a book now and again. If they are not presently all in use, of course."

Fulton laughed, "I like your pluck, Private. I'd be pleased to loan books to you, even without the gift of your sketch. I have a number of useful subjects for your consideration. Visit me at the commissary and you can choose among them."

Charles did follow up on Fulton's invitation. Their relationship evolved, the sergeant becoming something of a mentor. He commanded increasing measures of respect, not only from Charles but from the rest of the regiment as well. As commissary sergeant, Fulton was exempted from front line duty. Nevertheless, he made a point of personally distributing rations to troops under the fire of battle. Fulton also functioned as a free-lance correspondent for the *Pittsburgh Chronicle*. His accounts of military life were followed avidly back on the home-front.

* *

In March, Charles wrote to Barney of an impending, second draft. In his letter, he betrays the typical attitude of the day, especially among Irish-Americans, towards the free blacks inhabiting his home city. Though blacks in Pittsburgh could be found widely in the workplace, usually as stevedores and in unskilled laboring positions, they tended to reside in segregated neighborhoods—notably a section called Hayti, along Wylie Street in the old Sixth Ward. In the McKenna's home Fourth Ward, less than three percent of residents were blacks. Given their low social position, and the competition between black and Irish for unskilled jobs, it is not surprising that Charles exhibits low esteem for African-Americans. His language sarcastically mimics their dialect as well.

"If you are drafted I hope you will send a man in your place instead of paying $300, even if that man should be of the 'collod' tribe . . . I advise you to let 'Brudder' Woodson and his fellow countrymen go in your place . . . You must overlook the indiscretions of the veterans . . . such amusements as knocking 'collod gemen' down, cleaning out saloons, raising rows generally, . . . whiskey is to blame . . ."

Spring arrived with the promise of a renewed military campaign. President Lincoln traveled to Falmouth to review Hooker's army and discuss military strategy for the approaching Spring campaign. With one hundred thousand men to pass in review, the event took all day of April 7th. Private McKenna recorded the event with another of his drawings.

Lincoln and General Hooker Review the Army of the Potomac
Sketch by Charles F. McKenna

During the following days in Camp Humphreys, Charles McKenna was often assigned to picket duty along the north bank of the Rappahannock. So extended and quiet were conditions, he and other Union pickets regularly exchanged gossip, newspapers, and tobacco with the Confederate pickets on the south bank. One such day in late April, Charles sat in the shade of a willow close to the riverbank. The protracted serenity of picket duty had lulled him and his mates into abandoning the constant pacing more familiar for such assignments. The brown waters below still ran fast from the recent spring rains. Charles stretched his body in an attempt to shake off the lethargy of mid-afternoon.

"Hey, bluecoat! Got any tabac on ya?"

Charles started at this sudden interruption, a call from the opposite bank. "Sorry, Johnny, I don't use it . . . . You fellows running low?" Charles stood now to get a better look. He searched the scene before him but his correspondent remained hidden from view.

"Just a little bit lately. Where ya from, Yank? Ain't ya homesick yet?"

The voice seems to be coming from behind a mound of honeysuckle. "Pennsylvania, . . . but I'm managing reasonably well. Where's home for you?"

"Nottoway—sou'west o' Richmond. Plenty tabac at home, I reckon . . . . When ya boys gonna head on home and leave us'ns alone?"

"Not too soon, I'm thinking . . . But I expect Jeff Davis can hurry us along . . . by crying uncle."

"Yeah, well don't ya Yanks count on that happenin' . . . . Seems like ya should be tendin' to Pennsylvania and leave us tendin' to our own affairs down heah."

Charles puzzled a moment as to whether or how to reply. This didn't seem the time or place to conduct a political debate. "I suppose that works most of the time, friend . . . . But my citizenship doesn't end at the Pennsylvania line. There's a whole country . . . and it belongs to all of us. You folks pulling away makes our country smaller and weaker than it should, by rights, be."

"Smaller might jes be better!"

This is getting tiresome. No way to change minds shouting across a river to someone I can't even see. "Well, friend, let's just enjoy the rest of our day. Be glad there ain't folks dying in battle just now."

"That, Yank, I kin agree to do."

When the order to begin the march to Chancellorsville came, the 155th was divided into two wings. The left wing was directed by Lt. Col. John Cain. The right wing was led by Major Alfred Pearson. The latter included Company "E." Private Charles McKenna was appointed acting Sergeant Major. Their line of march took them across the Rappahannock on pontoon bridges, and thence to the Rapidan River. There, the men stripped off their clothing and waded through the chest-high, rapidly-flowing waters to the south bank.

Without belaboring the details of the battle of Chancellorsville, suffice it to say that it was a costly stalemate for both sides. The battle lasted from May 2nd through the 5th. The Confederates lost their heroic General Stonewall Jackson, long the nemesis of Union efforts in northern Virginia. General Hooker was severely wounded on May 3rd, depriving the Union forces of decisive leadership. Finally, a general retreat back to Camp Humphreys was undertaken in rain and mud. The 155th remained at this camp until June 3rd, when a series of marches and forays through northern Virginia ensued amid extreme heat, sunstroke, and occasional heavy thunderstorms.

Battle at Chancellorsville
Sketch by Charles F. McKenna

Back in Pittsburgh, there was a general state of alarm among citizens and the authorities. Knowing of Lee's intent to invade the Union territory again, their concern was for the protection of the Allegheny Arsenal, the Fort Pitt Foundry, and the manufacturing capacity of the city, upon which the Union depended for much war materiel. From mid-June till early July, there was construction of a twelve mile ring of thirty-seven fortifications (earthen redoubts, battery sites, and powder magazines). Miles of trenches were dug to connect many of these sites. Hundreds of businesses provided thousands (from 4,000 to as many as 11,000 at times) of volunteer laborers, working in the peak summer heat. It was expected that there would be reimbursement for these men at $1.50 per day, and boys at 62¢ per day. But both businesses and citizen volunteers were greatly disappointed when the Federal authorities refused payment on grounds the Pittsburghers were simply protecting themselves and their city. Only in 1905 was the long running dispute settled when Congress voted to pay the claim, but at the face amount—without the forty-two years of accrued interest.

* *

By the 26th of June it was known that Lee's main forces had moved into Maryland and, perhaps, Pennsylvania in an apparent attempt to cut Washington off from its supply routes to the north. Hooker's army was on the march in hot pursuit. They reached the outskirts of Frederick, Maryland on the 27th. Marching past beautiful, green fields of corn stalks and grain, and past orchards showing early signs of their fruits, the Union troops progressed between thirty and thirty-five miles daily. But Hooker's injuries from Chancellorsville necessitated his resignation. He was replaced as commander of the Army of the Potomac by Gen. George Meade on the 28th. Gen. George Sykes succeeded Meade at Fifth Corps. Within that Corps, Charles' 155th regiment was moved to the Third Brigade under the command of Brigadier Gen. Stephen H. Weed. Colonel Edward Allen, formerly of the 155th, now returned from his extended sick leave, hoping to resume his command. But his debilitated state required that his former regiment remain the responsibility of Lt. Col. John Cain.

As Meade pressed his pursuit of Lee through the Maryland countryside and into Pennsylvania, his army was greeted by nearly one hundred school children singing the *Star Spangled Banner* and other patriotic songs. Also turned out were enterprising, if not generous, civilians selling bread, pies, cakes, and bottles of milk. Jimmie O'Neill nudged his comrade in the march. "Now look at these fellows, Charlie. Many seem young and fit. Shouldn't they be defending their homes and the Union instead of squeezing the last coins out of a soldier's pocket."

"Your point is well-made, Jimmie . . . . Still, such rich fare is not to be found in our army rations. No one is forced to buy if the price is too dear."

O'Neill just shook his head in disgust. "Well, if it were up to me, I'd draft these farm boys on the spot!"

Generally, though, the morale of these Pennsylvania troops was high as they were off to defend their home state. Their resolve was unshaken, even when they encountered gruesome scenes of prior conflict between opposing cavalry units. Then, on July 1st, an urgent dispatch was received that Union and Confederate forces were already clashing outside of Gettysburg, Pa. It was imperative that the Fifth Corps arrive in time to maintain control of the high ground already seized at great cost by Union cavalry. Within ten minutes a forced march was launched. At 1:00 a.m. the next day, exhausted soldiers were allowed to make their bed in the roadway for a three hour respite, and then on to Gettysburg.

There were many stragglers during the forced march. Often these soldiers were unable to wear their shoes due to severe foot blisters. Privates McKenna, Jimmie O'Neill and others of the 155th were among those seen with their shoes dangling from the muzzle of their muskets.

The regimental surgeon stopped them a few miles from the impending battle. "You men may stand down until you can wear those shoes again."

Charles exchanged glances with his comrades before making reply. "Thank you, sir, but no. I guess if Johnny Reb can fight barefoot, we might do the same."

"Nevertheless, Private, I have passes for you and they are meant for just such a purpose. If you ruin your feet, you'll be of little use in the fight. Here now, take these passes!"

Grudgingly, they accepted the passes but, as the surgeon passed on, they donated them to other weary soldiers.

Having become separated from their unit during the night, they hurried on, arriving at the Peach Orchard just in time to help reinforce other units under their Corps commander, General Sykes.

The rest of the 155th was halted two miles outside the town of Gettysburg and assigned to reserve duty behind the positions of the First Corps. They rested at Power's Hill till afternoon, within earshot of cannon fire to the west. This brief period was filled with rest, sleep, meals, and song. General Weed and Col. Patrick O'Rorke of the 140th New York even joined in the singing. They would be dead within the hour.

A strategic hilltop position, called Little Round Top, had been designated a signal point by General Meade earlier in the day.

Detecting the approach of Longstreet's Confederates, General G. K. Warren, Meade's Chief Engineer, signaled Meade and requested that Fifth Corps occupy Little Round Top and positions around it. A grizzled captain wholly unknown to them addressed Privates McKenna, O'Neill, and Pangburn of Company "E," and Sergeant Collner of Company "G." "You men fall in with these others . . . . Our orders are to capture those heights over yonder. Captain Hazlitt must get his artillery pieces up top as soon as possible, but his horses are useless for such a climb. You'll be given some rope to use in the hauling. Now, all of you, get to it!"

Little Round Top (foreground)
(www.old-picture.com)

Upon arriving at the foot of Little Round Top, and despite heavy enemy fire, this mixed squad physically hauled four heavy cannon up the steep slopes. Soon other Fifth Corps units, including the main body of the 155th, hurried to help secure Little Round Top. Confederate Gen. James Longstreet now diverted his attack on Third Corps to contest for control of Little Round Top. He sent his sharp shooters to take up position in a nearby area of boulders later known as the "Devil's Den." They immediately trained their sights against those on Little Round Top. Sadly, General Weed received a Confederate bullet in the chest shortly upon his arrival. Artillery Capt. Hazlitt bent down to hear Weed's last words, "I would rather die here than that the rebels should gain an inch of this ground." As he did so, another "minie ball" took Hazlitt's life. Col. Patrick O'Rorke was also mortally wounded by this intense rebel fire. His 140th New York regiment sustained heavy losses as Longstreet sent various Texas and Alabama units to overrun the hastily-established Union positions.

The 155th took up position on the right flank, atop the west face of Little Round Top. On the left flank, the 83rd Pennsylvania and the 20th Maine were bravely repulsing attacks from the southwest. Stationed upon rocky, tree-covered heights, the 20th Maine, under the leadership of Col. Joshua Chamberlain, made a protracted defense, eventually exhausting their supply of ammunition. Desperate to prevent their position from being taken, Chamberlain ordered his men to fix bayonets and led them in a courageous charge down treacherous slopes against their relentless foes. This audacious maneuver routed the enemy and saved Little Round Top from almost certain capture. Chamberlain would subsequently receive the Congressional Medal of Honor for his valor on this day.

General Joshua L. Chamberlain
(www.old-picture.com)

Meanwhile, 155th and others from Fifth Corps improvised stone bulwarks against the enemy fire. They would raise their caps on the end of their bayonets, above these battlements. This would draw fire and thus expose rebel positions at Devil's Den. Pennsylvania sharpshooters, using telescopic gun-sights, were then able to target their fire with considerable effect.

Because most of the 155th was still using the old "buck and ball" ammunition, their fire was not so effective at distance. So they held their fire and quietly waited. A Texas brigade, under Jerome Robertson, assumed this absence of Union fire indicated a breach in the Union defenses. When they came within twenty yards, they were subjected to a withering fusillade. It took thirty minutes of pitched battle before the Texans fell back, leaving both sides with heavy losses.

In the ensuing lapse in enemy pressure, the still-infirm Col. Edward Allen was seen moving across the line of battle on improvised crutches, encouraging those he once commanded. Charles turned to his mess-mate, Thomas Tomer. "Hey, Tom, look! No one can shade Colonel Allen for persistence, eh?" Receiving no reply, he advanced to where Tomer had been positioned. The Color-Corporal lay slumped in a heap. McKenna found him severely wounded, but alive. He draped Tomer over his shoulder and gingerly carried him to a rear area where surgeon's staff rendered rudimentary first-aid.

Over meager rations late that evening, Charles and Jimmie O'Neill comforted their mess-mate George Tomer on the wounding of his brother. The four of them had been inseparable since those first days at Camp Howe, sharing tents, sharing meals, even confiding hopes and fears on occasion. Now, each was greatly distressed.

"He's been moved already to the field hospital and I'm told he should recover," O'Neill reported.

Charles touched his friend on the shoulder. "Your brother fought bravely, George. He never faltered in protecting our colors. Our friend John Mackin was with him. Both Color-Corporals, both wounded today. I pray they'll heal quickly."

Ironically, George received a medical discharge two weeks later. His wounded brother returned to duty after a period of convalescence.

The next day was quiet till around mid-morning. Then there was an exchange of artillery fire, but without great effect upon the Union positions on Little Round Top. Gradually, both sides ceased their barrage. Around 1:00 p.m., a massive Confederate advance, known now as Pickett's charge, was launched against the Union position on Cemetery Ridge. Wave upon wave of rebel infantry marched across open field and uphill slope in a desperate attempt to repeat the familiar pattern of Confederate success. This time, however, they were repulsed decisively with overwhelming artillery and rifle fire from forces under General Winfield Hancock. Canister and grape shot swept the rebel lines in appalling carnage. Only a small remnant of Pickett's entire force ever reached the Federal positions and these were rapidly overcome. The grisly scene to the north was easily observed by Private McKenna and his comrades. They were stunned to silence by the wholesale slaughter of Confederate forces.

Major Alfred Pearson was visited that afternoon by a delegation of local farmers, demanding immediate payment for hay and straw taken by Union soldiers for use at their field hospitals. Incensed, Pearson, spat upon the ground at their feet. "Get out of my sight you worthless excuse for citizens! I'd sooner burn your barns than accede to your greedy demands. If I hear from you again, I'll see you all court-martialed!"

Meanwhile, the enemy riflemen at Devil's Den appeared to have withdrawn in the aftermath of Pickett's failed attack. Given the absence of enemy fire, Irish immigrant Private James Finnegan of Company "D" decided to visit the Devil's Den late in the afternoon. Perhaps he was in search of souvenirs, but he neglected to bring his rifle with him. As he toured the site, he suddenly encountered four hapless Georgia sharpshooters. Apparently abandoned by their comrades without warning, they immediately threw down their weapons in surrender. Finnegan collected their rifles and marched them back to his own lines.

Devil's Den, Gettysburg Battlefield

A bemused 1st Lt. Edward Montooth received the prisoners. After having them marched off under guard to the rear, he questioned Finnegan closely. "So, Private, explain this to me. How was this capture accomplished—what with you being unarmed?"

Finnegan stroked his chin briefly in thought. Then he beamed a smile. "Begorrah, sir, I surrounded them!"

As evening arrived, Charles huddled under a rock outcropping. The evening had become cool and rainy. By the light of his pitiful, little fire, he pulled out his pencil and paper to sketch from memory a scene from the day's battle. As he did so, the goateed Noah Pangburn crawled in beside him and peered at the emerging image.

Charles looked up from his work. "Hi, Noah."

Pangburn sat down and drew his knees till they touched his chin. He pondered the sketch for a minute, then broke his silence. "Charlie, could you believe those Johnnies today—the way they just kept coming? . . . I didn't know if I should laugh or cry. It was the damnedest sight I ever did behold."

Charles set his sketch aside and looked out into the darkening scene below. Thousands of little campfires lit up the field of conflict here and there. Shadows moved about collecting the wounded, blue and gray, and carrying them to waiting ambulance wagons. "I didn't cry, that's for sure. I kept thinking about Tomer and Mackin . . . all the men we lost yesterday and today."

"Was it courage or were they just foolish, marching right into the . . . ?"

Charles didn't let him finish. "Certainly it was foolishness! They were done in by their generals, including the great Bobbie Lee! . . . Those boys really thought they could lick us one more time. When you believe something as hard as you can, it gives a certain courage, I suppose."

Pangburn looked off to his right, lost in thought. "I hope I can . . . we can believe like they did. We showed them here that we are finally a real army."

Also that evening, Col. Cain, mindful of the inadequacy of the "buck and ball" cartridges carried by his men, ordered that proper

Springfield rifle cartridges be recovered from the field of battle and distributed to his men. Cain would soon thereafter resign his commission and be replaced by Alfred Pearson, now promoted to Lieutenant Colonel.

Charles McKenna and his comrades awoke the next day, the weather having made no improvement. As they consumed what passed for a breakfast, Pangburn broke the dreary silence. "Today is the fourth of July! . . . It's Independence Day."

Jimmie O'Neill raised his tin cup of watery coffee grounds and toasted. "A good day to mark a great victory! Maybe now the war will end and we'll be goin' home."

"Don't I wish it were so?" Charles whispered to himself.

News of the Union success swept the nation, bolstering popular support for the war effort and Lincoln's re-election hopes for the coming year.

The Fifth Corps spent the balance of 1863 in various movements within northern Virginia; but as winter set in, Meade's army began an encampment near Warrenton, Va. that would last till May, 1864. Once again, the soldiers were housed in three-man log huts, this time with canvas roofing. When bitterly cold weather set in that January, rye whiskey was distributed to the men, a quart for every twelve soldiers. Charles McKenna, a confirmed teetotaler like his brother Barney, reluctantly declined his ration.

The winter encampment was relatively quiet. Perhaps the saddest moment came that January when Capt. Joseph Sackett, commander of Company "E," drowned while crossing Kettle Run, having been thrown and kicked by his swimming horse. The entire brigade turned out for Sackett's formal military funeral and for the mournful march to the rail station, from where his body was shipped home. His replacement was Captain George Laughlin.

The time in winter camp was not wasted, however. The new brigade commander who had replaced Stephen Weed was General Kenner Garrard. He initiated a rigorous training program of "Zouave" drills and bayonet tactics. The original Zouaves were North African units of the French army from the 1830s even unto

World War I. Their distinctive, oriental style of dress became quite popular in the United States during the run-up to our Civil War. Charles McKenna had participated in a militia-like organization back in Pittsburgh called the Park Zouaves. During the war, selected Northern units were authorized the use of such uniforms in recognition of bravery under fire, or other worthy accomplishments.

So successfully did Garrard's brigade master these battlefield skills, he recommended that they be awarded the Zouave uniforms, to be purchased directly from Paris. But Garrard was soon promoted to Brigadier General and transferred to the Western Theater before the uniforms arrived. Lt. Colonel Pearson continued the regime of Zouave drills within the 155th. It was he who would distribute the fancy garb to his troops. The uniforms consisted of wide, dark-blue knee breeches, a jacket of heavy, blue material trimmed in yellow at the collar, waist, and down the front. A long red sash, trimmed in yellow wrapped around one's waist. White canvas leggings and a red fez with blue tassel completed the ensemble.

Private McKenna in Zouave Uniform
Image from "Under the Maltese Cross"

Their first parade in the new attire occurred on February 11, 1864. As they first donned these exotic costumes, there was much laughing and joking within the ranks. Placing a fez at a rakish angle upon his friend's head, Charles chided the former seminarian. "Not as awesome as priestly vestments, Jim. But dashing enough, I'm thinking."

Zouave Bayonet Drill, Private James P. O'Neill

Sketch from "Under the Maltese Cross"

Chapter Ten

In March, Charles wrote to brother Barney:

"Your probable alliance with the haberdasher's daughter, and your sign up at 'No. 24' (Irwin Street) *as successor to James McShane, Grocer, are events that may yet transpire . . . Success, Barney, is my wish . . ."*

Someone in the family, probably not Barney himself, was sharing with Charles news of the deepening relationship between Barney and Mary McShane. Still, obstacles to marriage remained in place. Mary's father's health continued its slow decline. Her forty-eight-year-old mother, Ann Daugherty McShane, had had eleven live childbirths, of which only six survived early childhood. Mary being the eldest of those remaining at home, her youngest siblings still needed her care and supervision. Until her only brother, thirteen-year-old James, attained adulthood the store and family life would require Mary's full attention.

Barney continued as an iron moulder, though no longer a journeyman. Now twenty-two, he moved to Mitchell's Foundry at 194 Liberty Street. Despite his experience, the wages paid to Irish labor still lagged far behind the skilled, typically Protestant, iron puddler and master moulder. Taking upon himself the responsibilities of wife and family would prove difficult financially. His volunteer fireman position offered no reward beyond a network of contacts and the grateful respect of the community. So, despite Charles' enthusiasm, a wedding was not in the offing for the foreseeable future.

Eddie had left his clerk's position and was now working as a brass moulder. James had risen to the position of chief clerk at the post office. Patrick apparently had gone through a period of illness the prior year. Whatever his illness, it was grave enough for him to leave his clerk's job at the Pennsylvania Railroad. Now somewhat recovered, he launched a new career as a tobacconist at the corner of Liberty Street and Virgin Alley. In April, Charles wrote:

> *"I am glad to know that Patrick's health has improved so much . . . and I hope God will continue this blessing to him. It pleases me also to know that he has started so well at his new business and I would like success to crown his efforts. I think, if I ever return, it will be trying temptation to resist his fine cigars . . . ."*

Annie and Catherine were still fully engaged in running the boarding house at 281 Penn Street. Besides themselves, other family members in residence included Uncle Bernard, James, Patrick, Eddie, Barney, and a cousin James McKenna, son of Uncle Charles. And then there were the boarders: four being stone-cutters; there was one tailor, one salesman, one laborer, and one surveyor. Some of these would stay on for some time, whilst others would come and go in a few months. So, there was always an effort to maintain a full house. Between boarder revenue and the contributions from family breadwinners, Annie was probably comfortable in economic terms. Now approaching her mid-sixties, her health seems to have been satisfactory also.

****

With the appointment of General Ulysses Grant to head the Army of the Potomac, further reorganizations were announced that spring. The 155th was again transferred, this time to the First Division of the Fifth Corps, commanded by General Charles Griffin. It was Griffin who adopted the Maltese Cross as the insignia for his unit, a mark worn proudly by his troops throughout the remainder of the war. Charles describes it in his letter of April 25th:

"I have received a beautiful one as a present from my friend Edward Sackett of our company which will answer very well. It is made of small white beads on red velvet, which I intend sewing on the breast of my pocket."

Major General Charles Griffin & staff (with Maltese Cross banner)
(www.old-picture.com)

Efforts were expended in re-enlisting soldiers whose terms of service were expiring. Those agreeing to do so, together with new recruits and draftees, helped to repopulate units that had been decimated in previous conflicts. Charles describes the diversity of his company thus:

"Our company is composed of miscellaneous specimens of humanity who all agree well—Fayette, Armstrong, Westmoreland, and the rural districts of Allegheny (counties) *have their representatives . . . while the city of smoke is not 'irrepresented' in privates and 'ossifers'. Farmers, millers, miners, moulders, topers, clerks, students, pedagogues, cobblers, loafers, barkeepers, and travelers compose the motley crew . . ."*

On May 1st, Gen. Grant ordered his army to de-camp and to cross again the Rappahannock in search of Lee's Army of Northern Virginia. At the intersection of Germanna Plank Road and the Orange Court House Pike, the army made a pleasant encampment on the 4th of May.

The following day, inexplicably, two great armies chose to meet in battle in an area called The Wilderness. This twenty-square-mile thicket was nearly jungle-dense, with few roads and many deep ravines. Even seeing one's enemy, never mind maneuvering, was nearly impossible. The Confederate forces had already taken up established positions for their riflemen. About 9:00 a.m. Union skirmishers encountered rebel musket fire. At noon, the bulk of Union forces were ordered into the woods, only to face difficult going and continuous disruption to their lines. Paralleling the Orange Turnpike, the 155th advanced, as best they could, passing through their own pickets and skirmishing with rebel counterparts.

Generals Meade and Grant, directing events from The Old Wilderness Tavern, were under the impression that the enemy was not present in force, and that Lee's army had fallen back from the Union approach. To their chagrin, their army encountered a fierce and numerically superior foe. The exchange of volleys was so intense that it seemed to be raining leaves and twigs. Soon exploding ordnance set the tinder-dry woodlands on fire, trapping and often incinerating many of the unfortunate wounded left behind. That night was horrific for Charles McKenna and his comrades as they sleeplessly listened to the anguished cries of those beyond their reach.

"Dear Jesus," Charles prayed, "can't you just take them right now? Surely, a merciful death is better than the scrap of life they're clinging to now!"

Jimmie O'Neill, overhearing his friend, grimaced. "I'd do anything for those poor bastards, . . . even give 'em a friendly bullet."

The next day, the 155th established a skirmishing presence facing a large force of rebels massing for attack. As the foe emerged from the trees into a large clearing, the skirmishers waited for good targets, fired in force, and then fell back. Company "E" lost a number of comrades in the ensuing battle. Privates John Hunter and Jacob Friend, both severely wounded, were captured by the enemy and spent eleven months at the infamous prisoner-of-war camp at Andersonville, Ga. Sergeant Hugh McGimpsey and Corporal Michael Lemon, wounded and left for dead, were subsequently rescued when the ground where they had fallen was regained. Private McKenna had an extra reason to be grateful for Lemon's recovery. The preceding night he had entrusted a packet of family photos and letters to Lemon for safe keeping in his knapsack.

As the Confederate advance continued, the regular army units of Gen. Ayres' brigade, being disoriented as to the position of the 155th, opened a mighty fusillade against the approaching rebels at an angle that brought his own forces under heavy, friendly fire. Livid at this needless assault, Col. Alfred Pearson, commanding the 155th, launched a withering, verbal attack upon Ayres, his immediate superior. So vociferous was his protest, he was temporarily arrested and relieved of his command. Though no charges were filed against him, it was nearly forty-five days before he was re-instated and his regiment transferred away from Ayres.

As the regiment regrouped at battle's end, Theo Callen came, head hung low, bringing disturbing news. "Our friend John Mackin is among the wounded. Shot again in the same shoulder as at Gettysburg! Seems to be quite serious this time."

Charles was pouring forest debris from his shoes. He turned and faced Callen. "Not Johnny! . . . He came back full of beans and confidence. Said, 'lightning don't strike, but rarely, in the same place.' . . . I remember when his father, the Pittsburgh flour inspector, visited John at Fredericksburg."

O'Neill, now sporting a trim mustache, paused as he cleaned his rifle. "So do I. The old fellow had been to Washington, . . . talked his way into getting a pass to our camp. Shoot, nobody in my family would do that for me!"

Callen couldn't repress a chuckle at his comrade's complaint. "My pa might wish to visit, but he'd never be wantin' to join in the attack! But old Mackin was game. Col. Allen turned him down flat."

"Yes," Charles nodded with a smile. "But he did get to see John. And they shared an embrace before we crossed that pontoon bridge."

Color Corporal John Mackin died a month later in a Washington hospital.

* *

The battle of The Wilderness was a tactical draw, with heavy losses on both sides. But Grant, unlike his predecessors, did not retreat to safety. Rather his plan for grinding down Lee's smaller army through a war of attrition was fully joined. He ordered Meade to immediately leave the Wilderness and begin a night march to Spotsylvania in pursuit of the Army of Northern Virginia.

On May 8th, the Fifth and Sixth Corps engaged the enemy again at Alsop's Farm, skirmishing to identify Confederate lines of battle, breastworks, and weak points. The 155th took heavy casualties later that day in over-running rebel entrenchments. Charles McKenna's mess-mate, Jimmie O'Neill, was wounded in the abdomen. Bleeding profusely, and in a state of near-hysteria, O'Neill ran to General Griffin's position, collapsing only after providing details of enemy strength and location. Company "E" Capt. George Laughlin ordered McKenna to personally conduct O'Neill to a nearby field hospital. Praying desperately, Charles half-walked, half-carried his good friend. "Don't you go dying on me, Jimmie," he demanded upon delivering his friend to the regimental surgeons.

"Is it a choice I have, Charlie?" his friend groaned in reply. This was the last they would see of each other till after the war.

The rest of the month of May was spent in strenuous marches and intense fighting through oppressively hot, humid weather. By the end of the month the Fifth Corps again confronted Lee's army in a seven mile front from Bethesda Church to the Chickahominy

River. On June 2nd, Griffin's Division responded to a call for reinforcements from the new Fifth Corps commander, General Gouverneur Warren. They took to breastworks at Bethesda Church in time to face an assault by Confederate forces under Gen. Jubal Early. Finding the previously entrenched rebels now in the open, they threw themselves at the enemy, driving them back to their previous defensive battlements. There were heavy losses on both sides.

That night, a Company "E" squad of four lookouts were assigned to a picket station just outside of the regiment's breastworks. A schedule of rotating watches involved Privates Charles McKenna, Theophilus Callen, Newton Hipsley, and Robert Douglas, under the supervision of Corporal John Lancaster. It was 10:00 or so when McKenna began the first "vidette" in an advanced position at the foot of a large tree. He dug a foxhole to protect himself from the continuing volleys from rebel sharpshooters. At the end of his watch, he heard a low signal whistle. It was Callen, there to take the next watch.

Detail for Vidette Duty—Hipsley, Douglas, McKenna and Lancaster
Image from "Under the Maltese Cross"

Leaving his cover, Charles crawled out to meet him. "Theo," he whispered. "I've got a hole for you just over yonder. But please, stay low! Them rebs are making it mighty hot out here."

Callen nodded and moved off to take up his position. Charles slowly skittered his way back to the picket station and promptly took to his bed-roll. I sure hope I get some decent sleep. 'Tis little more than four hours till my next watch!

Two hours passed and Private Hipsley's turn came. When he received no response to his whistle-signal, he searched impatiently for Callen's position—but without success. Under sustained rebel fire, he returned to post and reported the possible loss of Private Callen. Corp. Lancaster quickly aroused McKenna. "Charles, wake up! We can't find Theo! He doesn't respond to Hipsley's whistle. You must come show us. Only you know where you left him."

Charles immediately agreed to return to the foxhole. Maybe he's fatigued and fallen asleep. When he reached his prior position, Theo indeed appeared to be sleeping. Charles reached forward and shook him, only to encounter a cool, rigid corpse. "Ach, God, no!" Returning to Corp. Lancaster, he reported the loss. They both then sought out the company commander.

Capt. George Laughlin frowned, his heavy, dark eyebrows merging into a solid line. "I can't order any of you to recover Callen's body while we're under such heavy rifle fire. But . . . if there be volunteers, I'll not object."

Charles stepped forward and addressed his captain. "Certainly I will go. I must go. Only I can show where he lies."

"We'll go as well!" Lancaster, Hipsley and Douglas volunteered. It was now nearly 3:00 a.m. The still-bright moonlight made targets of each. Moving on hands and knees, they used trees to shelter themselves from rebel bullets. Upon reaching their destination, they found Callen with a head wound judged to have killed him instantly. His musket chamber was found to be empty and his cartridges depleted to only a few rounds. They rolled him into a blanket. When scudding clouds overtook the moonlight and obscured their movements, they dragged the body back to camp.

Eighteen-year-old Private Theophilus Callen was buried by his fellow pickets near a peach tree in the yard of the Bethesda Church. Later, Charles drew a sketch of the boy's resting place. It, and a letter of condolence from Corp. Lancaster, was forwarded to Callen's family in Westmoreland County.

* *

While the Fifth Corps was busy repulsing the enemy at Bethesda Church, much of Grant's army was assaulting Lee's fortifications at Cold Harbor. Despite the protests of his chief of staff, General Humphreys, that such an attack over open ground was doomed, Grant persisted. He would later write, "I have always regretted that the last assault at Cold Harbor was ever made. No advantage whatever was gained to compensate for the heavy loss sustained." So desperate were the losses accumulated in the nearly constant fighting of that month, Grant ceased offensive activity. He sent a flag of truce to Lee so that the Union dead lying before the Confederate positions might be gathered and buried.

As the fighting ground to a halt, the 155th received their portion of a shipment of shoes purchased by General James Wadsworth from his personal funds before his death at The Wilderness. With so many soldiers having been without shoes for months on-end, Wadsworth's gift to the Fifth Corps would be enshrined in bittersweet memory.

Grant now ordered a swift and hidden withdrawal across the James River. Under the personal direction of General Warren, the entire Army of the Potomac, along with its numerous supply trains, livestock, and artillery pieces, was successfully spirited away under Lee's nose. All this was accomplished without the loss of a single soldier, gun or wagon. Then, while the Fifth Corps made a feint towards Richmond, Grant led his other 150,000 troops to Petersburg, the main transportation hub south of Richmond, from whence Lee was receiving most of his supplies of food, clothing, and ammunition.

On the 16th of June, Union forces commenced their attack on Petersburg in what would become a long, bitter siege. The Fifth Corps entered the fray two days later under heavy artillery fire. The 155th participated in leading the attack, even launching a bayonet charge to within twenty feet of the enemy breastworks. Finally, they had to fall back in the face of heavy casualties. Col. Joshua Chamberlain of the 20th Maine, hero of Little Round Top, was severely wounded in the hip and groin. Surgeons voiced the opinion that his wound was mortal, but the former college professor overcame that prediction. At Warren's recommendation, Grant promoted Chamberlain to Brigadier General in recognition of his continued bravery under fire. Indeed, all of Griffin's Division—including 155th—were commended for gallantry in the attack.

Within days, Grant concluded that Lee's Petersburg's defenses were impregnable. He, therefore, instructed the Second Corps and Griffin's Division of the Fifth Corps to disrupt the routes of communication and supply between Petersburg and points south. Private McKenna and his unit spent much of the rest of June seizing and holding segments of the Weldon Railroad against severe Confederate resistance. Later, they were assigned to digging trenches and establishing breastworks from which the siege of the city would be prosecuted.

****

In early July, Company "E" commander, Cpt. George Laughlin was promoted to the staff of General Griffin. At his recommendation, Private Charles McKenna was assigned special duty in the headquarters of the Fifth Corps, reporting to Lt. Col. Fred Locke, the Assistant Adjutant for General Warren. Leaving trenches he had helped to dig came as a great relief to McKenna. Weather and the change of seasons would make trench warfare terribly unpleasant, dangerous, and debilitating.

The Corps headquarters was situated quite near the Union firing line. It was housed in the fine, old, colonial-era Avery Mansion, which had been abandoned by its owners. The house showed considerable damage from Confederate artillery. Its spacious parlors, rooms, and grounds hosted a diverse staff of between three and four hundred officers and enlisted men. These included Quartermaster, Commissary, Provost Guard, Medical, and Signal Corps units. There were also mail clerks, teamsters, escort cavalry, sharpshooters, orderlies, clerks, contraband cooks and servants in attendance. Here also, horses, mules, ambulances, and wagons of the Corps were maintained and protected.

One might suppose that Private McKenna enjoyed considerable safety in this remove from his unit back in the trenches. But such was not fully the case. Artillery exchanges were common nighttime occurrences, and shells penetrated the roof and windows of Avery Mansion occasionally. Just the noise of these explosions was a considerable impediment to a good night's sleep.

In a September letter to his family, Charles wrote from a successive headquarters location, the Yellow Globe Tavern near the Weldon Railroad:

"Today, as I write, the sound of not distant cannonading reaches my ears. It is from Hancock who is again trying his best to gain advantages over the enemy, and I hope will succeed. The fall of Atlanta I think was a matter the country might well rejoice about . . . Recruiting I also hear is very good at home; our regiment received 200 a few days since. I firmly believe if the people at home have patience and sustain the armies in the field now, by word and deeds, that the end of the needless and unjust Rebellion will be before Christmas.

I had a notion to try and get home lately on recruiting service, but as the length of time the job would last; my certainty of losing this situation I am now in; and the uncertainty of getting on that duty were considered by me, I gave up the notion."

145

Annie McKenna sat at the kitchen table in the quiet of afternoon shelling peas for the evening meal when this letter arrived. She read it privately and was tempted to rejoice in Charles' forecast of victory. Shakily handing the letter across the table to daughter Catherine, she said, "Please God! Could it really be over by Christmas?"

Catherine scanned the letter quickly and shrugged. "Let's hope that it is so, Mother. But there have been such predictions in the past. Each of these has left us disappointed in the end. We must be grateful that Charles serves the General's staff. At least, he is not confronting the rebels personally."

Annie buried her face in her hands momentarily. Then, she raised her eyes to heaven. "Two years my boy has been at war . . . and for two years he has been saved from harm. Daughter, let's pray that God's protection continues."

Catherine was correct in asserting that her brother was not typically under fire in his staff capacity. As he attended to the administrative duties assigned him by Col. Locke, he was always aware that his comrades in the 155th were actively engaged in battles throughout that fall and early winter. Being at the center of command, he saw the orders issued and knew when his old unit was facing enemy assaults or attacking Confederate positions. He knew when they were continuing the destruction of rail communications, rendering them useless in resupplying Lee or the Confederate capital in Richmond. He sympathized with their physical hardships as the weather turned wet, cold, and often icy as winter approached.

Addressing the impending presidential election of 1864, Charles wrote to his brother James:

"Had I a vote however, I would be sure to cast it for the general, the patriot and statesman McClellan, who desires to end this war or rather bring about the accomplishment of what the war was inaugurated for on our part—I mean the

Preservation of the Union, the Constitution, and the complete
subjugation of the rebellion."

But eight days later, he wrote to his friend Jimmie O'Neill who
was back home in Pittsburgh convalescing:

"There seems to be a prevalent opinion here that the
Democratic party, or its leaders are opposed to the war; wish
for an armistice now that our success seems not far distant;
and generally fail to appreciate the valor or sacrifice of our
armies; and finally, pronounce this unholy war to be a failure.
In addition to this, they place the blame wholly on our side,
and consider all the blood shed by our men as in vain. I know
General McClellan is far from entertaining any such views—
but the journals of that party as well as the speakers (at the
convention) *express no other sentiments . . . it is in the Army*
the real longing for peace is; but only for such a peace as is
honorable and effectual. They will show in November. I take my
leave of McClellan and his party very sorrowfully indeed . . .
I think the Administration have done their whole duty this last
campaign and I believe they can end the war effectually in
six weeks, as becomes a great nation and without dishonor or
disgrace to the efforts of our armies."

Turning from politics, he adds to O'Neill:

"I have very little work to do and have fine, gentlemanly
officers, but for all that I feel lonesome, or want of being at
home as I would in the company. I think I will not serve out my
time in this office . . . (I) visit the company nearly every night
till I am afraid of being a bore to them . . . All the boys are well,
and never fail to inquire the latest from 'Jimmie' . . . . (Sergeant
Robert) *Thompson* (who assumed command of Company "E"
with the departure of Capt. Laughlin) *has not his commission*
yet and appears to be a supernumary (sic) *Serg't."*

There was one incident at headquarters for which Charles had an excellent point of observation. It occurred in the second week of December as Warren's Fifth Corps returned to the Union lines outside Petersburg from their raids upon the Weldon Railroad. A murdered Union soldier was discovered pinned to the ground by a stake driven through his mouth. Then, at the Sussex Courthouse, the bodies of six Union soldiers were found stripped of their clothing and lying by the road.

"This is clearly the work of bushwhackers—rebel civilians whose lack of honor and humanity disgusts me." General Warren raged as he paced impatiently before his staff. "Far be it from General Lee or any of his commanders to allow such to be the work of their soldiers."

Turning to Col. Locke, he continued, "I want orders issued to Division and Brigade commanders. This Courthouse and all public buildings in this village are to be burned to the ground! Houses, barns, and storehouses within a half mile of our line of march are to be put to the torch!"

Locke blanched at his instructions. "But sir, there have been many locals who have been courteous, even sending their darkies to the road with buckets of cold water and dipping ladles for our thirsty troops. Must all these suffer for the sins of their neighbors?"

Gouverneur K. Warren, Major General
(www.old-picture.com)

Warren blinked in amazement, not accustomed to having his instructions questioned. He sighed a great sigh and approached his Assistant Adjutant. "Colonel, I must remind you that war is a cruel occupation. We have no time to sort out from among the general population the guilty bastards who committed these barbarous acts. It is not my preference to wreak havoc upon civilians. But there must be notice given. Bushwhackers will not be tolerated! Perhaps their betters will prevail upon them in light of this retribution."

Standing at some distance, Charles was able to hear this exchange and shuddered at the thought that he would now be inscribing the requisite copies of Warren's orders.

Upon returning to the Union lines outside Petersburg, the 155th regiment withdrew to a camp a short distance away. Given the effect of winter weather upon the dirt roads, they were ordered to construct accommodations for the duration of the season. By the 20th of December, they were housed in the best and most comfortable lodgings of their time of service. Even the winter clothing they had packed and shipped to Washington for storage last spring now arrived to the joyful appreciation of all. When Christmas arrived, the enlisted men were presented with a large apple, or two small ones, gifts of the United States Sanitary Commission. At the New Year, the enlisted men marched to Warren's headquarters to personally convey their compliments to their respected commander. He greeted them warmly and feasted them as best as he could. The afternoon was marked by games of ball, boxing, and wrestling matches.

Throughout these weeks of winter stalemate, a stream of Confederate deserters presented themselves for surrender and respite. In squads of five or six, they came complaining of the raggedy state of their half-starved army. They admitted plainly their belief that the end of hostilities was near.

Chapter Eleven

Winter camp did not last as long as the men had hoped. By February they were perplexed to be on the move again, despite terrible weather conditions. Moving to Hatcher's Run, a new winter quarters had to be constructed. When the weather improved in mid-month, Warren's Fifth Corps approached the Southside Railroad, the last umbilical of supply for Lee's Army of Northern Virginia.

The Fifth Corps' record of bravery and success presented a mixed blessing to its soldiers. Promotions were frequent and Col. Pearson was made a Brevet Brigadier General. But as they wrested fortifications from the enemy, Warren enforced his engineer's discipline by having them expanded and bolstered so as to become impregnable. These were then turned over to units from other Corps. His own men moved on to their next target. The bravery and arduous labors of his soldiers were demonstrably appreciated by their commander. Should the general encounter a novice recruit at a loss in the fine art of pick and shovel, Warren would dismount, climb into the trench, and instruct the hapless soldier in the proper technique.

In late March, Lee stripped troops from both Richmond and Petersburg to reinforce his defense of the Southside Rail Road. Grant ordered General Philip Sheridan's cavalry to flank Lee's position. When they encountered heavy resistance near Hatcher's Run, the 155th went in to reinforce the attack and protect essential artillery placements. The Confederates began to flee their positions at the Quaker Road, and General Pearson seized the regimental colors and led the charge in pursuit, taking between fifty and sixty prisoners. His bravery would earn him the Congressional Medal of Honor.

After much maneuvering and fierce engagements over the next three days, the city of Petersburg fell into Union hands. At the

Battle of Five Forks, acting battle commander Phil Sheridan laid out a plan to advance against forces under Confederate General George Pickett. He assigned a left flanking action to the Fifth Corps. In the course of battle, heavy resistance produced delays in the ordered movements. Lines of battle became disconnected here and there. Capt. Laughlin, formerly of Company "E," gallantly rushed forward to restore order, rally the soldiers, and fill the gaps detected.

General Samuel Crawford's Division, moving into woods on the right flank, inadvertently created a breach in the line of battle. General Warren personally led a desperate charge into the gap, replacing Crawford's troops. He had his horse shot from under him, but his timely efforts turned the tide of battle. Yet, because of Sheridan's (and Grant's) suspicion of Warren, and erroneous reports received regarding Warren's position and performance at Five Forks, General Sheridan was greatly dissatisfied. He summarily removed Warren from command of the Fifth Corps.

In the ranks of the 155th, there was initial disbelief of what seemed a wild, baseless rumor. When it was confirmed, however, there was nearly universal indignation. Private McKenna and his fellows on the headquarters staff were stunned at Warren's dismissal. They gathered around the ashen-faced Lt. Col. Fred Locke as he confirmed the report.

"General Griffin is now our leader and we must confer upon him the loyalty and respect we have heretofore rendered to General Warren."

The men turned away, grumbling in discontent. But Charles was still distraught and he queried Locke privately. "It was General Warren's personal bravery that snatched the victory for us, was it not? How can this be?"

Lt. Colonel Fred T. Locke

The New Yorker's face twisted into a bitter scowl. "You know that, Private. I know that, and so does the defeated George Pickett! I have tried to tell Sheridan, but he would hear none of it. He even ordered that I should inform General Warren of his removal instead of doing so himself. It was the worst assignment I've ever been given."

It would take nearly sixteen years before Warren succeeded in getting a military court of inquiry. Though it would fully exonerate him, Gouverneur K. Warren would die three months before his vindication was achieved. "I die a disgraced soldier" were his last words.

* *

The day following the battle at Five Forks, the 155th was rushed towards Richmond to exploit Lee's reverses and the vulnerability of the Confederate capital. While enroute, however, word of the fall of Richmond was received. Turning south again, they moved to rejoin the rest of the Fifth Corps in the pursuit of Lee's forces and to prevent their escape into North Carolina.

On April 8th, Sheridan's command, including the Fifth Corps, arrived at Appomattox Station on the Lynchburg Railroad. There, they intercepted four supply trains trying to re-supply Lee's debilitated army. The following day, the 155th and the rest of the Third Brigade were ordered to establish a skirmish line on a ridge overlooking the village of Appomattox Court House.

Private McKenna described the dramatic succeeding events of April 9th thusly:

We were exhausted from the urgent marches of the last few days, taking no time to prepare a hot meal. The day was, again, sunny and very warm. Confederates, thinking that they had encountered only a smattering of cavalry, gave us heavy rifle fire. But upon witnessing cavalry left and right and our infantry brigade in the center poised to attack, the rebels began to fall back into the wooded area beyond the village. Shortly thereafter, a mounted courier brandishing a white flag of truce galloped out of the woods and directly toward our lines. I was not there to observe this first indication of surrender, as I was engaged at General Griffin's field headquarters just above the Old Turnpike and behind our line of battle. However, I am told that Sergeant-Major William Shore intercepted and guided the rebel emissary to Gen. Chamberlain, who then redirected both of them to General Griffin.

Shortly after their arrival at field headquarters, Griffin dispatched his aide, our own former Company "E" commander, Capt. Laughlin, with an order for total cease-fire. But scattered Confederate rifle fire persisted a while, so the cease-fire order was rescinded. Finally, the enemy stood down and the cease-fire was re-established. Sadly, in this interval of Confederate confusion, Private William Montgomery of Company "I" was mortally wounded by a rebel cannon ball. Only fifteen years old, and in service for a few months, he was, I believe, the last combat fatality in the Army of the Potomac.

As an expectant quiet fell upon the battlefield, I and several of the other headquarters clerks advanced to the ridge where our regimental comrades were positioned. It was nearly 2:00 in the afternoon. We enjoyed an excellent vantage of the village of Appomattox Court House, a modest cluster of, perhaps, a half-dozen houses arrayed upon a single, dusty street. The most commodious of these was the home of one Wilmer McLean, where negotiations were underway between Generals Lee and Grant. About 4:00, we saw the Confederate leader, our long-time nemesis and skillful opponent, emerge from the house in his resplendent gray and gold uniform. He mounted his fine gray horse and slowly returned to the rebel position north of the village. Moments later, a Union artillery battery opened fire in an intended salute, rejoicing in the long-awaited victory. But General Grant immediately ordered them to desist. He made it clear that there was to be no gloating over the vanquished. My only thought was to rejoice that, someday soon, I would be returning to Mother, Catherine, and my brothers. How long I have awaited that happy day.

McLean House, Appomattox Court House, Virginia
(www.old-picture.com)

Three days later, having shared nearly 30,000 rations with the near-starved rebel soldiers, there was neither a cracker or a bean to be had by the soldiers of the 155th Pennsylvania Volunteers. Now, a proper ceremony of surrender was undertaken. General Griffin was given the honor of receiving the formal surrender and General Joshua Chamberlain, hero of Little Round Top, was designated to receive the Confederate arms and colors. At 9:00 A.M. the 155th, the 20th Maine, and the rest of the Third Brigade took up position along the right side of the Lynchburg Road leading into the village. On the left side was Pearson, temporarily assigned to lead the First Brigade at the surrender of arms. About thirty minutes later, the first of the Confederate brigades arrived to stack their arms and deposit their cartridge boxes before moving off. This process was repeated over and over by ensuing rebel units, only completing around 5:00 P.M. While most of the former rebels conducted themselves in a most dignified manner, there were some so distraught that they threw their cartridge boxes to the ground in disgust. There were tears flowing within both armies that day.

* *

On Saturday, April 15th Private McKenna and his comrades had their joy diminished amid a national sorrow.

How shocked we were when news was had that our beloved President was dead, victim of a cowardly assassin. A martyr to the cause of national unity, he was betrayed and struck down, on Good Friday no less. Only days before, Lincoln had visited General Grant's headquarters at City Point, just southeast of Richmond. Though our regiment was not present, we nevertheless felt honored by the attention and praise he bestowed upon the Army of the Potomac on that occasion.

About three weeks later, General Griffin, to his great credit, arranged a parade review of the entire Fifth Corps for its former commander, General Warren. Warren, appointed military governor of the city of Petersburg by General Grant, was greeted warmly by Griffin and the Brigade commanders he had led so long and so well. It was the long and heart-felt ovation from the rank and file that caused emotions to swell among those on the reviewing stand.

What thoughts and emotions swept over us on the march back to Washington. We passed scenes of battles fought, sieges laid, and the graves of convenience where our late comrades lay in unmarked repose. Our passage through Richmond, silent and unwelcomed by it citizens, was interrupted by a review for Army chief General Halleck. This man had commanded the entirety of the Union forces, but no great respect from us, the foot soldiers. Finally, on May 12th, our march brought us within sight of the city of Washington. The unfinished dome of the Capitol building loomed in the distance. We promptly sent up cheers for the nation saved, for ourselves, and for the victory wrought. We went into camp at Falls Station on the Orange and Alexandria Railroad to await further ceremonies within the capital. Oh how we hated those days of waiting, thinking only of home and family reunions delayed.

On the 24th of May, there was a Grand Review of the Union forces within traveling distance of Washington, D.C. (Grant's Army of the Potomac and General Sherman's Armies of Tennessee and Georgia). It was attended by the new president, Andrew Johnson, his Cabinet officers, many members of Congress, and the Washington diplomatic corps. In their march down Pennsylvania Avenue, the 155th regiment, in their brightly-colored Zouave uniforms, stepped smartly to the enjoyment of local citizens. The shattered staff of their regimental colors attested to the fierce action they had endured in nearly three years of service. The parade of troops took the entire day amid a general outpouring of gratitude and joyful welcome from the crowds lining the broad avenue.

The Grand Review of the Army, Washington, District of Columbia
(www.old-picture.com)

It would be recorded later that Charles McKenna's Company "E" had fought in 32 battles, suffered 17 killed in action, 21 wounded, 11 died on duty of other causes, and 44 were medically discharged. Only 38 survivors were on hand to participate in the Grand Review.

Two more weeks in camp were necessitated by the preparation of muster-out rolls, certified and rendered in seven copies. Games and informal glee clubs helped pass the time. The tedium of which Private McKenna complained was only broken by the spontaneous night-time processions of farewell to the Brigade, Division, and Corps headquarters. With lit candle stubs replacing the bayonets at the end of their rifles, nearly six thousand soldiers voiced, in sequence, their affection and esteem to the Generals under whom they had served. General Griffin, too shy to respond personally to the calls of "Speech! Speech!" deferred to General Joshua Chamberlain to make an eloquent reply and tribute. The procession continued until it was cut short by the exhaustion of the candle supply.

On June 1st, the regiment received orders to report to Camp Reynolds in Pittsburgh for final pay and muster-out. Back in Pittsburgh, Mayor James Lowry and the city fathers determined to mount a public reception, dinner and parade for the two hundred and fifty surviving members of the 155th, most of whom were sons of the city.

At ten o'clock on the morning of June 5th, the regiment arrived in the city from Camp Reynolds under the command of General Alfred Pearson. Quickly forming up into parade ranks by company, they set off from Liberty Street Station, preceded by Young's Military Brass Band and platoons of uniformed city police. The Mayor and members of the city council followed in open carriages. The soldiers, joined by members of the 26th Michigan (just arrived in the city on their journey home), made their way via Smithfield Street to the Monongahela House Hotel. There, speaking from the balcony Lincoln had used on that rainy night in February, 1861, local dignitaries made speeches of welcome and tribute. Later, in formal ceremonies of welcome at City Hall, the veterans were subjected to a further stream of oratory.

The happy soldiers were then ushered into the City Hall where the Pittsburgh Subsistence Committee, aided by numerous volunteers, served an elegant catered dinner. More speeches were now supplemented with war and camp songs performed by the regimental glee club, including General Pearson, Captain Edward Montooth, and (now finally 1st Lieutenant) Robert Thompson. After dinner, a last parade followed across the St. Clair Street Bridge to Allegheny City. There a promised demonstration of Zouave bayonet and battlefield tactics was performed for the public.

All this parading and ceremony brought out crowds of fathers, mothers, sisters, brothers, children, and sweethearts of the returning heroes. From Pittsburgh, Allegheny, and the countryside beyond, they streamed to the venues and lent their cheers and tears to the welcome home. Not surprisingly, Annie McKenna and other family members lined the parade route seeking a glimpse of Charles. When he did come into view, the press of the throng, the sound of the brass band, and cheering of citizens prevented a meeting of their eyes.

"Dear God, he looks so different!" Annie gasped as his company passed by. "He's grown so . . . and is brown as a boot."

Barney was equally taken aback at the sight of his younger brother. "Aye, he's looking rather fit too. I'll not be challenging him to any of our old games of boxing!"

"You'd better not, Brother!" Catherine teased. "We will make a grand homecoming for Charles with all the family and his old friends as well. How soon will they release him, I wonder?"

Barney shrugged. "I've heard not till Thursday, but no one seems sure. There must be a general payday and a surrender of their weapons. Charles has told us that things move slowly in the army. We might be safe to plan our welcome for Saturday. That's when most folks will be free to attend."

Annie waved a hand of dismissal. "Never mind the party now. I just want my son in my arms again. Praise be to God, he's come back to us whole and healthy . . . . So many have not."

It was, in fact, late on Thursday—after prolonged reminiscences, heartfelt farewells, and promises of continued friendship among comrades—that Charles finally made his way back to 281 Penn Street from Camp Reynolds. Now nearly twenty-one years of age, he was no longer the boy who had left home in 1862. He had grown to a height of about five feet, nine inches, though still slender at 140 lbs. He preferred to be clean-shaven, though the military life had oft-times interfered with such. He had a straight nose and his left eye was somewhat closed compared to the right. His chin was marked by a pronounced dimple that would charm the ladies until he adopted mustache and goatee in later years.

Awaiting Charles' arrival, the family designated Eddie to keep watch through the afternoon. Being twins, Eddie and Charles had always maintained a special closeness. And Eddie's sense of missing his brother through the war years was only eclipsed by that of their mother. When he saw Charles approach, still attired in his colorful Zouvave military garb, he let out a shout and ran to greet him. The passersby on busy Penn Street were both amused and congratulatory at the sight of the returning veteran. Shouts of "Well done!" and "Welcome back, soldier" rang out as they walked, arm in arm, back to the boarding house.

There, the scene became even more chaotic. The boarders, family members, and neighbors made a clear path for Annie— all in tears—to apply her kisses and give a prolonged embrace. After that, it was a free for all as Uncle Bernard, James, Patrick, Catherine, and Barney swarmed forward. Most of the boarders were strangers to Charles, though the aged, pipe-smoking, retired laborer, John McKeon, was a familiar face. Tears and shouts of joy finally gave way to feeding the war hero the home-cooked meal he had dreamed of for so long.

The welcome home party, two days later, was equally festive, though less fraught with emotion. The family was now joined by Uncle Charles' widow Ann and her children. To Barney's delight Mary and the rest of the McShane family joined the festivities. Charles was saddened to learn that Will McKeever, his father's great friend, had passed away earlier in the year. His widow (and Annie's sister) Catherine and her young boys were among the guests. It was also Charles' first introduction to brother James' fiancée, Ellen Collins. The celebration ran from mid-afternoon until well into the night. There was music and singing, a bit of dance, an occasional speech, and—though Charles and Barney were abstainers—a drop or two of whiskey was consumed by other men-folk.

As the evening wore on, Charles called for attention to voice his thanks while all were still present. He stood upon a chair so that everyone might see and hear.

"My dear ones," he began. "I am humbled at the outpouring of affection and good wishes that you have given me this day. Each of you I have called to mind and included in my prayers during my time away. It was thoughts of you and the blessings of home that helped sustain me. I realize that the war has brought sorrow and loss to those at home as well as to those on the battlefield. I have prayed and continue to pray for poor Ellen and Catherine who were lost at the Arsenal. I give thanks to our heavenly Father, and to all of you. I am richly blessed."

Chapter Twelve

"So, are you goin' back to Mr. Shuchman and the lithography trade?" James inquired of his younger brother as they walked home from St. Paul's after the Sunday Mass. It was a beautiful summer day as they descended Grant's Hill. Both of them were still a bit bleary-eyed after the festivities of the preceding evening. Other family members had taken a carriage with Annie. At her age, she appreciated the prerogative not to walk to and from worship.

Charles, now dressed in civilian attire loaned to him by brother Barney, hesitated in answering. For several days, he had warded off such inquiries, pleading that he was undecided. In truth, his thoughts had been taking shape for over a year. "Don't laugh at this, please. I know it will seem a bit presumptuous or grand . . . . I've been encouraged to study the law."

James stopped in his tracks. "The law!?"

"Yes, you know, become an attorney. During times in camp, one of our sergeants, George Fulton, tutored me. He is a well educated man and he gave me books to read. My friend Jimmie O'Neill also helped me. He had studied for the priesthood and knows his Latin backward and forward. It was Jimmie's idea I should take up the law . . . and I've a mind to pursue it."

James' surprised expression remained stamped upon his face. "Jaysus, that would be a grand profession . . . and Mother will be so proud. I'm certain you'd be up to it . . . . Won't you be needin' a bit more schoolin' though?"

"Well, that may be. But I'm told that most of learning the law is done while working for a lawyer in practice."

James clapped him on the back. "Good on you, lad. If I can help you in any way, I'm more than willin'."

Charles blushed a bit at such congratulatory sentiments. I haven't even begun my studies yet, he reflected. "Thanks for that. I may well be calling upon you. There's two things I'm needing just now. I must find a lawyer who will take me on as an clerk. And I need a job to supplement the modest wage of an apprentice of the law."

James nodded gravely and paused. Then, he beamed a smile. "You should talk this out with Barney! Since he joined the fire company, he's very tight with any who's well placed in the ward. He may know where you might find a suitable position . . . . Yes, I'm thinkin' he would."

James' advice did not come out of the blue. He had been contemplating a career move of his own. While he had risen to chief postal clerk, further progress would require a political appointment. Now, his impending marriage to Ellen prompted him to consider moving into the business world where better rewards and chances for advancement might be had. At Barney's suggestion, he was put in contact with a gent named Rogers. Together, they were planning to enter the business of refining oil from the petroleum fields of Western Pennsylvania. For a few years, brother Eddie would join them in what became McKenna, Rogers & Company, at 211 Liberty Street.

Barney, meanwhile was still an iron moulder, now at the foundry of Mitchell, Stevenson & Company between Pike Street and Duquesne Way in the area known as The Strip. His interest in promoting the rights of workers had developed steadily during the war years. His winning personality, humility, and diligence made for a rapid advance within the moulders' union local. Indeed, when in 1863 the International Iron Moulders Union (IIMU) held its first national convention in Pittsburgh, Barney attended with other members of the Pittsburgh local. In the following two years, the IIMU grew from fifteen locals in eight states to fifty-four locals in eighteen states. It tripled its membership to six thousand. Due to the manufacturing requirements of the war effort, the iron workers were in a relatively strong position to seek improvements in wages and working conditions. And progress was achieved without significant strike action.

But with the end of the war, demand for iron declined rapidly and industry leaders began to impose wage reductions to offset the falling prices for iron products. The wage cuts were severe, erasing all the previous gains and more. Barney's role expanded as he assumed the position of treasurer of the union local. In 1865, Barney was also elected Captain of the Allegheny Volunteer Fire Company. His influence and political connections within the city continued to expand as well.

The Allegheny Company firehouse, a clapboard two-story structure topped by a belfry, stood at the north end of Irwin Street. A large brass bell hung in this perch to summon the volunteers from their homes and work sites within the neighborhood in the event of a fire alarm. The aging building was fronted by two large bays, one for the steam engine and the other for the hose wagon. Behind these bays, a large work area was devoted to equipment maintenance. Horses were stabled in an adjacent wing at the back of the building. Upstairs, firemen on watch spent their waiting hours sleeping, eating, and playing cards. It was a Saturday afternoon when Charles visited the old neighborhood and the fire house where Barney was on duty.

A grizzled, old fireman greeted him. "Well, the returning war hero! . . . You'll be findin' your brother upstairs, lad." Though his face was familiar, Charles couldn't recall his name. Nodding and smiling in greeting, Charles entered the work area where men were coiling hose. He climbed the wooden staircase and found Barney alone, reading the *Gazette.*

"Hello, Charles. What brings you to the old neighborhood?"

Charles looked around, the scene vaguely familiar. "I don't think I've been up here since Hugh was with the Company. I was probably six or seven at the time . . . . I came to ask your help, Barney. Can we talk?"

Barney collapsed his newspaper and pointed to a vacant chair. "'Course we can. Sit." He struck a match and lit his third cigar of the day. Since Patrick's entry into the tobacco business, Barney had developed a strong attachment for his "stogie."

Charles described his plan to study the law and the need to find a sponsoring attorney. "I was hoping you might have some contacts within the legal profession—someone I could call on with your introduction."

Barney was readily supportive; any feelings of resentment at being deprived of the military career enjoyed by his brother had been put away, at least for the time being. "Not to worry, Brother. I know a few attorneys and they know many more. We'll certainly find someone who'd welcome a bright, young law clerk—especially a returning soldier. But will you not continue your work as an artist? Your sketches from the war seemed very good to me."

Charles beamed in pleasure mixed with some embarrassment. "I'll always enjoy drawing. But an artist, particularly one without formal training, usually leads an impoverished life. It seems best to me to strive for a profession where one can do some good and make a proper living as well."

"You thought this through, haven't you. I'm happy to be asking around, Charles." He paused and studied his cigar pensively. Then his eyes lit up with enthusiasm. "What of your former regimental commander, Alfred Pearson? He practiced law here in Pittsburgh before the war. Surely, he would welcome a query from one of his troops as to where one might get on."

Charles struck his forehead in chagrin. "Glory be to St. Patrick! How stupid of me. Though I was only a private, I had many occasions to deliver messages to him when I worked in the Corps Headquarters. I'm sure he'll remember me! Thanks for the suggestion. I'll seek him out at once."

Barney laughed and re-opened his newspaper. "Good, you do that . . . . Let me know how it works out."

It took two days for Charles to trace Pearson's association with the law firm of Edward P. Jones. The office was at 64 Grant Street, down near the Monongahela riverfront. It was late afternoon when he called upon the firm. As he approached, the shadow of John Roebling's Smithfield Bridge fell upon the street. It was a welcome respite from the glare and intense heat of the summer sun. Taking a deep breath, Charles knocked at the office door.

"I'm afraid Pearson is not in at the moment," said the forty-three-year-old Jones. The attorney drew on his frock coat, clearly making preparations to leave at the end of the day. "Perhaps there is something I can do? What's your name? Have you a case you wish to bring?"

Charles was flustered at first. He hadn't expected the head of the firm to answer the door. "I'm Charles McKenna, sir. Sorry to have troubled yourself, as I have no case to bring. I served under the General during the war and wished to seek his advice."

"Legal advice, is it?" Jones raised an eyebrow.

"Not exactly, sir . . . . Well, I guess it might be, indirectly. It has to do with the legal profession. You see, I was hoping the General might refer me to a law firm in need of an apprentice clerk."

"Well, we have no opening here. But, if you'll call again in the morning, Alfred will be in. I'll tell him to expect you."

With that, Jones walked him out. Turning to lock the door, he added, "So you want to be an attorney, eh? Well, good luck, soldier."

The next morning, Charles returned and found Pearson in civilian attire: waist coat and jacket, winged collar, and cravat. His brown hair was combed back, revealing a high, broad forehead. His face was clean-shaven, save for his familiar, droopy mustache. The man was still in his mid-twenties.

Brigadier General Alfred L. Pearson

"Well, Private McKenna! Late of General Griffin's headquarters, as I recall. No need to stand at attention now, lad. Have a seat. I understand you wish to take up the law."

Charles relaxed his accustomed military stance and moved to the straight-backed wooden chair. "Yes, sir. I studied some Latin. And Sgt. Fulton tutored me in several subjects while in camp. He thought I showed some promise."

Pearson leaned back in his more comfortable chair and steepled his fingers together. "Your work on staff was well regarded, McKenna. I have little doubt that you can master the law. But as you know from Mr. Jones, we have no openings here."

Charles leaned forward. "So I understand, sir. I thought, perhaps among your acquaintances within the bar, there might be someone in need of a law clerk."

Pearson frowned. "Off hand, I don't. I'm sorry. I've been away from the city for so long . . ."

Charles sighed heavily and rose to leave. "Well, thank . . ."

But Pearson brightened suddenly and interrupted, "There is someone who might help. You might recall the name Thomas Howe. He was Assistant Adjutant General to Governor Curtin when our regiment was formed."

Charles resumed his seat and smiled in relief. "I do recall, sir. Camp Howe was named in his honor."

Pearson's mind was racing. He rose and began to pace the room. "Correct . . . Tom and I are friends, you see. And he is married to the sister of Judge Sam Palmer. It is said that the Judge is not well. He recently announced his departure from the bench. But, I understand he plans to continue in private practice. It may be he can use a bit of assistance from an energetic clerk . . . I'll speak to Tom. Perhaps he can arrange an interview with the Judge."

Charles flushed with excitement. His leave-taking was a blur of thanks and pumping the General's hand. Out on the street, he fairly flew up Grant's Hill and back to Penn Street. He couldn't wait to share his news with his mother and the rest of the family. A week later, he was sitting for an interview with Judge Samuel Palmer.

Charles was surprised to find the man was only forty-two years of age. Given reports of poor health, he had expected a more elderly man. Though pale in appearance, Palmer was nevertheless animated in conversation. He had earned great esteem within the legal community and beyond. As a young attorney, Palmer had personally traveled the length and breadth of Allegheny County soliciting relief supplies for the victims of the Irish famine. He was known for his legal knowledge, his precision, integrity, and his eloquence in pleadings. Based upon the recommendation from Pearson, and the endorsement of Thomas Howe, the judge readily accepted Charles as apprentice clerk.

"You'll take much of your instruction from my long-time partner, John Mitchell. But I'll give you assignments occasionally as well. You can begin tomorrow. Now, let's get you introduced to John."

John J. Mitchell turned out to be a few years older than the judge. He welcomed Charles as his understudy. He would mentor him over the next three years, imparting lessons of case law and legal procedure. He was also a devout Catholic and highly active at St. Paul's Cathedral parish, where he was a member of the finance committee.

Several weeks into his service, Charles was busy researching a precedent in Pennsylvania case law beyond the normal end of office hours. As he was leaving for the day, Mitchell stopped to chat. "Putting in some extra time tonight?"

Charles looked up from a pile of books and the notes he had taken. "Yes, sir. But I'm almost finished. I'll be leaving shortly."

Mitchell fingered his keys absent-mindedly. "Your work has been first-rate, Charles. Do you feel you're getting along well here?"

Charles stood now, sensing more conversation was coming. "Oh, yes sir. I'm very happy with the work. And you and the judge have been most patient with my lack of experience . . . . I suppose my only concern is that I might be distracted. I'm seeking a second job, you see, to make ends meet."

Mitchell laughed, "Not paying you enough are we? . . . No, don't apologize. I know a new clerk's salary is modest at best. Have you found a position yet?"

Charles shook his head, his face reddened in embarrassment. "Not yet, sir. It must be an evening job and not so demanding that my work here shall suffer."

"Yes, rightly so. Well, good luck. Lock up as you leave, will you?"

"Yes, sir. Thank you. Good evening."

Several days later, to Charles' surprise, he received an invitation to present himself at the offices at St. Paul's Cathedral. There, he was informed that on Mitchell's recommendation he was being offered the position of librarian at the newly-established Catholic Library at Wood Street and Virgin Alley. Between the two jobs, Charles would now be able to support himself. And the library turned out to be the perfect place to study during his evenings.

Mitchell was a friendly, garrulous person. One day, again as the time for closing approached, their conversation turned to personal backgrounds. Mitchell queried Charles to share some of his experiences from the war. After a bit of that, it was Mitchell's turn.

"Of course, I was never called to serve in the military," he began. "But I did once meet a great hero of our war of independence. It was in 1824; I was just five years old. That was the year that the Marquis de Lafayette was touring the United States at the invitation of President Monroe. Of course, he was an illustrious major general who had served with George Washington. When Lafayette visited Pittsburgh, my father—who was a French-American; Michel was the name originally—took me to the parade of welcome. As Lafayette passed by, father spoke a few words of French to him. Lafayette was surprised and stopped briefly to respond. Before leaving, he patted me on the head. I'm afraid that's as close as I have ever come to the military life."

* *

Charles F. McKenna, Aspiring Attorney
Image from "Under the Maltese Cross"

While Charles was getting on with his legal career, it was
increasingly a time of challenge for brother Barney. The iron
workers of Pittsburgh were about to defy the imposition of a 20%
reduction of wage rates announced in December, 1866. His union
endorsed a nationwide strike at their convention in Boston the
following month. A strike fund of $40,000 had been established to
support the strikers at $7.00 per week for married men, $5.00 per
week for those who were single. It was Barney's job to distribute
such relief to his members. In response, the owners of the iron

companies launched an industry-wide lockout. Mills and factories from the east coast to the mid-west closed their doors to all workers. There ensued six months of work stoppage.

One Saturday in July, Barney walked Mary McShane home after an evening stroll along Duquesne Way. The breeze off the Allegheny's waters was pleasant relief after the heat of home and store. His slumped shoulders and somber mood allowed Mary to read his disappointment and despair. Taking his hand, she stopped their promenade. "Bernard, I hate to see you so worried."

He raised his head from its downcast posture and looked at the expression of concern on her pretty face. "Oh, Mary dear, I fear the end is now upon us in the union. I paid out the last of the strike fund this week. Heaven knows the men are desperate, desperate for rent and grocery money. Their families were suffering, even beforehand. Everyone wants to go back to work, but our defeat leaves a bitter taste . . . . As for myself, I can't be a burden any longer. My family has been so generous to me these many months."

She took his hand and kissed it. "I'm so sorry . . . . You all did your best. None can fault the efforts you've made. I pray that better times lie ahead, though today we can't see how. Let's not be unhappy, you and I. We still have each other."

"Someday, we will, darling. Someday, we will."

* *

In 1868, Charles finished his legal studies and was admitted to the bar. Knowing his experience fell short of commanding partner status, he decided to enter private practice on his own and he quickly succeeded in attracting clients. John Mitchell had been deeply impressed with McKenna's logical mind, his written briefs, and his ability to marshal his case into a forceful, eloquent presentation. On the strength of his recommendation, Charles secured certain legal assignments for the Catholic Diocese of Pittsburgh, then headed by the second bishop of Pittsburgh, Rev. Michael Domenec. The following year, Charles was also functioning as the Secretary of St. Paul's Orphan Asylum, a charity of the diocese. Needless to say, the flow of legal work required by the diocese would provide significant demand for Charles McKenna's services—a relationship that would last nearly a quarter century.

The post-war years were a period when some of the McKennas moved out of the rooming house operated by their mother. Perhaps they wanted a lifestyle of their own. Perhaps their presence placed too great a burden upon the aging Annie and their sister Catherine. Certainly, as the city grew, their Penn Street location was changing. The neighborhood was no longer so residential and was now more a part of the expanding, downtown business district. First, Patrick relocated to Allegheny City in anticipation of his marriage to Mary Grimm. After their union, he moved his tobacco business to York, Pennsylvania where they resided for ten years. James and Ellen had also left to establish a home of their own.

Eddie left next, taking his wife Margaret and their son Edward to Allegheny City where they would share a residence with Margaret's mother and younger brother and sister. Clearly, the time was approaching when the operation of the family rooming house had to be called into question. It was Charles who took the initiative, but Barney followed in close support. One evening after supper, their boarders having dispersed, they addressed their concerns to Annie and Catherine.

"Mother," Charles began, "we are concerned that your efforts with the business are now too great a burden . . ."

Noticing a stiffening of Catherine's posture, he quickly added, ". . . and that's no reflection upon Catherine's efforts. Everything continues to be well taken care of. It's just that . . . well, we are well into our careers and have sufficient earnings to create a normal household, away from the noise and stench of the city center."

Catherine, now somewhat mollified, the tension drained from her posture. "'Tis true, Mother, soon you will be seventy. You deserve to lay down this business that has occupied you for nearly forty years."

Annie frowned impatiently. "I don't need my children to remind me that I am no longer young . . . . Still, I will admit that I wouldn't miss risin' each mornin' to do a breakfast for a dozen fellows who may stay a month, or maybe a year . . . . Charles, does this mean we will all go our separate ways, as did your brothers? Will I be havin' any family about me?"

"Ah, Mother," Barney interjected. "We wouldn't leave you and Catherine alone. We're thinking to find a nice place for the family, for all of us. Perhaps it should be in Allegheny, so you can see Pat, Eddie, and your grandson whenever you want. I know Charles will like Allegheny as Miss Virginia White also makes her home across the river."

Charles blushed and became irritated. "Barney, that's got nothing to do with it!"

Barney laughed but returned to the question at hand. "Of course, we must give our boarders a decent period of notice. And a buyer for this house must be found. In the meantime, Charles and I will undertake a search for a fine house in Allegheny that will suit you and Catherine."

"So, Mother, Catherine, are we agreed?" queried Charles.

Annie took Catherine's hand in her own. "Daughter, are we agreed?"

Catherine nodded and gave her a squeeze in return. "Yes, Mother, I think so."

Later that evening, Catherine came into her mother's room to say goodnight and noticed right off that Annie seemed teary and upset.

"Mother, what is it? You're not having second thoughts about the move are you?"

"Oh, Catherine, how we will do all that must be done? When we moved here from Irwin Street, we had little choice. Then, I had the energy and could handle all the details. Now, I hardly know where to begin."

Catherine embraced her mother. "You must let us think it through for you this time, Mother. The boys and I will carry the load. Change is never easy, is it?"

Annie looked about her bedroom, still slightly overwhelmed. Then she dried her eyes and raised her head. "I've managed my share of change, dear, . . . from Anacramp to Pittsburgh, from wife to widow, from Irwin Street to here, from mother to grandmother. But yes, you are right. It never was easy—though the good Lord always did provide."

* *

In 1870, the family successfully transitioned to their new home at 88 Robinson Street in Allegheny. They rented a pleasant, but modest, row house in a residential area, somewhat removed from the furnaces and factories that lined the north side of the river. Annie, Catherine, Barney, Charles, and their fifteen-year-old domestic Katie Flynn constituted the new household.

For a time, all was well. But a few months later, James' wife Ellen was struck by the cholera and passed away. It was a shock to all, but for James it was the end of the world. Broken-hearted would be to put it too mildly. He moved into the home on Robinson Street, but his appetite disappeared and he lost all interest in his oil refining business. His family looked on helplessly as his health failed. Within a year, James followed his young wife.

Charles was especially affected by James' passing. As he comforted his mother, she saw the agony in his eyes. "He was the eldest, your big brother. Is it that what you're thinkin'? You look so desperate sad."

He heaved a grand sigh and patted her hands. "When I was in service, James was always my most faithful correspondent. I'll never forget the many letters he wrote to give me the news of home and brighten my days when I missed you all so much. I owe him a debt I never acknowledged to him. I should have done."

Annie put her hand on his arm. "I'm thinkin' he knows now."

With James' death, Eddie left the oil refining business and took a position as warehouseman for the Pennsylvania Railroad. He, his pregnant wife Margaret, and their two children moved back into the McKenna household. Sadly, Eddie's wife Margaret was taken sick the following year and died, leaving her husband with now three young children.

Once again, the rearing of children became a duty largely shouldered by Catherine and, to a lesser extent, Annie. The losses of a son and two daughters-in-law were difficult, no doubt. But the presence of grandchildren in her home was a joy to Annie. "Wasn't I so busy with the boardin' house, I nearly missed the blessin's of my own youngsters?"

Not long after removing to Allegheny City, Barney faced a major change with considerable effect upon his personal life and his work. The city fathers and the citizens of Pittsburgh reached a consensus about that time to replace the system of volunteer fire companies with a paid, municipal fire department. Enabling legislation was passed by the Pennsylvania legislature and the Pittsburgh City Councils. It took most of 1870 to put the organization and equipment in place. But by January 1871, the new fire department was up and running. Staffing the department meant that veterans of the volunteer companies had to choose to join up or relinquish their firefighting duties.

Barney McKenna, especially, was pressed by the choice. As a volunteer, he had the time and ability to work as a moulder and continue with his union activities. To become a paid, full-time fireman would mean stepping away from these other occupations. And the decision no longer impacted himself alone. There was Mary, now his fiancée.

Aged twenty-eight, she was an attractive brunette, with dancing eyes and a pleasing disposition. Barney had been courting her for over five years, but her father's death in 1866 had left her more tied than ever to the family grocery and to attending to her younger siblings. Recently, however, her brother Frank (James Francis) had taken on the grocery. Mary was now free to begin the life of which she and Barney had dreamed.

As Barney lived on the North Side, his visits with Mary were often upon a Sunday afternoon. This day's visit was marked by pleasantly crisp, autumn weather. Clouds scudded across the sky, throwing occasional shadows and darkening the waters of the Allegheny. He crossed the St. Clair Street bridge and on to Irwin Street, only a fifteen minute walk. Mary was outside waiting for him to take her for a promised treat in town. They chose P. Schildecker's, a restaurant and "ice cream saloon" on Diamond Street. After the waiter left with their order for ice cream sundaes, Mary pressed Barney on the choice between union and the fire department.

"Ah, Mary, I hate giving up the union. 'Tis clear there will be more strife. Leaving our members now feels like I'm deserting my post."

Mary's face lost its pleasant smile. "Now Bernard, listen to me! You've always put your union duties before your own career and the members know that! . . . Besides, I can't imagine you'll be missing the foundry after all."

"Ach, that's the truth. There'll be no advancement for me as long as I'm a union man. At least with the fire company, I might rise to engineer."

"You'll not be facing strikes and lockouts either. It will be a comfort to me that you'll be secure in your position."

Taking her hand and pulling it close, he teased. "So, you're happy to be the wife of a fireman, then?"

"I'd like that very much. Shall we now be setting a date?"

* *

Barney and Mary did wed early in 1872, taking residence with the rest of the family at 88 Robinson Street. Barney's decision to join the new city fire department provided him with a starting annual salary of nearly $800, enough to start a family of his own.

He was assigned to Engine Company No. 2, having its station house at Smithfield Street, between First and Second Avenues.

Charles was also married in 1872 to Virginia White, the girl of whom Barney had once teased him. Her father, Norval White was an Allegheny City physician. Her mother, Annie Flick White came from Blacksburg, Virginia, where her daughter was born and from whence the name may have been taken. Virginia's uncle was the highly-esteemed and prominent Pittsburgh attorney and later judge, J.W.F. White. It was at a reception hosted by his law firm, White & Slagle, that Charles chanced to meet the vivacious lass, six years younger than himself. Charles now presented a somewhat flamboyant appearance. His still-dark hair was longer and swept high upon his head. To this, he added a dark mustache and generous goatee. Perhaps it was this dramatic aura which attracted the attention of the tall and elegant Miss White. In any event, it would seem that she might have taken the initiative in establishing an acquaintance with the up and coming attorney.

In October, 1873 Mary presented Barney with a son, Charles Bernard, named in honor of both uncle and father. Now a family, Barney and Mary began to feel the pinch of close quarters at 88 Robinson Street. One evening at supper, Barney announced proudly, "Everyone listen now, I have some good news to share. The chief called me aside this afternoon—for a little chat, he said. Well, to my surprise, he told me I am to be promoted to first hoseman!"

Everyone joined in with their congratulations, and Annie bragged on her son. "Praise be to God, Barney! I'm so pleased for you. Before you know it, you'll be making chief somewhere." But Mary just beamed quietly. Her serenity was prompted by more than her husband's promotion. Later, as they prepared for bed, she shared her secret satisfaction with her husband.

"Perhaps, Bernard, we might afford a place of our own now? I love being with your family, especially dear Annie—she's always treated me as a daughter of her own. But it would be grand to have a place just for us . . . someplace nearby."

Barney dropped his suspenders, surprise written on his face. Then he shrugged. "I know what you mean, dear. Sometimes I wonder if our little Charles will know his mother from his grandma or aunt. And with Eddie's three wee ones, it seems a circus here some days . . . . I think with the raise I'll be having, we could look for something here in Allegheny."

But finding the right place took some time. It was May, 1874 when Barney and Mary finally moved to 37 Fayette Street in Allegheny's Fifth Ward. It wasn't exactly close to the rest of the family, perhaps fifteen city blocks distant. But it was a neat little house away from the foundries, and the rent wasn't too dear. It was only four weeks later when Eddie showed up unexpectedly at the Smithfield Street fire station. He burst in, huffing and puffing in exhaustion. "Barney, come home quickly!"

Barney and his crew were just coiling a length of hose for the next call of duty. "What is it, Eddie. Is Mother all right?"

"It's not Mother; it's your boy. Mary says to come right away. He's running a wicked fever and cannot be consoled. Catherine has gone to fetch Dr. Shaw."

Barney dropped his end of the hose and rushed to the street. The two brothers found a cab and urged the driver not to spare his horse. They flew across town, over the St. Clair bridge, and into Allegheny City. By the time they reached the house, Annie and sister Catherine were there, calming Mary as best they could. Dr. Thomas Shaw had also arrived and was examining the nine-month-old child. When he emerged, the physician led Barney away from the others.

"Mr. McKenna, your son is very sick. Unless I'm quite mistaken, he has come down with the cholera. As you will know, this is very grave for one so young. I haven't a great deal of hope to offer. A day or two will tell the tale."

"Cholera?" Barney protested. "The boy isn't yet weaned! I thought it's bad water that causes cholera. How could this happen?"

"It usually is. But it can be a piece of food gone bad. Though it's rare, a mother's milk can turn. Has your wife been ill, or under a strain?"

Barney gazed, unseeing, out the window. "Well, we have just moved house . . . last month. I don't . . ." His voice trailed off as the desperate situation overcame him."

Shaw turned to take his leave. "The child will be plagued with diarrhea, probably some vomiting also. He'll be ravenously thirsty. Give him all the water he wants, but boil it first. Feed him nothing. Keep him warm, but not too hot. I'll come around again in the morning."

Barney went to console Mary, but consolation was not to be had. Annie and Catherine had brought along Katie Flynn to tend the house and fix meals for the grieving couple. Several days later, on June 12th, little Charles succumbed to his fever. He was interred at St. Mary's Cemetery in Lawrenceville, the same grounds where Barney's father and brother rested. Even old Hugh, Barney's grandfather, had been re-interred at St. Mary's when the city's growth encroached upon the old burial plots of St. Patrick's.

The boy's uncle Charles shared the devastation of his brother and sister-in-law. Regrettably, Charles and Virginia were destined to be childless. To fill the void, Charles had doted upon his namesake nephew. Only in 1877, when Barney and Mary had a second son, James Francis, he would transfer his attention and affections to Frank, as this new nephew would be known.

* *

In the earliest years of their marriage, Charles and Virginia shared the family residence at 88 Robinson Street. But they, like Barney and Mary, were anxious for a quiet place of their own. In 1874, being now somewhat more affluent, Charles was able to take rooms down the street, at number 108 Robinson. They would remain in Allegheny City for nearly ten years. They were highly social and active in numerous community organizations.

As Charles progressed in his legal practice, he became the solicitor for the Western Pennsylvania Humane Society, originally founded with the mission of preventing and remedying cases of child and spousal abuse.

He also began a long and distinguished participation in the periodic reunions and encampments of the Union veterans of the Civil War. The first of these was a reunion of the 155th Regiment of the Pennsylvania Volunteers held at Lafayette Hall in Pittsburgh in September, 1875. Joining with him on the Ways and Means Committee were his former commander Alfred L. Pearson and former Regimental Adjutant, Major Edward Montooth. Pearson's return to legal practice culminated in 1868 when he was elected the district attorney for Allegheny County. Some years later, however, health problems forced an exit from elective office. Ed Montooth, also a Pittsburgh attorney, was now the current district attorney—having followed in his commander's footsteps. It was a grand occasion Charles shared with his war-time comrades. Mess mate Jimmie O'Neill was now a Pittsburgh journalist. Also present was Charles' former mentor of the war years, George Fulton—now the principal of the Highland Schools in the East End. As Charles shared with Virginia later, "It was most pleasing to see so many of my comrades. But O'Neill and Fulton will always be special. I might never have found my way into the legal profession were it not for their kindness and belief in me."

Ways and Means Committee, First Reunion
Charles McKenna, Alfred Pearson, Edward Montooth
Image from "Under the Maltese Cross

The legacy of Charles' service during the war was not entirely benign, however. Beginning with the earliest days of their marriage, Virginia was frequently awakened in the middle of the night by raving monologues Charles conducted in tortured sleep. It was always difficult for her to awaken him fully. He would sit up and converse in vague response to her questions, but was, in fact, still asleep. In time, however, she learned the content of these episodes was a revisiting of war scenes from his youth.

Virginia had led a sheltered existence as a child. Her physician father had been diligent in his protective efforts. She was largely untouched by any appreciation of the horrors of the war that raged during her early teen years. This may have been in deference to her mother's southern ties as well. A further stumbling block to her understanding was Charles' reluctance or inability to discuss, during his lucid daytime hours, the details of these nightmares. In any event, Virginia developed a growing impatience for the frequent, nighttime disturbances. Her response was retire to separate sleeping quarters.

The visions that plagued her husband were always the same—the fields of Antietam. It had been his first exposure to the carnage that would mark his three years of service. Though more painful losses of close comrades would follow at Gettysburg, the Wilderness, and Bethesda Church, it was the sheer scale of death and destruction at Antietam that replayed over and over in his memory. Torn and staring bodies, many of which had been lads younger than his seventeen years, lay in profusion along the Sunken Road where he and Jimmie O'Neill had picked their way across the littered battlefield. Now, tangled sheets, sweated nightclothes, and anguished cries were the evidence of his struggle—a struggle he could not or would not share with his wife, or even his war-time friends.

****

The city of Pittsburgh had changed dramatically during the late 1860s and 1870s. The community of Lawrenceville was annexed in 1867. Then in 1872, several communities on the south side of the Monongahela were annexed into the city, raising the population to well over 100,000 souls. As suggested earlier, the downtown business district encroached increasingly upon the residential areas of the center city. Many of the more affluent citizens were moving to the leafier suburbs of Oakland and the East End. Even Allegheny City, which had attracted the McKennas, was increasingly blighted by industrial activity and the accompanying pollution of the water and the air. Conditions would continue to deteriorate in "the smoky city" as the transition from iron to steel now got underway.

"The Point" of Pittsburgh was an especially poverty-stricken district, home to a largely Irish immigrant community. These post-famine arrivals hailed mostly from the poor western counties of Ireland, districts where the worst of the famine impacts were felt. Most speaking the Irish language only, they clustered together and clung to the traditional, rural customs and values they brought from home. A new parish, St.Mary's, was established to serve them, the Masses being conducted in Gaelic.

For most working-class Irish-Americans, the neighborhood saloon functioned as the center of their social life. It was the source of neighborhood news; it functioned also as a hiring hall, a political club, and occasionally as a bank. In the 1870s, fully a third of the saloons in Pittsburgh were operated by Irish-Americans.

However, the Irish-Americans who arrived in an earlier era, like the McKenna family, were now often to be counted as middle class. They populated the boards of their churches, fraternal associations, and benevolent societies. Sixty percent were merchants, proprietors, or professionals. Eighty percent had shops or offices in the downtown district. They were strongly loyal to the Catholic Church and the Democratic Party. And many within this community, including Barney and Charles McKenna, supported the Catholic Total Abstinence Union of America. There was a chapter of this national temperance movement to be found in virtually every Catholic parish in Pittsburgh.

It was in this milieu that Barney McKenna finally felt ready to undertake the political career to which he had long aspired. He and Mary had returned to 88 Robinson Street after the loss of their first-born. Now blessed with an infant daughter, Catherine, and living again with the extended family, Barney first had to sell the idea to his own. He started with Annie one evening in early 1875. "It will mean another move, Mother. But if I'm to run for alderman, it must be in the Fourth Ward where friends and former neighbors may support me. Mary and I hope that all of you will join us, but if you choose to stay here, we will understand. You'll still have Catherine and Eddie and the grandchildren about you."

Annie stared off into space momentarily. Then she laughed, "Ach, you're just like your father was—bound to be a politician whatever may be! I remember him usin' all his blarney on me so to buy the house on Irwin Street. 'Twas just so he could be runnin' for them old Whigs!"

Barney fidgeted, anxious for a decision. "I know we've had less than five years here, so leaving Allegheny will be a nuisance . . ."

"Oh, don't you be worryin' after me. I'll be glad for the old ward people again. Of course, I'll not be speakin' for your sister or your brother. If Catherine is dead-set against it, then I don't know."

As it turned out, Catherine and Eddie offered little objection. "It's been your dream all along, Brother," was her reply. Eddie's position was more self-serving. "I'll be closer to the job."

And so they went, settling at first in a house at 306 Penn Avenue.* Shortly thereafter, Barney announced his candidacy for alderman of the Fourth Ward. In those days, an alderman was the equivalent of a justice of the peace. They issued warrants (executed by the ward's constable), held hearings, and rendered decisions in cases consisting largely of petty crimes and civil disputes amounting to $300 or less. The position was largely remunerated by the fines and court costs imposed. This, of course, left the position vulnerable to unprincipled occupants who based their decisions on the outcome most likely to maximize their earnings.

Having been a life-time resident, and serving for years at the volunteer firehouse on Irwin Street, Barney was well-known and popular among citizens of the Fourth Ward. The campaign consisted of retail politicking at its best, visiting voters in their homes, in their saloons, and at meetings of the fraternal associations. When the votes came in, the incumbent, Squire James Donaldson, was defeated soundly. Resigning his position at the fire department, Barney took up the aldermanic office at 188

---

* (*Many of the street names in the city had been renamed numerically. St. Clair was now Sixth Street and Irwin Street, first home of the McKenna family, was Seventh Street. Penn Street and Liberty Street were now re-designated avenues.*)

186

Penn Avenue and began a judicial career without the benefit of any legal training. Before long, however, he demonstrated himself to be a man of extraordinary judgment, patience, and a refreshing sense of humor. It was soon clear to all that his political career was well-launched.

Chapter Thirteen

The year 1877 proved to be a momentous one for Pittsburgh, but also for the McKenna family. Barney, the de facto head of the family, took a larger residence at 263 Penn Avenue, a home he would continue to share with the extended family. His brother Patrick and his wife Mary also crowded in, probably for economic reasons.

Barney was in his second year of a five year term of office. He was now about to be swept up into events that shattered the civic landscape as dramatically as had the Great Fire of 1845. The seeds had been planted several years prior when, in response to the financial panic (recession) of 1873, the Pennsylvania Railroad (PA.R.R.) had arbitrarily reduced their workers' wages by ten percent—a not uncommon labor practice employed by industry during the nineteenth century. The railroad's actions affected not only the employees of their own lines, but also the employees of other railroad companies they controlled. In the spring of 1877, it was understood that a further ten percent reduction would be announced in the near future.

In May a committee of employees met with Thomas A. Scott, President of the PA.R.R. He told the delegation that the planned reductions were a consequence of the general decline in business and that wages might be increased when improved business conditions permitted. Though the employee committee went away somewhat mollified, they were unprepared for the reaction of the rank and file workers. The railroad did not recognize any union organization of their employees; however, there did exist a secret, oath-bound society called "The Train Men's Union," pledged to protect its members by lawful means, including strikes.

In June, the wage reduction was officially announced. This action provoked the expected call for a strike, which was set for noon on June 27th. The strike plans extended beyond the PA.R.R.

and would affect other major railroads in the East as well. When word of the intended action leaked to railroad management, the strike was postponed for the time being.

But now, the PA.R.R. management twisted the plunged knife. On July 16th, they announced that freight trains, which previously consisted of seventeen cars and one locomotive, would be replaced with trains of thirty-four cars and two locomotives. The so-called "double-header" would result in a nearly fifty percent reduction in workers required. Freight conductors, firemen, brakemen, and flagmen suddenly found themselves with the proverbial pink slip.

On the appointed effective date, July 19th, Robert Pitcairn, general agent and superintendant of the Pittsburgh Division of the PA.R.R., left Pittsburgh on an early train (the first doubleheader) on personal business. David M. Watt, his chief clerk, was left in-charge during his absence. At 8:40 a.m., the second double-header was due to leave Pittsburgh for points east. But before the crew could execute their orders, twenty to twenty-five strikers took control of the switches within the rail-yard—effectively blocking the train's departure. They also chased away the train crew.

When advised of the situation, Mr. Watt sent a request to Mayor William McCarthy for ten policemen to protect those employees willing to work. The mayor politely declined, pleading the city's own reduction in their work force left them with insufficient staff. McCarthy, aware of the great wave of public sympathy for railroad workers, may also have wished to avoid putting the city on the side of railroad management in their labor dispute.

Even Pittsburgh's business community had their own grievances with the PA.R.R. over their anti-competitive pricing and the resultant distortions in the freight rates. Two examples worth citing are these: It was cheaper, according to the railroad's rates, to ship goods to California from Pittsburgh via Boston rather than to ship them directly. Also, it paid a shipper in Chicago to send his Pittsburgh-bound goods via Philadelphia, even though they would pass through Pittsburgh on their way to Philadelphia. Many business leaders were, therefore, largely supportive of the railroad workers.

Despite his concerns, McCarthy eventually offered to dispatch ten recently-sacked police officers, if the railroad would bear the expense. This was agreed and the police contingent set off for the 28th Street Outer Depot under the leadership of Officer Charles McGovern. Meanwhile, Mr. Watt attempted to personally open a track switch to enable a train's departure. But a crowd of one hundred or so had gathered, roughly half of these being spectators—supporting the stoppage or simply amused at the stand-off. Someone in the crowd struck Watt in the eye and others chased him away. The time was between noon and 1:00 p.m.

Upon reaching the Twelfth Ward police station, Watt wired a second request to the mayor asking for more policemen. The mayor promptly sent five or six men, insisting he could spare no more. At 5:00 p.m., Watt issued a further request for more police officers, but found the mayor to be out of the office, attending his sick wife. The mayor's clerk pled no more available men and suggested trying Allegheny County Sheriff, Hugh Fife. Late that night, Fife went to the main switchyard at 28th Street and ordered the strikers and crowd to go home. But he was jeered by the now five hundred or so men and boys—rail workers, discharged workers, laborers from iron, glass, and textile mills, and riff-raff also. They told Fife to go back to his home. Feeling helpless before such numbers, the sheriff retired from the scene.

On the following morning, Watt requested Mayor McCarthy come to company offices at Union Station for consultations. The mayor refused, effectively capping municipal involvement in the protection of life and property. Watt then, together with the PA.R.R. solicitor John Scott, traveled to Sheriff Fife's home. Together, they composed an urgent message requesting military intervention and wired it to the Pennsylvania Adjutant General James W. Latta (Governor Hartranft being off in Wyoming, vacationing at the railroad's expense).

Latta immediately wired General Alfred L. Pearson, Charles McKenna's friend and former commander. Pearson, then commanding the Pittsburgh units of the Pennsylvania National Guard, was ordered to take charge of the situation. But he was able to assemble only 250 of the 326 men of one regiment of the Sixth Division by 4:30 a.m. Saturday morning. These were dispatched to the Union Station depot. He later ordered the 14th and 19th regiments and the Hutchinson Artillery Battery to 28th Street to protect life and property. But these numbers proved to be inadequate also. Many of these guardsmen retired to the Union Depot where they joked and fraternized with the strikers, their arms stacked harmlessly nearby. They were also warned by the strikers that any movement to release trains would be resisted vigorously.

Pearson was properly dubious that his Pittsburgh-based guard units would use force against their friends and neighbors. By now, the crowds at 28th Street numbered four to five thousand, including many women and children. He therefore requested that Latta dispatch two thousand soldiers from the National Guard at Philadelphia. Latta agreed and ordered Major General Robert M. Brinton to lead these guard units by rail to Pittsburgh. General Brinton, only thirty-five years of age had, coincidentally, served as Adjutant General to Major General Charles Griffin in the last stages of the Civil War. As such, he and Charles McKenna would have known each other very well.

Brinton was eventually able to assemble eight hundred men and left for Pittsburgh on the morning of July 21st. Stopping at Harrisburg, his forces picked up two Gatling guns. They arrived in Pittsburgh about 1:00 p.m. Brinton gave his men orders to avoid firing unless they were subjected to attack. But there was a long-standing rivalry between Pittsburgh and Philadelphia, bitter on both sides. It was rumored that the Philadelphia Guard units were spoiling for a fight and boasting "they would clean up the workingmen's town."

While Barney McKenna's Fourth Ward was well removed from the scene of the strike, he was, nevertheless, greatly concerned for his constituents—railroad employees and those citizens being swept up in the tidal wave of anger. When his brother Charles called at his aldermanic office that Saturday, he voiced these worries. Striding back and forth in the cramped hearing room and puffing furiously on his cigar, Barney was clearly agitated. "There must be something I can do! . . . But I'm not certain what that might be," he admitted.

"Well, Brother, I share your concern," Charles replied calmly, his feet propped up against his brother's beat-up wooden desk. "The railroad seems hell-bent to force an outcome that ignores the workers' grievances. They've already bought up most of the key political figures in Harrisburg, so the state government will always be on their side."

Barney stopped pacing and faced his brother. "It's not the railroad I fear, Charles. It's the Guard from Philadelphia. You've heard some of the rumors?"

"Aye, I've heard. Still, I'm somewhat comforted that Alfred Pearson can contain the crisis. If anyone can, he will."

Barney stubbed out his exhausted stogie. "I hope you are right. The crowds at the Outer Depot swell by the hour . . . and tempers are running high."

Charles rose to take his leave. As he reached the door he turned and gave warning. "It is a good place to avoid, Barney. Stay clear, just in case things get out of hand."

Meanwhile, Pittsburgh's mills and factories typically released their workers at noon on Saturdays. A number of manufacturers had approached PA.R.R. Vice President Cassatt that morning with the request that no action be taken against the strikers until Monday, when their workers would be back on the job and unavailable to support the strikers. But Cassatt refused, insisting that it was the duty of the government to re-open the line immediately, "regardless of the consequences."

A meeting between strikers and community leaders was convened shortly thereafter. Dr. E. Donnelly addressed the rail workers, describing the Philadelphia soldiers:

> *"They are not, you may say, your brothers. . . . These men will come here strangers to you, and they will come here regarding you as we regarded the rebels during the rebellion, and there will be no friendly feeling between you and them. For this reason, I implore you, for God's sake, to stand back when they arrive. . . . I have been informed by the men who are leading the strike that they will exercise the greatest caution and forbearance when the soldiers arrive, and I entreat you to stand back and let them manage the thing in their own way."*

Donnelly's remarks were greeted by cheers, and the strike leaders adopted and announced resolutions promising no interference with passenger or mail traffic on the rail line. They also offered to release freight then being held in the rail yards and intended for Pittsburgh deliveries. They thanked the public for their expressions of sympathy for the strikers' cause.

At about 5:00 p.m. the crowd at 28th Street's Outer Depot heard a cry, "Here they come!" The eight hundred guards from Philadelphia were advancing from Union Depot towards the Outer Depot with fixed bayonets. Superintendant Pitcairn (now returned), Sheriff Fife, and numerous constables and police led the march. They were carrying a warrant for the arrest of unnamed strike leaders on the charge of riot. As the Philadelphia troops arrived at the Outer Depot they were deluged with jeers and scorn, from women as well as men. Members of the Pittsburgh Guard were present, arrayed on the hillside above the rail yard. Others mingled with the crowd, urging the arriving Philadelphia guardsmen to "take it easy."

Chaos and confusion reigned. Those at the back of the crowd pushed forward to see what would happen. Those in front attempted to talk down the confrontation. Some in the crowd even grabbed at the bayonets poised in their faces. Suddenly, an order was given to the Philadelphia "Dark Blues" to charge with fixed bayonets and clear the obstructed tracks. A number of protesters were stabbed, reeling back, blood oozing from their wounds. The crowd roared its outrage. Stones rained down upon the soldiers. In seconds, an order "Fire!" was heard and the Guard troops began firing point blank into the crowd. Pandemonium ensued. Men, women and children scattered in all directions, seeking to escape. In the pell-mell rush, bodies of the wounded were stepped on as they writhed in pain upon the ground. Members of the Pittsburgh Guard units were flushed with anger. They had to be restrained by their officers from firing in retaliation at the Philadelphia phalanx. Frustrated, many tore off their uniform blouses and ground them under foot.

As the firing ceased, the dead and wounded were lifted and carried to undertakers, physicians' offices, or to private homes. At least twenty persons were dead, including a woman and three small children. One of the dead was a Pittsburgh guardsman. An additional twenty-nine were wounded, many grievously. News of the "massacre" spread like wildfire throughout the city. Thousands of angry workers poured into the streets to make their way to the scene of violence. Denunciations and threats of revenge filled the air of the still-crowded rail yard. Meanwhile numerous shops throughout the city were stormed by angry citizens eager to seize weapons and ammunition with which to confront the Philadelphia guardsmen.

28th Street Outer Depot, Site of Shooting
(University of Pittsburgh Library)

Barney McKenna's worst fears were being realized. The family was at supper when the word came. Besides Annie and Catherine, Barney and Mary, there was their three-year-old daughter Catherine and their youngest child, five-month-old Frank resting in Mary's lap. Their meal was interrupted when Eddie dashed in carrying news of the massacre.

"You weren't there, were you?" his mother challenged anxiously.

"Oh, no, Mother. I was on my way here when a crowd came streaming down Liberty. They were crying and cursing and ready for mayhem."

His sister Catherine was moved to tears and promptly made the sign of the cross. Barney left the table and went to the parlor with Eddie. He questioned him closely for details. But, heeding Charles' advice of that morning, Barney resisted the temptation to proceed to the scene of conflict. But when additional reports were received of further mob activity, he finally relented. He rushed to city hall and volunteered his services as an auxiliary policeman. Along with other volunteers, he was assigned to protect the downtown district from being caught up in the widening conflict.

Later that evening, Barney was patrolling along Market Street. A shopkeeper shouted to him. "Alderman McKenna! They're setting fires over on Liberty Avenue!"

Anxious to respond, Barney immediately made his way to the stationhouse of Engine Company No. 2, his old unit of two years prior. Together with engine and hose wagons, Barney and the firefighters advanced to the scene of arson activity. They found the Rush House, a Liberty Avenue hotel in flames, though not yet fully engulfed. A rank of thugs blocked their way. Grabbing a fireman's ax, Barney pushed his way through the now-intimidated rioters. The firefighters followed his lead and began to extinguish the blaze. When the fire was out, Barney returned to his home, physically and emotionally exhausted.

Around 8:00 p.m., the Philadelphia Guard at the Outer Depot, sensing their jeopardy, took refuge in a nearby roundhouse. It immediately came under siege. A wagon of food, intended for the barricaded troops, was quickly seized by the mob. With the Pittsburgh National guards virtually in desertion, no police remaining, and the Philadelphia guardsmen cowering, the crowd ruled the city. And they would do so for some time.

The incensed rioters began to put to the torch all forms of railroad property—buildings, locomotives, freight cars, passenger cars, etc. Freight cars were first broken into and stripped of goods before being burned. Women frequently took the lead in the looting. They could be seen scurrying away with bolts of cloth, brooms, hams, bacon, etc. They even carried away quantities of loose flour in their upturned aprons. "Sure, we're savin' it all from bein' burned," one woman explained. One of the freight cars was filled with wine and spirits. These quickly fueled what would become a drunken spree.

Fire alarms rang at various firehouses throughout the city at about 10:15 p.m. Station No.7 at Penn and Twenty-third was the first to respond to the Outer Depot with three engine companies and one hose company. But before they could advance more than several city blocks, the mob blocked their way and doused the fires in their steam engines. Threats of murderous violence were made against any attempt to save railroad property.

Back at home, Barney continued to receive updates from police patrols. He lay in the parlor, having refused entreaties from Annie and Mary that he get to bed. It was around 11:00 p.m. when Dan Eckels, engineer from Fire Company No. 2 pounded upon his door.

"Barney, there's more trouble. Firefighters are being held hostage by the crowd at Outer Depot. The whole rail-yard from Union Station to 28th Street is ablaze! Shots have been fired! The rioters told Commissioner Coats not to bother turning out other companies."

Mary, awakened by the excited conversation, came to the head of the stairs in her night-robe. "Bernard, what has happened now? . . . You won't be going out again?"

He strode to the foot of the stairs. "Go back to bed, dear. There is someone I must see at the fire company. I won't be gone long."

"Please, Bernard! No! You mustn't continue to be mixed up in this! You could be killed just stepping out onto the street."

Barney pulled on his jacket. "Mary, I must go. I will be careful. Now go back to bed. We mustn't wake the children. I will be back as soon as I can."

With that, he and Eckels left the house and advanced up Liberty Avenue, paralleling the railroad right-of-way. Despite the hour, the sky was brightly lit by the bank of flames on their right. As they passed St. Philomena and St. Patrick churches, their shadows and those of the crowd danced on the walls beside them. Just beyond, a knot of women were busy serving tea and coffee to the rioters. Barney and Eckels reached 23rd Street where they were informed that William Coats, one of the five fire commissioners, and his men were up ahead, but still being held in check. They continued their march till they found Coats.

As they approached, the commissioner suddenly recognized the alderman and former fireman. "Jesus, Barney, what are you doing up here?"

Barney grimaced in embarrassment. "Hello, Bill. I want to help . . . if I can. How do things stand at the moment?"

Looking around at the mayhem, Coats threw his hands up in despair. "We can't fight these fires! My men are at risk of their lives. Some son-of-a-bitch just took an ax to our hoses. Frankly, I was just about to order No. 7 to retire to their station house. But, the fires are spreading now along Liberty, including a lumber yard. Soon those houses on the bluff will go up as well."

"Is there anyone in charge?—among the rioters, I mean."

"Not really, but a big fellow with the black beard was over here before. Seems to be a leader of sorts. No names are being given, of course."

"Let's have a word with him."

Before Coats could respond, Barney began to proceed further up Liberty. When the large, bearded gent was sighted, Coats pointed him out. He was over six feet tall, with a girth nearly as big. Barney was feeling intimidated. Heavens! This lad's arms are as big as my thighs!

He approached the man cautiously, his empty hands outstretched. "Sir, may I have a word?"

The giant glowered at him. "And who might you be?"

"My name's McKenna. I'm alderman in the Fourth Ward. I'm not here to defend the railroad, nor the troops that fired today. Can we just . . . . ?"

"Glad to hear it. I told the firemen, and I'll tell you the same—there'll be no savin' railroad property!"

Barney persisted. "Aye, I've got that. But look now, there's private property going up in flames across Liberty. Folks on the bluff are about to lose their homes, their jobs. That's not what you men wanted. Can we agree that the firemen pass freely to fight the blazes beyond the rail yard? Can they be assured they will not be shot for protecting the city from another Great Fire?"

The bearded fellow paused, uncertain. "I dunno. I'll have to talk to the others."

"Yes, please do. Every moment lost increases the damage and possible loss of innocent lives. Surely, enough folk have died already today!"

"Wait here." The bearded fellow then walked into the crowd, towards 28th Street.

Barney turned to Coats. "If they say yes, will your men step up?"

"I don't know Barney. They're a nervous bunch just now and I don't blame them."

"Can I talk to them?"

Coats shrugged. "Be my guest." He called his crew together into a tight circle. "Gather round! Alderman McKenna would like a word with you men."

Barney took a deep breath. Lord, give me the right words! He looked into the eyes of the firemen for what seemed a long interval, saying nothing. Then, he smiled and began.

"Rough night, eh? . . . . You must know I don't come to you tonight as Alderman McKenna. No, I spent too long in the Allegheny Company and in Engine Company No. 2. I come as a firefighter . . . well, at least a former one. I know each one of you simply wants to be able to do his duty. And you don't want to be killed by some crazy drunk for doing it. Am I right?"

Murmurs of assent passed through the knot of uniformed men.

"Now, we're waiting word from their leaders. I've asked them if we can be allowed to spare those homes up on the bluff, and the private property along Liberty as well. I told them we must have safe passage—no more bullets, no more axes. Now, if they agree, can I count on you all to do what's needed?"

A red-headed fellow, a hoseman, spoke up. "What if they break their word? . . . What if they can't control these blockheads with the rifles?"

"In that case, you will return to your station house immediately. I'm not here to get any of you killed."

"What about the railroad property?" the hoseman pressed Barney.

"Let it burn! That's the feckin' railroad's problem."

A few of the firemen laughed. But they had reached a consensus. They would fight the blazes on private property, if allowed.

It was nearly midnight. The rioters were sending rail cars of burning coal and petroleum down a track to an out-building adjacent to the roundhouse where the Philadelphia guardsmen were imprisoned. The out-building went up in flames, but the roundhouse was preserved when the soldiers discovered a railroad water-bib and hose and doused the approaching flames.

Shortly thereafter, the bearded emissary returned from his mission. "They agreed, mister. We'll pass the word through the crowd. But that will take a bit of time. Now, only private property, mind you!"

"Thank you, sir. We'll start with the homes on the bluff . . . . Bill, let's get the other companies moving up above. By the time they get there, the cease-fire should be in effect. Let these men attend to that lumberyard."

Coats nodded and turned toward the "Independent" station house. Barney thanked the firemen and shook a few hands. "God be with you, men." With that he hurried to join Coats in the walk back down Liberty Avenue.

The burning and looting continued through the night. No opposition from military or police was mounted. Their leaders had absented themselves from the chaotic scene. Fire companies struggled to save the private buildings on Liberty Avenue; but they had to move continuously towards town to keep up with the firing of rail cars across the way. Their efforts were largely successful, save on Quarry and Fountain Streets, immediately adjacent to the rail yards.

About 6:00 on Sunday morning, conditions at the roundhouse had become even more desperate. The Philadelphia guardsmen hadn't eaten for nearly twenty-four hours. And they were increasingly choked by clouds of acrid smoke. General Brinton concluded that their only chance of survival was to break-out and retreat from the scene. At 7:30, he gave the order and the companies, in double-quick fashion, raced to Liberty Avenue and what they hoped would be safety. Unfortunately for them, they met sporadic gunfire from windows and doorways along the street. As they moved towards Lawrenceville, the soldiers returned fire as best they could, wounding many and killing several bystanders. The soldiers crossed over to Penn Avenue, and thence on to Butler Street, anxious to evade the still-large mob.

Ruins of Freight Cars
(University of Pittsburgh Library)

When General Brinton and his troops arrived in the center of
Lawrenceville, they sought refuge at the Allegheny Arsenal. Later,
giving his account to a newspaper reporter, Brinton described his
reception by Commandant Buffington.

> *"All I ask is cover that my men may not be shot down," said the*
> *General.*
> *"You can't stay here," was the reply.*
> *"But they are being shot down in the street."*
> *"Well, this is United States property, and you can't stay."*
> *"But we are here in place of United States troops."*
> *"It makes no difference, you must get right out."*

They resumed their march, making for Sharpsburg, on the
opposite side of the river.

One daring rioter in shirt-sleeves pursued them closely, darting
from doorway to doorway. This lone gunman dogged them, firing
his pistol at the retreating soldiers with considerable effect. Though
they returned fire, the avenger seemed to have a charmed existence,
constantly eluding the bullets sent his way. At Forty-ninth Street,
he captured a straggling soldier who had tripped in his haste. The
prisoner pleaded for his life. His captor granted this request, but
took possession of his weapon. He then turned it upon the trailing
ranks of soldiers, shooting two fatally. He dodged into side streets
and continued his attack until the guardsmen had crossed the
Sharpsburg bridge.

Brinton claimed six killed and twenty-three wounded among
his men. They finally found succor at the Allegheny Poor House.
There, the superintendant provided their first meal since their
arrival on the previous day.

Back in Pittsburgh, the arson-minded mob continued their
spree. The Union Station housing the railroad offices, the Keystone
Hotel, and the passenger terminal had been set ablaze. Employees,
travelers, and hotel guests barely escaped the rapid conflagration.
A nearby grain elevator, the tallest structure in the city, was also

consumed. Various machine shops, freight transfer stations, and separate rail companies' facilities suffered the same fate. These blazes were beyond the capabilities of any fire department.

Meanwhile, the story of riot and ruin was being told in newspapers across the nation. Shock and outrage was the typical editorial reaction, branding the strikers as the guilty parties. But the strikers themselves assured the city fathers and the citizen's committee of defense that their members had no wish to see the railroad destroyed. It was their source of employment. They claimed to have abandoned the field after Saturday's massacre. It was the plundering mob that was to blame.

Nearly every city and town in Pennsylvania experienced mass meetings of angry citizens voicing their support for the strikers and their animus toward the railroad. Strikes of sympathy broke out in Steubenville, Ohio, Johnstown, Altoona, Reading, and Philadelphia.

Destruction Of The Union Depot And Hotel At Pittsburgh
(Harper's Weekly—August 11, 1877)

In some cases crowds obstructed the passage of military reinforcements headed for Pittsburgh. The worst of these incidents occurred when state militia troops fired on a largely peaceful assembly of citizens in central Reading with great loss of life. Meanwhile strikers in Allegheny City, though fully in support of their Pittsburgh brothers, maintained a non-violent posture and protected railroad property from destruction. Similar strikes occurred on the Erie, New York Central, and Vandalia Railroads. Even as far west as Chicago and St. Louis, strikes against the railroads ensued. Separately, Pennsylvania coal miners, reduced to starvation wages by abusive coal operators, took strike actions of their own.

Though conditions in Pittsburgh returned to relative calm by Monday—there was little railroad property left to burn—it would take nearly a week to put down strikes and civil disobedience and reopen the lines of the Pennsylvania Railroad. Federal troops, joining with units of the Pennsylvania National Guard moved from the rail strikes to the coal strikes to restore order and return these industries to nearly normal operations. In the end, the violence in Pittsburgh destroyed 39 buildings, 104 locomotives, and 1,245 rail cars of various types. Over forty persons were killed and many more wounded.

Chapter Fourteen

In 1878, Charles McKenna demonstrated that there was more than one politician in the family. He, like Barney, was a strong Democrat. Despite his busy law practice, he was an active member of the relatively new Chamber of Commerce. Both party and chamber friends urged him to run for Congress as an anti-boss candidate and against "ringers" who were minions of the Republican political machine. His opponent was Tom Bayne, the Republican former district attorney for Allegheny County.

Barney also encouraged his brother. "You'll probably lose, Charles, but the message you carry to the voters is important. With repetition from illustrious candidates like yourself, perhaps folks will wise up."

Charles cast a baleful glance and muttered. "That's very comforting! Nothing like being a sacrificial lamb. I'll be lucky if Virginia's family will speak to me after this."

Given the Republican party's dominant position in this era, the results were as predicted. Charles didn't wait up for the returns. He read the result in the morning paper at breakfast the next day; Bayne garnered 9,104 votes to Charles' 5,621 votes.

"Well, it made for an interesting autumn," Charles remarked to Virginia. "I met a lot of people and saw some new parts of Allegheny County."

"You did your duty, dear. Besides, I didn't want to live in Washington, anyway."

* *

The late 1870's were also a difficult time, again, in Ireland. Especially in the western province of Connaught, continued potato blight and severe winters produced another economic crisis for peasants. Rising rents and mass evictions of tenants then resulted in a grass-roots protest and reform movement. In October, 1879 it was organized as the Irish National Land League, a coalition of nationalists and reformers. Its first president was the Protestant parliamentarian and home rule advocate, Charles Stewart Parnell. The League established two goals, the reductions of rents and the replacement of "landlordism" with the opportunity for land ownership by its Irish tenants.

In Pittsburgh, as in much of the United States, there was great sympathy among Irish-Americans and others with the proposition that the Irish peasants ought to have the right to purchase the land they worked and which was their only source of sustenance. The following year, working with various Irish-American organizations, Parnell organized the Irish National Land League of the United States. Its purpose was to provide moral and financial support for the movement in Ireland. Quickly hundreds of League chapters sprang up around the country, including Pittsburgh where nearly eleven percent of the population was of Irish descent. Even beyond the Irish-American Pittsburghers, the Land League movement attracted broad public support, especially from the labor movement.

The men of the McKenna family were not immune to this call. They had heard from Annie and Uncle Bernard the history of their family's forced emigration and the tragic circumstances for those left behind. So when Parnell visited Pittsburgh in 1880, Charles McKenna rushed to join the first of many Pittsburgh chapters of the National Land League. Among those joining in League affairs were the reform-minded mayor Robert Liddell, James J. Flannery, the prominent Grant Street undertaker, and John O'Neil, a prominent liquor merchant. Flannery and O'Neil were also politicos in the Democratic party and close associates of Barney McKenna.

Though Barney was a member—how could he desist when nearly twenty percent of his Fourth Ward constituents were Irish-American?—it was his brother Charles who rose within the chapter hierarchy. Early in 1881, Charles helped organize "The Indignation

Meeting" at the Fifth Avenue Lyceum, a rally of local League chapters from all of Allegheny County. The indignation was over the arrest by British authorities of League leaders within Ireland, including Parnell. Later that year, Charles was elected the President of the Allegheny County Land League at its November 21st public meeting at Lafayette Hall. The meeting's featured speaker was the fiery Galway member of parliament, T.P. O'Connor. He was one of thirty-five Irish members expelled from the British Parliament for exercising their rights to speak freely for land reform in Ireland. The meeting resulted in unanimous support by all Land League chapters for the "No Rent Manifesto" of the Irish League. They also promised to intensify fund-raising efforts, hoping to eradicate the "blighting curse of landlordism" in Ireland.

※※※※※※※※※※※※※※※※※※※※※※※※

But Barney had more personal issues to distract him from the troubles of Ireland. In July, 1880 he and Mary were forced to re-live the horror of infant death. Their fourteenth-month-old son, Charles Francis, succumbed to diarrhea and lung congestion. Once again, it was Dr. Thomas Shaw who had the wretched duty to advise the sorrowing couple that this youngest son, a second Charles, was at death's door. Their grief was shared acutely by Annie McKenna. As the internment at St. Mary's Cemetery concluded, the eighty-one year-old matriarch, now quite frail, walked slowly from the gravesite to a waiting carriage. The summer day was warm and muggy and Barney could see his mother was struggling emotionally and physically. He helped his mother and wife into the carriage, then turned to thank and bid goodbyes to other mourners.

After catching her breath, Annie commiserated with her daughter-in-law. "God love us, Mary! How cruel this life can be, at times. We expect our children and grandchildren to outlive us. I have seen sons and grandsons taken . . . . Yet here am I, in my old age. It doesn't seem right!"

"Dear Annie, it is very sad. And so many families endure these terrible losses. Yet, who can judge the will of God? I just thank Him that we have Catherine and Frank, whole and healthy as they are . . . . Someday, we may have another son. But,—and you can call me superstitious—there will never be another Charles in our family!"

That night Mary found her husband seated on the steps of the front porch, escaping the heat in their upstairs bedroom, she surmised. As she approached, however, he blotted his eyes with a rolled-up sleeve. She leaned forward and caressed his yoke. "You were very brave, keeping it all within yourself at the church and at the cemetery. But it's good to let your grief come forth, even if it's only in front of me."

"It's for you I cry, Mary. I know our son—our sons—are in the arms of their Savior. It's the grief that you must bear that brings these tears."

"Dear Bernard! I have you and Catherine and Frank. My broken heart will heal as it did once before."

* *

In the days that followed, Barney could take but little time for grieving. His term as alderman was about to expire. If he didn't wish to become unemployed, a re-election campaign had to be mounted in the fall. There was no real debate in his mind, nor within the family. His first term had been very well received within the Fourth Ward and beyond. Citizens still told the tale of how "Judge Barney" had faced the mob during the railroad strike and helped prevent greater loss to the city. That November, the voters returned him to office for another five years. His responsibilities as head of the extended family at 263 Penn Avenue would continue as well. But the composition of that extended family was about to change again.

It was February of 1881. Winter was again wreaking its bitter cold upon the region. Cutting winds coursed along the rivers and into the adjacent neighborhoods within the "triangle." Perhaps it was the cold, or maybe it was just that the appointed time had arrived. Whatever the cause, old Annie passed away quietly in her sleep on the last day of the month. Her increased frailty had provided ample warning to the family that her time was getting short. But losing this remarkable woman still stung the sensibilities of family, neighbors and friends.

Her passing seemed to impact her daughter Catherine most of all. Long a spinster, she had spent her life assisting her mother and serving family and boarders alike. Strengthened my her deep religious faith, she was not one to fall to pieces in such emotional circumstances. Rather, she signaled her loss by voicing her love and admiration at the wake held in the family home.

"How much Mother had accomplished—a young widow providing for her family! How much she had seen—from the leave-taking from Anacramp, through the emigration journey, to adjusting to life in this great, dirty, often-mean city of Pittsburgh. She lost her husband early on, one son to adventure and another to untimely death. But for us, she was a rock of stability and continuity. Now, she is gone. God bless her soul, as we all surely do."

The wake was well attended. Uncle Bernard, an unmarried laborer now living alone on the Southside, was there—the last surviving family member linked to old days in Anacramp. Ann, the widow of Uncle Charles, came with several of her sons and daughters. Of course Eddie, now a toll collector, was there with his daughter and two sons. Patrick and his wife Mary traveled back from their new home in Springfield, Ohio. Charles and Virginia, now living at the Central Hotel in Pittsburgh, helped Barney and Mary with all the arrangements and hosting that ensued. Various close friends joined the occasion, including members of the McShane and McKeever families. Among the latter, was old Will McKeever's thirty-three-year-old son, Edward, now an ordained priest. Father Ed assisted at the funeral Mass at St. Paul's Cathedral. Annie was laid to rest beside her long-gone husband in St. Mary's Cemetery at Lawrenceville.

McKenna Family Members circa 1880
(left to right, Uncle Bernard, Charles, Annie, Patrick, Barney)

It was sad, but also merciful, that Annie McKenna's death preceded the first news of her second son, Hugh, since his departure for the California gold fields in 1851. It was Charles McKenna who received the letter dated September 21,1881. It was sent by Dr. Allen Hardenbrook, a physician, druggist, gold miner, and coroner in the mining community of Challis, in the territory of Idaho. It read:

> *Dear Sir,*
>
> *Your brother is dead as I telegraphed you. I surmised that he had seen better days and was well connected from the fact that he so sedulously concealed the names, or whereabouts, of his relatives, when dying. He seemed desirous that they should not know the circumstances of his death.*
> *Poor fellow! He got into a difficulty with two other parties over a mining claim and in the scuffle one of them stabbed him*

in the breast. He lived several weeks, but could not recover owing to internal bleeding. The murderers are in jail awaiting the action of the Grand Jury and will assuredly be indicted for murder.

Your brother received my careful attention and constantly was attended by nurses during his illness. He possessed absolutely nothing at the time except the mining claim under contention as aforesaid, and was buried at the expense of his friends. He was well liked among the miners, and there was much talk among them of lynching his assassins. The names of the latter are Ireland and Walker. Ireland did the cutting and has hired able attorneys to defend himself.

Court meets Oct. 17th/81. If you take any interest in their prosecution, address me at once.

Very truly yours,

Dr. A. Hardenbrook

P.S. The mining claim is said to be valuable but I know nothing of the merits or demerits of his claim to it.

****

In September of 1886, the surviving veterans of the 155th Pennsylvania Volunteers gathered at the battlefield at Gettysburg for the dedication of a regimental monument funded by themselves and friends from Pittsburgh and vicinity. A massive, yet plain, stone plinth was erected on Little Round Top, where they had mounted their gallant defense on July 2nd, 1863. Charles McKenna was selected by the members of the regimental association to give the oration of the day. Summoning an eloquence honed in courtroom pleadings, he began:

"It has been well said that from the beginning the living have paid homage to the virtues of the dead; for immortality is the dream of man. Scarce a city, town, or village but contains some monument designed to perpetuate the memory of one who has passed from earth. These earthly tributes can be of no service to the dead, but they form lasting records of deeds, held honorable among men; are strong incentives to noble acts in the present, and mark a steady progress toward that better condition which is the ultimate destiny of the human race. You are here today to formally dedicate to the memory of your fallen comrades this beautiful monument. . . .

Gettysburg! What memories cluster around that word! The great turning battle of the rebellion—the battle where thousands of brave men gave their heart's blood that the banner of their country should be unsullied, and always wave in undiminished glory."

Three years later, the state of Pennsylvania would appropriate an additional $1500 to erect further monuments on the battlefield. With an allocation from this sum, the monument of the 155th Regiment was newly topped with a marble statue of a private soldier, armed and dressed in a Zouave uniform.

Gettysburg Monument to the 155th Pennsylvania Volunteers
(155thpa.tripod.com)

Not far away, also on Little Round Top, a bronze statue of General Warren has been placed, looking out upon the field of battle. It commemorates Warren's initiative in commanding troops to seize this strategic position, thus assuring great advantage to the Union forces.

* *

Barney McKenna's rise in Pittsburgh politics coincided with the emergence of the Republican machine that came to be known as "The Ring." Its leader was Christopher Magee. Rising from fifteen-year-old clerk to City Treasurer at the age of twenty-three, he used his control of utility and transportation franchises, city deposits, and construction contracts to reward friends and punish foes. He left the Treasurer's position to become fire commissioner, where he could concentrate his efforts for political dominance by supporting various special interests. Wards became tightly organized and controlled through patronage, including the filling of city, police, and fire department positions. Together with his principal ally, William Flinn, an Allegheny County paving contractor, Magee's Ring interposed itself between the Pennsylvania Railroad's substantial donations to "worthy" political candidates. They co-opted labor leaders and even members of the opposition political party. They committed public funds to projects that would raise property values in favored neighborhoods while steering contracts and franchises to themselves and their supporters. Even property tax rates were skewed to favor the affluent suburbs whilst penalizing working class districts nearly devoid of city services and proper infrastructure.

Christopher Lyman Magee (1848-1901)

But Magee and Flinn were more than self-dealing power brokers. They rose from humble beginnings by hard work, considerable management ability, and undaunted persistence. Of course, they used their positions and political influence for selfish advantage. Nevertheless, their accomplishments were significant and often beneficial to the public. Magee developed the Pittsburgh street car services, opening various suburban districts as residential options to commuting workers. Flinn's contracting business, Booth & Flinn, Ltd. constructed the Mount Washington tunnel, adding a new residential district in the hills south of the Monongahela. And each gentleman undertook private efforts of charity to benefit the community. In a posthumous bequest, Chris Magee would fund the establishment of the Elizabeth Steel Magee Women's Hospital. Flinn would serve as president and trustee of that hospital, as well as functioning in support roles for Western Pennsylvania Hospital, the Industrial Home for Crippled Children, and the Pittsburgh Maternity Dispensary.

William Flinn (1851-1924)

Magee was the "good cop" to Flinn's "bad cop." Magee would reward, Flinn would punish. It is said that Magee sought power, while Flinn sought wealth. They proved an irresistible combination within Pittsburgh, a city too busy growing and prospering to question how government decisions were being made. To make the power of the Magee-Flinn regime complete in local affairs, they needed the cooperation of the political establishment in Harrisburg, in both the executive branch and the legislature. The man who could deliver such help was the Republican Party boss at the state level, one Matthew S. Quay.

The reader will remember Quay as the querulous Union colonel who lost his horse early in the Virginia campaign during the war of rebellion. It was Quay who Charles McKenna saved from a court-martial by the timely production of a receipt for the Colonel's replacement mount. Quay had left the 134th Pennsylvania Volunteers for reasons of health in early December, 1862. But upon learning of the impending battle of Fredericksburg, he returned to his unit and joined in the assault upon Marye's Heights. His selfless return to duty won him the Congressional Medal of Honor. After the war, Quay ran successfully for a seat in the Pennsylvania House of Representatives. He served as secretary of the Republican State Committee from 1869 until his death in 1904. He was Secretary of the Commonwealth in the mid-1870's and again in the early 1880's. At this time (1887) he was the state treasurer.

Matthew S. Quay (1833-1904)

Magee and Quay always had a rocky relationship, neither trusting the other. In order to secure the necessary alliance, William Flinn took the extraordinary step of drafting a written memorandum of understanding between Magee and Quay. The agreement pledged Magee's complete fealty to Quay in state and national political matters. In return Quay promised complete support for the Magee-Flinn Ring in county and city politics. This extended to the selection of candidates for virtually every elective and appointive office at every level, as well as to any legislative initiative in which either had interests.

Under Pennsylvania law, and the city charter of 1816, all legislative, executive, and administrative power was vested in the select and common councils of city government. The mayor was merely a peace officer with powers similar to that of alderman. There were no functional departments in the city government. All operations were conducted by committees of the councils. When, in 1886, the manipulation of the city common and select councils had become tiresome, Magee used Quay's influence to secure state legislation revising the city charter. The effect of the new charter of 1887 was to place most power in the hands of newly-established functional departments of city government. The heads of these departments would not be appointed by the mayor, but elected by the councils. When council seats came up for election, the department heads would use their powers of patronage to ensure the success of only "loyal" candidates.

In his article, *Pittsburg: A City Ashamed*, Lincoln Steffens reports the following example, among many, of the system of graft and corruption devised by the Magee-Flinn Ring:

> *"During the nine years succeeding the adoption of the charter of 1887, . . . one firm (Flinn's) received practically all the asphalt paving contracts at prices ranging from $1 to $1.80 per square yard higher than the average price paid in neighboring cities. Out of the entire amount of asphalt pavements laid during these nine years, represented by 193 contracts and costing $3,551,131, only nine street blocks paved in 1896, and costing $33,400, were not laid by this firm."*

Barney McKenna, having run successfully for a third term as alderman in 1885, was now approached by an ad hoc organization, the Citizens' League. They had spent the previous two years railing against the Republican machine, high taxes, monopolized utilities, poor city services and public corruption. Though they attracted significant support among the professionals and middle class of the East End, they had difficulty in converting the older city wards downtown and in the "Strip." In these wards, patronage jobs still held sway over notions of clean government. Given Barney's extensive network and personal popularity in the center city wards, they came to entice him to run for mayor in 1887.

Though the mayoral position was not a powerful one, Barney was inclined to acquiesce. One day he and Charles dined together at Kegel's Oyster House in Diamond Square. The restaurant was a Pittsburgh institution. With its time-scarred wooden tables and tall wooden booths, it was a place where one could speak freely without being overheard by other patrons. Barney had invited his brother to solicit his advice about the proposed political campaign.

"Someone needs to oppose Flinn's boy, McCallin," Barney insisted. "If I should win, well, Chris Magee and I can get along."

Charles laughed. "I'm sure you'll do better than I did when I ran for office." He paused to blow upon his very hot oyster stew. Then turning serious, he added, "I even know many disaffected Republicans who will support you. A lot of the members at the Chamber of Commerce are unhappy with what takes place at city hall. And you're right about Bill McCallin. He was fine as coroner and sheriff; but as mayor, he'll turn a blind eye to all of Flinn's shenanigans."

"Well, it may be a lost cause, Brother, as you found out. Being a Democrat is an act of faith in this state. Still, one hates to surrender the field without a fight. Being an old soldier, I'm sure you'd agree."

Charles sat back and regarded his elder brother with affection. "It won't hurt you to try, Barney. You've made a fine impression on voters throughout the city. That will stand you in good stead. I will certainly rally my forces for you as best as I can."

The mayoral contest that fall proved to be a fierce battle—though not for any bombastic rhetoric. Rather, it was the broad public support for "Judge" McKenna that made the race so close. But the labor movement was desperately divided and much of their support went to fringe candidates or to the Republican. In the end, McCallin won by 1500 votes, out of 25,000 cast. Still, this was something of a high water mark for a Democratic mayoral candidate.

* *

To Barney's great astonishment, several days after the election, mayor-elect McCallin called upon him at his aldermanic office.

The room had yet to be invaded by the daily stream of aggrieved citizens looking for vindication. Barney was seated at his cluttered desk in the hearing room, chewing on his first stogie of the day. McCallin was ushered in by the constable. Waving away the cloud of smoke, Barney rose and greeted his erstwhile opponent.

"Good morning, Judge," McCallin began. "I hope I'm not intruding upon your busy schedule."

"Not at all, Mr. Mayor, please have a seat. My first hearing isn't until 11:00 . . . . Allow me to offer my congratulations, once again. Your victory was hard-fought, but fairly so."

McCallin tossed his overcoat over the back of a chair and made himself comfortable. "Well, thank you, sir. That's very kind. Actually, my impressions of your campaign are similar. You have a reputation for integrity and fairness on the bench which carried the day with a great many voters. Frankly, my victory was uncomfortably close."

Barney smiled and leaned back in his chair. "Well, how may I help you today? I presume your visit was not for the purpose of consoling me in my defeat."

McCallin chuckled. "Quite right, Judge, though you may take some consolation if you choose. No, I came to ask you to serve as one of my first appointments. I want you as police magistrate in the Twelfth Ward. Your experience as an alderman equips you well for such a post. You'll find that the pay is better and more steady than the ups and downs of the fines and fees due an alderman. And you won't have to campaign for the position. What do you say? I'm confident the City Councils will approve."

Barney shook his head in disbelief, yet grinning from ear to ear. "Forgive me, sir. This comes as something of a surprise . . . . Of course, I will gratefully accept. It's just going to take me a while to get used to the notion."

McCallin rose and stroked the wispy goatee that decorated his chin. "I'm very pleased to have your agreement. Of course, I must be sworn before I can make it official. But this will give you some weeks to tidy your affairs here for your replacement . . . . Good day, Judge."

They shook hands and McCallin took his leave.

Barney spun around in his swivel chair and re-lit his cigar. "Jaysus, what will Mary say?"

Charles' prediction that running for mayor would enhance Barney's political standing was prescient. His brother's involvement in the Democratic Party and city politics increased as his reputation as an honest and effective magistrate spread. His demeanor was captured best, years later, by Grif Alexander of the Pittsburgh Dispatch.

> *"He is Barney McKenna to most people . . . . He may be a scholar, but the fact has never been thrown up to him. But he carries around with him big chunks of common sense and that's what counts in a police court; that and judgment and knowledge of human nature. B. McKenna had all these things . . . . He is a diplomat. He did a favor when he could. When he didn't he convinced the man who braced him that he couldn't. He kept square with the politicians whose friends were in trouble, on the one hand, and with the police on the other. This required skill. He has it.*
>
> *His Honor never drinks, but Old John Barleycorn has been his very good friend. John has made it possible for His Honor to do favors for a dozen men a day, and favors are not as soon forgotten as cynics would have us believe. A plain drunk would be 'jollied' and discharged. A 'disorderly' would be lectured sufficiently to justify the arresting officer and discharged. And there would be nothing commonplace in the way it was done, either.*
>
> *A case in point—A printer was arrested for being drunk. A reporter mentioned to His Honor that the man was a pretty good fellow, that he didn't often drink and that he made no trouble for the officer. This was before the hearing. When the man was brought to the bar His Honor said:*

'You are charged with being drunk.'
'Yes, sir,' said the prisoner.
'You are a printer, aren't you?'
'Yes, sir.'
'And you were drunk?'
'Yes, sir.'
'I don't believe it!' said His Honor positively. "Printers never get drunk. Discharged!'

This kind of thing usually amuses the policeman as much as the prisoner.

His Honor smokes strong, juicy tobies. He carried one in his mouth when he entered the station house and kept it there until the first case was called. It stuck up in the air, close to his nose. When the hearings were over he lighted up again and smoked while writing out informations. He had the toby in his mouth when the regular morning crowd rushed in from Cherry Alley the moment the door was opened, and he shifted it to one side to say 'Good Morning!' affably, a touch of humor which was always appreciated. There are those in the crowd who haven't missed a hearing in years . . . . Entertainment there was, and plenty of it. Sometimes it was the prisoner that provided it; just as often it was some droll saying of His Honor's that pleased the crowd.

. . . I'll take oath that B. McKenna is no saint, but, just the same, I am willing to declare, just as earnestly, that he is a pretty fair all 'round kind of a man, who plays square with his friends; and that he made as competent a Police Magistrate as any Pittsburg has ever known."

In those days, Barney and his Democratic colleagues, many of whom were childhood friends and/or former firemen, would gather for an evening's conversation about local politics and the issues of the day. This talk shop was conducted at the confluence of Sixth Street, Liberty Avenue, and Market Street, just around the corner from the Crystal Pharmacy. James Fahnestock, who owned the drug store, and undertakers John and James Flannery were among the many regulars. But it was Barney, William J. Brennen, and Thomas "Boley" Mullen who presided over these discussions at "The Steps," so called because they would sit and talk on the front steps of that corner building.

Bill Brennen was nine years younger than Barney. At the age of twelve, he had followed his father in work at the Jones and Laughlin steel mill on the South Side. He had been elected captain of his volunteer fire company in the district of Ormsby at the age of twenty-one. In 1876, he was the youngest delegate to attend the Democratic National Convention in St. Louis. He was elected to the City Council and, later, became alderman in the Twenty-Fourth Ward. Brennen would go on to study law and have a brilliant legal career. For many years, he served as legal counsel to the Amalgated Association of Iron and Steel Workers (AAISW).

William J. Brennen

Boley Mullen was also a fixture of Democratic party affairs. This status eventually led to his appointment as an assessor for the city of Pittsburgh.

Thomas "Boley" Mullen

In time, "The Steps" admitted members of the Republican persuasion as well. Charles Flinn, brother of the Ring boss William Flinn, was one. Also joining were Michael J. Feeney, a superintendent for Flinn's contracting business. But during his political career, Barney was the undisputed ruler at "The Steps."

In the early 1900s the meeting place was moved to a corner in the lobby of the William Penn Hotel. It also took up a new moniker, "The Amen Corner." It's charter members included many of the regulars from "The Steps," but the purposes of the gathering remained constant even as the venue and name changed. The "Amen Corner" continued its gatherings and deliberations right unto modern times. It was still a going proposition as late as 2010.

Chapter Fifteen

The 1880s were also a time of reaction to the disorder of labor unrest and attendant violence. A law and order movement emerged, prompting greater professionalism within the police department and, at the state level, the militia. This was relatively non-controversial, although the lingering perspective of labor was that state and local government were in the back-pocket of the industrialists, especially the railroads and coal operators.

But there was also a companion effort in various states, mounted largely by middle-class Protestants, pressing for temperance measures and Sabbatarian blue-laws. This was motivated by the belief that immigrants, many of them Catholic Democrats, were having a detrimental impact on society, given a perceived devotion to drink. In addition to being anti-liquor, these "law and order leagues" opposed the sale of milk, ice-cream, tobacco, newspapers and groceries on Sunday.

In 1887, the Pennsylvania legislature responded to the temperance forces by passing the Brooks High License Law. Beginning the following year, fees for liquor licenses were increased, as were the penalties for illegal liquor sales. A uniform scheme of regulation of breweries, distilleries, and saloons was included. Perhaps of greatest change was the transfer of licensing authority from local governmental commissions to the county courts. Though the political machine, and even the police department, showed little enthusiasm for the new law, the effect was to reduce the number of license holders in Allegheny County from 3500 to 389. In Pittsburgh itself, the reduction was from 1500 licenses to 223.

These restrictions, naturally, brought about numerous legal appeals from disenfranchised license holders, as well as manufacturers and distributors. And Charles McKenna found himself in the enviable, if slightly awkward, position of handling such cases in large numbers. The presumption of his clients was that McKenna might have added influence in his pleadings before County Court Judge J.W.F. White, who was Virginia's uncle. Virginia laughed at her husband's predicament as they sat at breakfast one morning at their Central Hotel residence.

"I have done nothing," Charles insisted, "to encourage the notion that Judge White will be more deferential to my clients than to those of other attorneys. Indeed, I protest to the contrary. Yet still these previous license-holders come to me in droves!"

"Dear me, what a problem you have! Everyone should know my Uncle John is far too much of a curmudgeon to give any special consideration on the matter of drink. Why, he even wants to outlaw the game of baseball! He says it undermines the productive use of time among our young men."

Charles shook his head at the lack of sympathy being offered. Then he grumbled. "Well, he is a fine lawyer, . . . but as an arbiter of social behavior he's lost somewhere in the Middle Ages. At least he knows that I don't drink. Perhaps that will provide me some standing in his court room."

In the years following the new liquor law, Charles' income rose handsomely on the back of these legal appeals. And despite Charles' busy law practice, he still found time to provide assistance to worthy causes. He continued his legal assistance to the Catholic Diocese of Pittsburgh and the Western Pennsylvania Humane Society. Then in 1889 he added to his duties those of Treasurer for the St. Paul's Catholic Orphan Asylum on Tannehill Street in the Eighth Ward.

That same year, Uncle Bernard passed away. This last surviving son of old Hugh had never married and rose no further than common laborer. Yet he was always a devoted member of the family, living in the boarding house of his sister-in-law for much of his life. Whatever trial or celebration came their way, Uncle Bernard always played his supporting role. In his last years, he did seek accommodation elsewhere. Perhaps a house full of young children was a little too much excitement for a man of his years.

Barney and Mary continued to host the extended family in their Penn Avenue residence. Cousin James McKenna, a son of the late Uncle Charles, was then living with them, while working as a plumber. And widower Eddie and his three children were still fixtures within the household. Eddie's eldest son, Edward J., had taken up study of the law. During these studies, he also worked as a notary. In 1890 he would be admitted to the bar and begin legal practice in partnership with his uncle Charles F. McKenna. The firm made their offices at 135 Fifth Avenue.

Eddie experienced a great change in his working life in this period. It had begun in 1885 when Barney used his political muscle to arrange his brother's appointment as a sanitary inspector for the Board of Health. Eddie would later bemoan the uphill battle he faced in this new position. But the pay was good, the work steady, and it was a less demanding physical challenge than had been his previous duties at the Standard Oil warehouse at Eighth and Duquesne Way.

For much of the century Pittsburgh had no organized effort directed toward public health. Conditions in most of the city were appallingly bad. The air was black with soot and smoke. The rivers, which functioned as the principal source of drinking water, were highly polluted. Streets were mostly unpaved, especially in the tenement districts. Housing density and overcrowding were extreme; and sewers were non-existent except in the most affluent neighborhoods. Garbage and ashes piled high in yards. Cesspools and privy vaults were allowed to seep their contents downhill, running into gutters and creeks. There was no organized system for trash removal and disposal.

Though constrained by limited funding from the city councils, the board of health was ultimately rejuvenated. Eddie, like his colleagues, would tour his district daily, identifying housing unfit for occupancy and cajoling reluctant residents to clean-up their damp, foul cellars, their alleys, yards, and privy vaults. Occupants of tenements, having little incentive to make costly improvements to property they did not own, proved reluctant. And most landlords, anxious to maximize profits, shared that indifference. It would be the 1890s before the board of health was reorganized, made responsible to the mayor, and the city would begin to contract for routine garbage collection and disposal. Little did Eddie suspect that Barney would have much to do with instituting these future improvements to the city health scene.

****

Pittsburgh's wealthy stratum of society led, in this era, a rarified and compartmentalized existence. The elite lived in stately mansions in the East End or in picturesque riverfront communities, such as Sewickley, in the western suburbs. Their children went to private academies and eastern universities. Families would travel to Europe in search of cosmopolitan, cultural experience. Everyday life involved the delegation of the mundane household tasks to large staffs of maids, butlers, gardeners, stable boys, coachmen, and the like. Rarely, if ever, did this class encounter working Pittsburghers, except in highly structured commercial relations. The classes at each extremity of the social spectrum had only the dimmest appreciation of the circumstances of the other. That ignorance promoted gross stereotypes that resulted in resentments, indeed significant hostility.

To enjoy their leisure within reasonable travel distance from home, a group of prominent Pittsburgh businessmen acquired property and built summer cottages, indeed mansions, around a man-made lake about eighty miles east of Pittsburgh, near the Cambria County village of South Fork. There, fifty or so magnates including Henry Clay Frick and Andrew Mellon established the South Fork Fishing and Hunting Club. The lake, really a reservoir on the Little Conemaugh River, had been constructed decades previously as part of the Pennsylvania east-west canal system. When the advent of railroads made the canal system obsolete, the property fell into disuse and the South Fork dam suffered deterioration. By the 1880s when the club was founded, the dam was prone to frequent leaks and received only cursory repair.

On Thursday the thirtieth of May 1889, a storm system from the Midwest arrived in western Pennsylvania, bringing with it a downpour exceeding any in recorded local history. It is estimated that six to ten inches of rain fell within twenty-four hours, and it continued into the following day. Friday the thirty-first, Barney McKenna was scheduled to attend an evening political meeting in Allegheny City. Sitting at supper, Mary voiced her concerns to her always easygoing husband.

"Bernard, must you go out on such a dreadful night? The rain has fallen in sheets all day. You will be soaked in minutes! Can't this meeting proceed without you?"

Barney put down his tea cup. He longed to light up a cigar after supper. But he had long ago surrendered to his wife the concession of no cigar-smoking in the house. His mind raced. Mary's right, it is an ugly night. Still, if I go out, a smoke might be had.

He folded his napkin and rose from the table. "I really should attend, dear. The Democratic Club in Allegheny has issued a rare and kindly personal invitation. If I don't show up, they will take it as an affront, I'm sure. I will take a closed carriage and wear my overcoat."

"Take an umbrella as well, if you really must go. I just hope you don't come down with something."

Barney left home at 6:45 p.m. Despite the overcast skies, there was lingering daylight at that hour. As his carriage ventured across the Sixth Street Bridge, he noticed how high the river was running, and flooding of low-lying areas.

Up in Cambria County, hills that had been logged aggressively were unable able to absorb the run-off of storm water. Trees, telegraph poles, and tons of debris were swept down the valley in a deluge, washing out rail lines and overflowing creek banks. That morning, Elias Unger, president of the South Fork Club, awoke to find their lake-reservoir nearly overflowing. Spillways, having been fitted with fish screens, were clogged with storm debris and unable to provide relief. Clearing the spillways was attempted, but with little effect. The lake continued to fill and threatened to crest the top of the dam.

Unger dispatched the club engineer, John Parke, on horseback to the village of South Fork to telegraph warnings to downstream communities. But the villagers, having experienced years of repeated warnings of the dam's vulnerability, were skeptical and neglected to transmit the warnings. At 1:30 p.m. Unger and his volunteers were exhausted and recognized that their efforts were useless. At 3:10 p.m. the dam collapsed, sending forth nearly five trillion gallons of water in a wall thirty-five feet high. It roared down the Conemaugh valley towards the city of Johnstown, some fourteen miles distant. Consumed in the path of this deluge were houses, barns, railroad cars, tracks, and ties, wild and domestic animals, trees, shrubs, mud and, yes, humans. At forty miles per hour, it took only fifty-seven minutes for the wall of water to reach and crush Johnstown.

Early that morning, Robert Pitcairn, the superintendant of the Western Division of the Pennsylvania Railroad, had left Pittsburgh on an east-bound passenger train. He wanted to inspect for possible storm damage to rail property. Pitcairn still held the same position he had occupied during the 1877 Railroad Riot. Many Pittsburghers still blamed him and his employers for the resultant destruction of life and property.

Pitcairn was well-situated in his private rail car as he traveled through the flooded countryside. In the driving rain, he proceeded only as far as the village of Sang Hollow, about four miles down-river from Johnstown. He arrived there about 4:05 p.m. A railroad telegrapher dressed in slicker and rubber boots entered the car. He stood there dripping until Pitcairn looked up from his paperwork.

"Beg your pardon, sir. We've lost much of our wires and have no contact with points east."

"Yes, I'm not surprised . . . . Guess I'll proceed to Johnstown and continue my inspections in the morning." Pitcairn rose to go speak with the conductor.

"May I suggest, sir . . ." The telegrapher nervously fingered the brim of the rain-hat held at his side. "The way to Johnstown now is very poor. It may be washed out entirely in sections. Even to proceed on foot seems rather treacherous."

"Hmmm . . . . Let's go have a look at the river." Pitcairn reached for his own rain-gear and the two of them marched from the rail-yard to the edge of the Conemaugh. Clusters of spectators had already taken up positions to observe the rising torrent. As they stood in the downpour, the roar of rushing waters filled their ears. Pitcairn peered through the gray, misty atmosphere. Suddenly he noticed there was considerable debris in the river where there had been very little, moments before.

Robert Pitcairn

"My God, those are telegraph poles!" The Superintendant nervously paced along the riverbank, his telegrapher trailing behind. Someone shouted and a man appeared in the river, clinging to a pile of debris. Soon more persons were sighted, men, women, and children rushing by, hanging onto poles, branches, and the remnants of smashed buildings. They were carried by so quickly that bystanders were largely unable to effect a rescue.

"Come with me!" Pitcairn barked at his employee. "I need to send a telegram back to Pittsburgh!"

His message addressed the editors of the city newspapers. He reported a disaster of unknown proportions. Being a member of the South Fork Fishing and Hunting Club himself, he suspected that the South Fork dam had failed. He ordered his train to back down to the village of New Florence where passengers might find accommodation for the night. There he waited. At ten o'clock, a message was received from Sang Hollow. One of his railroad employees from Johnstown had made his way to Sang Hollow on foot. He reported that the city was "literally wiped out."

Pitcairn now sent a second telegram to Pittsburgh proposing a public meeting be arranged for the next day to organize efforts of relief. Food, clothing, temporary shelters, coffins, and undertakers would be needed in great quantity. The materiel, he promised, the railroad would carry to the site at no charge, as soon as the way could be cleared. Shortly after 4:00 a.m. Saturday morning, he began his return to Pittsburgh, where he felt he could be of greater use to the relief effort.

Mayors McCallin of Pittsburgh and Pearson of Allegheny City quickly had their communities bedecked with placards announcing the disaster and calling a public meeting of response. It was set for 1:00 p.m. the same day, June 1st. Barney and Charles McKenna, having seen the posted announcement, encountered each other at the Old City Hall.

"Hello, Brother," Charles began somberly. "I'm afraid this is a very bad situation. Have you seen the river? It's full of debris!"

"Not today. Last night the Allegheny was in flood, but I saw no signs of wreckage. Jim Flannery tells me the dead may be a thousand or more . . . . God have mercy!"

Charles looked anxiously into the rapidly filling hall. "Let's get in and claim a seat. There is already quite a crowd." Once inside, he shared further. "I spoke this morning with my friend,

the reporter Jimmie O'Neill. He told me that eye-witness reports
confirm that Johnstown and several down-stream communities
have been devastated. There are dead everywhere. Survivors are
clinging to the hillsides . . . with little or no clothing, food, or
shelter."

Barney was about to reply when the meeting was called to
order. It began with an impassioned description of conditions
by Pitcairn. The superintendant hadn't slept for nearly thirty-six
hours. He was haggard, despite a change into fresh attire. Though
he was brief, he conveyed the horror he had personally witnessed
or that had been reported to him. The crowd was hushed in rapt
attention, astounded at the scale of destruction.

"In the center of Johnstown," he concluded, "there is a stone
railroad bridge. A great mass of debris is stuck against its pillars.
Somehow, the resulting tangle has caught fire. The smell of
burning flesh, animal and human, fills the air . . . . Now is not the
time for lengthy speeches. We must undertake immediate action to
save survivors and recover the deceased."

The assembly quickly agreed upon the appointment of an
Executive Committee of Relief. Then, Mayor McCallin issued
an appeal for contributions of funds and materiel. The over-
crowded hall promptly erupted in shouts of pledged support. The
prominent banker W.R. Thompson immediately began functioning
as committee treasurer. But he was quickly overwhelmed with
proffered cash, and bank drafts. He called for assistance in
handling the onslaught. McCallin and his successor-to-be, Henry
Gourley, joined in receiving and recording the donated funds.
After fifty minutes of bedlam, they determined they had received
$48,116.70.

The next day, Sunday, church collections aimed at flood relief
netted an additional $25,000. The local chapter of the Grand Army
of the Republic, at the urging of Charles McKenna and others,
collected nearly $2000. Across the nation, citizens of large cities
and small towns sent contributions to the relief committee that

eventually totaled over $800,000. This was in addition to similar donations directed to Pennsylvania's governor.

Ring boss William Flinn was prominent in quickly organizing physical relief efforts in Johnstown. Drawing upon his construction company, he directed an army of laborers, wagons, horses, and mules to the recovery of the dead and the clearing of debris. His assembled force of fifteen hundred employees and volunteers accomplished great feats in restoring a semblance of physical order in the first weeks.

Johnstown, Pennsylvania after The Flood
(Library of Congress)

Barney McKenna later observed to his friend, Bill Brennen, "I've never had much regard for Bill Flinn. But his work at Johnstown has caused me to reconsider."

"Some days a saint, some days a sinner. Just like the rest of us, I'm thinking," Brennen replied.

The Flannery brothers, close political allies of Barney, organized the efforts of the undertaker community. They deployed fifty-five members to wash, embalm, and prepare for burial many of the 2,209 victims. Some Pittsburgh businesses closed their doors to allow their employees to join the ranks of volunteers working in the affected communities. Henry Clay Frick was active on the relief committee and donated substantial personal sums as well. In time, Andrew Carnegie would replace the destroyed public library in Johnstown.

Though various members of the South Fork Fishing and Hunting Club were active with the relief committee, questions quickly surfaced about possible negligence regarding the integrity and maintenance of the South Fork dam. It was generally agreed that the tragedy was triggered by an act of nature. But the foreknowledge of problems with the dam by the club officers prompted an eventual law suit. A defense team of Philander Knox and James Reed, both members of the South Fork Club, argued that there was no negligent party. Further, the club assets were minimal. Each member's property was separate from club holdings. These facts and the close relations between members of the business elite and the local judiciary resulted in the failure to hold anyone to account.

Barney complained bitterly to Charles after the suit failed. "You're a lawyer, Brother. Tell me how it is that such a failure of justice can occur. These tycoons live in a protected world of their own. If it was laboring men, they'd be off to jail in no time!"

Charles chuckled at his brother's angst. "You dispense an informal brand of justice as a police magistrate, Barney. But in a proper court room, the law is the law. It may be crafted to advantage the few; it may not produce what we would recognize as a just result. But the remedy, if one exists, lies in the hands of the legislature."

Barney cast his glance to heaven. "Oh, the legislature! You mean the one that is bought and paid for by these same industrial bosses? Jaysus, Charles! . . . You may be right, but you offer no comfort! The widowed, the orphans, the dispossessed of Johnstown are left to merciful charity? 'Tis a rotten system, you must agree!"

Charles raised his palms in a defensive gesture. "Look, Barney, I don't like it any better than you. The politics of our state are, indeed, corrupted by the influence of rich and powerful private interests. It is, however, the only system we've got, so it's up to politicians like yourself to try to fix it."

Barney stabbed out the dying cigar he had been nursing. "Would that I could do so, Brother."

Chapter Sixteen

If conditions were grim at home for the laboring class, they had gotten even worse on the job. Throughout America, but particularly in Pittsburgh, the nature and conditions of work had changed radically since the Civil War years. Previously, industry was largely conducted in small workshops and factories. The workers were often skilled in industrial arts through which they assured the quality and pace of output. A prime example was the large cadre of iron puddlers who transformed pig iron into malleable metal (wrought iron) through a process controlled by years of experience and practiced judgment. They had their difficulties with their employers over wages and working conditions but, as they were not easily replaced, they could exercise considerable bargaining power when united in labor organizations like the Sons of Vulcan.

However, there were changes afoot that would disrupt the balance between labor and capital. Essentially, these changes were three dramatic departures in how industry was conducted. The first of these was the unflagging pursuit of new and improved technologies whereby better products could be produced faster, cheaper, and in greater volume. In Pittsburgh, this change was exemplified by the adoption of the Bessemer process and open-hearth furnaces for making malleable metal (steel) from iron, without the low-scale, high art of puddling. The effect of these technologies, together with improved work space and work flow design, had the effect of tripling output. The second major change was the re-design of work, breaking the production process down into many simple, repetitive, and specialized tasks that could easily be taught to unskilled, often illiterate, laborers. These single-task-focused workers, unlike their puddler predecessors, could be fired, killed or injured, and replaced overnight. As such, their ability to bargain effectively for wages and working conditions was greatly reduced.

The third great change was the rise of a class of hired managers who now controlled the design, pace, quality and cost of production. Often schooled in engineering and/or cost accounting, they had the responsibility of increasing profitability and the scale of operations for the benefit of investor-owners who were uninvolved in the day-to-day business.

Capital came to view its workers not as partners in enterprise, but as expendable cogs in a great machine, elements of cost to be minimized, and, when organized in unions, as the enemies of progress in society. The "sacred" and unfettered rights of property and the accumulation of wealth, they thought, ought to reign supreme over any imagined rights of labor. As the Secretary of Carnegie Steel, Francis Lovejoy, stated it:

> *"Well, a man's work is worth just what he can get for it, . . . If there is something that only one man can do, he is sure to get big money for it, but if a hundred can do it just as well, he will not get any more than what someone else is willing to do it for."*

Meanwhile, laboring men saw themselves as free and independent agents who contributed their labor subject to a living wage, a reasonably safe work environment, and without the surrender of their dignity and individual worth. While they could no longer control how work would be organized, they believed that, when joined in union with their fellows, they could and should be allowed to bargain with their employers in a fair and balanced relationship of mutual advantage.

Regrettably, these disparate points of view between labor and capital were never reconciled in an open-minded, mutual consideration. Each party stood apart from their opponent, unable to see opportunities for bridging the gap. Between 1867 and 1875, Pittsburgh's metalworkers engaged in sixty-nine strikes, some of these being triggered by employers imposing reduced wages or reductions in force (as did the Pennsylvania Railroad in 1877). These strikes were won, lost or compromised in roughly equal proportions. In 1875, the Sons of Vulcan and several lesser metalworker unions combined themselves into a single national labor organization, the Amalgamated Association of Iron and Steel Workers (AAISW). Over the next ten years, there were ninety-three metalworker strikes in Pittsburgh. Only a third or so were won by workers or compromised. Most were lost. The changes described above were having their impact felt.

* *

By 1891, AAISW membership had peaked at 24,000 and a show-down was looming between the union and Andrew Carnegie's steel company. Its profit-focused company president, Henry Clay Frick, had been engaged in coke (a form of distilled bituminous coal used to fire steel furnaces) operations in southwestern Pennsylvania and, as such, was a major supplier to the Pittsburgh steel mills. Bitterly anti-union, Frick joined Carnegie Steel with a determination to free the company from any influence of organized labor. The company's principal mills were the Edgar Thompson Works in Braddock, the Duquesne Works, and the Homestead Works. All three mills were located along the Monongahela River just upstream from Pittsburgh. All three had a history of unionized labor, though Frick had broken the union at Edgar Thomson in 1888, cut wages, and re-imposed the twelve hour work day after nearly ten years of eight-hour shifts. Though Carnegie himself often publicly asserted his acceptance of labor's right to organize and bargain for terms of employment, his private views were betrayed by the actions he authorized and Frick gleefully carried out.

Henry Clay Frick, President of Carnegie Steel
(Penn State University Library)

In 1889, Carnegie had attempted to impose a new wage scale at the Homestead Works that would effectively reduce wages by 25% or more, depending upon job category. When the workers, acting through the AAISW, rejected the proposal, Carnegie imposed a lockout, closed the mill, and imported a trainload of black, Italian, and East European scabs to replace the striking workers. The citizens of Homestead and the workers, constituting a crowd of three thousand or so, precipitated a stand-off. They refused the replacements entry to the mill. They also blocked access by County Sheriff Alexander McCandless and 125 of his deputies. A twenty minute silent impasse was finally broken when a deputy ripped off his badge, threw it and his revolver to the ground, and announced he was going home. Soon other deputies followed his lead. By late afternoon, the deputies and the scabs had returned to Pittsburgh by train. Negotiations between Carnegie's managers and the union were resumed and a compromise settlement was reached in the form of a three-year contract. Though a sliding scale of reduced wages was imposed, the role of the union in bargaining and in filling vacancies with its members was enshrined in the agreement. Normal operations and relative peace were restored, for the time being.

* *

In late June 1892, Barney McKenna and his Democratic cronies were gathering at "The Steps" in their customary council on all things political. It was a pleasant Monday evening; the days were lengthening and the warmth of approaching summer proved comfortable for such outdoor gatherings. The regulars began to arrive, Boley Mullen and First Ward alderman Stephen Toole being the first. Then Barney showed up in the company of Mike Feeney and John Sweeney, his replacement as alderman in the Fourth Ward. While Barney lit up a fresh cigar, the conversation focused mostly on the current prospects for the Pittsburgh Pirates baseball team. Barney had become a keen fan of the game and of Pittsburgh's five-year-old franchise. The team had had a losing season the previous year, but there was optimism that this season would be different.

Just then, Bill Brennen came rushing down the street, visibly agitated. Sensing that something was amiss, everyone suspended their discussion of the Pirates. There were real pirates to contend with, Brennen would assert.

"That bugger Frick has flyers posted all over Homestead! It's '89 all over again. The company will no longer contract with the union! Take it or leave it contracts with individual workers only! Wages are to be reduced by 10% to 30% for those paid by the tonnage produced."

Barney's expression turned grave as he absorbed the news. "I recall that Carnegie and Frick prevailed upon the Congress to raise the tariff on every steel product imported, except the four-inch billet. That's the product that they now use to calculate the wage scale. For that product only, the tariff has been removed, causing its price to fall, and thus the wages as well."

Boley Mullen snickered, "You fellows ought not be surprised that trouble is on its way! The company put up ten-foot fences

241

around Homestead Works, with barbed wire atop and gun ports! Fort Frick the men are calling it."

Brennen took a seat and paused to catch his breath. Then he ruefully answered the dig. "Aye, we knew there'd be trouble. Still, when you see it raise its ugly head . . ."

Barney turned to Brennen. "So Bill, the current contract expires on the last of the month. If the company will talk no more, it'll mean a lock-out. Scabs will be brought in, like last time."

Brennen stood and gave a snort of dismissal. "Ah, but the people of Homestead are as one! They'll hold the works like they did last time, even at the cost of their lives . . . . Barney, you must have a word with Chris Magee? He may be the only man who can head off the violence that's sure to come."

"I'd be willing, but I'm not sure he'd agree. What do you think, Mike? You're closer to Chris than I am."

Mike Feeney was William Flinn's right hand and could speak with some credibility on what might attract the support of his boss and Chris Magee.

"You boys are dreaming," Feeney replied. "Magee and Carnegie—ah, they're grand friends. As for Frick, he and Magee are partners in business. It isn't likely that he will cross Frick's plans for Homestead."

"I suspected as much," Barney muttered. "The workers caught management off guard the last time. Frick will not allow that mistake to be repeated. Bill, tell your union friends they must be prepared. It will go badly, I'm afraid."

Though Barney's prediction would prove correct, he needn't have worried about the precautions being undertaken by the AAISW and the citizens of Homestead. The union's Advisory Committee at Homestead was headed by Hugh O'Donnell, the leader of the successful strike of '89. A military-style plan of defense was developed. It included seizure of the works upon its July 1st closure, pickets at key positions, river patrols, and a system of warning signals to sound the alert in the event of approaching danger. They would need every bit of that. Frick was secretly busy contracting with the

Pinkerton National Detective Agency for a private army. It would consist of three hundred men—forty regular Pinkerton employees and the rest thugs recruited in Chicago, Philadelphia and New York.

On July 1st, the contract expired and a lock-out began. The workers took control immediately and, for four days, things were quiet. Then, on July 5th, the new County Sheriff, William H. McCleary, and two deputies visited the Advisory Committee at their improvised command post in the town of Homestead. The Committee conducted the sheriff around the works to demonstrate that all was peaceful and that private property was being protected. They even offered to supply deputized guards, though McCleary declined the offer. He did, however, pronounce himself satisfied that peace and order were being maintained. He promised to dispatch a small force of deputies to Homestead later in the day.

After a private caucus, O'Donnell announced the dissolution of the Advisory Committee. He told McCleary, "We'll assume no responsibility for the consequences if there be violence provoked by company action." With that, committee members removed their badges and burned them, along with their committee documents.

Hugh O'Donnell, AAISW Advisory Committee Leader
(Battle of Homestead Foundation)

At 10:30 p.m. that night McCleary, Chief Deputy Sheriff Joseph Gray, and Homestead Works Superintendent John Potter met the Pinkerton army as they arrived by rail in Bellevue, about five miles below Pittsburgh on the Ohio River. Waiting for them were two specially equipped barges—*Iron Mountain*, configured as a dormitory, and *Monongahela*, furnished as a kitchen and dining facility with twenty waiters. A river tug, *Little Bill*, would propel them upriver to the landing wharf at the Homestead mill. The leader of the Pinkerton force, forty-two-year-old Frederick Heinde, ushered his men aboard the barges along with cases of uniforms, ammunition, three hundred pistols, billy clubs, and two-hundred-fifty Winchester rifles. Under cover of night, the flotilla proceeded upriver. At 2:30 a.m., as they passed under the Smithfield Bridge, a union scout recognized the invasion force and telegraphed a warning to AAISW leaders in Homestead.

Before Heinde and his forces could reach Homestead, the union steam launch *Edna* approached the flotilla, fired several warning shots, and blew its steam whistle as further warning to the town and defenders inside the mill. Thousands of men, women, and children poured from the town, many armed, but most not. Mrs. Margaret Finch, widow of a steelworker and proprietress of the Rolling Mill Saloon, charged through the streets toward the mill carrying a club and shouting, "Let me get at 'em, the dirty black sheep!"

As *Little Bill* approached the landing at the bottom of a steep grade below the mill, shots rang out from a pump house and water storage tower some twenty-five feet above. Though Hugh O'Donnell and his committee men urgently cautioned the armed workers and town's people against violence, their pleas would be largely ignored by the incensed crowd.

Heinde showed himself at the head of a gang plank and announced, "We are coming ashore, . . . there are three hundred men behind me and you cannot stop us."

He was immediately confronted by Billy Foy, a town's man and Salvation Army member. "If you come, you'll come over my carcass," he responded.

With that, Heinde struck at Foy's head with a cane. Two gun shots followed immediately and both Heinde and Foy fell wounded. Then the Pinkerton men opened fire from the port holes of their barges, killing three steelworkers. They found a prompt reply, however, from armed defenders above the landing. Quickly *Little Bill* left the barges and conveyed Heinde and five other wounded Pinkertons across the river to Port Perry for medical attention. About 10:30 a.m. the river tug returned to rescue the two barges and their passengers, but a hail of gunfire prompted the abandonment of that mission.

In the meantime, Sheriff McCleary had gone into consultations with "Bosses" Chris Magee and William Flinn. The lawman was acutely aware that he owed his political career to these men. And yet he was reluctant to undertake operations that would turn working class voters against him. While this meeting was in progress, William Weihe, National President of the AAISW, rushed in to seek the politicians' intervention to avoid further bloodshed.

"You must prevail upon Mr. Frick to meet with a workers' delegation," he pleaded. But a flat rejection came back promptly from Frick. As Secretary Lovejoy stated to the press, there would be no "interference" by the company. "Our works," he said, "are now in the hands of the Sheriff."

By late morning, McCleary was desperate. The exchange of gunfire at Homestead was nearly continuous. Numerous mob efforts to torch the barges had, so far, proven unsuccessful. But the Pinkerton army was bottled up, without hope or medical attention. The sheriff, realizing that he was out-gunned and out-manned, telegraphed Pennsylvania Governor Robert Pattison requesting assistance and instructions. The governor's reply reflected the same political ambivalence that the sheriff himself felt. Pattison, a Democrat, was deeply indebted to Magee and Flinn for swinging the Pittsburgh vote towards him in the last election. (Magee had done so to spite his rival, Matthew Quay.) Yet the governor also wished to avoid alienating much of the electorate by a precipitous retrieval of Carnegie's chestnuts from the fires of labor unrest. His telegram of response read: "Local authorities must exhaust every means at their command for preservation of peace." Several more messages were sent by McCleary through the day, requesting a large force to meet the emergency. They were met with requests from Pattison for evidence of a good-faith, local effort.

Magee and McCleary suggested that Weihe attempt to negotiate the release of the Pinkerton force on the promise that they would leave peacefully, never to return. This he consented to do. It was late afternoon when he arrived at Homestead. He found the mill further reinforced by sympathizing steelworkers from the Edgar Thomson and Duquesne Works. When he put his proposition to the crowd, he was hooted down. Ultimately, however, the strikers and townspeople did respond to a white flag of surrender raised by the trapped Pinkerton force. Each Pinkerton agent, now unarmed, was assigned a steelworker escort and marched up the bank, through the mill yard, and towards the town.

Before they had proceeded very far, however, the angry crowd, emotionally overwrought by the loss of their killed and wounded, surged forward forming a gauntlet of two parallel lines about six hundred yards long. All along this path, Frick's hired vigilantes were subjected to spitting, cursing, kicks, and blows from fists or clubs. Their worker escorts tried, but proved unable, to protect them until they turned their weapons upon the crowd. Eventually, the captives made it to a temporary jail in the town's opera house. The celebrating mob now turned their attention to the barges on the riverbank. These were promptly burned to the waterline. About 6:15 p.m., "Honest John" McLuckie, a long-time labor leader and now Homestead town burgess, restored a semblance of order by promising the mob that the Pinkertons would be arrested and prosecuted for murder and aggravated assault.

Pinkerton barges burning at the Homestead Steel Works, July 6, 1892
(cargocollective.com)

Later that evening Bill Brennen, acting as legal counsel to the AAISW, joined Chris Magee, William Flinn, Sheriff McCleary, and William Weihe for a private dinner to discuss how to obtain the release of the Pinkertons from their captors. They then boarded a late train and traveled to Homestead, arriving about 12:30 on the morning of July 7th. Without explicitly accepting McLuckie's terms of release, they took custody of the Pinkertons and escorted them to a train bound for Pittsburgh. Only later the next day did the Homestead workers discover that the promise of charging and prosecuting the Pinkerton agents had been abrogated by the civil authorities.

The following Saturday, Bill Brennen convened a meeting of the Democratic Committee of Allegheny County. They unanimously adopted a resolution of support for the workers at Homestead and commended their efforts to "resist pauper wages." During the meeting many members expressed surprise that the Pinkerton agents had got off scot-free. They got put on another train and shipped out of the city. In reply Brennen admitted, "I didn't like it a bit; but what could I do? There was no way to resist the logic of it. How in God's name were we to distinguish between real murderers and the many innocent agents holed up in those barges? No court would take on such a case!"

The whole nation was watching events at Homestead. The national press was largely shocked and outraged by the use of the Pinkerton army. Reached at his vacation lodge in Scotland, Andrew Carnegie publicly deplored the violence, but he avoided speaking to the merits of the conflict. Yet he displayed his real feelings in a telegram to Frick. "All anxiety gone since you stand firm. Never employ one of these rioters! Let grass grow over works. Must not fail now."

Four days of mourning and funeral processions ensued at Homestead as they buried their nine dead and nursed their eleven wounded. Though still held by the strikers, the Homestead Works and town returned to relative peace and order. A delegation of AAISW leaders traveled to Harrisburg to assure Governor Pattison that law and order did not require his dispatch of state militia forces to Homestead. The governor pronounced himself skeptical, and there is reason to believe that he felt ultimately bound to respond to the Ring and its leaders Magee and Flinn. The union leaders pledged that, if the militia did arrive, there would be no resistance. At 9:00 a.m. on July 12th, more than 4,000 soldiers surrounded the Homestead Works. They quickly displaced the steelworker guards. Within a few days, Frick began to bring in strikebreakers recruited across the country. Many of these were blacks, which sowed the seeds of racial strife that would last for decades. By July 15th steel-making resumed on a limited basis.

Throughout the lockout and work stoppage, a great swell of public support for the striking workers was expressed, in Pittsburgh and elsewhere. Sympathy strikes broke out at Carnegie's Lawrenceville, Duquesne, and Beaver Falls steel mills. Contributions to the AAISW strike fund flowed generously into Homestead from donors across the country. Even members of Congress took to the floor to denounce the use of a private army to force men to choose between starvation wages or replacement by non-union recruits. However on July 23rd, an anarchist from New York named Alexander Berkman arrived in Pittsburgh and gained entry into the offices of Henry Clay Frick. Though Berkman had no association with the AAISW or the striking workers, he was bent upon the assassination of Frick. He shot and stabbed his quarry, but failed to deal a mortal wound. Frick recovered within a couple of weeks. But the attack had the result of turning public sentiment against the union.

As this shift in popular opinion became clear, Barney joined Bill Brennen over drinks at Dwyer's, a pub near Brennen's Wylie Avenue home. Choosing a relatively quiet table in a back corner, the magistrate ordered his usual—coffee, Brennen, a beer.

"Bill, it's so like what happened after the Pennsy riots of '77. It's always the excesses of the mob, or in this case a lunatic assassin, that tars the labor movement unfairly."

Brennen peered through his wire-rimmed spectacles, his beer glass raised to his lips. "Too true, my friend! I thought the union leaders at Homestead bent over backwards to protect life and property, to ensure law and order in the mill. But the press always loses sight of such when there's a more sensational story to tell."

Barney fumed a moment and then exploded. "It just galls me that the Republican machine has been bought and paid for by Carnegie and Frick. Even the Chief Justice of our state Supreme Court has conspired with Magee and the Carnegie attorneys. He would wrest control of these cases from our local courts. They have filed trumped-up charges against individual strikers. Murder! Riot! Even treason! Jesus, Mary, and Joseph, save us from such perversion of justice!"

Brennen winked to cool his friend's passions. "You sound just the same as you did after the Johnstown flood. Maybe you should run for office again."

"Ach, Bill, like you? Running for office every whipstitch and losing every time!"

Brennen jerked his head back, feigning outrage at insult. "I did get elected alderman, mind you! And wasn't it myself that served on the City Common Council?"

Barney laughed, admitting, "Right, you did win those; but you lost a lot of races. Anyway, I had my turn five years ago. Besides, I like being a magistrate."

"So, you don't really care to oppose the Ring. You'd rather bemoan injustice than attack it head on!"

Barney repressed an oath as a waiter stopped to freshen his coffee. Coffee now hot and emotion cooled, he responded. "Be careful there, counselor. I will do my part. You and my brother, attorneys both, sound the same tune. Great with advice for others!"

Brennan placed his hand on Barney's arm. "Now be serious, Barney, as I am now. I can't run! I'm the legal face of over a half-dozen unions in this town. That alone seals my defeat. But you could do it! You're known and respected in every ward. If you really want to push back against the likes of Magee and Flinn, this is your chance! . . . I happen to think you can win. So buck up and do it! You'll have the support of the entire Democratic Committee. I can promise that."

Barney mused silently for a moment, toying with his unlit cigar. Finally, he retorted, "By all that is holy, I just might! . . . I must talk it through with Mary. But, I might give it another try."

Brennen raised his beer in a toast. "To Your Honor!" They both laughed heartily.

Beginning in November, charges were brought against the entire AAISW Advisory Committee and numerous individual steelworkers at Homestead. The first of these was a murder charge against a striker named Sylvester Critchlow. The District Attorney for Allegheny County, Clarence Burleigh, headed a legal team for the prosecution that included at least two attorneys on the payroll of Carnegie Steel. The defense team included, among others, Bill Brennen and Edward A. Montooth, the former adjutant of Charles McKenna's 155th Pennsylvania Volunteers. The testimony from various Pinkerton agents was questionable, and Critchlow had a nearly air-tight alibi. The jury brought in a "Not Guilty" verdict after only a hour's deliberation. Two subsequent trials, of steelworker Jack Clifford and Hugh O'Donnell, on the same charge of murder produced the same result.

Recognizing that an Allegheny County jury would not convict any of the accused, Carnegie's legal henchmen agreed to drop all further charges in return for the abandonment of lawsuits leveled at Frick, Potter, Heinde, and other Carnegie and Pinkerton protagonists.

The strike was defeated, despite sporadic violence against scab labor at Homestead. It was now clear that steelworkers had to choose between destitution and re-applying for their old jobs—jobs without a contract or their former rates of pay. Initially, only 800 of the 3,800 strikers were rehired. But Charles M. Schwab, a new superintendant at Homestead, valued the experience and skill of displaced strikers. He gradually dismissed unreliable scabs and brought back many of the former employees.

In the end, Frick had crushed the AAISW. The steelworkers would be without representation for nearly forty years. But, the result was the loss of active participation and partnering of labor with their managers on the shop floor. Loyalty to the company and initiative from workers to improve production was extinguished. Further, the drastic reductions in wages reduced the economic incentive for management to invest in further technological innovations. These set-backs would only become apparent over time. For now, Frick and his colleagues basked in their triumph.

Chapter Seventeen

There was a bit of a tailing, political wind for the Democrats as 1893 dawned. Grover Cleveland had just been elected to his second, albeit not consecutive, term as President of the United States. And there was considerable optimism for the Democrats locally. On January 9th the local party gathered in nominating convention for city offices. Bill Brennen, still the long-time party chairman, was successful in smoothing the way for his preferred candidate for mayor. Jacob J. Miller, principal of the public schools in the Eighteenth Ward, gave a stirring speech describing the Democratic cause as a noble crusade against corruption and influence-peddling by the Ring. The vote went well for Barney McKenna.

In his acceptance speech and throughout the campaign, Barney hammered the issue of the rapid rise in city expenditures for public improvements. Per capita expenditures had risen from $8.53 to $14.36. These costs, he asserted, were heavily driven by contracts awarded to Ring supporters. Republican political leaders had bought up large tracts of suburban land in advance. The streets in these districts all required paving and sewers—"luxuries" woefully lacking in city center neighborhoods. Of course, William Flinn's construction company usually received the contracts for such infrastructure.

Further, franchises for street-car lines had been constantly awarded for service in these outlying areas of the city. Chris Magee's Consolidated Traction Company was awarded many of those franchises, and paid artificially low rates of taxation on his company property.

Feeling threatened by such public criticism, the Republican machine undertook a campaign of character assassination against McKenna. Fortunately, Barney was blessed by a reputation for fairness and integrity which "nearly immunized" him to such baseless attacks. His Republican opponent, John S. Lambie, proved to be a bit lackluster as a campaigner. Though reputable and judged personally honest, it was expected that he would turn a blind eye towards the plundering of others. The election was held on February 21st and Barney polled 15,497 votes to Lambie's 14,117. McKenna had overcome the strength of the Republican machine and several minor candidates as well.

A celebration at 817 Penn Avenue on the evening of February 22nd was a joyous affair. Well-wishing neighbors, brothers and sister, political allies, and hangers-on, all crowded into the family residence. Mary received great assistance in providing hospitality from nineteen-year-old daughter Catherine and fifteen-year-old son Frank. A beaming Charles McKenna, and wife Virginia, arrived with a retinue of friends from the legal profession, at least those who were Democrats.

Early in the evening, Bill Brennen pulled Barney aside. His face glowed with enthusiasm and the effects of some earlier celebrating. "I told you, didn't I? You had it in you all the time. You just needed a good kick in the pants to get you started!"

Barney laughed and shook his hand. "I give all the credit to you, counselor. But now the hard part begins. Magee and his cronies still hold the councils, the department heads, and the controller's office. That's where all the power over spending resides. My title exceeds my powers of office, as you well know."

"Yes, of course," Brennen retorted. "But we won't leave you to wage the fight alone. The first thing we need to do is attack the city charter. It must be reformed!"

Just then, Mary approached the two of them. Behind her trailed ten-year-old son Bill, for whom the festivities represented an unaccustomed adventure. "I'll be wanting my husband back now, Mr. Brennen," she announced. "Everyone's asking for a few words from the mayor-elect."

Brennen pecked her on the cheek and placed his hand on Bill's shoulder. "You must feel very proud of your father, William. 'Tis a grand victory he has won."

The boy nodded with a grin, but his mother was ready with a response. "Of course, we're proud of Bernard—but we always have been. Just between us, Mr. Brennen, I'm having my fill of politics and cigar smoke at the moment."

The guests crowded all around clapping and cheering. "A kiss for the mayor," someone shouted. Presently, the demand spread throughout the assembly.

Laughing, Mary turned and gave her husband an embrace and prolonged kiss, to the great amusement and pleasure of the crowd.

"Speech! Speech!" they cried.

Barney took to the staircase and climbed a few steps to show himself more readily to those at the back of the room. Naturally a modest personality, he sheepishly complied. "Well, just a few words, then . . . . First, a special thanks to my lovely wife and family. And a grand measure of thanks to all my friends and supporters." He paused for a moment to gather his thoughts. "You all may have seen the audacious headline in today's Pittsburgh Post." The crowd laughed and cheered.

"If I recall correctly it read, *'The Day of Reckoning; Defeat of the Ring Ticket by Uprising of the People.'* Sounds mighty grand, doesn't it? And I guess it is, somewhat. For the first time in decades, the voters have made it clear they have had enough of bossism and corruption at city hall. But it's what happens next, once we're in office, that will tell the real story. I promise to give my total energies in serving the people of our fair city. But the adherents of the Ring will not be easily tamed. In that, I most assuredly need your help . . . and your prayers. God bless you all."

More cheers and good wishes followed. The festivities lasted well into the night. Mary went off to bed well beforehand. Barney finally closed the door on the last-departing guests well after midnight. As he slowly climbed the stairs, he pondered. I wish Mother and Da could have seen this day. I like to think they'd be proud.

* *

The first appointment Barney made upon his April 3rd inauguration was given to former mayor William McCallin. Returning a favor of six years prior, he gave McCallin the office of police magistrate in the Twelfth Ward that he now relinquished.

Throughout his time as mayor, Barney maintained his love of baseball and his support for the Pittsburgh Pirates. When the pressures of his office were sufficiently light, he could often be found at the ballpark of an afternoon. Early in his tenure as mayor, Barney was presiding over the usual gathering at "The Steps." Most of the attendees were regulars, but on this evening a newcomer appeared.

Barney removed his ever-present cigar and spoke to the stranger. "Welcome friend. Would you like to introduce yourself to the group?"

The handsome young man with piercing blue eyes stepped forward shyly. "My name is Patrick Donovan. I'm new to your city and after tryin' to figure out the politics of the place. I was told this is a good place for such schoolin'."

Bill Brennen offered his hand. "Welcome to Pittsburgh. Your accent suggests you're from the land of our fathers."

"I guess that depends upon where your fathers came from . . . . I was born in Cobh, which the Brits call Queenstown, in County Cork. But I've . . . ."

Suddenly, Barney stood up and approached. "Say, I know you! You're an outfielder for the Pirates. You're Patsy Donovan!"

Murmurs of name recognition swept through the group. "That I am, Mr . . . . ?"

"McKenna, Barney McKenna."

Boley Mullen corrected. "That's Mayor McKenna, actually. And a grand supporter of the Pirates, he is."

"Well, we can use all of them we can get . . . . A pleasure to meet you, your Honor."

"Ah, but the pleasure is all mine. We'll give you all you want of politics. You just give us another winning season."

In time, Barney developed a great friendship with the twenty-eight-year-old right fielder, who would go on to an impressive career with the Pirates, as player and player-manager. In 1899, he was traded to St. Louis where he would play and then manage for the Cardinals. He held this position later with the Washington Senators, and a predecessor team of the Brooklyn Dodgers. Ultimately, he became a scout and then the manager of the Boston Red Sox. In 1914, he was instrumental in Boston's recruitment of a pitcher named Babe Ruth.

Patrick J. (Patsy) Donovan

As mayor Barney now participated, for the first time, in a military remembrance of the type in which his brother Charles was so active and prominent. In 1894, as Vice-Chairman of the Citizens Executive Board, he issued a formal invitation to the Grand Army of the Republic (GAR) to hold their Twenty-Eighth National Encampment in Pittsburgh. When the great gathering occurred that September, Barney was designated an honorary Commander of the GAR. In that role, he joined the former Union generals in reviewing the grand parade of thousands of Civil War veterans from around the nation. In company columns, they marched through downtown Pittsburgh, across the Sixth Street Bridge and into Allegheny City. As Charles marched along with his comrades from the 155th, he chatted with his good friend and mess-mate, Jimmie O'Neill. The long-time journalist with various Pittsburgh newspapers had retained his whimsical sense of humor. As they passed the review stand, Charles pointed out his older brother, standing at attention and wearing a ceremonial sash over his blue business suit.

"You know, Jimmie, it does my heart good to see Barney up there with all the brass. He always figured he missed out during the war."

O'Neill sputtered in amusement. "Missed out? Was it the menu of stale hardtack and bad coffee? Perhaps it was the opportunity to get shot that he was missing?"

"Oh, you know; he was after serving his country . . . maybe testing himself in battle. Who knows? But it stuck in his craw that his responsibilities at home that prevented all that."

"Well, now he's a commander . . . and you're still a private! I think he might have got the better bargain. Besides, he's a mayor and you . . . well, you know how I feel about lawyers. I'd say things had worked out pretty well for your older brother."

Charles laughed. "I'll ignore that remark about lawyers. Still, it's a grand day for Barney. I hope he views it so."

The next morning Barney delivered the address of welcome to the General Assembly at the Grand Opera House on Fifth Avenue. It was a proud moment for him, but it was made bittersweet by the knowledge that Charles was not present to witness it. Conflicting schedules made it thus. Charles' old Company "E" had their own reunion that same day, as did many other units at various venues around the city.

Company "E" Reunion, 1894
Front row left to right—Morgan, McKenna,
Laughlin, Douglas, Pangburn, and Brown
Back row—O'Neill, Eicher, Wall, Evans, Lancaster, and White
Image from "Under the Maltese Cross"

The members of Company "E" gathered at the Monongahela wharf where they boarded the steamer *Katie Stockdale*. Of the one hundred and forty-nine soldiers who spent any time in the company, and the thirty-eight survivors who were at the Grand Review Parade in Washington in 1865, only twelve members were on hand twenty-nine years later. Setting out on a river day-trip, they stopped for a picnic lunch at Orchard Grove Park in the upriver town of Duquesne. As they lounged on the lush, green lawn, much reminiscing ensued. Private Robert Douglas was now a distinguished looking fellow with a white mustache and goatee, and showing his years. Sergeant John Lancaster carried his age more easily, though he suffered constantly from his war wounds. Some were dressed in their old uniforms, or the bits that still fit. Others came in civilian attire. Charles McKenna still looked to be in his prime, though his wavy pompadour and beard were now nearly white. He wore his favored Stetson-style hat, giving him his usual flamboyant appearance. Eventually, Lancaster turned to one of the sadder memories. "Do you men recall the night Theo Callen got shot at Bethesda Church?"

Robert Douglas was first to reply. "I sure remember. I was plenty scared that night! Poor Theo, he was just a kid . . . . I wish Isaac Hipsley was here. He was with us that night when we went for the body. Is he still living, does anyone know?"

"He's living somewhere in Ohio," Charles offered. "His poor health has prevented his coming. You'll recall he was wounded later that month near Petersburg. But he refused a medical furlough and stayed in company all the way to Appomattox. Isaac was a soldier's soldier, truly."

Lancaster returned to his subject. "Well anyway, after the war, Theo's father asked me to help him locate the body so he might bring it home. We went down into Virginia, recovered the remains, and brought them up to their village in Westmoreland County. The old man was in deepest sorrow, though he carried it with dignity. You might not know that, just a few months prior, Theo's sister Louisa had died of grief at the loss of her brother. I still have the letter she sent me after Theo's death . . . . Charles, she was mighty grateful for that sketch you drew of Theo's grave at Bethesda Church."

Grave of Theophilus Callen at Bethesda Church
Sketch by Charles F. McKenna

Charles cast his glance off to the river and blinked away a tear. "It wasn't much. I just wanted the family to have something . . . something to show we did our best for their boy."

"Theo's father gave me that sketch during my visit. I still have it at home. Would you want it back?"

Charles gave a dismissive gesture. "Oh, no, John. You must keep it. It should remain with her letter . . . as a remembrance."

Later that night, the Regimental dinner was held at the Banquet Hall at the Monongahela House. Alfred Pearson gave an address honoring the generals under whom the regiment had served. Charles McKenna then gave a similar address recognizing the various officers of the 155th. Memories of the fallen and the absent put a tinge of sadness on a memorable day.

* *

Barney's time as mayor was marked by success and failure. Unfortunately, the movement to reform the city charter proved to be the latter. The entrenchment of Ring office-holders proved to be an insurmountable obstacle to such reform. But Mayor McKenna was not without his accomplishments. As suggested previously, it was under his watch that the public health department was reorganized into a Bureau of Health reporting to the mayor. During his term garbage and trash collections were begun under city contracts. The south-side bridges were purchased from their private operators and the tolls eliminated.

The Carnegie Library of Pittsburgh, funded by a one million dollar donation by the industrialist and philanthropist, was built and dedicated in the district of Oakland. Combining reference, circulation, art galleries, and meeting rooms, the library would eventually provide for branch locations also. The city provided the land and assumed the operating expenses.

At the library's dedication, Andrew Carnegie gave a lengthy address on the duties of wealth and the challenges to effective philanthropy. In part, he said: *"Every thoughtful man must at first glance be troubled at the unequal distribution of wealth, the luxuries of the few, the lack of necessaries of the many. And giving away to feeling, without regard to judgment, he is very sure to commit many grievous mistakes . . . . To one to whom surplus comes, there come also the questions: What is my duty? What is the best use that can be made of it? The conclusion forced upon me, and which I retain, is this: That surplus wealth is a sacred trust, to be administered during life by its possessor for the best good of his fellow-men . . . . Mine be it to have contributed to the enlightenment and the joys of the mind, to the things of the spirit, to all that tends to bring into the lives of the toilers of Pittsburgh sweetness and light. I hold this the noblest possible use of wealth."*

Barney's private reaction was decidedly skeptical. Carnegie makes no acknowledgement that sweetness and light might not be at the very top of the working man's priorities, the mayor mused. But when the city receives a gift such as this, courtesy and decorum are the order of the day. In his public remarks during the ceremony, Mayor Barney adhered to this standard.

"As Chief Magistrate of this, my native city, I am pleased to receive for the people this beautiful building which you, at great expense out of your abundant means, have erected and designated that it shall be 'Free to the People.'

"Starting from the lower rung of the ladder, you have, by your indomitable perseverance and tact, raised yourself to a place among the great men of the world, distributing your wealth with your own hands, thus improving the condition of mankind. This, and other buildings of like character, erected by you, will stand as monuments to your memory, and the name of Andrew Carnegie will live in grateful remembrance.

"I know I voice the sentiment of all when I wish you long life; that you may live to know the benefits our people have derived from your generous and magnificent gift. I thank you in the name of the people of the city which you have helped to make great, and with which you have been identified from boyhood to mature age."

During his term of office, Mayor McKenna exercised as much influence as possible in correcting the use of city funds for public works. When Boss Magee's cousin and ally, Edward M. Bigelow, Director of Public Works, pushed a $6,000,000 bond issue through the city councils, it contained no specifics for what the money was to be spent. Barney promptly vetoed the ordinance. When a successive ordinance including the desired specifics was passed, it received the mayor's unreserved support.

Bigelow was a man of great vision and energy. His creation of the network of municipal parks represented a great enhancement to the civic life. In 1889, he had convinced Mary Schenley, heiress to the estate of James O'Hara, her grandfather and an early Pittsburgh settler, to donate three hundred acres in Oakland for what would become Schenley Park. That same year, he negotiated the acquisition of numerous parcels of land on heights over-looking the Allegheny River in the East End. Spending over $900,000, he constructed Highland Park around a city reservoir.

In the summer of 1895, Barney was approached by Chris Magee, then serving as a state senator. The legislature was in recess. Though they had tangled frequently over political matters, Magee's easy-going demeanor allowed for a pleasant, personal relationship. Chris and his wife Eleanor frequently hosted business and political figures in their home. Magee penned a note reading in part: "Mr. Mayor, Eleanor and I would deem it an honor if you and Mary would join us for dinner at The Maples."

"The Maples" was the Oakland estate that Magee had built with wealth that office and influence had afforded him. Barney and Mary, being of modest means, were somewhat awed by the grandeur and formality of the surroundings in previous visits. On this occasion, they were the only guests, making for a rather intimate evening. Eleanor personally greeted them at the door.

"Good evening your Honor, . . . Mary. Welcome. I'm so glad that you could join us. Chris is looking forward to seeing you both."

Leading them into a reception room, Eleanor requested refreshments from a liveried butler. "Chris will be down in just a moment . . . . Mary, you must bring me up to date on your beautiful family. How is Catherine?"

Mary took a seat beside Eleanor on the settee while Barney admired oil paintings on the opposite wall. A set of French doors stood open at the end of the room, allowing a welcome breeze to penetrate the room.

"Well, Catherine's friends are all calling her Kitty. She is twenty-one now, and she's seeing a young man. Frank is still a student; he's eighteen. And then, there's our youngest, Bill; he's thirteen. Sure, with them and the rest of Bernard's family, it keeps my hands full. But I'm blessed that Bernard's sister helps me run the household."

"How lucky you are! . . . Oh, here's Chris now."

Magee strode into the room, beaming his familiar smile. After twenty minutes of drinks and social chatter, dinner was announced. The dining hall was a large room of dark wood paneling. There was a large fireplace at the center of the back wall. Candelabra of silver and china dinnerware graced a long mahogany table flanked by rather gothic chairs. Only when dessert and coffee arrived did the evening's conversation turn to a matter of substance. Magee held his agenda till the serving staff had been dismissed.

"Mr. Mayor," he began, "Eleanor and I have been pondering an issue that I'd like to share with you. As you well know, I have been fortunate in business. The traction company, the Pittsburgh Times newspaper, and my stake in National Tube have left me with a wealth I couldn't have imagined as a clerk at city hall twenty-five years ago."

"You've done very well, Chris. I trust good fortune is not too heavy a burden." Barney offered a wink and a smile. Mary frowned at her husband. "Just kidding, Chris," he quickly added.

"Actually, there is one aspect of such riches that has us perplexed. As you know, unlike you and Mary, we have no children who might be heirs. We've had to give extra thought as to how to dispose of our surplus. There are several ideas that we have in mind, but there's one such that involves the city."

At this, Barney quit conjuring cute ripostes. He exchanged surprised glances with Mary. There was, after all, a serious purpose to the evening. "How can I help?" he replied.

Chris shifted his chair back and crossed his legs. "We'd like to make a gift to the city that has been so good to us. I've been discussing this with Ed Bigelow and I believe we have devised a suitable project. Eleanor and I would like to provide a zoological park for the city. Ed suggests the ideal venue would be at Highland Park."

Mary's face brightened. "What a wonderful idea! How good of you both!"

"We wanted to provide something that would be educational, and yet full of fun for the children," Eleanor explained.

Barney replied cautiously, tamping down his surprise. "It's very generous, Chris. I don't have any idea what scale of an undertaking this might be. Have you any notion of what will be required?"

"Ed has done a bit of research for me. It would appear that a reasonable facility, together with the animals required, can be had for something in the range of $125,000. Of course that presumes the city contributes the land and that operating costs are assumed by the parks department. If upon examination, the city concurs, I am prepared to underwrite that amount."

Barney repressed the urge to whistle at the estimable sum. "Thank you for your most generous offer. I think I'll want to put together a citizens' committee to develop a plan that the city and you can agree upon. Perhaps you will suggest a few names for us to consider?"

As Barney and Mary rode home in the taxi carriage, they laughed and talked about the evening and its unexpected ending. "How many folks think to make a gift of a zoo?" Mary asked in amusement.

"Well, it certainly is a surprise. Still, it will be a welcome addition to the city. I always knew Chris had a good heart, even if he and Flinn have fleeced the city coffers over the years."

Acting as chair of the citizen's committee, Barney would eventually accept the proposed zoo on behalf of the city. It opened to the public in June, 1898, two years after Barney left the office of mayor.

Chapter Eighteen

In 1896, the movement for political reform that had powered Barney into office had matured significantly. Organizations like the Civic Club of Allegheny County and the newly created Citizens' Municipal League redoubled their efforts to confront the power of the Republican Ring. When it became clear that they would push to nominate one of their own leaders, George Guthrie, for mayor, Barney decided not to split the Democratic unity and to forego another campaign. The Magee-Flinn machine responded to the challenge with additional patronage and increased organization at the ward level. Their candidate, Henry P. Ford, was a career accountant who had served as the Eleventh Ward's representative on the City Council for fifteen years, the last eight years as its presiding officer.

It was a close election, but Ford prevailed with a six hundred vote majority. In recognition of McKenna's integrity and long public service, Ford quickly nominated him to return to the office of police magistrate. This time, his position was in the Central Police District on Grant Street. He would continue in that post with the support of four mayoral successors.

Nationally, the year was marked by the presidential contest between the Republican William McKinley and Democrat William Jennings Bryan. The nomination of Bryan presented a political dilemma for Charles and Barney McKenna. Both had been life-long Democrats. Only in the contests of 1860 and 1864 had their allegiances swung to President Lincoln. But Bryan's stand on issues such as the protective tariff and sound money were seen as hostile to Pittsburgh's industrial well-being. Both McKennas threw their political support behind McKinley. Charles even led a revolt of Democrat war veterans. As chairman of the Allegheny County Soldiers for McKinley, Charles visited the presidential candidate at his home in Canton, Ohio that fall. He also joined a delegation of prominent Civil War veterans undertaking a speaking tour throughout the West on behalf of the McKinley ticket. Some years later, these measures of support would prove most consequential to Charles' career.

It was during Barney's time as mayor that he began to look for a residence in the East End. The downtown generally, and Penn Avenue particularly, had become increasingly commercial. With the economic security of office, he could now afford to remove to the leafier, suburban areas of the city. After a brief time in temporary quarters, he moved his family to 6018 Howe Street in Shadyside. As in prior years, his household still included his sister Catherine, brother Eddie, Eddie's son (Edward J.), and several housemaids.

In 1897, Barney and Charles received frightful news. That September, the home of their elder brother, Patrick, was demolished by a natural gas explosion. Both Patrick and his wife, Mary, were severely burned. Several days later, Mary succumbed to her injuries. Both Barney and Charles traveled to the Beaver County township of New Brighton to attend the funeral. In that sad journey, they were accompanied by their long-time family friend and cousin, Rev. Edward McKeever. Patrick, at that time sixty-three years of age, was terribly scarred. Childless, he would remain in New Brighton until 1899, when Barney prevailed upon him to return to Pittsburgh and move in with the family.

Also in 1897, Mayor Ford summoned Barney to his offices at City Hall. Barney found the invitation curious as his responsibilities as police magistrate were strictly apolitical. What is Ford up to, he thought as he climbed the stairs he knew so well. In the corridors, he was greeted warmly by many city staffers and political figures. "Good morning, Judge." or "Good to see you again, Barney" were repeated numerous times before he reach the office that had been his just months before. As he entered, Mayor Ford rose from his desk and gave him a firm, two-fisted handshake.

"Thanks so much for your time, Judge. Have a seat. Can we get you a coffee or a glass of water?"

"Coffee would be great, Mr. Mayor."

Barney doffed his overcoat and took a chair facing the mayor's large, ornate desk. But Ford didn't retire to his desk. Rather, he pulled over another visitor's chair and sat close, facing Barney. Pleasantries passed the minutes till coffee arrived.

"Judge," Ford finally admitted, "I asked you here because I need your help."

Barney's eyebrows arched in surprise. "I'd be pleased to help if I can . . . though I'm quite happy in the magistrate's position."

"Oh, I wouldn't ask you to leave your office as magistrate. What I have in mind is a part-time task, lasting a few months at most. Let me explain. You've read about the Pennsy's plan for a new rail station?"

Barney set his coffee cup aside. "Glory be to St. Patrick! Yes . . . and it's about time! The city has struggled with that temporary structure since the riot of '77."

"I agree; we've needed a proper station badly. Twenty years is a long time to wait. The railroad has recently engaged the famed architect Daniel Burnham to design and manage the project. Last week, they presented their plans here at city hall."

"Well . . . Burnham may be the best! He made quite a success of the Chicago Exposition."

"Yes, and the railroad is sparing no expense!" Ford beamed his enthusiasm. "The drawings were most impressive. But here's the rub. The design calls for a significant re-grading of the streets adjacent to the station site. When the merchants along Liberty Avenue, Eleventh Street and Elm heard that the area would have to be re-leveled, they became most upset. They have complained to the Chamber of Commerce. Now we have a resolution from the chamber opposing the plan!"

Barney nodded in appreciation of the merchants' concern. "Of course, we've already had several reductions of the grade on Grant's Hill . . . with considerable disruption, I might add."

"Yes, well anyway . . . the City Councils have passed an ordinance establishing a commission of citizens to resolve the issue between the merchants and the railroad. Judge, I'd be forever in your debt if you'd agree to head that commission. Everyone here at city hall thinks you'd do a splendid job of it."

Barney rubbed his chin, his mind racing. This is a fine kettle of fish! There will be plenty of folks mad at me whichever way it goes. Still, we must have the new station . . . . "Well, Mr. Mayor, I'll do it on one condition."

"And what might that be?" Ford asked with furrowed brow.

"You must agree to fully support the recommendations of the commission and bring the councils along as well. I don't want to get in the middle of a donnybrook without the backing of city hall."

The mayor sighed in relief. "You have my word, Judge. There'll be no problem from our end. And I'd welcome your ideas as to who should serve with you. Of course, most business leaders want to see the project go forward. I'm sure we'll have their cooperation."

Ford was as good as his word, though there wasn't much controversy in the end. It took several months, but the commission patiently heard from everyone involved, as was Barney's style. They then hammered together a package of concessions from the Pennsylvania Railroad to mitigate the disruption to nearby residents. Financial assistance was made available to those businesses where the re-grading required relocations. There was a general consensus that the result was fair and the project went forward. The new Union Station (later renamed Penn Station) turned out to be a brilliant architectural achievement and a boon to Pittsburgh transportation.

Daniel Burnham's Union Station, Opened 1903

Just a year later, Charles McKenna was another who needed his brother's help. For almost ten years, Charles had acted as Treasurer for the St. Paul's Orphan Asylum. As the number of youngsters to be served increased, the financial resources had not kept pace. As a result, many orphans had to be placed in other institutions, or left unserved. Christmas and "orphans' week" collections in the parishes had proved inadequate and Archbishop Richard Phelan charged the board members to undertake additional fundraising to correct the situation. It was determined that the annual benefit picnic would be rejuvenated. It would be held in mid-July at the Calhoun Amusement Park, just southeast of the city limits. Executive committee chairman Hugh Murphy looked to Charles McKenna to ensure that the business and political leaders of Pittsburgh would throw their support behind the project, ensuring the desired turnout and financial success. Charles knew where to go for help. On Sunday, after Mass at Sacred Heart Church in East Liberty, Charles pulled his brother aside.

Old Sacred Heart Church circa 1875

After explaining the situation, he added, "Of course I'll be after the legal profession and the members at the Chamber of Commerce. But I'd like you to handle the political community. Many of them are Catholics, and those who are not can still make room in their hearts for the orphaned boys and girls."

Barney threw his arm over his brother's shoulder and laughed. "When we get done, there'll hardly be a politician in the city whose gone missing. Put me on one of your sub-committees. I'll even draft my sons to pitch in."

Within a week, Barney had enlisted his cronies from "The Steps." James and John Flannery; Charlie Flinn; City Controller John B. Larkin; Chief of Police Roger O'Mara; John C. Reilly, Fifth Ward Alderman and many more agreed to serve. Charles did his part as well, enlisting among others, Charles M. Schwab, now president of Carnegie Steel Co. The large German-American community was also well represented. Leopold Vilsack and Aloysius Frauenheim, proprietors of the Iron City Brewing Company, were both active on the executive committee.

When July 14th arrived, the weather was awful. A downpour of rain persisted all morning, and further showers threatened into the early afternoon. Barney, stationed at the "contests" booth, worried at the poor turnout so far. When the rector of the orphanage, Father P. J. Lynch, came by Barney told him, "Better say your very best prayers, Father. This rain has everyone a bit down."

The priest nodded and raised his eyes to the still dark heavens. "'Tis a great test of faith, your Honor! Still, I'm putting my rosary to good use. The Lord will yet provide. In the meantime, let's do our best for those who have braved the elements and give them a good time."

"So we shall, Father."

About 2:30 the sun emerged and gradually cooked the skies clear. The grounds began to dry-out and the traffic picked up. Trolley cars, stuffed full, disgorged visitors. For the next four hours, men, women, and children poured through the gates. Sporting events, music and dancing, and various contests were ready and waiting for them. It was estimated that over 15,000 visitors took part, a significant increase over prior years. Charles confided later to Father Lynch, "I'm hopeful we may clear $9,000 on the day."

Barney's son Frank was working at the dance pavilion. Frank was a serious fellow, tall, thin, with short dark hair, his father's nose, and somewhat large ears. Like his father, he couldn't be described as handsome. But his eyes attracted one's attention and obviated his less attractive features. They had a penetrating character, yet without hint of glare or staring. Rather, they conveyed intelligence and keen observation.

Working with him were two of the Vilsack sons, August and Anthony, and Joseph Frauenheim. These young scions of the two brewer families were good friends. They took Frank under their wing, promising to secure an attractive dance partner for him.

Frauenheim kidded Frank repeatedly. "I can't believe you have no young lady today . . . . A notary's life must be a dull one . . . . Don't worry, though. We shall match you with a suitable female before the day is done."

Late in the day Joseph's parents, Aloysius and Catherine Frauenheim, arrived at the pavilion. With them were Aloysius' sister Mary Frauenheim Heyl and Catherine's brother William Heyl and their two eldest daughters, Anna and Elizabeth. After several minutes of pleasantries, the two older couples made for the dance floor, leaving the young ladies chatting with cousin Joseph. "Now's your moment!" the Vilsack boys whispered in Frank's ear, pushing him forward. Suddenly, Frank found himself inserted into the nearby conversation.

Joseph adeptly smoothed the way. "Ah, ladies, allow me to introduce our co-worker, Mr. Frank McKenna. He's an aspiring attorney, the son of our former mayor. He says he knows how to dance but, as yet, we've had no proof of it."

Frank's visage turned rather crimson. He glared at the well-meaning Frauenheim.

"I'm sure we all should enjoy a dance," Anna chirped. "As Mother and Father are still on the floor, we may as well join in."

"Come along then, Anna." Joseph took her hand, leaving Frank and Elizabeth to themselves.

Frank watched them leave, silently struggling with how best to proceed. Finally he mustered his courage. "I'm afraid, Miss Elizabeth, that Joe has exaggerated my experience at dance. But if you'd enjoy a turn, I'm happy to give my best efforts."

With her own shyness, she replied, "All my friends call me Bess, so you might as well do so. And yes, I'd be pleased to have a dance . . . . Between you and me, I haven't much experience either."

In the days that followed, the benefit picnic would be remembered as a great financial success, especially considering the weather. But Frank McKenna would recall its success for personal reasons. He and Bess would marry in 1906.

Frank & Bess on their wedding day

In 1899, Frank's sister Kitty (Catherine) married her long-time beau, Edward T. McNulty, a bookkeeper. The young couple set up house on Lang Avenue, also in Shadyside. The following year, they had a daughter, Mary, named for her maternal grandmother. They would later remove to Washington, Pennsylvania and thence to West Virginia, ultimately raising a family of ten children.

In December 1900, Barney's brother Eddie passed away, having suffered for over a year with the symptoms of hypertrophy (enlargement of the liver) and arterial sclerosis. He and his son, Edward J. had been living on Kentucky Avenue in the East End at the time of his death.

Frank was studying the law in the offices of his Uncle Charles and cousin Edward J. McKenna. He continued in those years to earn his keep as a notary. He would be admitted to the bar in 1902 and promptly enter the family practice. His younger brother, Bill, still a student studying medicine, aspired to become a general practitioner.

Edward J. McKenna

* *

As the twentieth century dawned, Pittsburgh was continuing to experience rapid change. The population had risen to over 321,000. A system of water purification was now in place with salubrious benefit to community health. Its creator, public works director Edward Bigelow, turned next to the creation of rapid, limited-access roadways from the eastern suburbs to the downtown. The first of these was Grant Boulevard. Carved out of the still-wooded Bedford Hill, it was opened to traffic on July 1, 1900. Shortly thereafter, the Magee-Flinn Ring received a major challenge when Bigelow, pressed by the forces of political reform, insisted upon a proper competitive bidding process in the awarding city contracts. This rankled his former patrons after years of rigged contracts. The breach with Magee and Flinn soon led to Bigelow's forced resignation. That proved to be a great mistake as Bigelow enjoyed great popularity with the public.

But it was the reaction of Bigelow's brother, Thomas, that delivered retribution to the entrenched bosses of city government. He went to our old friend, now U.S. Senator, Matthew Quay, still the Republican Party boss at the state level. Quay had been in perennial quarrel with Magee and Flinn. Thomas Bigelow prevailed upon Quay to engineer the passage of a "ripper bill" through the Pennsylvania State legislature. This law allowed the Governor to remove or "rip out" of office municipal recorders (mayors). The day after the bill became law, Christopher L. Magee died after a lengthy illness.

Quay then had Governor Stone "rip" out of office Mayor William J. Diehl, successor to Mayor Ford and a political ally of William Flinn. The Governor then appointed common pleas judge Adam M. Brown to fill the vacancy. But when Brown showed too great an independence, he was ripped from office as well. In his place, Stone installed Joseph O. Brown (no relation to his predecessor) who had been serving as Pittsburgh's Director of Public Safety at the time. Pittsburgh citizens were outraged when they learned that William Flinn and his Ring had raised a substantial fund to reward the Governor for this latest appointment.

But Thomas Bigelow was not yet done. In December, 1901, he led a campaign of "Stalwarts" in creating a Citizens' Party to contest the election of February 1902. Their stated objectives were "to defeat efforts to elect dishonest and incompetent men as public officers, prevent the perpetration of fraud upon the taxpayers, and to secure and maintain economic and efficient government."

The Ring fought back, manipulating as usual the voter registration lists, offering bribes to "purchase" Citizens' Party candidates, and hiring gangs of "repeater" voters from Philadelphia to come and vote "the regular ticket." Nevertheless, the reformers, Democrats as well as the Citizens' Party, easily elected John B. Larkin as city controller (chief financial officer). They also captured the Common and Select City Councils. In the Mayoral race of 1903, Bigelow's reform candidate, William B. Hays, was elected. The long-standing regime of the Republican Ring came to an ignominious close. William Flinn was quoted as saying, "When Magee died, I died politically too."

Chapter Nineteen

Sadly, all the political turmoil and controversy of these days transpired without the involvement of Barney McKenna. Still serving as police magistrate in 1902, he began to experience significant discomfort and fatigue early that autumn. He mentioned this in passing to Mary but was disinclined to be a complainer. His wife, however, was having none of it.

"Bernard, I am greatly worried for you," Mary insisted, hands on hips. "You must see a doctor and the best you can find!"

"I suppose I should . . . . Perhaps I'll call on Dr. Koenig. He attended Eddie and I liked him very much."

"God help us! He should be more successful than he was with Edward," Mary mumbled as she left the room.

Barney went back to his old Fourth Ward and visited Dr. Adolph Koenig, a second generation Swiss-American physician with offices on Duquesne Way. Koenig, now in his late forties, was a serious looking fellow. He wore a trim mustache, but no beard. His brown hair he parted severely in the middle. He was a most highly regarded member of his profession, being a Professor of Materia Medica and Botany at the Pittsburgh College of Pharmacy for many years. In 1895, he helped found the Pittsburgh Medical Review and served as its publisher and editor. He would later serve as president of the Pennsylvania Medical Society. But given the tools at his disposal, a precise diagnosis of Barney's ailment proved difficult.

"I could be wrong. I hope so," he opined. "Your symptoms are rather similar to those which afflicted your brother, though there can be various causes. Prolonged exposure to various chemical fumes seems likely to me. We're in Pittsburgh after all."

"Dear, Jesus!" Barney whispered, as his chin sunk to his chest. His mind raced back to the shop conditions he had endured as a young iron molder.

278

"Judge, I believe you should take a rest from your duties as magistrate . . . . Take Mary and find a quiet spot for a vacation. When you return, come see me and let's see how you're feeling."

So Barney and Mary spent six weeks at the seaside in New Jersey, but the relaxation had no great effect upon his symptoms. Early in 1903, Koenig confirmed the suspected enlargement of the liver. He could only offer palliative treatment.

When William Hays became mayor, he declined to reappoint Barney to the magistrate's position, perhaps because of these health issues. Still, Barney took what pleasure he could in the rising fortunes of his beloved Pittsburgh Pirates and their star player, Honus Wagner. Barney attended games whenever his energy allowed and he was a familiar sight at Exposition Field on the North Side. On these occasions he was often accompanied by one or both sons, Frank and Bill. But as the season progressed, Barney's health continued to decline. On June 1st, he made his last visit to the ballpark. A newspaper account recorded:

"Those who saw Judge McKenna there realized, many for the first time, that his span of life was almost run. He was wan and nervous, and time and again got up from his seat and paced up and down the aisle at the back of the grandstand. One of his old companions at the games in former years was Robert H. Lindsay, long chief ordinance officer for the city. It was his habit, unless the game was unusually exciting, to get up at the end of the sixth inning, always the sixth, and slip home. After Judge McKenna had paid intermittent attention to the game . . . for three innings, he whispered to his son and rose in his seat. He turned to a group of friends seated behind him and said with a sad, little smile: 'Boys, I guess I'll have to do the Bob Lindsay act.' Then leaning heavily on his companion's arm, he left the stand."

Barney would never see his team go on to compete that year in baseball's first World Series.

Exhibition Park, Allegheny City
A crowd overflows the playing field prior to
Game 3 of the 1903 World Series

He was soon confined to his bed at his home at 6325 Marchand Street in East Liberty. It was a new residence, only occupied by him ten months prior. Realizing the end was near, Barney had Koenig desist from administering stimulants. He requested that Rev. Francis Keane, pastor at Sacred Heart Church, come to perform the last rites. On June 12th, Barney lost consciousness, but lingered until Thursday, June 18th. Then, surrounded by Mary and members of his extended family, he peacefully slipped away as the clock struck noon.

Anticipation of the event had somewhat steeled the family against the emotional blow. Now, Mary and Barney's sister Catherine prepared the body and dressed him in a dark suit and tie. After placing him on the large, leather couch in the judge's library, preparations were made for the next evening's wake. From 4:00 p.m. until 11:00 June 19th, over five hundred relatives, friends, political associates, and—perhaps—a few of those he dealt with kindly in the magistrate's court, all came to pay homage to a most beloved citizen.

On Saturday, June 20th, a Requiem Mass was conducted at Sacred Heart Church. Rev. Keane was assisted by Father Edward McKeever. Among the honorary pallbearers were former mayors, William McCallin, Henry Ford, and William Diehl. Also included were John C. Reilly, Roger O'Mara, Robert H. Lindsay, and Michael J. Feeney. Thomas "Boley" Mullen had pre-deceased Barney by five months. Actual pallbearers were Bill Brennen, John Flannery, Tom Foley, John Kearns, and Aldermen Stephen J. Toole and John J. Sweeney.

Bernard J. McKenna (1842-1903)

The burial took place at St. Mary's Cemetery in Lawrenceville. It had been a warm Spring and the day was blessed with sun and comfortable temperatures. The green hillside, where Barney's father and mother, even grandfather Hugh, rested was fully leafed-out. As at the church, the crowds at the cemetery were large, yet respectfully dignified. As brother Charles and wife Virginia left the gravesite, he remarked, "What an impressive turnout Barney has received . . . . You know, dear, my brother always envied me for the service I saw during the war. I wonder if he suspected how much I envied him—for the love and respect he received from all who knew him."

Yes, Virginia ruminated silently. I too envied Barney—and Mary, for the blessing of children, loving, happy, healthy children.

* *

Mary, her sons, brother-in-law Patrick, sister-in-law Catherine, and nephew Edward J. continued to live together at Marchand Street.

Charles McKenna now became the de facto head of the extended family, though without the communal style of living his brother had maintained. Charles and Virginia, having moved numerous times as well, were now renting an apartment at 5723 Fifth Avenue in Shadyside. As previously noted, he was the lead partner in the successful law practice with his nephews Edward and Frank. Some years earlier, he had become so busy that he felt compelled to resign his position as solicitor for the Archdiocese of Pittsburgh and for several Pittsburgh banks. Indeed his reputation was such that Arthur Burgoyne, artist and poet, profiled Charles in his book, *All Sorts of Pittsburgers.*

This is a pleader—a limb of the law;
In a spoilt reputation he'll heal any flaw,
Be you ever so wicked, just put up the fees,
And he'll wrestle with justice as nice as you please.

In his boyhood he valiantly shouldered a gun,
And for three weary years to keep on the run
The rebels—confound 'em—and great was his glee
On the day that brought round the surrender of Lee.

In pleading a case he'll try every resort,
He can crack a broad smile or shed tears by the quart;
He is funny, pathetic, or tragic at will,
And works on a jury with marvelous skill.

Cross-examining is a diversion for him,
He gets hold of a witness and makes his head swim;
Of the district attorney he's certain to speak
As a bloodthirsty miscreant grinding the weak.

But although he sticks up for the crooks many a time,
He's a square man himself, with no liking for crime,
And when death comes along he need feel no alarm,
For he'll play on a harp with a wonderful charm.

Charles had taken a prominent and active role in furthering a long-standing proposal for the erection of a suitable memorial to those citizens from Allegheny County who had served as soldiers or sailors during "the war to suppress the rebellion." The idea, sponsored by the G.A.R. and other veterans' organizations, quickly attracted broad public support. The original thought was to fund the memorial by private donation. But on further reflection, it was later decided that the project merited the support of the taxpayers of the county. It was Chris Magee, then a state senator, who generously agreed to introduce and shepherd legislation through the General Assembly. This he successfully accomplished in 1895. However, Allegheny County courts found the act to be defective and required an amending action by the General Assembly. They further suggested that if, instead of a monument or shaft, a memorial hall became the target of remedial legislation, they (the court) would heartily approve the necessary initiative by Allegheny County to fund the enterprise. This suggestion was embraced readily by the veterans groups, the Chamber of Commerce, and the press, resulting in a general consensus among the citizenry.

Early in 1903, Charles McKenna took a prominent role as the solicitor of the newly-formed committee for the purpose of securing the remedial legislation required to authorize the county to erect a Soldiers' and Sailors' Memorial Hall. He also chaired the supporting committee of the Union Veteran Legion. As solicitor, he appeared before the state Senate Committee considering the proposed new legislation. He subsequently appeared, with others, before Governor Pennypacker, who approved the Act that April. County-level approval was secured by June.

But Charles' involvement in the project was curtailed in the Spring of 1904 as his career was about to take a turn. President Theodore Roosevelt had succeeded the assassinated William McKinley three years earlier. His Attorney General, Philander C. Knox, was now looking for a candidate for the Federal District and Circuit Court in the territory of Porto (now Puerto) Rico. Knox, a Pittsburgher and formerly an attorney for Carnegie's steel empire, immediately thought of Charles F. McKenna.

Early that April, Knox arrived at the White House to review with the President several vacancies within the Federal judiciary. He found Roosevelt in his rectangular West Wing office (the famous Oval Office not yet conceived and constructed by successor President Taft). Stepping away from a large standing globe, the President greeted Knox and returned to his desk which was buried in books, papers, and decorative items. Roosevelt was dressed in his customary cut-away suit and vest. A pince-nez rode upon his rather large, bulbous nose, below which grew a reddish-brown, drooping mustache.

Knox passed over a green velum folder containing the briefing papers. The President spent several quiet minutes reviewing the list of vacancies and candidates. Removing his pince-nez, he looked up to query the Attorney General. "Why are we replacing Judge Holt in Porto Rico? He's only been there for three years and a bit. Is he unhappy there? Are we unhappy with him?"

Knox, a balding, round-headed fellow of almost fifty-one years, tugged at the starched, upright shirt collar he favored despite the changing styles of the day. "Sorry, Mr. President. I meant to point out that the judges in the territories are appointed for fixed terms of four years. Only federal judges residing within the United States proper receive life-time appointments. Holt has served well; still, I believe he will be happy to come home."

Roosevelt resumed his pince-nez. "I see. Now this fellow McKenna . . . it appears he's a life-long Democrat."

"That's true, sir. But he supported the McKinley ticket in '96 and in 1900. In addition, he has a distinguished war record. He was one of the co-founders of the Pennsylvania Bar Association back in '95. I'm confident he will prove to be an excellent jurist."

"Hmm . . . I think I recall him," Roosevelt replied. "He was here at the White House with a group of veterans. Seemed a good chap . . . . Let me make a few inquiries. I'll get back to you on this one. Who else do we have to discuss?"

The President later solicited input from the Republican congressman from Pittsburgh, John Dalzell. He received the same warm endorsement of McKenna for the post in question. Roosevelt was a man who, when he knew what he wanted, cared little for soliciting additional advice. This was particularly true when it came to Congressional advice. Thus, having made up his mind that Charles McKenna was his man, he truncated the selection process without having any consultation with the two Republican senators from Pennsylvania, Boies Penrose and Matthew Quay.

Perhaps senators from any state would consider this an egregious slight of senatorial prerogative. The senators in question were of a mind to take particular offense at the slight. McKenna's background as a long-time Democrat further rubbed salt in their wounds. Worse yet, the two often viewed Representative Dalzell, who was now championing McKenna, as a rival within the Pennsylvania party hierarchy. Dalzell had run twice against Quay for the party's senatorial nomination. All of this did not bode well for McKenna's nomination, of which Charles was still unaware.

He first heard word on April 26th as he attended the license court in his continuing representations on behalf of those aspiring to be holders of liquor licenses. While waiting for a hearing for one of his clients, he was accosted, somewhat aggressively, by a reporter for the Pittsburgh Leader newspaper.

"Mr. McKenna, the Associated Press has a dispatch from Washington. You've been nominated by President Roosevelt to the federal district court in Porto Rico. Will you have a comment?"

Charles raised his bushy, white eyebrows. "Are you telling me that to cheer me up after listening to the license court?"

The astonished reporter replied, "You mean you did not know?"

"It is a surprise to me," Charles admitted, somewhat embarrassed. "The boys of the Union Veteran Legion must have been booming me."

"Were you not an applicant for a federal appointment?"

"No, sir"

The reporter sat down on a bench in the waiting room, a quizzical look on his face. He pulled his notebook from his breast pocket. *"To what do you attribute your appointment?"*

Charles looked around the room to see who might be overhearing their conversation. In a lowered voice he replied, *"It must have been at the instigation of Attorney General Knox or Congressman Dalzell, as a recognition of the Union Veteran Legion."*

"Will you accept?"

Charles thought for a moment, then laughed. "Is acceptance compulsory?" He then added, "I cannot tell. I have a partner, a lady who might be interested. Mrs. McKenna might not care to go so far south . . . . Before taking any action or saying anything except what I have said, I shall await official notification that I am the man referred to."

The next day, Charles received a visit from John Dalzell. The congressman, powerful chairman of the House Ways and Means Committee, had been admitted to the bar just a year before Charles. As young attorneys making their way in Pittsburgh, they had become good friends, despite their different political allegiances.

Charles rose from his desk and greeted him. "Well, my representative comes calling! Welcome, John. How is Mary Louise?"

Once having seated his visitor, Charles listened to entreaties to accept the appointment being conveyed. He paced the area behind his cluttered desk. "Don't take the notion that I am ungrateful, John, but I don't think so. I'm not sure this is the right position for me."

Dalzell jumped to his feet. "Good God, man! You sound like an old maid whose been invited to a charity ball . . . . When the President of the United States asks your service to the country, even pays you the honor of requesting you for an exalted position— one doesn't refuse."

Charles sighed, his shoulders slumped. "Yes, I know that you are right . . . . Still, there is Virginia to consider. Her mother's family are southern folk and Virginia was raised according to their customs and beliefs. Porto Rico is a land of darkies and, frankly, I don't know how comfortable she'll be spending four years in those circumstances . . . . But, as a courtesy to you—and to the President—I will give a prompt and firm reply tomorrow."

The congressman shook his head in exasperation. "You micks are a hard crowd. Anyone would think this is an honor to be jumped at . . . . But all right, I'll wait until tomorrow."

John Dalzell, 1904

That evening, Charles broached the subject with Virginia. He waited until they had finished supper. He then reviewed the offer and several reasons for his reluctance. "I will have to leave my practice, largely in the hands of Edward and Frank. They are bright attorneys, but still inexperienced. Further, we will have to leave friends and family . . . move to an island in the Caribbean of which we know nothing . . . . It's been less than a year since Barney passed away. Mary and the family may need our assistance now and again."

Virginia pushed her plate aside and looked at her husband with admiring eyes. "Charles, I accept everything you've mentioned as legitimate reasons to say no. But you haven't said a word about the reasons to say yes. Once you have been on the federal bench, who knows what opportunities might come your way . . . . You've been a trial lawyer for over thirty years. Perhaps the change would be pleasant, even invigorating. Besides, it may be that a few years in the tropics would be fun. At the very least, I wouldn't miss the Pennsylvania winters."

Charles rose and came around the table to stand behind his wife. He placed his hands on her shoulders. "There is another item to consider, my dear. The people of Porto Rico are all black and brown. As the second ranking American in the country, after the governor, I will have certain diplomatic obligations. We'll be expected to entertain community leaders in our home."

Virginia turned and looked up at her husband. "I suppose, Charles, that is something I'll be able to accommodate . . . if you can."

Charles looked surprised and befuddled. "I was sure you'd say no . . . . You still surprise me after all these years."

* *

Dalzell, not one to be put off, went and polled the members of the Allegheny County Bar Association on the question. He received a unanimous endorsement of Charles' candidacy. Immediately, Charles' attorney colleagues began to deluge McKenna's office with messages urging his acceptance. When Charles relented and passed his decision to Dalzell, neither man realized what obstacles lay ahead.

The next day they found out. Senators Penrose and Quay would exercise the tradition of senatorial courtesy—that no nomination may be advanced without the support of at least one of the candidate's home-state senators. Together they visited the White House that morning and informed the President that the nomination of Charles McKenna would not go forward. When Charles received word, he opined—perhaps this is a sign that it wasn't meant to be.

But the senators had not accounted for the outpouring of support for the appointment from the members of the G.A.R. and the Union Veteran Legion. Letters piled high upon their senatorial desks. Quay, at the time confined to his sick bed, was particularly struck by one letter he received from a former member of the 155th Pennsylvania Volunteers.

"Do you not recall, sir, the misfortunate day that you were summoned by General Humphreys to a court-martial? You stood accused of the misappropriation of Federal property, to wit, a horse. Perhaps time clouds one's memory. A private, then assigned as guard at the military stockade, produced the receipt given upon the issuance of said horse. Do you recall that this evidence resulted in your exculpation? And do you not recall the name of that dutiful private? Surely, you must have forgotten that he was Charles F. McKenna, the same person whom President Roosevelt now requests be made Judge for the Federal District Court for Porto Rico! The surviving veterans of his former regiment earnestly request, in the name of justice, if not gratitude, that you withdraw your objection to this worthy appointment."

In the face of this letter and others like it, Senator Quay notified President Roosevelt that he was withdrawing his opposition to Charles' nomination. This decision left Senator Penrose with little ground to block Senate consideration. For Quay, his action was one of his last. One month later, he was dead.

* *

Announcement

CHARLES F. McKENNA having accepted the appointment of Judge of the U.S. District and Circuit Court of Porto Rico, desires to announce the dissolution of the firm of C.F. & E.J. McKenna, and the formation of the law firm of McKenna & McKenna, consisting of Edward J. and J. Frank McKenna. Unfinished business in the hands of C.F. & E.J. McKenna will be looked after by the new firm who will continue the general practice of law in the offices at present occupied, Maeder Building, 433 Fifth Avenue, Pittsburg, Pa.

On Saturday September 3rd, the eve of his departure for Porto Rico, Post #3 of the G.A.R., Encampment #1 of the Union Veteran Legion, and the members of the Allegheny County Bar Association sponsored a gala banquet as a fond farewell. It was held at the modern Hotel Henry, which had a banquet hall that could accommodate the over three hundred guests. The toastmaster for the evening was Charles' first regimental commander, Colonel Edward J. Allen.

Aside from Charles, the most celebrated attendee that evening was President Roosevelt, who had traveled from Washington in an uncommon tribute to his appointee. Other notables included Barney's old friend and political ally, William J. Brennen, Congressman Dalzell, Attorney General Knox, Robert Pitcairn of the Pennsylvania Railroad, and the former Ring political boss William Flinn. But Charles was more gratified by the presence of four of his former comrades from Company "E." Most regretted in their absence were Charles' closest war-time comrade Jimmie O'Neill and his last regimental commander and long-time friend Alfred Pearson. Both had passed away in the two years prior.

The next day, Charles and Virginia made their goodbyes to family members and started upon the train journey to New Orleans from where they would travel by steamship to the island of Porto Rico. There Charles embarked upon his four year term of office. He found himself in what had only been a possession of the United

291

States for a little over five years. It had been ceded from Spain to the United States at the end of the Spanish-American War.

Upon their arrival, Judge McKenna and Virginia were transported from the beautiful natural harbor by horse-drawn carriage. Old San Juan, founded in 1521, still retained its historic walled appearance, though it encompassed an area of only seven square blocks. The McKennas were struck by the bluish hue of the cobble stones, originally brought from Spain as ballast in colonial sailing ships. Though the main plazas and principal buildings were charmingly picturesque, there was plentiful evidence of dilapidation and poverty—signs of years of colonial neglect. The country was only now emerging from the economic damage of a devastating hurricane some five years prior.

La Fortaleza, San Juan, Puerto Rico

It was arranged that, initially at least, they would take occupancy in the recently vacated residence of Judge William Holt, Charles' predecessor. The court chambers were located at 54 Fortaleza Street, close to La Fortaleza, the 16th century fort and now the Governor's Palace. Arriving just as the heat of summer neared its peak, Charles and Virginia discovered that tropical breezes might be over-rated. From July through November the rainy season added humidity without dissipating the heat. But they were determined to withstand the discomforts. With winter, a more temperate climate offered some respite.

By 1905, they had truly settled in. They enjoyed a social network consisting of American military and civil servants, along with various Porto Rican political and business figures. Always active socially, this aspect of their tenure was, perhaps, the most rewarding. The traditional siesta took some getting used to, as did the formality of calling cards and visits by the curious, or lonely, expatriate community. They especially enjoyed the company of thirty-year-old Governor Beekman Winthrop and his wife Melza. They had arrived in San Juan just a few months prior to the McKennas. Winthrop was a hardworking diplomat, anxious to improve the social conditions of the island. And he cultivated the Spanish language, though he was no match for his fluent wife.

Though Charles' official duties were reasonably taxing, he had sufficient free time to join with locals in organizing a chapter of the Benevolent and Protective Order of Elks in San Juan. But when the climatic cycle came around again, discomfort gave way to physical decline. At Virginia's urging, Charles sought medical advice over his lack of energy and the pain in his joints.

"Do not be alarmed, Señor McKenna," his elderly Porto Rican doctor offered after a thorough examination. "It is not an unusual reaction to the tropics for visitors from the mainland. Unfortunately, I can offer you only partial and temporary relief from pharmaceuticals."

"You mean there is no cure for my condition?" Charles grumbled.

The physician smiled a patronizing smile. "You will find, I think, no better cure than a return to your home in Pittsburgh."

Charles shook his head vehemently. "No, Doctor, the President has sent me down here to do a job, an important one. The greater pain for me would be having to explain to him that I cannot perform my duties because of a bit of physical discomfort."

Charles soldiered on through that year and most of the following. But Virginia was worried and repeatedly suggested that it was surely not the President's intent that Charles should ruin his health. She encouraged him to travel back to Pittsburgh in the summers of 1905 and 1906 for reunion gatherings of his old regiment. During these visits, he experienced some amelioration of his ailments.

Later in 1906, as the rainy season returned, Charles' defenses started to crumble. It was becoming painfully difficult to navigate steps or walk even reasonable distances. That November, President and Mrs. Roosevelt were due to arrive in San Juan on the heels of their historic visit to the Panama Canal, then under construction. Charles was sure to see him during his visit.

President Theodore Roosevelt's arrival in Puerto Rico, 1906

The presidential party arrived at the southern port of Ponce on November 21st. They then traveled the eighty-odd miles to San Juan overland by automobile. As the President recounted at that evening's reception at the Governor's Palace, "It is shameful! But the harbor here in San Juan is so silted our battleship, the *Louisiana*, could not put in here . . . . Still, what a bully journey!"

294

He laughed. "Why, at one point, we were bogged down in mud in the middle of a river. I had to get out and push!"

Later in the evening, the president found Charles for a moment's private conversation. "Judge McKenna, I have nothing but the best reports of your service here." Then his demeanor turned grave. "I must say I am alarmed at your diminished physical appearance. Are you receiving adequate medical attention?"

Charles grimaced in embarrassment. "I appreciate your concern, Mr. President. I'm afraid it's the climate, not my duties, that wears on me. In another eighteen months or so, my term will expire."

Roosevelt shook his head and barked, "It looks to me like a race as to who or what will expire first . . . . I will not order you, sir. But if I receive your letter of resignation, I will accept it promptly and without prejudice. You must keep your health!"

****

And so it happened that, reluctantly, Charles relinquished his post. He and Virginia returned to their Pittsburgh home on Fifth Avenue early in 1907. Though the process was gradual, Charles' health, his energy, and mobility returned. Almost immediately Charles re-entered legal practice, joining his nephews at the offices of McKenna & McKenna. But his consuming interest over the next few years was his work on behalf of the veterans of the war, especially his old regiment.

In April, 1907 Charles wrote to Andrew Carnegie on behalf of the Civil War veterans of Allegheny County, delivering resolutions *"expressive of goodwill and gratitude of the veterans for your public benefactions and especially for your advocacy of International Peace."*

It had long been Charles' desire to capture a record of the 155th Pennsylvania Volunteers and to do so while sufficient survivors remained to offer their accounts and reminiscences. Acting as a co-editor and contributor, Charles joined a Regimental Committee on History and began to collect and assemble the material for what would become the definitive account. Using the title, *Under the Maltese Cross: Antietam to Appomattox, The Loyal Uprising in Western Pennsylvania 1861-1865*, the final product ran to 794 pages including hundreds of portraits, photos, and sketches. It would consume almost four years of effort and was received to universal acclaim by scholars and veterans alike. One of its notable merits was the inclusion of personal anecdotes, by various regimental members, of camp life and numerous tragic or humorous episodes.

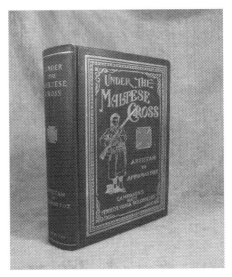

Under the Maltese Cross, 1910

It was, perhaps, Charles' work on the regimental history that influenced his second involvement in Civil War commemoration. In June, 1907 the Pennsylvania legislature enacted and sent to Governor Edwin Stuart a bill providing for the erection of a memorial to the Pennsylvania's soldiers who had participated in the battle of Gettysburg. Shortly thereafter, Governor Stuart appointed Charles McKenna as one of nine members of the Gettysburg Battlefield Memorial Commission. It began its efforts in April, 1908 and would take two years to plan, design, and construct the memorial. The result was the largest and most glorious of all such remembrances placed upon the site of the battle.

Pennsylvania Battlefield Memorial at Gettysburg

Charles' return from Porto Rico also afforded him the opportunity to rejoin the effort he had left three years prior, the Allegheny County Soldiers and Sailors Memorial Hall. In the time he had been gone, there had been much nattering between Allegheny County authorities, the state legislature, and citizens—for and against the public expenditure. Now having settled these controversies, land in Oakland had been purchased, architects selected, and specifications agreed. It was decided that the laying of the cornerstone for the Memorial Hall should take place in October, 1908 as one of the final ceremonies marking that year's Pittsburgh Sesquicentennial.

At 9:30 on the morning of October 2nd, a parade of Civil War veterans from all of Allegheny County set off from Meyran

Avenue, up Forbes Avenue, and then down Fifth Avenue to the selected site. At the head of the assembly of G.A.R. and Union Veteran Legion elements, Chief Marshall James E. Porter was accompanied by a chief of staff, an adjutant general, and five military aides, one of whom was Charles McKenna. It would take two more years to complete the construction of the hall, but its position as a jewel of civic architecture and patriotic remembrance was securely established.

Allegheny County Soldiers and Sailors Memorial Hall

* *

But the spring of 1908, filled as it was with veterans' affairs, was a very sad period for Charles and his nieces and nephews. That April, in a sad coincidence of consecutive days, his elder brother Patrick and sister Catherine passed away. They had survived into their seventies, outliving each sibling, save Charles. Both had lived in the home of brother Barney for much of their lives, and lastly with Barney's widow, Mary. Catherine, in particular, was mourned as the devoted aide to and surrogate for her mother in the raising her younger brothers and in assisting in the boarding house operations. Some speculated that Catherine's demise was prompted by the loss of her brother the previous day. Conscious that he was the last surviving grandchild of old Hugh McKenna, immigrant from County Tyrone, Charles soon began to delve into family history and to record, as best as he was able, the persons and events of prior generations.

Having been consumed by the various veterans' projects, Charles' devotion to the practice of law was rather restricted in these post-Porto Rico years. But his interest in jurisprudence was undiminished. With this in mind, the new Governor of Pennsylvania, John Tener, selected Charles to become a judge in a newly established Allegheny County Court. The June, 1911 appointment was temporary, until an election could be mounted in the autumn. In light of the appointment, then ex-president Theodore Roosevelt sent the following message to McKenna dated August 22, 1911:

"My dear Judge:

Pray accept my heartiest congratulations. I particularly appreciated your service in Porto Rico and I am glad that you are now to serve on the bench in our own country.

Faithfully yours,

Theodore Roosevelt"

In November, Charles was elected handily, with a majority of over 30,000 votes, for the prescribed term of ten years.

Chapter Twenty

Judge Charles F. McKenna

Prior to his ascension to the bench, Charles indulged himself in researching and writing about local history. Sometimes these writings would appear in the magazine of the Historical Society of Western Pennsylvania. It was an area of interest which he shared with his long-time family friend and cousin, Rev. Edward M. McKeever. Father Ed was the youngest son of Will McKeever, farmer of Anacramp, fast friend of Charles' father, and brother-in-law to Charles' mother. Ed, four years junior to Charles, had studied for the priesthood at Mount Saint Mary's College in Emmitsburg, Maryland. Shortly after ordination, he took up pastoral duties at Sts. Simon and Jude Church in Blairsville, Pa., about forty miles east of Pittsburgh. He served there from 1873 till 1889. During those years Ed had little contact with the McKenna family, save at family funerals. But in 1892, he became pastor at the church of St. John the Baptist in Lawrenceville. There, he was able to renew his McKenna family contacts, especially with Charles. They would often consult over items of local history. Father Ed later became one of the first chroniclers of Lawrenceville's history.

Ed was turning sixty-two in 1910. He was a cheerful soul, with graying red hair and the spectacles of a scholar. Of medium height, he kept himself trim and fit by his penchant for taking long walks, nearly daily. He had a down-to-earth manner that put ordinary folks at ease, despite his clerical black suit and white, Roman collar. The McKenna family invited him to a birthday celebration in his honor at the home of Mary, Barney's widow. She had moved to a new residence on Euclid Avenue with her son, Dr. Bill, now a licensed physician and surgeon. Her still-single nephew Edward J. and her widowed, younger sister, Alice McShane McCullough lived with her as well. Her eldest son, Frank, and his wife Bess, along with Charles and Virginia, rounded out the guest list.

Though Barney and Charles had been life-long teetotalers, Frank and Bill did not follow this practice. Even Father Ed would enjoy an occasional drink. That evening, at pre-dinner cocktails, Frank began to chastise his younger brother.

"Bill, God and man like a hard-working doctor; but you could use a bit of a social life."

His brother laughed, unperturbed. "I'm quite social, Brother. I see lots of people every day. Perhaps more than even a busy attorney . . . . Actually, since I've taken this surgical position at Pittsburgh Hospital, my time for society is a bit limited. But I suspect you have a recommendation for me, a prescription to improve my social standing. Is that not so?"

Frank raised his glass in salute. "Ach, you know me too well. As a matter of fact, I do. You know that Mother is working again this year on the benefit dinner-dance of the Ladies Catholic

Benevolent Association. As before, it will be a command performance for all of us."

"Don't I know it," Bill said with a grimace. "Last year was a frightful bore."

"Well, this year could be different—if you have a proper partner on the evening."

"And I suppose you have such a partner in mind. You may have your hopes too high, Frank."

Undaunted, Frank pressed on. "Come now, Bill. At least consider the possibility. Bess' younger sister Clementine will be there, but as yet has no escort. We'd make a grand foursome! Wouldn't you consider . . . ?"

Just then Father Ed came over and the discussion took a different turn. But Frank reported to Bess over dinner, "At least he didn't say no."

When the singing of "Happy Birthday" concluded and the birthday cake was eaten, Charles and Father Ed retired to the parlor with their coffee. Once settled, Charles began the discussion of their mutual interest—local history. "How's that piece on Lawrenceville history coming, Ed?"

The priest shook his head slowly, his face betraying feelings of dejection. "I'm afraid time for my research is hard to come by. But I do want to write something for the historical society . . . . I'm still at a very early stage and there's so much material, too much for a magazine article. I must lower my sights a bit and just deal with the earliest days."

"I'm keen to see it finished. Just what you've shared with me so far suggests it will be a most interesting article. I hadn't known that Stephen Foster's father was a founder of Lawrenceville."

"What about you, Charles? What project have you embarked upon now that the regimental history is finished?"

Charles, relaxing in Barney's old easy-chair, stroked his now white beard. "Nothing so taxing, I assure you. Actually, since the deaths of Barney, Patrick, and Catherine, I have been assembling a bit of the family history. Once I am gone, much of what is known about our ancestors will be lost unless I record it."

Ed placed his now-empty cup beside the colorful Tiffany lamp at his side table. "You are right to do so. Would that I had written down the stories of the old days Father used to tell us—how our families lived together back in Anacramp, how we are tied by marriage, and of the journey made to America."

"Yes, I remember . . . . He was my father's best friend. If Will had not bought the drayage business, our family's lives would have been quite different."

Father Ed now came to the edge of his chair, a gleam in his eye, and with excitement in his voice. "Charles, I have, for some time, given thought to the notion of visiting Ireland . . . . I guess it was Father O'Shea, my assistant, who put the thought in my head. I would like to go back to see Anacramp and Caledon. It would be grand to have a look at these places . . . to walk the land of our fathers."

Charles' expression also became animated. "That's a capital idea, Ed! If you think you could ever get away from the parish . . . I'd love to go with you. It would be a boon to my research. Jaysus, wouldn't it be fun as well?"

Ed sat back again and mused a moment. "Of course, I'd have to consult Bishop Canevin. It isn't unheard of for a pastor to be given leave for a sabbatical period . . . . I feel sure Father O'Shea would be happy to cover for me. I'd make the request, if you are serious."

Charles rose from his chair, empty cup in hand. "I am more than serious! Come, let's see if there's any coffee left."

* *

For weeks thereafter, Charles investigated potential travel arrangements while Father Ed awaited clearance from the chancery for a leave of absence. Charles calculated that six weeks would generously cover the travel time and the touring of the country. The itinerary he planned would take them from Pittsburgh to New

Jersey by rail, by ship from New York to Liverpool and thence by ferry to the city of Belfast. As soon as Father Ed's availability was confirmed, Charles made the appropriate bookings.

It was early May when Charles kissed Virginia goodbye. "You know you'd have been welcome to join Ed and me. It would be a grand vacation from the smoke and the soot."

Virginia looked at Charles with amusement. "No, dear. I have a feeling that this is more than a vacation. It seems a journey of the heart. You and Ed need to do things that are yours and yours alone. If I were with you, there would be fussing over how I should be entertained. I am very happy that you'll have this experience."

Charles' nephews had their own reasons for not joining in—the press of the law and medical practice for sure. Also, Frank and Bess had two young children, Mary and J. Frank Jr. And another was on the way. So, it was just the two travelers who left Pittsburgh for their ancestral home.

In New York, they waited overnight to board the steamship *Celtic*, operated by the White Star Line. The vessel was of modern design, built in 1901. It was over 21,000 tons and carried hundreds of passengers in relative comfort—a great improvement over the McKenna voyage of 1830. It was a gray, misty morning at the ships' terminal on the Hudson River. But the weather was unable to dampen spirits as the travelers marched up the gangway and searched out their cabins. Happily, there were only a few days of rough seas on the North Atlantic during their five-day voyage to Liverpool.

S.S. Celtic of the White Star Line
(Courtesy of The Ships List.com)

Each morning Charles would join Ed for his routine, morning walk. Together, they would march several circuits around the open, upper deck. This morning, skies were blue and the winds blustery. Ed took a deep breath of ocean air. For a Pittsburgher, such clean air was a most unfamiliar, yet welcome, experience. "I'm just curious, Charles. Why do we arrive at Liverpool? It seems these days most of the liners for Britain go to Southampton?"

Charles shrugged his shoulders, "I'm not sure why Southampton is preferred. I booked for Liverpool as it offered the most direct passage to Belfast."

Just then a gust of wind threatened Charles' signatory, white Stetson. Quickly he clamped it with a hand till they made the turn to the leeward side of the ship.

"My father came through Liverpool on his way to America," ruminated Ed. "It will have changed a great deal, I suppose."

Three days later, they arrived in Liverpool. Indeed the port had undergone many changes, but the overall impression would have been familiar to old Will McKeever. It was still a chaotic scene of ships, ferries, cranes, steam-powered donkey engines, rail spurs, horse-drawn freight wagons, stevedores, crowds of arriving and departing passengers, ticket agents, porters, and hawkers of every description. The noise and the smoke, however, were familiar, reminiscent of the mills along Pittsburgh's riverfronts. They made their way through the press of the landing stage and onto the Strand. Sorting out an overnight ferry took most of the morning, but left plenty of time in the afternoon for a proper meal before departing for Belfast.

They found a tea room several blocks into the city. Its warmth and shelter was most welcome on the cool, drizzling day. As they waited to be served by their sullen Irish waitress, Charles raised a subject he had deferred too long. "Ed, you know well the strife that prevails, sadly, between Catholic and Protestant residents of Ireland. Indeed, the worst of it seems to take place in Ulster."

Ed raised his eyebrows in curious and impatient response. "Yes, of course I do. What of it?"

Charles cleared his throat nervously. "Well, I was just wondering what sort of a reception we might receive when we get there. You know, I mean, with you in your priestly attire. We might make fewer waves during our visit if you adopted a more civilian appearance."

Ed laughed loudly enough to draw stares from those seated nearby. "So that's it, eh? Are you afraid I'll be tarred and feathered by the Orangemen—and you along with me? What would the martyrs of old have to say if I trim my sails and sneak about pretending to belong to the Church of Ireland?"

"You're having me on! Don't act like I'm advising apostasy. I just think you might get by a few days without the Roman collar."

"Sure, sure. I'm giving you the needle. If you'll feel safer, I can do my impersonation of a layman. Now you may sleep soundly tonight on the ferry."

But, though the crossing of the Irish Sea was unusually calm, sleeping on the ferry proved to be difficult, for both of them. They sat up through most of the night, alternating between dozing and quiet conversation. Father Ed stared out the window into the dark void that shrouded the Irish Sea. "I know, Charles, that you are compiling a history of your family; but I sense that your interest is broader than that. Am I correct?"

Charles ran his fingers through his white pompadour and paused before answering. "I suppose you are right . . . . Perhaps some of my interest in visiting Ireland has nothing to do with family. You may know that years ago I was active with the Irish National Land League. It was rather big in Allegheny County. I had become concerned with the plight of the Irish peasants being evicted from their homes and from the land they had worked for generations. It seemed an encore of the wretched days of the famine, though I was just a babe when that took place."

Ed shook his head in sorrow. "Yes, I've heard the stories too. Many in the parish are those who came to Pittsburgh on the back of such evictions. They don't make a show of it. Most won't discuss it at all. But sometimes, in the confessional or at a funeral, it will all come out."

"Yes, same thing for my colleagues in the Knights of Equity. It brings me near to tears to hear their experiences at the hands of an Anglo-Irish landlord . . . . I hadn't quite acknowledged it to myself before you asked. But I guess I am keen to see what the conditions are like today . . . how the British deal with those who they are determined to retain as part of their United Kingdom, but who they refuse to treat as equals."

"It must be the religious divide, don't you think?"

"In part, I suppose it is. Still, there are many native Irish of the Protestant faith, or of none at all, who share the lower status of their Catholic brethren. I sense that much of it is grounded in economics. The Irish and their lands have long been easy, nearby targets for British exploitation. The religious differences are largely a veil cast over the conflict by a government that cannot admit its real motives."

"I am afraid," Father Ed admitted, "that our own Catholic Church in Ireland has been largely complicit in that ruse. Of course, it is only Christian to preach against sectarian strife. But the bishops know well that the modicum of freedom allowed them by the British government comes with what you lawyers call a *quid pro quo*. If they join in the chorus for home rule or, at greater risk, outright independence, their property and position may be jeopardized."

"Well, it will be interesting to have a personal look at these issues and hear what our own people in Tyrone have to say to us about them."

* *

Charles and Ed arrived in Belfast early in the morning and took a Hansom cab to the Royal Hotel on Donegall Place. Though the conditions were less than royal, the establishment was the once stately townhouse of the Marquis of Donegall. After their extended travel, the two spent forty-eight hours restoring themselves before setting out for the Tyrone lands once inhabited by their forebears. This respite also allowed them to visit the Church of St. Malachy on Alfred Street, a short walk from their hotel. There Father Ed was permitted to say a Mass. The old church had originally been planned to be the cathedral for the diocese of Down and Connor. But those plans were scrapped so as to divert funds to relief efforts during the Great Hunger.

The following day the travelers made their way to the Great Victoria Street Station for passage by rail to their destination in County Tyrone. The Great Northern Railroad—Ireland operated a route from Belfast southwest through Portadown and Armagh. At the village of Tynan they hoped to make a transfer to a spur line into the Clogher Valley. But because of delays their arrival was too late to make the desired connection to the town of Caledon, one stop west.

Great Victoria Street Station, circa 1900
(National Archives of Ireland)

As the hour was getting late Ed suggested walking. "It's less than a couple of miles. Surely, we can leg it out."

Charles looked at the priest as if he were mad. "I admire your faith, Ed; but I question your prudence. With our suitcases to carry and it coming upon supper time, I vote for finding a ride."

It did not take long to find a young fellow willing to hire himself, horse, and carriage to drive these strange, American visitors the twenty minute journey from County Armagh into the southeast corner of County Tyrone. As they crossed over the Ulster Canal and then the River Blackwater, Charles queried as to what inn or hotel might accommodate them while in Caledon.

The callow driver turned and stared at his passengers. He struggled for words. Finally he shook his head and replied, "Oh, no, sirs. We've none of that in Caledon. You must stop at the pub. 'Tis they who may know of a house that will take in a traveler."

Charles and Ed grimaced to each other. This was a complication Charles had missed in their travel planning. "Very well, sir. Please drop us at the pub."

Main Street, Caledon circa 1910
(www.caledon.org.uk)

In actuality the term pub seemed a bit generous when describing the establishment before which they later found themselves. The edifice was really a fractional section of a stonewalled structure on the main street. It had a slate roof which, along with the color of the stone walls, presented a drab, gray image. Inside the decor was brighter, with plain white walls and a plank floor. A cluster of simple wooden chairs and a large matching table were arranged in a cluster before a coal-fired hearth. Despite its modest appearance, the warmth and cleanliness of the room produced a general sense of comfort and welcome. A young woman in her early twenties greeted them, introducing herself as Nellie.

"Good evening, Miss Nellie," Ed began as he removed his black fedora. "It has been suggested to us to inquire here where one might find lodging for several nights. We are visitors from

America. My name is Edward McKeever. My friend here is Mr. Charles McKenna."

Nellie's friendly smile slid off her face, replaced by widest eyes and a gaping mouth. "Ye must speak to my Da! I will fetch him," she sputtered and dashed nervously from the room.

The two visitors exchanged puzzled expressions at this strange departure. From deep within the house excited voices were heard, raised, then lowered to a buzz. Presently three other persons, together with Nellie, arrived in the front room. One was a man, tall and lean, appearing by his age to be Nellie's grandfather. A short round woman of middle age and a young girl, not yet in her teens, accompanied him. At first, none of them said a word. They simply stared at their visitors until the silence became awkward.

"Which of ye is called Charles McKenna?" the old man inquired in a deep, gravelly voice.

Charles moved closer and replied, "That would be me, sir. May I have your name?"

At that the old man broke into a grin and laughed. "Sure, ye already do. I am Charles McKenna!"

Charles and Ed were silenced in shock. They looked at each other and then joined the others in peals of laughter. Even Nellie's smile returned as her previous bewilderment dissipated. When the laughter subsided Charles stretched out his hand to the old man.

"It is a most pleasant surprise to make your acquaintance. My friend here is Edward McKeever. We have just arrived in your town after a long journey from America."

Charles avoided using the honorific "Father" or "Reverend" as had Ed in making introductions. Ed shook hands now and the old man introduced his wife Sara, and youngest daughter Mary.

"Ye have already met Nellie," he concluded.

Charles nodded. "Yes, we were just explaining to Nellie that we are in need of room and board for several nights. We were advised to stop here in hopes that you might know of someone here in Caledon who will take in a traveler or two."

Sara affected an awkward curtsy. "Our home is not grand, sir. But we might make room for ye here." She gestured with her hand. "Isn't that so, dear?" she confirmed, looking at the old man.

It now dawned upon Charles and Ed that the old man was, despite an age difference of easily twenty years, her husband and the father of the two girls. He nodded in reply to his wife and ordered the girls to take the suitcases, coats, and hats to an upper room. After a visit to the "necessary," the two travelers were refreshed and settled. Glasses of stout were produced for their host and Ed. Charles made do with a cup of tea. The old man peppered them with questions.

"We are from a city in America called Pittsburgh," Charles explained in response. "Both Mr. McKeever and I are descended from farmers in the townland of Anacramp. We are on holiday, but we also have come to learn a bit more of our families and the world they left behind."

His namesake nodded. "Ye are not the first from America to come around for the same purpose. Sure, there are still McKennas about, though the greater number are across the river in County Monaghan. I'm unaware of any by the name McKeever in the parish. Was it long ago yer people left?"

"It was. My grandfather, Hugh McKenna, was a widowed man. He left with his sons in 1830. Ed's father came along a year later with his wife and several of Hugh's daughters. They were tenants on the estate of the Earl of Caledon."

"As I have been for over fifty years. Of course, 'twas here in the townland of Caledon where I had my small farm. In these last few years Sara and I took to the spirits business as I'm no longer able to manage the acreage I once did."

"Of course we will wish to visit Anacramp while we are here," Charles continued. "Also, the grave of my grandmother, Catherine. She was a McMahon. Perhaps you can direct us to the place called Donagh?"

"Now 'tis the Catholic church what ye're after now?"

"Oh yes, our people were all Catholic, McKenna and McKeevers."

"Ach, man, Donagh is over in County Monaghan! Were her people from there?"

"I shouldn't think so." Charles took on a puzzled look. "This place, Donagh, is just a name I heard my mother mention years ago."

"Ach, ye haven't any Irish. Most of us cannot speak it ourselves. The word donagh is Irish; it means church. I expect yer mother was using the term for the chapel nearest Anacramp. That would be Derrygooly in her day. Course, they might have gone to Aughnacloy, but 'twould be a greater distance."

"Well, we shall look at Derrygooly then. Is there a parish priest who might help us?"

The publican shook his head. "No, not at Derrygooly. Sure, that chapel hasn't been used for over fifty years. There's our church, St. Joseph's, on the Minterburn Road. Father Francis Ward is our pastor."

"Thank you. You have saved us a bit of wandering, I'm sure," Charles replied. "Are you a Catholic family also?"

Their host nodded. "Aye, we are—all the way back to St. Patrick, I'm thinkin'."

"Well, I should explain then, my friend here is a parish priest back in America. We thought it best that he not travel in his Roman collar."

Father Ed looked up from his drink, sheepish at Charles' disclosure. "My Charles McKenna is a cautious man," he said with a wink.

＊＊＊＊＊＊＊＊＊＊＊＊＊＊＊＊＊＊＊＊＊＊＊＊

The next day was clear and mild. After a leisurely breakfast, Charles and Ed set out for Anacramp by way of the Clogher Valley Railway. The narrow-gauge route followed the Derrycourtney Road through a countryside of green, gently-rolling hills. Their

313

destination was the station at Ramaket, just three miles out from Caledon. As they slowly rode along, Ed broached a conversation to pass the time.

"You know, the Catholics around here remind me of the Hunkies back in Pittsburgh?" he observed, referring to the Slavic immigrants who had fled the Austro-Hungarian empire, only to find menial work and wretched housing in the steel city.

Charles wrinkled his nose. "What do you mean? How are they alike? I don't see it."

Ed stopped and looked Charles in the eye. "Perhaps you need to look a bit closer, cousin. It seems to me that, though the Catholics here are many, they live their lives on the fringes of this society. The town of Caledon looks to be owned and operated by citizens of the Protestant faith."

"Subjects, Ed, subjects, not citizens. Yes, but that should not surprise you. The Brits have always reserved land and position for their own. It's the same throughout Ireland. What's that got to do with Hunkies?"

"It just seems to me that the Catholics here are the Hunkies of Ireland. It's easy for us to resent the treatment of Catholics here. But how different is it for the Hunkies back in America?"

Charles sniffed, "They're not the worst off, friend. There's always the niggers."

Ed let the subject die in awkward silence.

They reached Ramaket in mid-morning. As there were no signs announcing Anacramp, they were told to look for the old school house on the right side of the road. "The farms of Anacramp are along the boreen opposite the school," Caledon's Charles McKenna had advised.

"My mother and father would have received their schooling here," Charles observed. "Perhaps yours did as well."

They took the well-beaten path south by southwest, where they encountered a young farmer in his late twenties driving a few sheep. Doffing his flat cap, he introduced himself as Peter McMahon. He was visibly suspicious of these strangers in their

314

finely tailored attire. Only when he learned they were Americans did he become friendly and relaxed.

"Me mother is a widow. I keep the farm whilst me brother Thomas works at the woolen mill. I have a sister Ellen who is a dressmaker."

"How many houses here in Anacramp nowadays, Peter?" Ed asked.

The dark-haired fellow rubbed his chin and counted to himself. "Now, there's Shannons, they run the model farm up by the road. Then there's the Woods, the Culls, Hugh McMahon, the Mullans . . . . Eight, I'm thinkin'."

"Sweet Mother of God! How many people might that be?"

"About thirty, give or take a few. The postmistress in Caledon can give a good figure, sure."

"My father, Will McKeever, lived here eighty years ago. He said there were nearly a hundred-fifty souls in Anacramp. Did they all emigrate?"

The young man looked skeptical. "Many did, of course. Still, 'tis hard for me to imagine a hundred and fifty in little Anacramp . . . . I've never known a McKeever hereabouts."

Charles interrupted now, somewhat excited. "My grandmother was also a McMahon, Catherine. She married Hugh McKenna and they raised a large family here. Did you ever hear those names among your family?"

Peter slowly shook his head. "I could ask me mother. But there still be McKennas here. 'Tis a farmer Joseph, wife Bridget, and two babies. There's a hireling too; he's also a McKenna, but from Monaghan."

Charles and Ed next paid a visit to the McKenna household, but with similar results. Joseph, a lean friendly fellow in his fifties stated, "We may be kin to yourself, sir. But I couldn't say for sure. I can't recall hearing of a Hugh McKenna around here."

Feeling dejected, Charles thanked the farmer. "Can you direct us to the Mullan farm? My mother was a Mullan. Perhaps they'll know of her."

Fifteen minutes later, he and Ed were seated around the kitchen table of James Mullan, a farmer of sixty-odd years. The craggy widower had a few rogue, white hairs that projected from a large Adam's apple. He lived with his son and two daughters, all adults. The youngest girl, Margaret, busied herself stretching the midday meal to accommodate their guests.

The old man explained, "Me father was also named James Mullan—a stone mason by trade. He had two brothers, Pat and Michael. Then, there was four sisters, Ann, Catherine, Mary, and Sarah. Sarah, the youngest, was the only one of the girls to stay on here in Ireland."

"Ann was my mother!" exclaimed Charles triumphantly.

Catherine was mine," Ed added, beaming a great smile. "Charles, this fellow's aunt Mary must have been Ed McShane's wife."

"We are your cousins, sir, I am convinced of it," Charles assured his host.

Mullan looked perplexed at the thought of being visited by American cousins he never knew existed. As they chatted away, he confirmed what they had heard about the old chapel at Derrygooly falling into disuse. "We go to the church in Drumess, St. Joseph's. But I was baptized at Derrygooly. I'm thinkin' that's where ye'll be findin' yer people."

The farmer had little knowledge of his long-departed aunts. And there was little family lore to be shared. He spent most of the dinner table conversation describing his own generation. "Do ye know of any Mullans in Chicago?" he asked. After the meal, he had chores to perform, so Charles and Ed offered profound thanks and went on their way.

The trip back to Caledon was a quiet one. Though both of them were gratified that they had made contact with a distant relation, Charles sensed that Ed was a bit disappointed to discover no trace at all of the McKeevers. That evening at McKennas' pub, Charles gave a report to his host of their findings in Anacramp. The older

316

man noticed that Father Ed, as he now called him, was unusually subdued.

Addressing the priest, he offered, "Ye must query Father Ward tomorrow when ye visit Derrygooly. Perhaps he will know of yer people."

Ed smiled and raised his glass of stout. "That I will do, Mr. McKenna. Though it's possible that my father's family were not native to this part of Tyrone. Anyway, it's a good suggestion."

Charles moved to change the subject. "I noticed the population at Anacramp is now quite small compared to former times. Is that the case, generally, around the county?"

The publican looked up from attending the coal fire. "Since I was a boy I should think we've lost near to half our people. Ye must understand that turnin' tilled land to pasture took the bread out of the farmer's mouth. Even the flax and other textiles are down. Those who could left for America, England or Canada. 'Tis sad but true."

After supper their host inquired, "Are ye fine to walk to Derrygooly tomorrow? I can sort out a ride if need be."

Charles looked at Ed with pleading eyes. But the priest laughed. "We'd be pleased to have a bit of a walk, sir. Surely, the Catholics here in Caledon must walk to the church for the Mass."

* *

And so the next morning Charles and Ed set out on the Minterburn Road. Their first stop would be St. Joseph's Church in the townland of Drumess. The pastor had been given notice of their desires and would be awaiting their arrival. The day was warm enough but a bit overcast. An ordinary day for the season they were informed.

They found Father Francis Ward in his residence. The housekeeper, Jane Devlin, showed them into the parlor of the small, but comfortable, dwelling. The priest rose from his chair, setting aside his breviary.

"Good day, gentlemen, and welcome! God's peace be upon you," the priest greeted. He was a young man—mid-thirties perhaps—about the same age as his housekeeper. He was of medium height, with short, brown hair. The beginnings of a paunch suggested future corpulence. His smile was warm and his eyes twinkled with delight at the arrival of guests from America. "I'm Father Francis. And which of you might be Father McKeever?"

Charles and Ed introduced themselves and explained their interest in visiting the chapel and grounds at Derrygooly. "I'm sure it will seem somewhat strange to you, Father Francis, for us to come all the way from America to visit a disused graveyard," Charles added. "It's just a small part of assembling as completely as possible the story of our families. Something to pass along to future generations."

"Sure, 'tisn't strange at all! You're not the first Yanks wishing to trample about an Irish cemetery. There's few parishes in Ireland without family ties to America. I've set aside the morning for yourselves and I'm pleased to be your guide. Shall we have a cup of tea before setting off?"

Shortly Miss Devlin reappeared with a tray of cups, biscuits, and a ceramic pot. Once they were served Father Francis continued, "Derrygooly isn't far at all. Of course, the church here has served our people for sixty years or more, so I rarely visit the old chapel. It's not in good repair, I'm afraid. When we're finished our tea I must show you our new shrine to the Blessed Mother. The parishioners themselves did all the work and 'tis very grand, we think."

After tea there was the obligatory inspection of the church, grounds, and the aforementioned shrine. Then all three men walked the narrow country lane as it wound its way past deep-green pastures bordered by overgrown walls of stone and earth. The distance was not great. As the road rose before them, Father Francis indicated a turning through tall grass to a cluster of trees at the top of a hill. There a stone building, surrounded by overgrown hawthorn, stood sadly dilapidated. Behind the chapel they found the long-neglected cemetery, deep in grass and weeds. It was so overgrown that caution was advised by their host.

"Don't be twisting an ankle on headstones hidden below."

Charles and Ed bent down to push aside the tall grass hiding those markers that were still standing. Some were tipped at an angle, while others had fallen flat. Where inscriptions could be found, most were so weather-worn as to be illegible. Only where a headstone was tipped inscription-side down could the legends be discerned. Father Francis wandered over to the derelict chapel while Charles and Ed conducted their searches.

After twenty minutes of fruitless inspections, they looked at each other in despair. "The names, when you can find them, ring familiar. There are even McKennas, McMahons, and Mullans here and there. But the dates and the given names, I do not recognize," Charles complained. "I just have the feeling that Catherine lies here somewhere. If only I knew where to look."

Father Francis, who had quietly returned from his sojourn, interrupted. "Many of our people would not have had the means to purchase a headstone. Often a small wooden cross would have to suffice. Decades of weather have consumed these completely. Would you care to see the mass rock at all? 'Tis where our people secretly heard the Mass during the days of the Penal Laws."

"You go ahead, Ed. I'm not quite done here. I'll join you in a few minutes."

Left alone with his thoughts Charles sauntered back and forth, tracing the graveyard border to border. He made no further effort to read inscriptions. Rather, without consciously articulating his purpose, he focused all his senses in search of a sign, a clue, a feeling. Yes, a feeling would do.

I know you're here Catherine, and maybe others of our family as well. I wonder if you know what became of your beloved Hugh and your many children. My mother, Annie, kept a memory of you to share with her children. It seemed to us she loved you dearly. She would have wanted you to know that your family did well in America. Though she lost James far too soon, he gave her a fine home and seven children who were her pride. Perhaps she has told you of her son who became the mayor of our great city . . . . Our lives today are very different from your own. Your hardships we can only imagine. But we try to keep your memory, and that of old Hugh, and of Father. We are the products of your making in ways we cannot fully describe or appreciate. But we know they are real. Though I haven't found the spot where you rest, I'm glad we've had this visit. God bless!

Epilogue

August, 1946

The Catawba Island juts into Lake Erie, pointing north towards Canada like a big thumb. Small farms of peaches and corn intersperse with the modest cottages of fishermen and summer refugees from overheated cities. In 1900, William Heyl, father-in-law of J. Frank McKenna, was one of a group of Pittsburgh Knights of Columbus taking the ferry from the village of Put-in-Bay on South Bass Island to Catawba. It was from Put-in Bay that that U.S. naval commander Oliver Hazard Perry set off on September 10, 1813 to engage British vessels in the Battle of Lake Erie during the War of 1812.

In later years, the village became a popular recreational locale. So taken was Heyl with the bucolic atmosphere on Catawba, he and several of his fellow knights purchased waterfront property on the east side of the island. Their intent was to create summer vacation cottages as a retreat for families and friends. In time, a cluster of dwellings was erected to comprise a tiny settlement they named Little Pittsburgh. There, on the edge of the lake, Heyl commissioned a large, Victorian residence of eleven rooms which he named *The Heylands*. It was a clever wordplay, combining his own surname and the name of a popular pilsner beer from Germany—his wife being a Frauenheim, the offspring of the German-American family of brewers in Pittsburgh.

The Heylands on Catawba Island

It was here at the Heylands that Bill McKenna and his family joined his parents, Frank and Bess for a week's holiday that summer of 1946. Late one afternoon, while the women and children were taking their second or third swim of the day, Bill and his father relaxed over glasses of whiskey. Seated on the screened-in, wrap-around porch, they enjoyed a panoramic view of the blue waters of the lake, dotted with sailboats passing between Catawba and the off-shore islands.

Lighting one of his innumerable cigarettes, Bill turned the conversation. "Do you remember, Father, the talk we had at your office last fall? We ended up discussing your father and your uncle Charles."

Frank set his drink down and turned to face his son. "Why, yes! I've thought of that chat several times. I was sorry that we didn't have the time that day to carry it a bit further. I sensed you were interested in learning more."

"I was . . . . You know, the only one of that generation I ever met was Charles. I must have been seven or eight at the time. To me, he was just a kindly, white-haired, old man. I had no appreciation of who he was or what he had accomplished in his day. I guess I still don't fully. Just that he was a county judge and had fought in the Civil War."

"He was a man of many accomplishments, Bill. He gave me my start in the legal profession, me and my cousin Edward. Not only a county judge, but a former Federal judge as well. When he ran for re-election in 1921, he was so highly regarded they couldn't find a candidate willing to oppose him. Before becoming a judge, he was an eminent advocate in the courtroom. But he was also an author, an artist, a great supporter of the Church and the community. When he died in 1922, the funeral was so large they had to move it from Sacred Heart to the cathedral just to accommodate the crowd of mourners."

"Do you think he led a happy life? Did he seem satisfied?"

"I suppose . . . . He never shared that much with me . . . . I know it was a great disappointment to him that he and his wife were unable to have children. After he died, she removed to her family's homestead in Blacksburg, Virginia. We never saw her after that. I guess without children, and none of her family left in Pittsburgh, there was nothing to keep her there."

"Freshen your drink?"

Frank nodded and handed him his glass. Upon returning to his chair Bill asked, "With all that Charles accomplished, of what do you think he was most proud?"

His father laughed, "Oh, that is easy to say. He often mentioned it. When you entered his law office, there was a picture prominently displayed upon the wall behind his desk. It was a sketch he had made himself. It was set at the fiftieth anniversary of the Battle of Gettysburg, the first ever reunion of both Union and Confederate survivors of that battle."

"Gee, it must have been a very emotional time—to sit across a table from those who tried to kill you and your comrades!"

"I'm sure it was. Anyway, the War Department had arranged to distribute special medals to the surviving members of Charles' regiment who had fought at Gettysburg. They made the presentation at the site called Little Round Top. Charles captured the ceremony, as he remembered it, in this drawing. It was clear that his proudest role was that of soldier-patriot."

Bill went quiet momentarily, gazing off into Erie's blue expanse. Finally, he observed in a subdued voice, "I guess I can relate to your father's mixed feelings. It's kind of hard to compare oneself to such achievements, though Barney was no slouch himself."

Frank sipped his drink and paused in thought. Finally he broke the spell.

"We don't get to control what the fates have in store for us, Bill. All we can do is make the best job we can of what is dealt to us. I like to think that old Hugh McKenna, my grandfather James, and grandmother Annie did that. They weren't famous or acclaimed. But they did their best and laid a foundation from which Barney and Charles benefitted. By what they did and who they were, they made possible what was to follow. Not a bad legacy, I'd say."

* *

Glossary

Abattoir—a synonym for slaughterhouse

Ach—Interjection with a hint of sadness (Hiberno-English)

Arrah—Interjection meaning "now, but, really" (Hiberno-English)

Bakelite—A brand name for any of a series of thermosetting plastics prepared by heating phenol or cresol with formaldehyde and ammonia under pressure: used for radio cabinets, telephone receivers, electric insulators, and molded plastic ware.

Barmbrack—A loaf of bread with currants in it.

Boreen—A country lane or narrow road.

Brevet—A commission promoting a military officer to a higher rank without increase of pay and with limited exercise of the higher rank, often granted as an honor immediately before retirement.

Cess—Luck, possibly a contraction of "success" (Hiberno-English)

Chandler—a dealer or trader in supplies, provisions, etc. of a specialized type. A ship chandler

Clachan—A small village or hamlet.

Cottier—A peasant renting a small piece of land, awarded to the highest bidder

Demesne—An estate or part of an estate occupied and controlled by, and worked for the exclusive use of, the owner.

Flummery—Oatmeal or flour boiled with water until thick. Fruit custard or blancmange usually thickened with cornstarch.

Fooster—To fuss, a to-do.

Hansom—A low-hung, two-wheeled, covered vehicle drawn by one horse, for two passengers, with the driver being mounted on an elevated seat behind and the reins running over the roof.

Hawker—A person who offers goods for sale by shouting his or her wares in the street or going from door to door; peddler.

Iron Puddler—An iron puddler or a 'puddler' is an occupation involved in the manufacture of iron. Puddling was an improved process to convert pig iron into wrought iron with the use of a reverberating furnace.

Knackered—Exhausted; tired out.

Knights of Equity—The Knights of Equity (KOE) is an Irish-Catholic fraternal organization established in the U.S. in 1895 and still in active operation in the 21st century. The group is among the oldest Irish-Catholic membership associations in America. With some 65 local chapters, called "courts," during its period of greatest influence, the group was an important Catholic political and fraternal benefit society.

Left-footer—A Protestant; folklore of Northern Ireland had Catholics using the right foot for digging with a spade and the Protestants using the left foot.

LST—(Landing Ship, Tank) An oceangoing military ship, used by amphibious forces for landing troops and heavy equipment on beaches.

Mamó—Irish word for grandmother, granny.

Minie Ball—A cylindrical bullet with a hollow base, invented by the French Army officer Claude-Etienne Minié.

Nappies—Diapers.

Orange Men—Members of a society founded in Ireland (1795) to uphold the Protestant religion, the Protestant dynasty, and the Protestant constitution. Orange Lodges have since spread to many parts of the former British Empire. After William of Orange.

Orderly—An enlisted soldier assigned to perform various chores for a commanding officer or group of officers.

Ordnance—Military supplies, especially weapons, ammunition, etc.

Poteen—Illicit spirit, often distilled from potatoes.

Praities—Potatoes.

Quid Pro Quo—(Latin) One thing in return for another. Something that is given or taken in return for something else.

Quoits—A game in which rings of rope or flattened metal are thrown at an upright peg, the object being to encircle it or come as close to it as possible.

Skirmishers—Small bodies of troops, especially advanced or outlying detachments of opposing armies.

Sláinte—Gaelic toast used in Ireland and Scotland meaning (good) "health."

Spalpeen—An itinerant seasonal laborer.

Supernumerary—One in excess of the usual, proper, or prescribed number; additional; extra. Associated with a regular body or staff as an assistant or substitute in case of necessity.

Sutler—A person who followed an army or maintained a store on an army post to sell provisions to the soldiers.

Toper—A hard drinker or chronic drunkard.

Vidette—Sentinel stationed in advance of pickets. The duty or post of such a sentinel.

Bibliography

Alexander, Grif *Bits with M'Kenna*. Pittsburgh Dispatch, April 12, 1903

Altenburger, Christine *The Pittsburgh Bureau of Police—Some Historical Highlights*. The Western Pennsylvania Historical Magazine, January, 1966.

www.amen-corner.org

Baldwin, Leland *Pittsburgh—The Story of a City 1750-1865*. University of Pittsburgh Press, 1937.

Bates, Samuel P. *History of the Pennsylvania Volunteers 1861-1865 Vol.4*. Harrisburg, 1870.

Blaxter, H.V. & Kerr, Allen H. *The Aldermen and Their Courts. The Pittsburgh Survey—The Pittsburgh District—Civic Frontage*. The Russell Sage Foundation, 1914.

Boucher, John Newton *A Century and a Half of Pittsburgh and Her People*. Pittsburgh, 1908.

Burgoyne, Arthur Gordon *The Homestead Strike of 1892*. Rawsthorne Engraving & Printing Co. Pittsburgh, 1893.

Burgoyne, Arthur Gordon *All Sorts of Pittsburghers*. The Leader All Sorts Co. Pittsburgh, 1892.

www.caledon.org.uk

Catholic Historical Society of Western Pennsylvania *Catholic Pittsburgh's One Hundred Years 1843-1943.* Loyola University Press, Chicago, 1943.

Cebula, James *The Glory and Despair of Challenge and Change, A History of the Molders Union.* International Molders & Allied Workers Union. Cincinnati, 1976.

Census of Ireland, 1851, 1891, 1911.

Connelly, Frank & Jenks, George C. *Official History of the Johnstown Flood.* Journalist Publishing Co. Pittsburg, 1889.

Cook, Donald E. *The Great Fire of Pittsburgh in 1845.* The Western Pennsylvania Historical Magazine, April, 1968.

Couvares, Francis *The re-making of Pittsburgh—Class and Culture in an Industrializing City 1877-1919.* SUNY Series in American Social History, State University of New York Press, 1984.

Dahlinger, Charles W. *Old Allegheny.* The Western Pennsylvania Historical Magazine, Vol. 4. October, 1918.

Dawson, Charles T. *Our Firemen: The History of the Pittsburgh Fire Department from the Village Period Until the Present Time.* Henry Fenno, Publisher. Pittsburgh, 1889.

Day, Angelique & McWilliams, Patrick (Eds.) *Ordnance Survey Memoirs of Ireland, Vol. 20—Parishes of County Tyrone II 1825,1833-35,1840.* Institute of Irish Studies, Queens University. Belfast, 1993.

Diffenbacher, J.F. *Directory of Pittsburgh and Allegheny Cities 1881-1897.*

www.eriecanal.org.

Fahnestock, Samuel *Pittsburgh Directory, 1850.*

Fleming, George Thornton *History of Pittsburgh and Environs.* American Historical Society, Inc., 1922.

Foner, Philip S. *The Great Labor Uprising of 1877.* Monad Press. New York, 1977.

Fox, Arthur B. *Pittsburgh During the American Civil War 1860-1865.* Mechling. Chicora, Pa., 2002.

George, Henderson *A Country Boy Begins Life in Pittsburgh.* The Western Pennsylvania Historical Magazine, 1920.

Gettysburg Battlefield Memorial Commission *Pennsylvania at Gettysburg.* Wm. Stanley Ray—State Printer, 1914.

Harris, Isaac *General Business Directory of Pittsburgh & Allegheny, 1841, 1847.*

Hays, Agnes M. *Old Penn Street: The Old Fourth Ward.* Gilbert Adam Hays. Sewickley, Pa., 1922.

Hays, Samuel P. (Ed.) *City at the Point—Essays on the Social History of Pittsburgh.* University of Pittsburgh Press., 1989.

Henderson, James A. *The Railroad Riots in Pittsburgh.* The Western Pennsylvania Historical Society, 1927.

Hudson, Samuel *Pennsylvania and Its Public Men.* Philadelphia, 1909.

Jordan, John W. *Encyclopedia of Pennsylvania Biography, Vol. 1.* Lewis Historical Publishing Co., 1914.

Kaufman, Eugene *A Pittsburgh Political Battle Royal of a Half-Century Ago.* The Western Pennsylvania Historical Magazine, Vol. 35, No.2. June, 1952.

Killikelly, Sarah Hutchins *The History of Pittsburgh—Its Rise and Progress.* B.C. & Gordon Montgomery Co. Pittsburgh, 1906.

Kleinberg, S.J. *The Shadow of the Mills—Working Class Families in Pittsburgh 1870-1907.* University of Pittsburgh Press. 1989.

www.knightsofequity.com *History of Court Nine, Pittsburgh.*

Krause, Paul *The Battle for Homestead 1880-1892: Politics, Culture, and Steel.* University of Pittsburgh Press. 1992.

Maspero, G. *The Twentieth Century Bench & Bar of Pennsylvania, Vol. 2.* H.C. Cooper. Chicago, 1903.

McCollester, Charles *The Point of Pittsburgh.* Battle of Homestead Foundation. Pittsburgh, 2008.

McEvoy, John *Statistical Survey of the County of Tyrone.* The Dublin Society, 1802.

McKenna, Charles F. *The Soldiers' and Sailors' Memorial Hall of Allegheny County—Sketch of its Origins and Organization.* Pittsburgh, 1908.

New York Times *Strain Senatorial Courtesy—Pennsylvania Senators Defeat Appointment of Charles F. McKenna.* April 29, 1904.

New York Evening Post *Matthew S. Quay—The Kind of Man This Republican Leader Is.* 1893.

Pennsylvania Election Statistics—1682-2006 Wilkes University. Wilkes-Barre, Pa.

Pennsylvania 155th Regimental Association *Under the Maltese Cross—Antietam to Appomattox—The Loyal Uprising in Western Pennsylvania 1861-1865.* Pittsburgh, 1910.

Pennsylvania Report of the Committee Appointed to Investigate the Railroad Riots in July, 1877. Harrisburg, 1878.

Pittsburgh Catholic, page 9. *Orphans Picnic.* July 20, 1898

Pittsburgh Daily Post *Reign of the Mob.* July 23, 1877.

Pittsburgh Daily Post *Land League Leader.* November 22, 1881.

Pittsburgh Gazette *Appalling Disaster—Explosion at the U.S. Arsenal.* September 18, 1862.

Pittsburgh Gazette *Bernard M'Kenna, Former Mayor, Passed Away.* June 19, 1903.

Pittsburgh Leader *Judge Charles F. McKenna.* July 24, 1904.

Pittsburgh Press *The Steps—A Historic Spot in History of Pittsburg.* March 29, 1908.

Pittsburgh Times *Death Comes to B. M'Kenna at His Home.* June 19, 1903.

Pittsburgh and Allegheny Directory 1898-1920. R.L. Polk & Co.

Rutherford, Samuel Thayer *The Department of Charities of the City of Pittsburgh 1888-1923.* M.A. Thesis University of Pittsburgh, 1938.

Siebert, P.W. *Old Bayardstown.* The Western Pennsylvania Historical Magazine, Vol. 9, No.2. April, 1926.

Steffens, Lincoln *Pittsburg: A City Ashamed.* McClures Magazine. May, 1903.

Strassburger, Eugene B. *Remarks before the Allegheny County Bar Association—Ceremony of Induction Into Office of Honorable J. Frank McKenna, Jr. as Judge of the Court of Common Pleas of Allegheny County, Pennsylvania.* Pittsburgh Legal Journal. January 6, 1959.

Swetnam, George *Labor-Management Relations in Pennsylvania's Steel Industry 1800-1959.* The Western Pennsylvania Historical Magazine, Vol. 62. No.4, 1979.

Szarnicki, Rev. Henry A. *Michael O'Connor—First Catholic Bishop of Pittsburgh 1843-1860.* Pittsburgh, 1975.

Thurston, George Henry *Pittsburgh As It Is.* W.S. Haven. Pittsburgh, 1857.

Thurston, George Henry *Pittsburgh and Allegheny in the Centennial Year.* A.A. Anderson & Son. Pittsburgh, 1876.

Walsh, Victor A. *"Drowning the Shamrock": Drink, Teetotalism and the Irish Catholics of Gilded-Age Pittsburgh.* Journal of American Ethnic History, Vol.10, No.1/2. 1990-1991. University of Illinois Press.

Walsh, Victor A. *Across "The Big Wather": The Irish-Catholic Community of Mid-Nineteenth Century Pittsburgh.* The Western Pennsylvania Historical Magazine, Vol. 66. 1983.

Walsh, Victor A. *"A Fanatic Heart": The Cause of Irish-American Nationalism in Pittsburgh During the Gilded Age.* Journal of Social History Vol. 15, No. 2. 1981.

Wudarczyk, James *Pittsburgh's Forgotten Allegheny Arsenal.* Closson Press. Apollo, Pa. 1999.

Wudarczyk, James *Guns for the Union.* Lawrenceville Historical Society, http://www.lhs15201.org/articles_b.asp?ID=13